Winds
of Love

Winds of Love

Antonio Casale

iUniverse®

Winds of Love

iUniverse books may be ordered through booksellers or by contacting:

iUniverse
1663 Liberty Drive
Bloomington, IN 47403
www.iuniverse.com
1-800-Authors (1-800-288-4677)

ISBN: 978-1-4917-5876-2 (sc)
ISBN: 978-1-4917-5877-9 (e)

Library of Congress Control Number: 2015900772

Printed in the United States of America.

iUniverse rev. date: 01/31/2015

Acknowledgement

This book is a fiction. Any name, place, event, ideas, words and people are purely coincidental.

To Professor Pallotta,
my mentor and friend.
He taught me honesty,
intellectual integrity,
and professionalism

Prologue

Since time immemorial, humanity has been debating on the 'liber arbitrium' and its connections with our destiny. What are the main ingredients for our happiness or unhappiness? According to some psychology experts, there are two types of people: those who create happiness and those who pursue it. But, that is not always the case, as we shall see in this novel. For some, it is a transition from sweet romanticism to nuptial responsibility; for others, it becomes an endless, tempestuous enigma where microscopic components play a crucial role on the unpredictable human stage. Love was and remains a mystery. Those who pretend to hold the code that unravels its truth, are, perhaps, dreamers themselves in the inscrutable, cosmic vortex of human feelings. Each individual reader, at one point, will have to draw his or her conclusions. Is life a dream and, therefore, we are passive and impotent witnesses of human events? Or, are we the controllers of our destiny under the wisdom of an inscrutable, universal architect?

Please, follow me in this enjoyable voyage and let us forget, for the time being, our problems.

Contents

CHAPTER I

The Missing Section

In 2013, I traveled to Russia, with a group of tourists. I barely managed to pay for the trip. I was eager to visit so much of that vast and icy country that I used all of my savings. While sojourning in Vladivostok, one morning, around eight o'clock, I purchased a copy of the international renowned newspaper, Kommersant. On the front page, an uncommon announcement called my attention. It was written in three languages, Russian, English and Italian. This spared me the inconvenience of asking the tour guide for translation.

A local tycoon of about sixty years of age was easily recognizable for being a huge man with blond straight hair and blue eyes. He was very rough in his demeanor, but with his family, he was a model of gentility. He had one daughter, the opposite of her father in her physical composition. She was slim and extremely timid. Her parents were overprotective of her. After the university studies, she dedicated her time to writing. She was about to publish her first novel when she fell ill with an incurable disease and, shortly after, died. To honor her memory, her father decided to go ahead and publish the manuscript. Unfortunately, he was unable to carry out his desire. According to the editor, the middle part was missing. Subsequent inquiries revealed that the girl, in a moment of deep pessimism, cast the manuscript into flames and only the prompt intervention of her maid saved the first and last section from total extinction.

The wealthy man was not going to surrender so easily, ergo, he recurred to the mass media to achieve his objective. He appealed to any author, who would be interested in recreating the missing section. The reward of one million euro was too appetizing to refuse. I dialed a number and talked to the secretary. Immediately after, I raised my hand to a taxi passing by and left.

At his opulent house, the gentleman welcomed me affably. "So, you want to take on this enterprise?" He queried with an expression that appeared both doubtful and curious."

"Yes, I am ready to start," I answered self-assured.

"What makes you so confident that you can construe the interior of the manuscript in a way that it blends in with both the beginning and the end?"

"Sir, If I were doubtful, I would not be here wasting your precious time and mine," I replied, raising my head and staring at him straight in the eyes.

He spoke no more. He turned to one of his lady assistants and winked to her. The young lady grabbed a bunch of papers and began to explain to me the legal implications in the completion of the agreement. I understood that she was a lawyer and I nodded. Then, she excused herself and spent the next ten minutes scrutinizing my credentials on the computer. While she was absorbed in her work, I looked outside and noticed a long line of candidates. I was proud I had bitten all of them on the clock. The legal secretary or lawyer opened some documents and read a couple of them. I understood the legal sanctions in the event of a withdrawal and signed the contract. I saw her raising her eyes and looking outside, "You are a lucky man," she exclaimed. "Many dogs came around this bone, but you were the fastest." Her boss smiled from behind the desk. I reached for his hand in a euphoric state. The lawyer said, "Make sure you do a good job and keep in touch." I bowed in deference to both of them and went on the sidewalk waiting for a taxi. The lady secretary came over and asked, "What are you doing? Our chauffeur is waiting right there to take you back to your hotel." I thanked her ostentatiously and rushed to the car. I waived at her a couple of times. She shook her head and smiled.

CHAPTER II

The Innocent Kiss

The sky was a sheet of aluminum paper. Not a cloud, big or small, not a light streak of them disturbed the terse cosmic vault. The wind had stopped brushing the tree tops. Not even the grass blades trembled. The water was bubbling up against the rocks and the pebbles of the tortuous riverbed at the foot of the mountain looked remarkably white. The sun changed the running water into a sheet of an elongated and flexible mirror. Esperanza was sitting complacently on the left bank, staring at her own image beneath the water surface. Her eyes were light blue and disheveled blond hair streamed down her face like golden filaments. She was a bit short for her age, but stocky. She rated the prettiest among her four sisters and, probably, the most attractive in her village. Occasionally, she threw a twig into the water, which splashed and distorted her reflection. Once in a while, a frog would croak and distract her from her thoughts. She took pleasure in splashing the water with her feet making them oscillate like a pendulum. She accompanied the movement of her legs with her head, left and right. Once in a while, she smiled and quickly covered her knees with the end of the skirt that she had temporarily pulled up.

At that time, Esperanza was ten years old. In school, she did not excel and she could not after spending the rest of the day on the farm or at home for house chores. Despite her brightness, her father had determined her future role. Being the eldest, she was supposed to help him on the farm, while her younger sisters could continue their education. Esperanza never complained or objected to her father's decision. He was 'Padre e padrone.' When she had a few minutes

3

free from domestic responsibilities on Sunday, she preferred to go to the riverbank nearby her house and live with nature. Sometimes, passers-by heard her engaged in a soliloquy with water, "Where do you come from? Where are you going? Why do you run away from me? Are you afraid? I will not harm you. Stop for a moment your race. Oh, what a fool I am. Indeed, you do talk to me. You give me your music, your movement, your joy of living. You are always happy. You feed seeds, plants and vegetables. Birds come often to you in summer to abate their thirst. The same do the cows. Children enjoy taking a dip in your bosom and the son changes your color and temperature." Her monologue was suddenly interrupted by two hands that covered her eyes. She shivered and gave a jolt. A male voice, behind her, said, "Guess, who I am?" She got scarred and hastened to cover her legs. "Who are you?" She protested, trying to free her face from the hands of the intruder.

Again, the newcomer asked, "Guess!"

Espera did not appreciate the invasion of her privacy, but to avoid any unpleasant surprise, at least for the time being, she tried to cooperate. "You are Ernie," she said.

"Come on! Take another guess."

"First, take your hands off my face or I am going to scream." The boy withdrew his hands and exclaimed, "You did not guess!"

The friendly face brought a sigh of relief to Espera who replied a bit annoyed, "What are you trying to do? Scare me, Felix?"

"What made you come here, anyhow?" he asked in an inquisitive tome.

"I took my chance. My parents are in the field and I like to spend my little free time alone on this river edge." She took a pause and added, "Why, don't you tell me, instead, your reasons for following me." "Well, really, I was not following you. I was only trying to protect you," he replied with an innocent accent.

"You know, you are crazy! Boys don't stay with girls all alone."

"We are classmates and neighbors. We live right there, behind the elm tree. I can see you from my window. We are friends. Why? Did I really offend you? I am sorry. I did not mean it. I was alone and I wanted to be with you."

Espera blushed. "I better go home right now. Do you know what happens if my mother sees me with you? I never hear the end of it"

"We are not doing anything wrong. Listen! Let us talk about school! Tomorrow,

Mr. Pollito, the science teacher, is coming back from a long sickness. We have a lot of fun with him. He has such a long nose. He looks like Pinocchio. Remember?

"Yea, last time, I got punished because of you."

"Me? I did not throw the tomato on the board and I did not blame you. John, "the lizard, did it. That ugly puss causes many problems. When I see him, I am going to smack him. He gets many people in trouble. He almost got me suspended one day, because he put a mouse in the teacher's desk drawer. John looked at me when the teacher asked the class who did it. Too bad, the lizard' could not keep his mouth shot outside of the school, Mr. Pollito found it out, and the next day he gave him what he deserved

"John is stupid! I do not understand why they do not kick him out of school. He is a waste."

"Well, his father has a tomato business, you know. In addition, he thinks he can play any prank. Eh, he even comes to class without stationary. I have to lend him paper and pencil every day. I am tired of it."

"What is he going to make out of himself?

"Beats me! I do not get involved in people's business. I can only tell you what I am going to make out of myself. In the future, I want to be a mechanic, a good one and make lots of money."

"Mechanics do not make a lot of money."

"Are you kidding? Did you see a German tricycle in the display window in the main square? I am going to fix it."

"As for me" replied Espera. She did not finish the sentence. Her face became dead serious. When she realized that Felix was waiting for an answer, she said, I am going to be a farmer. That is all."

"Why that? Don't you like school? Felix replied with curiosity.

"It is not that. My dad has made up his mind. It is written in my destiny"

"What's that?"

"You know our customs about the eldest daughter. Why do you ask me for?"

Felix lowered his head. "I am also aware that the youngest daughter should take care of the old folks. Do you get it?"

5

Espera nodded. "Maybe that's why my twin sisters are going to college."

"That's not fair. I don't care." In saying that, he laid his right hand around her shoulders. She did not even feel it. Felix got his mouth closer to her ear and whispered to her,

"Someday, you will stay home. No more this hard work... Espera, you will be always my friend, my best friend, my..." He stared at her eyes and kissed her hair. Espera got startled. She looked at him with a troubled heart and blushed. She got up and slapped him on the face, "Do not try to do that again. I mean it!" She warned him. She jumped on her feet and hurried back home.

Felix made an attempt to pursue her, but desisted. Instead, he shouted, "I will never forget you!" The wind carried the words to her. She stopped and turned around. She passed her right hand on her face and took it down. She smiled with malice, then, made a 'good-by' gesture with her hand and ran toward the street.

Espera was surprised to see her parent home. Her father was waiting on the threshold of the door. "Where have you been you little scoundrel!" he shouted, spelling out every single syllable.

"I stopped on the river for a little while."

"And who was there with you?"

"Daddy, honest, I didn't call him. He came on his own." Crying and talking was one thing for Espera.

"I do not want you to be in his company ever again. Do you hear me? He is bad news."

"But, he didn't do anything to me. He is a good boy. We are classmates."

Her father was not in a mood to listen to alibis. He grabbed her by the hair and pulled her inside. There, he took off the strap of his pants and hit her on the legs and on her back many times, 'till the girl became livid and began trembling. The cries called the attention of her oldest brother, who came at her rescue. "The next time I see you with that boy, I am going to break your neck with my bare hands." He pronounced the last sentence in a threatening and unequivocal tone. Then, he added, "Tomorrow, you will not attend school. You will be confined in your room for the whole week." He straightened out his pants and shirt and told his wife in a domineering tone, "Put her in the cellar. I have to go downtown for business. As soon as he left, Espera's brother pleaded for her to his mother, but she brushed him aside. Instead of listening to him, she gave a stern look to her daughter and said, "What are you trying to do? Create more problems between our families? And, what is this business of being alone with him in an isolated area? At your age, you should be thinking about sowing in your spare time. If my father ever saw me with a boy at your age, it would have been the end of it. One day, I looked at a boy and I could not even go back home. Grandma kept me at her house." She looked outside to assure herself that her husband was out of sight and continued," This new generation is going out of hand. And this war does not help either. With the Germans here and the Americans coming pretty soon from Sicily, who knows what is in store?" She turned around waiting for a reply, but her daughter was shivering. She laid a blanket on her and put her to bed. I am not going to punish you yet, but your father's wishes must be respected," she added.

In a backyard of scenic serenity, Espera's mother had ignited an environment of resentfulness, hatred and vengeance. No one could foresee the consequences of maternal cruelty that invaded and usurped innocence in its purest state. Undeterred by any external repercussion, this woman was emblematic of a parental authority that created around her and her husband a halo of impunity.

Across street, a similar scene was occurring. Felix's mother, her eyes looking like burning charcoal, shouted at her son "Your thick head, good for nothing! When are you going to learn that we do not want to have anything to do with that family? Did you forget already that we are enemies forever?" She grabbed a broom and hit him on his legs. "We can hear from here what's going on in their house. What are you trying to do? Add gasoline on fire?" As if she were not content with the broom, she grabbed the pole used to lock the door at night and began to bang it on her son's shoulders. The boy cried out, "Mom, I did not do anything. Honest! Quit hitting me! Espera is in my class."

"Do not even mention her name in this house; otherwise I crack my knuckles on your scalp."

"Can I find out why you hate her so much? What did she do to you? How can she harm you? She is a little girl."

7

"Oh, yea? Right now, take this." She picked up the 'zoccolo' from her right foot and hit him hard on the head. "From now on, I will order your father not to give you any spending money at the end of the month. It is not much, but you can buy an ice cream."

"What money do you ever give me? I can't even buy the pencil," answered the boy, crying.

"Shot up, your fat head!"

"Mom, you can do whatever you want to me, but you do not say anything against that girl. In five years, I am going to leave this house. I am going to be a mechanic. I won't need anyone anymore."

"As far as I am concerned you can hit the road now. You are only an expense to me."

Felix kept on crying. His mother pushed him out into the street. Some peers saw him and clustered around him to console him. Her husband took part in the disciplinary action with a pole that he used many times on the back of a defenseless son.

Felix was a stocky young boy of eleven years of age with brown eyes and smooth dark hair, which fell in all directions. The skin too was of an olive color. He was intelligent, strong and assertive. He worked on the farm every day of the week after school, except on Sunday when he enjoyed some free time after feeding the animals and milk the cows. He told his friends that he had to get out of the house as soon as possible, maybe attend a mechanic school. One of his friends promised him that he would mention it to his father. Felix's eyes glittered. "You will?"

His little friend nodded, "I sure do."

Felix tried to clean his nose with the back of his hand, while his friends stood there in silence turning their emotions in tears.

CHAPTER III

Love under Duress

The day after Espera and Felix received the brutal beatings, Felix went to school with black eyes. His friends started to mock him. One of them, a short red hair girl, said, "What did you do? Did you paint them with black color because you want to be like the Indians?"

A fat boy reprimanded her, "Stupid, they used mostly red color."

A third boy joked around, "Giorgio gave him a licking."

This kind of psychological harassment continued in the classroom until the Mr. Pollito's arrival. He noticed Felix's swollen face and, even though he suspected that it was family related, did not make any remark. He overheard some unsympathetic remarks and scolded those students who made them. He reminded them to observe a civic behavior in and out of the classroom. Then, he proceeded with the attendance. When he called Espera's name, nobody answered. He scouted the room with his big eyes, but she was not there. Nobody knew or heard anything about her whereabouts. A couple of students threw in some guesses, but were quickly overpowered by negative shouts/

In dismissing the class, the teacher paid special attention to comments that might have led him to make some logical assumptions in regard to Espera's absence. One by one, the students passed by him at the door and bid good-by, except Felix. The teacher held him back by the arm and asked him how he got the black eyes. The boy lowered his head and stood there motionless. Mr. Pollito did not insist and without making any further inquiry that would have hurt his sensitivity, made a gesture with his right hand that meant permission to leave. Felix didn't even raise his head and left in silence. The teacher followed him with his eyes and muttered, "Mala tempora currunt."

Later, in the day, a couple of girls attempted to pay a visit to Espera. Her mother did not appreciate the visit and told them that her daughter was unavailable. One of the girls attempted to look behind the fence, but the lady yelled at her and ordered them to leave the ground. The insisted that the time was inappropriate and her daughter could not be distracted from attending the animals. The girls did as it was demanded to them, but when they were out of sight, the same girl, a bit more inquisitive and daring, than the second, returned from another direction. She stopped at the opposite side of the backyard, and hid behind a mound of hay. She stood in a squatting position for about two minutes to peruse the area. The air was tense. Traces of chickens and cows left over were everywhere. She smelled something offensive and looked at her shoes. They were smeared with cows' excrements. An exclamation of disgust barely made it to pass the lips. She pressed impulsively the right hand on the mouth to suppress her displeasure. A distant lamentation reached her ears. Her mind went on the alert. She perked the ears even more and, this time, she detected clear cries coming from the cellar. Using extreme caution, very peculiar for a teenager, she approached a small window across from her. The window was dirty and precluded any visibility to the interior. Nobody wondered in the vicinity. The rough cloth that held together her ponytail fell down. Without thinking twice, she used it to clean the glass. Now, the sun's rays illuminated the interior of the cellar and, for the first time, she was in a position to scrutinize it. The rubbing on the window, somehow, did not pass unnoticed and reached the kitchen where Espera's mother was peeling potatoes. Being sensitive even to the slightest noises around the house and fearing that foxes or thieves were attacking or stealing chickens, she abandoned her task instantly and grabbed the rifle from behind the door. The sight of the gun petrified the girl, who made it just on time to catch a glimpse of her classmate tied on a table and fled. The stranger's passage put on the run the animals in all directions. Espera's mother, alarmed by the disorderly conduct of the animals, cried out, "To the thief! To the thief! " Not seeing anyone, she pointed the rifle toward the pile of hay and pulled the trigger. The bullet ended up on a tree behind it. Determined to pursue the offender, she checked every inch of her backyard. At the end, she gathered the animals in their dominion and locked the gate. By then, she was satisfied that she had averted a theft and resumed her previous domestic chores.

The girl arrived home breathless. Her parents, alarmed by her puffing and panting, inquired about the cause of it. For a few minutes, she was unable to talk, which frightened them. As soon as she resumed the normal breathing, she recounted in details her experience. Her father rebuked her, at first, for having transgressed somebody's private property, but her mother stood there in her defense. "Don't tell anyone what you saw."

Her father warned her, "If you do, you won't be going out for a month,"

The following day, the girl went to school and did not open her mouth. Espera was absent for the second day.. When the class was dismissed, Felix called his friend on the side and asked her, "Do you know where Espera is?"

The girl turned her head left and right in a sign of denial, "No, but if you are so interested in her well being, why don't find it out on your own?"

Felix let out a deep sigh, "I have no friends anymore. I can't trust anyone. I am all alone against everybody," he answered.

The girl looked at him straight in his eyes as to invite him to rationalize and said, "Felix, do not be a fool! You may get in a lot of hot water."

He started to scratch his nails. He was undecided. "Thank you for being so nice to me," he said. Then, he added, "Felix, do not be facetious. You talk to me as if you do not trust me. Aren't we friends?"

"Yes, we are." She looked at him with compassion and said, "We all know who did that to you. But if you are really crazy, go to the barn and look through the cellar window."

"Now, you are a real friend." He opened his arms and hugged her. "Please, don't spill the beans; otherwise, my father will kill me."

Felix put his forefingers on the lips and tightened them.

Felix waited 'till dark before he tried to make a move. He had to act with the maximum secrecy. He grabbed a pail and told his mother that he was going to fetch water at the public fountain. There was only one streetlight in the corner. With the aid of darkness, he squatted down and moved slowly around Espera's house. Finally, he reached the window. A trembling candle flame was casting a scanty light in the cellar. He lay with his stomach down and raised his head. Espera was there agonizing. He was tempted to knock. A dog smelled his presence and ran over in an aggressive posture. The boy was lucky. He pulled out a bone from his pocket and threw it to him. At least, for the time being, he appeased the animal's anger

Felix tried to catch Espera's attention by moving his hands across the windows. Espera was very uncomfortable in her position and did not see him. Felix knocked lightly on the window. She made a jerk and turned around. She looked toward the window and saw a hand making gestures. At first, she got scarred. Shortly after, she recognized Felix and motioned to him to leave. She looked pale and was barefoot. A small shirt covered her upper body, while a sultry, long skirt protected her legs from flies. Her friend's appearance gave free reins to emotions and tears started to flow down her cheeks. They rested there for some time until the heat dried them out.

Felix was undecided on the next step to take. Espera, with a movement of her head, signaled to him u to leave immediately. She was aware that either of her parents would eventually discover his presence. He was not in favor of complicating the matter even further and told her that he would visit her again the following day. He bid good-by to her and threw her a kiss. Soon after, he realized that the back of his hands were wet. A couple of tears had found their way down. He wiped them against his chest and began to rotate his eyes clockwise to ascertain that no one had seen him. He assumed an erect posture and began to take distance from the house with extreme caution. In that moment, a harsh voice lacerated the evening peace, "I caught the fox in the trap, the one that comes here to spoil my soup!" The sarcastic comment and a sonorous laughter preceded a big bang and a loud cry. The woman hit Felix's shoulders with all her strength. The pole broke. She repeated the second strike with the remaining part left in her hands. The boy rolled over his body on the ground and barely managed to dodge it. He got up quickly and gained access to the path that led to the main street. The woman pursued him up to the sidewalk where she abandoned the prey for fear that she would alarm the neighbors. Felix felt relieved from the chase, but the back pain was unbearable. He reached the fountain, took hold of the pail of water and slowly proceeded toward his house. His parents were behind the door waiting for him. Espera heard a noise and a scream all the way from across the street and feared for the worst.

As a result of Felix's daring adventure, Espera's mother accused her of premeditated escape with the boy and deprived her of food and hygienic necessities for three successive days. Espera became emaciated, weak and devoid of any desire to live.

The following day, Felix was not walking straight on his way to school and his friends got concerned and asked him all sorts of questions. He ascribed his condition to an accidental fall on his way down the stairs. His teacher was skeptical to the latest 'accident.' The bell rang at the end of the day and the teacher dismissed the class. When Felix was at the door, the teacher held him back and said, "Not you...Today, you are going to be spend extra time here for not having done the home work."

The boy protested, "I can't stay, sir. My parents are waiting for me on the farm. If I don't show up, they will get worried and search for me."

"Well, I have to talk to them, then."

"Honest, Mr. Pollito, they need me. If I do not go to work..." The boy dropped his head in a sign of disappointment and disconsolation.

"Ten minutes of your delay will not undermine the crop," insisted the teacher.

"But, I can't," cried out Felix.

"Well, let us make a deal. I will help you to do the homework, now, so that, you do not have to do it at the end of the day. Agree?"

Felix raised his head in a sign of surprise and consented to it even though he was worried about his parents' reaction.

The teacher paused for a few seconds and exclaimed, "No, I changed my mind. I want to do something better than that for you. Maybe we can postpone the homework to a later date if you can help me to understand why Espera has been missing classes"

At that point, Felix began to be dubious about his teacher's intentions and said, "Why do you ask me that? Am I her brother?"

"That I know it, but you live across the street from her. You have friends, don't you?

13

Friends talk to each other. Don't they? They reveal secrets. If you heard something from them, it would make my job much easier and, maybe, I could help someone."

"Even if I knew something, I would not tell you," he replied in defiance.

"Yes, Yes, I am aware of the feud between both families, but I am interested in the education of the girl."

"And I am interested in her safety and mine."

Mr. Pollito pulled down the glasses from his eyes and placed them on the desk. He got up from the chair and pointed the index finger to the boy, "What do you mean by that?" he asked in a serious tone.

"You are a teacher and you ask me to explain it?"

The teacher got a bit bothered by the challenge. He did not wish to deteriorate the conversation. "Are you concerned about Espera?" he asked.

"Don't you think I should? We are friends."

"Very well, then, we both aim at the same target."

"What do you mean by that? What do you expect me do?"

"Help me understand what is going on."

The boy took was in no mood to cooperate. In fact, he expressed concern over the disclosure of Esperanza's family situation, His teacher said, "You are afraid it could become public affair and the repercussions would widen even more the gap between both of you. .. Right?

"Right!"

Mr. Pollito sat again and fell back on his chair. He was made aware of the boy's internal turmoil and did his best to assist him. He scratched his head many times and straightened the body to an upright position. He felt uncomfortable\ sitting down for too long. He got up for the second time and said, "Why are you so obstinate. If you care for her, then, let me help her. Let's cooperate."

The teacher's rationale rang the right bell in the young man's ears and Felix opened up 'Pandora's box.' Immediately after, both observed a long and tortuous silence. The boy was getting nervous for an answer that never came. Finally, Mr. Pollito recomposed himself and said, "Rest assured that what you just revealed to me will stay between us."

Felix welcomed his teacher's firm commitment and was ready to leave.

Mr. Pollito said in a low tone, "The Italian law has not changed since the Roman Empire. A parent is the supreme authority in the family and there is nothing that can be done about it. However, you and I can do something."

"What? Call the police?" answered the boy anxiously?

"No, not yet...At this time, it is more prudent to invent other alternatives. We must operate with caution and diligence. For instance, you could deliver some food to her."

"Where am I going to get it?"

"Don't worry! I will provide it. Allow me fifteen minutes. I run home and prepare it. Do not run away. Time is the major factor. If we do not act promptly, our project will fail. The boy was pleased to have support from a strong, public, institutional representative who shared his aim and would put his reputation in at the stake. He looked at him and nodded eagerly.

"I have another idea," added the teacher. "Wait for me, behind the school. I will be back shortly."

"We must do it in a hurry. Her parents are on the farm, but I do not know if Espera's mother comes back early to cook," reminded him.

"You are absolutely right."

The teacher did as he said. In less than half an hour, he was back with a package under his arms. He handed it to Felix and said, "Pay close attention to what I am going to tell you. Do not stop any place or talk to anyone. I will be going ahead of you. When you reach the curve, look at the tree in front of you. I will be there with this newspaper in my hands. Give me the time to get a close look at Espera's backyard. If I keep the paper wide open, that means that the area is safe and you may go directly to the target. Depending on the outcome of this operation I will decide on whether it is convenient to talk to her dad. The success of this plan depends on how well we keep our lips tight. Agree?"

The boy felt that his teacher had given him ample assurance of his sincere intentions and replied with confidence, "Agree."

"Good boy!"

Felix looked at the teacher's newspaper. It was open, but he exercised extra precautions. Once again, he checked if anyone was in the backyard. The traffic was scarce at that hour. He got nervous and almost gave up the plan. The sweat was raining down his forehead and brows. He wiped it with the back of his hand and then he made the move. He slid alongside the wall and reached the cellar window. The heat was intense. To his surprise, the window was open. He dropped the package and whispered to Espera a few words of caution. She picked up the package and hid it underneath of the blanket. She urged him to run away immediately and not to place his person in danger on her behalf. He stretched his hand down the window. She touched it with her. A warm feeling ran through their bodies. He said to her, "I will never abandon you. She looked at him with her big blue eyes and said, "You will always be in the mirror of my mind." She released the hand and begged him to leave before one of her parents would come back unexpectedly. Felix threw her a kiss. She watched him until he took off. Espera went to the stairs and stretched her ears. There was no noise or movement upstairs. She opened the package and found cheese, bread and fruit. She was feeble, but gained the residue of her strength and avidly devoured the food. She lit a match and burned the paper in the fireplace. She lay on the bed and slept for hours.

In the main street, Felix made the thumb up to the teacher and the two departed in different direction to their respective houses.

The Communist Party headquarter was in the main plaza. The president, Monsieur Serafine, was surprised to see him at his office in the middles of the week. As usual, he welcomed him with great effusion and deference. The teacher's customary visit was on Saturday, but the circumstances required a change. The secretary prepared a coffee that both enjoyed with gusto and the conversation assumed quickly a serious tone. The president asked his friend the reason for the abrupt anticipation of the traditional get-together and the teacher mentioned evasively a case which displayed a great deal of parental recrudescence. The president was shocked to hear that, but made it clear not to expect any commitment to investigate on his part. He stressed the fact that he did not wish to antagonize anyone because it would have negative repercussions on the next mayoral elections. Furthermore, he felt that any personal involvement in family matters would be considered a breach of privacy.

The teacher left the office disconsolate and disillusioned. While he was walking back home, he stopped and brought the right hand on his forehead. It was a sign of having forgotten something. At home, he picked up the bicycle from the garage and went out for a ride. In the narrow and dusty streets of the countryside, he ended up in many ridges caused by the daily passage of oxen carts and had hard time riding. Occasionally, hungry dogs attacked him from all sides and he had to use all of his skill to keep the wheels under control. Only at one point he was going off balance, but he managed to avoid the fall.

The weather was fantastic. The trees foliage did its best to filter the sun's rays still warm by the end of a working day. At an intersection, the teacher slowed down. He recognized Espera's parents carrying bales of hay close to the edge of the road. At the sight of the teacher, the two spouses interrupted temporarily their task and exchanged the ritual greetings with him. They spoke about crops and the lack of rain in the past month. The conversation, eventually, fell on Espera and the teacher inquired about her health, "Espera has been missing from class for the whole week. I was wondering if she is sick or what? Some neighbors hypothesized that you have a great need of help."

Espera's mother looked at the teacher and dropped the fork on the ground. She got closer to him and said, "My neighbors are usually wrong. This time they have guessed wrong once again. My daughter has been sick."

"But, don't you think that you should have informed the school principal? We could have sent the homework to your house."

"Now, I don't understand your reasoning," replied the woman a bit irritated. "How could she have done the homework if she were sick in bed?"

"Well," answered the teacher with calm, "It depends from the type of pathology."

"And, what do you mean by that?"

"If the infirmity relates to the foot, arm, knee, for instance, the child can still study even though, he or she is unable to move around and perform menial work."

The lady did not quite understand him and answered, "Good heavens! Luckily, you did not speak Latin; otherwise, it would have been a blackout. If you know what I mean." She leaned over the fork handle and added, "She is feeling better. In other words, she is moving around and by now she may be preparing supper."

The teacher was a man of great intelligence. Instead of continuing the conversation with her, he turned his attention to her husband.

"Sir, I am sure that you are aware that education is power. As we all know too well, parents have a great responsibility for their children's future, and, I surmise that you are unquestionably concerned about them."

The farmer considered his position to be far from his interlocutor and approached the edge of the road to respond, but his wife intervened, "Teacher, we are honest and proud farmers. As you can see, we live off our land." We do not ask anything from nobody. My children will do well. I am teaching them the proper way. If they miss school at times, it means that we have a lot of work here."

"I am not questioning your dedication to the farm neither I wish to interfere with your family private life. As an educator, I have the tremendous responsibility of educating the children how to be better citizens and have success in life. Likewise, parents, being natural teachers, have the holy duty to raise their children with respect, love and wisdom. Children are our future. I must address this issue because too often some parents act as tyrants and not as unselfish and loving guides."

The couple stood there speechless and marveled by the teacher's flow of ideas. The farmer, however, had a quick moment of reaction and replied, "Wait just a minute now! What is your business of being too private? I have never been a teacher and I never will be. I don't even know how to read or write. So, don't come here and try to trap me with strange words." He was going to add something else, but his wife intervened, "don't bother, honey, this guy is a book boy. He does not realize the tough life we live on the farm."

The teacher bit his lips and bid good-by to them. Both of them followed him turning around and disappearing behind the street corner. The lady did not appreciate the teacher's tough language. She exchanged a few ideas with her husband, cleaned up in a hurry and hastened home.

Felix was still in pain, but having suppressed the hunger pranks, she felt much stronger. Her mother arrived and unlocked the cellar's door. She moved her eyes around with suspicion and gave a sigh of satisfaction. Espera did not talk until her mother ordered her to go to the kitchen and help her to prepare supper. The sudden change in her mother's mood and action was welcomed by Espera with cautious optimism. The girl told her that she would be there right away. With some efforts, she climbed the stairs and reached the stove where she began to peel potatoes.

Felix's house was located across from Espera. Every day, he looked down the street to see if the teacher might pay a visit to her parents. His face brightened when he noticed Espera walking through the backyard. He could not believe it! He wanted to call her, to signal her with his hand that he was there watching her, but decided that it was too imprudent.

The next morning, an emaciated Espera, disheveled and without stationary, showed up in the classroom. Her classmates, especially the girls, rejoiced at her return and tried to find out the causes of her absence. The teacher was euphoric. He could not believe how his visit to her parents had such a positive impact on them. To celebrate the event, he moved the students to the school garden, changing the nature of the class from purely literary to recreational. Knowing how hungry she must have been, he grabbed his lunch and her and Felix inside. "Here, eat! I stay outside with the rest of the class."

The classmates vied in catching Espera's attention. She looked dazed and withdrawn. There were times when she and Felix exchanged intense glances, but did not dare to talk to each other in public. Aside from the fact that he was interested in averting unnecessary publicity on her account, he did not wish to spoil her moments of joy. The sandwich was consumed rather fast and the two returned to the garden. Felix grabbed a ball and threw it to the teacher. He caught it with his right hand and smiled. Felix shouted, "Great job! You made it!"

The teacher winked at him. He approached Felix and said in a low voice, "If it were not for your active cooperation and involvement, she would not be here today. You are a tremendous asset to school and to society."

Felix was unwilling to accept all the credit, "Let us say that we both did it."

The teacher hugged him. Both were getting emotional. The students looked at them, but did not know the reason for being so friendly.

At the end of the school day, Felix was the last one to leave the class. His back was still excruciating. *To allay the pain he resorted to massaging the area, but the benefits were all* temporary. The principal informed by the teacher and called Espera in his office to ascertain that her condition had returned to normality. Her friends were waiting on the school grounds. On her way out, she spotted Felix who quickly rose to his feet and asked her about her health.

"I am much better here than in that dungeon. By the way, where did you get the food?"

"It is not hard. He did it all."

"The teacher? How did you dare to tell him?"

"I did not. He wanted to find out the reason for being absent. Unfortunately, nobody provided him any information. At that point, he took action on his own. He planned the rescue operation, at least on paper, bought the food for you and went also to the farm to talk to your parents."

"Why did you do that for me?"

"I guess it is because he is our teacher. You know, many people teach, but a few know how teach. When he talks, he got fire in his words. His energy is infectious. I had many teachers in the past years, but he is the only one who affected my life."

"For sure, he knows what he is talking about and puts so much passion in his work and has so much charisma..."

Espera looked around to make sure no one was spying on her. Her friend was doing the same. Their friends left one by one. It was then that Espera turned her attention to him and asked him, "By the way, did my mother hurt you? I heard a crack..."

"Yeah...She broke a pole on my back. It still hurts."

She hugged him and kissed him on the forehead. "How can I ever forget what you have done for me? You pains are my pains."

Felix lowered his head and said, "When you suffered, I was suffering along with you."

A couple of tears fell down her cheeks. "I must go now, before somebody spies on us. Be careful and take good care of yourself. You hear?"

Felix asked her, "Why are you crying for?"

"These tears," she said, "Are the only gift I can offer you now. They are my pledge for eternal love to you."

"I will mirror in them during the most difficult moments of my life wherever I will be."

Espera's face brightened at the sound of those words and said laughing, "And you, what do you give me?"

"I have no gold and no silver. I am penniless, but I am the richest man in the world because of your love. I can only say that you are my April flower and I can only offer you my heart."

"Well, in that case, I will keep its perfume and fragrance in my heart as a reminder of you. Do you like it?"

Felix' eyes were radiant with joy, "I love it."

Espera added, "Felix you are my morning sunrise that will warm me up in the winter days of my life. I will always cherish your love."

"I will always love you."

He took her hand and put it on his heart. "No matter where I go, you will always feel this beating for you."

She attempted a half of a smile, blew a kiss to him and walked back home.

From inside his class, the teacher was following the scene with pride.

The following Sunday, the events took a new course. Espera's mother was beating a drum up and down her street, singing, "I got the fox. I got the fox. He wanted to spoil my soup, but I got him for good." The neighbors at the sound of the drums thought it was the town crier announcing some new municipal laws or doing advertisement for the market vendors. To their dismay, they saw a scene completely different from any ordinary one. Their astonishment grew deeper when they did not know what to make of the word 'fox,' in what context it was used and to whom it was referring. In less than half of an hour, a crowd gathered around her. The lady gave no explanation of her metaphorical language. Soon, people started to crack jokes at her. Her husband, who was observing from behind the curtains of his bedroom, could no longer accept the ridicule to which his wife was being subjected, and took action. He hurried to the street, grabbed his wife by hand and dragged her inside. The reverberations of her unique and rare exhibition became the talk of the town in the subsequent days and a Neapolitan singer drew inspiration from that song to launch a new, revised version of it that had a lot of popular success.

As the time went by, Espera's family turmoil became a note of the past. In school, the class atmosphere returned to its normality, but not for too long. Another dark cloud hovered on their heads and caused significant consternation among students. The teacher, previously mentioned, got seriously sick and was substituted by a young woman with a long chin and a raspy voice. With her, the children's behavior took a turn to the worse. They despised her disciplinarian attitude and, soon, their behavior exemplified defiance under different connotations.

One Monday morning, before she arrived to class, Felix put a package in the central drawer of her desk. Upon her arrival, during preparation time, she opened the central drawer to check if everything was in order and saw a box wrapped in a red decorative paper tied with a ribbon. She opened the card where it was written, "To a Great Substitute," but did not show any emotion. She pulled a tiny knife from her pocketbook and pierced the box. The blade point landed on a soft body that caused a shrieking sound. In that instant her mind went on a mechanical devise. Suddenly, one, two, three, six mice escaped and took refuge in different directions. The poor woman jumped on her feet and began screaming. Her face had the color of wax. The rodents terrorized her to the point that she fled to the corridor letting the classroom turn into a pandemonium. Being without guidance, the students took control of the classroom and got rowdy.

Many of them jumped from seat to seat laughing and shouting; other were running all over, throwing books left and right. No object was immune to vandalism. The class was in a complete chaos. The loud noise reached the adjoining rooms. The teachers interrupted their teaching and looked outside of the doors to find out what was going on. The situation became more dramatic when their students reversed in the corridor to be part of the ongoing theater. Obviously, the soap opera could not last too long. The janitor informed immediately the principal who rushed over with the vice-principals to restore order.

The acts of irreverence toward the substitute did not end there. On a Friday, a boy dropped an aunt on Espera's ear. As soon as, she realized that something was crawling around her head, she tried to shake it off with the paper. Her classmates jumped at the opportunity to get out of hand. One of them poked her from the back and asked her, "Guess who I am?" Espera grabbed the boy by the arm and threw him on the floor. This imprudent act generated a second turmoil. Half of the class sided with the boy and the other half with Espera. The sub, unable to control them, went to the corridor asking for help. In the meantime, Felix stood on the teacher's desk and yelled, "If anyone will touch Espera, he is going to be dead meat." At that firm threat, all the students returned to their seat. At the news of a second mass disobedience in a matter of a week, the principal's eyes became fiery and banged his fist on the desk. This time he did not waver. He was determined to put down the rebellious behavior once and for all by expelling them all until they returned with their parents. His rage turned into astonishment when he entered the classroom. Everyone was seating peacefully in his seat doing the homework. He looked at the substitute with a mixture of incredulity and self-control. It was June and he concluded that it was in everybody's best interest to play down the insubordination.

One last incident that threatened the school peaceful atmosphere occurred on the last day of school. Before that class started, a boy tried to lift up Esperanza's black apron to uncover the knees. Her reaction was rather immediate and harsh. She took off her shoes and kept on hitting his head with both hands. Felix was livid, but did not say a word. During a visit to the restroom, he stopped briefly at his locker. Later, the same boy fell asleep. Felix squatted and moved toward him on the tiptoes. While the teacher was writing something on the board, he carried out his secret operation.

The bell rang and the boy woke up, but he could not move. Felix had tied him around the desk. The boy moved like a lion in a cage, but could not disengage himself. The class went into a delirium. The sub, suspecting that someone was playing a prank, ordered everybody out. Only the tied student remained in his place full of anger waiting for her to untie him. The sub was unaware of his predicament and wondered why he was not leaving. The boy lowered his head in sign of shame. It was then that she shook her head and made a few steps to untie him. Unfortunately, she stumbled against a desk and fell on the floor on her back and with the legs up in the air. A group of students from behind the door was laughing and making all sort of funny comments. They were talking so loudly that the janitors spotted them from the end of the hall and rushed over. That part of the corridor was crowded of unruly spectators. The news soon reached the principal's office. He slumbered on the chair and did the sign of the cross. Eventually, the janitors untied the boy and helped the teacher to stand on her feet. The order was restored with the assistance of other staff members and the class resumed without further interruptions.

The end of June came and it was time to distribute the elementary school diploma. It was on this occasion that Espera had one of the rarest moments of serene conversation with Felix. After the ceremony, the two withdrew to an empty lot behind the school and sat. Felix said, "Tomorrow, I start my mechanical apprenticeship."

"And I go back to the farm for the rest of my life."

"What do you mean?"

"My father has made up his mind."

"Which is...?"

"Oh, only my sisters can go on studying."

"That's not right."

"Well, according to him, I am the oldest one."

"That's crazy!" He looked in the space as if he were waiting for an answer from somewhere in the galaxies. The answer did not come. He turned the attention to her again and said, "Someday, I am going to pull you out of the farm. You will not have to work hard anymore. I promise you."

"Someday..." she murmured in a discouraging tone.

"It won't be too long. Eight or nine years, the most.... My mother got married at the age of eighteen."

"My mother was sixteen. Her father's second wife mistreated her. But, he did the same."

"Are you joking?"

"He tried more than once to raise her skirt, so, she got married quickly."

"I can't believe it!"

"Many unpleasant things happen within families. These are the untold stories."

"I guess you are right. What I don't understand is why your mother is so rough with you."

She shook her head and said, "I do not know. Life is hard. As for us, we may not see each other anymore."

He covered her mouth with his left hand and said, "Do not say that ever again. I am going to work a few miles away. I will be near you. Don't worry about it. We find a way and the time to talk."

"It is going to be very difficult."

"Let's give it a try."

"I have my doubts. Good-by and good luck to you..."

"Don't kill me with those words. I will be here for you."

She hugged him. He did not want to break up the moment. She disengaged herself and said, "Forget me.

There is no sense to continue in this way. It is our destiny."

He stretched his hand to reach her shoulder, but she pulled away.

"Someday, I will be a great mechanic!" he shouted.

A year flew by and Felix was finally accepted in to attend an apprenticeship shop in a nearby town. There was one only one spot open and he grabbed the opportunity. After all, it was not easy at all to gain a space in a garage and learn the trade. Without friends or a political assistance, a young man would never get the chance. There was a time when, Felix thought of working for the Americans once they arrived in town, but the dream never materialized,

At the beginning of his mechanical experience, the boss assigned Felix to minor duties. He was assigned to clean motors, sweep the floor, hand tools to the master mechanic or go to a nearby café' to buy a lemonade for the manager's wife during hot days.

The learning process proceeded at a turtle's pace. Felix understood that it was not sufficient to be on the job every day. He realized quite early that he could only achieve his goal by watching as much as possible the master mechanic, which was not easy, due to many menial jobs he had to perform.

Being a journeyman was a long, tedious and unrewarding process. A boy started at a young age and finished in the twenties. The shop owner was very attentive to preserve his reputation, that's why none of his pupils would be leaving his garage without proper knowledge and experience. Conversely, in our contemporary society, for better or for worse, rules have changed. An aspirant barber in the United States, attends a sex month course and, voila', he becomes a licensed barber. In Italy, during that span of time, the apprentice would learn only how to put on the apron, hand the tools to the master barber and apply the shaving cream.

Every morning, Felix got up early and walked five miles to get to his working place. In winter, it was especially hard to walk in the cold and snow, unless he was lucky to get a ride on a horse and buggy going by. He expected the future to be tough and the road to success full of trials, but he was determined to hold on his dream.

...And, now, let us pick up the action someplace else in the Balkans, where I am going to introduce you, my friend reader, to two interesting traveling companions.

CHAPTER IV

Costantia

Costantia is a treasure city of Rumania that rests on the Black Sea. It was founded by the Greeks conquerors in 500 B.C. who called it Tomis in honor of their queen who beat Cyrus the Great. The Romans occupied it in 29 B.C. In the fourth century B.C., they changed the name to Costantia in homage to emperor Costantine's step sister, Costantia. Emperor Augustus despised passionately the well known poet Ovid and exiled him on the Black Sea. Ovid's friends pleaded to spare the agony of the exile to the famous poet, but the emperor was unmoved. Unfortunately, Ovid could not bear staying away from Rome and died homesick eight years later in this fascinating city.

Before the war, Costantia was a prosperous port that rivaled with others in the Balkans. Today, it has regained her splendor by judiciously administering her touristic spots. Mamaia beach is thirteen kilometers long and is a major vacation attraction. In those days, the beach was equally attractive despite the fact that it did not receive the attention that it deserved.

Here, the gypsy children walked barefoot searching for lost objects or begged for the sake of survival. The adults managed to beat the hunger and social discrimination by engaging in fortune telling or by entertaining with dancing and singing. The major source of earning came, however, from illegal business that they carried on the neighborhoods of Mangalia and Novedari where the police presence was scanty. In fact, their visibility was so negligible that the hotel owners hired their own agents to protect tourists.

Costantia enjoys also mineral spring waters a short distance from the beach. Both were and are the main source of attraction and income for the local economy. The touristic ministry has added more glamour, charm and games to the beach to make the area a center of economic revenues all year around.

CHAPTER V

The Gypsies

Many macabre stories have been floating around for centuries about this race. Some of them have become myths. In reality, there are many inaccuracies in those accounts. Gypsies did not originate, as was believed traditionally, from Egypt. This false assumption led the Spaniards to call them 'Egiptanos,' hence, the word 'gypsy.' It is important to clarify this aspect because the gypsies do not share the same somatic features as the inhabitants of the Niles River. In fact, the gypsies have straight or curly hair and the nose is not arched like most of the Arabs. The only common characteristic that they have is the dark complexion.

A swift glance to the past makes us realize that a mass migration of the gypsies began in India before the year one thousand. Initially, they laid the tents in the Balkans. Being restless and dissatisfied, after some decades, they moved to Turkey, Palestine, Egypt, Spain and the rest of Europe. By their quasi continuous wandering, they framed for themselves a nomadic lifestyle. No doubt, in the course of their itinerant transmigration, they left behind scores of old or sluggish residues from every tribe, a pack of independent minded individuals. These roots became, later, a generational virus, so that, in every country where the exodus took place, the older folks lacked the stamina to pursue the new itinerancy process and objectives and, so, remained behind. The migration process was reactivated when a new generation grew up. This gave rise to cultural and linguistic diversities within the same stock. A tribe that overgrew in fifty years broke up and ramified in different countries creating a lack of cohesiveness among them.

In a social, religious or political context, the ramification did not create a profound diversification among them because they lived in the suburbs, yet, they still had to abide, to a certain extent, to the local laws. The only basic connective wires that the many tribes maintained among them were of somatic and social nature, which were the color of the skin, the color and hair texture and their lifestyle. Unwilling to forge a sedentary identity, they lacked the will to attend schools or learn a trade.

The gypsies' impact on the economy was somewhat minimal on a large scale. The local population considered them a burden to society and kept them at a distance. For historical veracity, it would be erroneous to depict the gypsies completely dependent on public charity. They earned their living mainly by practicing divinatory arts, by mending bellows or fixing pots and pans in streets around the villages or cities they dwelled temporarily and improvised street or courtyard fire to carry out their artisan activities. Some of them even supplied manual labor in the farms to fill in for the local youth who considered harvest of wheat or the picking of fruit and vegetables too demeaning for them. It is curious to note that a similar attitude has been manifested by American and European youth who has deserted farms or manual jobs for higher education. This contempt for less remunerating job activities has favored in part the establishment of illegal immigration eager to fill in any available vacancy.

Other characteristic features of their culture were singing and dancing. They moved from town to town and performed in the main squares. The rare entertainment broke down the daily life routine of the villagers, especially on Sunday. They gathered around the artists and watched with humor mixed with fascination their performances. In return, they rewarded them by dropping coins in a hat that the band leader passed around.

The gypsies' social role, however, was more predominant in the fortune telling business. They boasted being the recipients of special divinatory gifts bestowed upon them by Mother Nature. They used tarot cards or palm reading to foretell the future in exchange of monetary or food compensation. To be more credible, they transformed these activities in actual professions. Firmly and deeply believing to have been blessed by supernatural powers, they boasted to be the producers of many benefits to the people. For instance, they claimed that by citing certain magic words they promoted the alleviation of mental distress or the healing of specific physical ailments. The credulous and superstitious people, especially in western countries, such as Italy, France, Germany and England were the easiest prey of their 'sirens." They became victim of 'a modus operandi' that in our contemporary society has won the government legal approval. We should bear in mind that these types of practices were not confined to the populace, but they extended to the high social, political and intellectual strata.

It should be stated, for the sake of truth, that not the whole population succumbed to the gypsies' controversial purported cures. A more sophisticated social sector, regardless of its structured ranks, remained utterly skeptical about the purported gypsies' prophetic powers; In fact, most of the local people wasted no time in denigrating those members of the nomadic tribes who purported divinatory power and made some victims even among politicians. To discredit the fortune telling profession and their clients, the skeptics insisted that the whole fortune telling profession was not immaculate. They presented cases of blatant deception and invoked the application of the law to stem down uses and abuses. In most instances, the impostors escaped the ax of justice simply by changing residence.

To depict the gypsies' life as idyllic, it would be a distortion of truth. The first serious and ominous anti gypsy movement took roots in Spain even before the Catholic kings conquered Granada in 1492. Unwilling to forge a sedentary identity or to submit to the new religious obligations, society labeled them outcasts. The lack of education and trade made them stagnate at the bottom of the social and economical scale. Their life style did not allow them to attend schools or learn a trade. It was not hard, therefore, to accuse them, often, of crimes which they may or may not have committed. And, so, the word 'gypsy' became synonymous of 'criminal.' Hunted like dogs, they fled to the fields or left altogether the country during the Inquisition.

The most prominent gypsy clan was the Roma. This group transmigrated in the ninth century along with other minor tribes. Obviously, their nomadic style of life, which they preferred, was not conducive to permanent settlement. Relegated in ghettos, they lived at the margin of the social, educational and economic progress. With the imposition of the Inquisition, they joined other itinerant groups fleeing in the farming areas throughout Europe. The two gypsies who concern us were originally from the Roma clan.

CHAPTER VI

Theft of the Orphans

Two men were confabulating with animosity at Poarta Albia in Constantia. They were debating for half an hour with alternating success. At times, the taller man seemed to have the upper hand; other times, it was the shorter guy to be more assertive. Worse yet, there were moments of crisis during which each threatened to break up the meeting and leave. The dispute was, finally, ironed out when they agreed to elaborate an action plan completely different from the first and from which both participants would equally benefit. Three kisses on two cheeks sealed the agreement putting an end to the acrimonious contention. The scheme that they had planned was dangerous and fraught with insidious traps. Even a negligent distraction could have cost them a long prison term or death. What they feared the most, though, was to miss the next mass migration that would take place sometimes that summer with their aim West Europe.

One of the two gypsies was tall and slender, like a string bean. The black, wavy, long hair rested on his unsteady shoulders. Whenever he made a jerky movement, it would fall foreword covering his face. In that case, he was forced to brush it backward with the back of his hand in order to be able to see. The eyes were similar to the charcoal and the lips were very pronounced, each departing in the opposite direction.

(My dear reader, even some anatomical parts of the body, at times, does not coexist pacifically! The nose was unusually long and bore a cicatrix alongside the septum. We will call him Scarman.

His friend shared the same dark complexion. His unruly, but smooth and uncultivated hair was very thick. When it was wet, it descended on the dark eyes, stopping at the eyelashes and partially precluding the vision. The nose was straight like a billiard stick. The chin had the shape of a V that was more common among girls. Unlike his companion, he was short and robust. He bragged of being the object of desire on the part of the girls of his clan and behind. His love rivals disputed the claim affirming that it was a figment of his imagination. He boasted also of being a high class man. In reality, his claim had no support, except for an over ironed suit that shone like a mirror and he wore every evening on the main street while he scrutinized the beach. He was recognized, however, for his athletic prowess. He was able to sustain his body on one finger and make somersaults in the air. He was very sleek in markets and shops. Excluding these reason, we will call him Barabbus. The read will understand...

At eight o' clock sharp, one evening, the shorter man was climbing, with some difficulties, the stairs leading to the second floor of Ovidiu Orphanatropy. He carried a big bag. On top of it, one could easily see apples and oranges.

An older nun greeted him with a faint smile at the door and inquired about the motives of his visit. Barabbus genuflected slightly and expressed the desire to distribute the fruit to the unfortunate children. The nun, a clever and mature woman around sixty was listening with justifiable apprehension and suspicion. She explained to him that it was not necessary to enter the premises and, therefore, he could leave the bag on the desk. Another nun would make sure that the distribution would occur at dinner time. Barabbus begged her to let him go on his own because it gave him a great sense of self-satisfaction. The nun acquiesced with some reservations and cautioned him not to trespass the boundary line at the end of the hall. It was the ward of the newly born babies. She imposed on him a ten minutes deadline.

The man twisted his lips and inquired, "Sister, forgive my ignorance. This is not a hospital. Pregnant women don't come here to give birth. I do not understand why you would have newly born babies here. They cannot chew fruit. They don't have teeth."

The nun realized that she was dealing with an ignorant gypsy and said, "All sorts of heinous acts occur under the vaults of heaven. Human nature is so degraded in some folks that they show their true fragile conscience when they have to meet their responsibilities."

The gypsy hardly grasped the significance of her talk. The nun smiled and said, "The babies were not born here. They were abandoned in the streets, in the fields, in the garbage cans."

The gypsy replied, "I see, some men like to put girls pregnant and, then, disappear. Am I right?"

"That's only one of the reasons. Financial or conjugal difficulties among couples or unwedded moms rank high on top of the list," she continued, "However, if you ask my personal opinion, I would reply without hesitation that we are confronted with vile acts of egoism. It is a human tragedy.

The gypsy once again was at loss with her language, but for the sake of carrying on the conversation he said, "Sister, excuse my poor education, but some people, not all though, are real animals"

"I just told you that in a different way," exclaimed the nun in a defensive gesture.

"They will never win!" rebutted the gypsy with emphasis by raising slightly his voice.

The nun frowned in her approval and the man added, "Life is far better than death." He raised the head toward the ceiling and exclaimed, "Lord, forgive us."

The nun replied, "Children are a Lord's blessing. In fact, he said, "Let the children come to me for theirs is the kingdom of heaven."

The man answered, "You are not kidding!" Then, he lowered the eyebrows and the head.

He beat his chest various times. The nun's face began to show a certain degree of curiosity. In her view, the man exhibited strange Christian rituals. Barabbus noticed the shift in her demeanor and stated, "I would like to listen to you more, sister, on this interesting subject, but I must confess to you that I did not read your Book. I do not know how to read or write."

"You mean you are an illiterate?"

"If it means the same thing, I say, yes."

"Maybe, I can teach you if you are willing…"

The man looked at her perplexed, "No, no, sister, that's impossible. I belong to another world."

The nun began to wonder about the man's real faith and was about to ask him when the Mother Superior called her. She excused herself momentarily and urged him to hurry in his tour of fruit distribution.

The other gypsy was impatiently waiting in the garden. He kept gazing upward constantly. From time to time, he touched his neck to ascertain that the nerves did not freeze. Every second that passed by the fear increased. It was a race against time. In a couple of occasions, he cursed his companion for being as slow as a turtle and made up his mind that he would drop him as a partner if the operation failed. He was on the verge of calling off the plan because the mosquitoes were biting him all over the body, when the window suddenly opened. He saw some movement going on and stretched his eyes and ears. The man from upstairs tied a rope around a steel beam and lowered two baskets with the prize in them. As soon as his friend below grabbed the baskets, the one from above untied the rope and dropped it on the ground.

With aplomb, he dashed out of the room and resumed the fruit distribution.

The nun returned and met the visitor on his way out. "I thank you, Sister, for giving me the chance to help these children." He had just finished the last word that cries and shouts lacerated the air and shattered the normalcy of a traditional, quiet environment. For the first time since its foundation, the orphanage experienced internal turmoil. The chaotic scene did not abate and Mother Superior immediately ordered to lock doors and windows. She sent word to the staff to engage in the emergency rules and ordered the guards to search for clues in every room that could lead to the discovery of the illegal activity. Barabbus asked the sister if he could be of any help. With a stern look, she ordered him to stay put and appealed to the custodians' professional responsibility to check the exits and the doors that led to the attic and roof.

One of the custodians came right back and whispered something to the sister's ear. The nun was not a novice. She gave the chastity vow long time ago. Without waiting further ado, she ran to Mother Superior's office and conferred with her rapidly, "Mother, I do not wish to be disrespectful, neither to appear arrogant, but may I find out what is the cause of this rambunctious movement?"

"It is more than that," she replied in a tone that hid an internal turmoil."

"As I understand, two babies have left the premises if the information I received is correct. If you confirm it, it means that we are dealing with a colossal mismanagement and crisis.

Mother Superior looked straight in her eyes and said, "I confirm that two babies of the opposite gender have been abducted."

"Who? Why? How?" Responded the nun in an evident state of uncontrollable anxiety. Alarm! Alarm! They stole two babies from the orphanage! She yelled.

Mother Superior stood there motionless perusing every facial movement of her co-sister.

The nun realized that she needed to restore her poise to a manageable degree and made an effort to appear calm.

Mother Superior was satisfied with her demeanor change and turned her attention elsewhere. Her only aim was to find the culprit. The situation appeared grave. The gypsy remained in a stiff position knowing well to refrain from any comment. At that moment, Mother Superior pointed the finger toward him.

The other nun got closer to her and whispered, "With all due respect, Mother, it is highly improbable that he is guilty of any wrongdoing. I have almost the absolute certainty."

"How"? Mother superior responded sternly.

"He came alone with a fruit basket to donate to the children. He did not escape. I did not detect any improper behavior in him. I do not see any clue that makes him a suspect. I am leaning to believe that this abduction is not an isolated case, but the scheme of an international agency engaged in illegal, lucrative activities involving orphans."

Mother Superior looked to her almost with disdain, but did not proffer a single word.

The custodians finished the accurate inspection and returned. Their gloomy faces were the tacit manifestation of an impending catastrophe for the orphanage reputation.

. Mother Superior did not blink an eye. She motioned to them to inspect the gypsy's bag. It was empty. Using her index finger, she invited the nun on the side and whispered to her ear, "What did you say this gentleman is doing here?"

"As I told you before, he came to donate fruits to the children."

"Did he, indeed, have the fruits?" insisted Mother Superior.

"Yes, Mother, I can swear on it. I saw it," she replied emphatically.

"Did you search the bag at that time?" continued Mother Superior.

"No, I did not, Mother. I did not think there was any need since I saw the fruit. Are you implying that...?" The nun covered her mouth with her right hand in a sign of surprise and horror. In her opinion, Mother Superior's inquisitiveness was becoming pathological. The nun turned pale and ran to the restroom because of vomiting feelings.

Mother Superior showed no emotion. When the nun came back still under the trauma of being accused of negligence, her boss placed a finger on her lower lip and said, "I have an idea. Let us make a quick visitation to the garden. Maybe, the flowers will give us an answer or maybe they will tell us that we are on the wrong track."

The nun placed both hands on her head in a sign of despair. "The flowers...? What significance do they have?" she muttered while she accompanied her.

"Never mind!" said Mother Superior, who had heard her. I have changed plan. Before going to the garden, we have to inspect something else. First, I want the custodians to search the gypsy. They have to secure anything in his possession that may help us to unravel the mystery. Secondly, I, personally, want to search the whole area of the children's ward."

The custodians conducted an accurate search of Scarman and reported their findings to Mother Superior. She acknowledged that her doubts about the gypsy were unfound, but she did not elaborate. Immediately after, she put in motion the second part of her plan and walked straight to the scene of the abduction. Ten minutes of minute search did not reveal anything conclusive, but some objects disheveled and the open window led her to arrive at unequivocal fact. Something was out of order and the puzzle had to be recomposed. She descended the stairs and opened the door that gave access to the garden. She summoned the gardener and inquired if the scene was exactly as he left it an hour earlier. The man felt perturbed. In all the years of service, his loyalty had never been questioned. He raised his right hand as if he were under oath and stated, "Up to ten minutes ago, I was working on the other corner of the garden, Mother Superior pointed at the flowers, "Look at the petals. They are broken." Everyone in the group of the observers bent over to ascertain that it was indeed as she described them. "Look at the grass!" she continued. It is all messed up." She turned again to the gardener, "Are you absolutely sure that you did not leave this area in this messy condition?"

"I am very positive, Mother. The garden is like my house. I take pride in keeping it neat and clean. I take good care of it."

Mother Superior felt satisfied to have exhausted convincingly the preliminary phase of her inquiry. She was a woman of high intellectual acumen and was able to solve cases which seemed insurmountable to legal experts. In a mood of pride, she looked at the nun and said, "The next witness would be the visitor. Don't you think so?"

"Mother, haven't you already investigated him?" dared to say the nun.

"And if I wish to conduct an additional investigation, what's to you?"

"As you wish Mother..." Her words were permeated by a sincere feeling of obedience.

Mother Superior raised her voice for the first time and ordered to the whole staff," Where is he? Find him and bring him here without further ado!"

An assistant responded, "He was right behind me a minute ago."

One of the custodians felt so embarrassed that he confided to his colleague, "I thought he was part of the entourage."

The report was dismal and Mother Superior did not comment on the gypsy's disappearance. She claimed that her investigation had come to a close and no further inquiries were necessary. The audience did not know what to make of it because no perpetrator nor an accomplice was found. She assured them that she would turn over her findings to the police authorities and they would be responsible to conduct further examinations. She invited everyone to return to his duty and to stay calm. One custodian raised his hand and said, "In all of this chaos, I feel partially culpable, but I have one curiosity. If the gypsy was limping, how did he run away? He may still be hiding in the garden or in the building. Let us chase him."

Mother Superior responded, "You do not chase anyone, you simple minded man! I appreciate your rationale, but I guarantee you that he is not longer on these premises." She scrutinized him from head to toe and added, "Why didn't you bring to my attention this detail before?"

Nobody answered, but her comments assuaged their thirst for suspicion and curiosity. She caught their feelings and added, "From now on, we have to abide by strict rules. Any visitor entering or leaving this building must be checked thoroughly and escorted during the visit. Moreover, he or she has to sign before and after the visit." Everyone applauded. The only one who remained pensive was the nun.

Two ladies with their faces semi covered with a cloth were stationed at a short distance from the orphanage. The tall gypsy handed to them two baskets. "Hurry! Do not waste any time," he urged them. They pulled the content out of the baskets and placed them in their own. The man dumped the baskets behind the bushes and walked expeditiously toward the city center. The two ladies covered the baskets with a thin cloth and departed to opposite directions. They reunited near the public baths whose water comes in from ten kilometers away. They drank and washed their hands. From there, they proceeded to unknown destination.

The next day, the police raided the gypsy's camp close to the Genovese Lighthouse, but found nothing relevant. At the beginning of September, the gypsy Central Council, in light of the many police investigations, decided to keep a low profile and gave order to the tribes to stratify a bit more in view of a possible mass migration.

At Camp A, the two ladies were complaining to the two gypsies about lack of food and money. That evening, at Mamaia Beach, the most renown on the Black Sea and not far from the mineral water springs, many gypsies were gathering for the ritual beach screening operation. They looked through the sand for lost valuable objects or something that the sea vomited on the shores. Two men were sitting about ten feet from the water line. Their concern appeared to be of a different nature. The sea waves invaded rhythmically the sand leaving behind a host of debris that reached the bodies of the men. The conversation between them went on for a while despite the fact that the waves threw a lot of foam on them. At that point, they decided to wash up. The shortest man got up and the other followed suit. They took a dip into the water and emerged with algae all over their bodies. "We were better off before," complained the taller man.

A week later, two gypsies, their heads covered with a hood, rang the bell of an apartment on the second floor of the street Valu lui Trajan in Constantia, Rumania. The only window that looked toward the beach was open. It was seven feet tall. Whoever managed to enter through it would have landed on the stairs. The heavy, front door of the building was doubly locked. From the façade, reminiscent the classical style, one could see that only the upper flights were occupied. The taller man squatted and allowed the smaller friend to step on his shoulder to propel himself inside the window without making any unnecessary noise. Once on the stairs, the man tied a rope and returned it outside. Their faces shone from the pale color of the moon in a calm evening of August. The shorter man landed so hard against the door of an apartment that he coiled and pressed his hands on the stomach to alleviate the pain. As he regained his composure, he knocked at a door. The taller man, who arrived in the meantime, smacked him on the head reproaching him for lack of self-control, "You alert the residents from above if you are going to be that rough." The first man looked at him sternly while the blood started to gush to the brains. They resumed their friendly relationship pressed more by events than by their real intentions. A feeble voice came from behind the door, "Who is it?"

"We are government agents. We came to deliver a certificate of good citizenship to every family here," responded the shorter man in a fake, gentle tone.

The lady's response delayed a while and the shorter man was meditating to bust the door. The same feminine voice thwarted his devious plan. "I am sorry if you had to wait. I could not find the key. I am so happy to receive this recognition." She hardly finished the last syllable that the taller man forced the entrance and covered the lady's eyes and mouth with a cloth and tied her hands. The unfortunate woman did not oppose any resistance, old as she was. The bandits opened the drawers of the chest and threw clothes all over in the hope of finding money. The shorter man put a towel around the woman's neck and was about to tighten the news. The taller man pushed him aside and said, "Are you crazy? Do you spend the rest of your life in jail?"

His partner released the pressure. The lady held a large manila envelope on her laps. He grabbed it and opened it. He could not believe it! He untied her hands and joined his companion who was already on his way out.

Half an hour later, Scarman and Barabbus were sitting in front of their tent at the gipsy camp. They opened the envelope and pulled out a bunch of money. "This is incredible," said the taller man. We scouted the whole apartment and did not find a single penny. Who would believe that her treasure was hidden in this envelope?"

The shorter man was making his case before sharing the money, "I should get seventy-five per cent of the totals."

"Why is that?" The other responded with incredulity. "I thought we do fifty-fifty."

"Yes, but I almost broke my knuckles pounding on the door."

"Suppose that you are stupid."

"Eh, watch your mouth!" responded the man resentfully.

His companion smirked and brushed his unruly curly, black hair from the forehead.

"Either we stay in business or not," he responded in a serious tone.

"Of course, we are!" and accentuated his remark to affirm his adherence to the partnership. Then, he lowered his voice and said, "You seem to forget that we have to feed the two children."

His companion made the index finger rotate around the center of the temple to indicate that he forgot, "I did not think of them. You are right."

"I propose a quarter to you, a quarter to me and the rest we allot it for the children's care."

The taller man stretched his right hand and the other did the same to shake it. At the end of the agreement, the taller man became suddenly pensive. The shorter man asked him, "What's going on, man? Are you repented?"

"Of what?"

"Of the agreement?"

"No, I was thinking if we have to circumcise the baby boy."

"Don't come up with those big words. What do you mean?"

"I heard that among the Jews, circumcision is considered a cultural and religious rite whose practice goes back to thousands of years. I must add that each Jewish community follows a different method. The parents take the baby to a building they call temple and that's it."

"What do we care about that!" shouted the other man.

"The Muslim males are circumcised between the fifth and tenth year."

"I don't believe it! You are crazy."

CHAPTER VII

The Gold Chalice

Our two men met again to lay out another plan which they carried out with impeccable precision. On a typical day of July, while the priest of San Nicolao went to the rectory to eat lunch, they dashed through the back door of the sacristy and started to despoil the statues of all the gold and silver. The Blessed Mother statue was still covered with the money collected from a previous procession. Scarman licked his fingers. "We should have come here before. Where have we been?"

"Who is this lady?" asked the other.

"I have no idea; I do not write a list of the people we rob."

"I did not ask you about people. These are statues, not people, stupid!"

"How am I supposed to know it? Do you know this man hanging on the cross?"

"I have not the slightest idea.

"I don't either," responded the other dazzled by the gold that was shining all over. He paused for a moment, then, he added, "He may be one of the pagan gods."

"Eh, stop talking about their names, you fool. If we do not hurry, we may get caught by police and end up in jail where we will shoot breeze for a long time."

The pillage continued for another five minutes until they reached the altar. Scarman pointed at the Bible and asked, "What is this book doing here?" He handed it upside down to his partner and asked him to read something to find out if it contained some sort of secrets.

Barabbus did not even look at it and replied, "I am not interested in books."

The priest had left the tabernacle open. Scarman gave a glance inside and saw a chalice. He grabbed and turned it around to better appreciate the contour. "What is this for?" he exclaimed.

"Stupid, it is gold. We sell it and make easy money. I hope I answered your silly question."

"I see that it is gold. I asked you what they use it for."

"Who cares? They can use it for anything. I am concerned about the gold metal and not the use of it. Whoever buys it will decide for himself. Let's not waste time in matters that are not our concern."

The tall man did not like the rough response, but he was in a hurry. He moved toward the sacristy and hit his head against a giant crucifix. The gypsy fell backward and emitted a cry of fear, "Ah,ah,ah! There is a man there. Let's get him out of here!"

Barabbus replied, "What are you talking about idiot! It is a man carved on wood.

Don't you see it? You make one more unnecessary noise and, for sure, we end up behind the bars."

In the sacristy, the gypsies saw the priestly vestments in a closet. Barabbus put on one of them on and queried, "How do I look like?"

"You look like a clown. Are you happy now?"

"Do you think clowns can wear them? Maybe, we could sell all these clothes."

"Nobody would buy them unless he is a clown and around here I don't know anyone except you."

"Eh, watch out how you talk to me!"

Time was running out. Scarman stumbled and accidentally pulled the rope that made the bells toll. They realized to have caused a big problem for them and ran away. The ringing of the bell puzzled the parishioners because it was not the vesper yet. The priest thought that it was a joke and alerted the sacristan. The latter climbed seventy-seven stairs, but found no one there. He was short of breath and took time for the descent. He arrived in front of the altar and genuflected. The mess that he saw when he raised his head shocked him and ran to the rectory to inform the priest.

At the sight of such desolate spectacle, the priest placed his hand on the heart and fell on the floor. The assistant sounded the alarm and the help arrived within minutes. Some staff members and advisers were appalled at the disappearance of the gold and money from the statues. The priest was still lying on the floor next to the altar in a rigid position. His personal secretary began to weep. Others raised the priest from the floor and lay him on a chair with a pillow on the back of the head. The sacristan hurried to the rectory to get a bottle of vinegar. He embedded his handkerchief in it and placed it under the priests' nostrils. The first attempt to revive him failed. He had to repeat it various times. Finally, the priest began to show the first symptoms of revival. He was incoherent in his speech for a few minutes. During that time, people and police checked every inch of church to find clues. The tabernacle was open, but the chalice was gone. The money had disappeared too. The priest saw the grim spectacle and cried out, "Oh, my Lord! Oh, my God!" He laid his head aside and fainted again.

The sacristan got irritated, "Did you have to tell him that right now? Couldn't you wait until he recuperated his strength?" The young lady tried to defend her action by saying, "I did not realize that Father was so weak."

Another lady, who was checking the altar, exclaimed, "Look here! There is no chalice, no tray. It is all gone!"

"The money from the Blessed Mother disappeared, too," commented with sadness the sacristan.

"We better carry Father to the rectory," suggested the secretary. "He won't be able to bear the loss! It could kill him."

The rest of them sat the priest on a chair and dragged him to the rectory where they accommodated him on the bed. Soon after, they called for a doctor who rushed on the scene immediately. "Not even the church is secure anymore, let alone the priests," he said during the trip.

The police arrival drew the attention of a multitude of people who surrounded the church in a matter of minutes. The curious crowd was fermenting with emotions and generated the most disparate speculations. The police realized that they could not conduct their investigation outside of the temple with that human sea around them and evacuated the area. The bystanders dispersed. Some watched from a certain distance; others convened in the main plaza to discuss and analyze even further the bits of information that reached their ears from time to time.

The check up lasted about ten minutes. The patient's heart showed symptoms of rhythmic irregularity.

The doctor prescribed some medicine and ordered him to observe seven days of absolute rest in bed. The visits were limited only to his secretary and a nurse. He also forbade him to read the newspaper or watch TV. The two persons who were allowed to see him could not talk about the incident. He would examine the clergyman in a timely fashion to ascertain that his physical conditions normalized.

The medical report had a devastating impact on the people's morale. They mourned every single day their beloved priest's convalescence and organized prayer groups on this behalf, "How can Father stay off his feet that long? He is a very active man. It will kill him," commented an old lady.

Her sister replied, "What's the use to go to a doctor when you don't follow his advice?"

The real shock came the next day. The patient's conditioned worsened. He was breathing feebly and irregularly. The ambulance came and took him to the hospital. Nurses took him immediately to the emergency room where the doctors declared him clinically dead. A veil of sadness and silence fell upon the parishioners. The mood changed shortly after. A second announcement retracted the first medical report explaining that the heart had temporarily failed, but it started to beat again although with utter reservations.

Several employees expressed relief at the news and called it 'miracle,' but not all shared the same reaction and became victims of skepticism and gloom. The sacristan reproached them for their depressive demeanor and exhorted them to pray rather than make ominous predictions. Having said that and relying more on the second medical report, he rang the bells to summon the parishioners to prayer. The untimely sound alarmed most of the town and all reversed to the temple to find out the motive. The scene was reminiscent of the previous year when telluric vibrations sent all the residents in panic from their abodes. The news of the priestly purported death soon reached their ears and women, children and old folks dropped on their knees raising to heaven their deeply felt for the priest's health. The congregation prayed incessantly around the clock for three consecutive days hoping for a lasting miracle. Many politicians and businessmen, as the two gypsies, responded to the call and gathered in front of the church to show their concern for the priest's health. At sunset, a third the medical report gave an end to all speculations. The priest was definitely dead.

The body was placed in the casket and brought to church where people could pay their respect. Unlike the overwhelming majority of the mourners who bowed or murmured something passing by in silence, even Scarman and Barabbus showed up as representatives of their gypsy clan. They paused a moment and noticed a mark on the priest's forehead. Their strange behavior did not go by unnoticed,

The funeral was set for the following day. The funeral was very elaborate. The whole city was being represented in all its main administrative and cultural groups. Each one displayed a large banner. In the last row, Scarman and Barabbus were holding one with the emblem of the Roma gypsy camp.

The funeral procession was long and silent. The cart with the casket was drawn by eight horses. Behind it, a band of fifty musicians played a somber march. Once the carriage reached the cemetery, the procession stopped. Being the last day of the week, the pallbearers pulled the casket with evident difficulties and carried it inside the wake mortuary hall at the entrance of the cemetery. The mourners lined up around the casket manifested their devotion in different ways. Some of them beat their chest and wailed; a couple fainted. While others got ecstatic and ran into convulsions. The priest's closest associates threw themselves on the casket and would not release the grip. It was an emotional scene where young and old wept openly, chanted hymns and threw flowers to the casket... A few tears streamed down the faces of the two gypsies. One reporter commented, "Look, how they loved him!" The police, who participated at the funeral, with its own band, stood on military attention during the moaning time. They paid the last respect, along with the political officials and left. The custodian locked the doors and went on his business.

The following Monday, the quiet town woke up at the usual sunrise. The main square was unusually in ferment at that hour of the morning. The only coffee shop in the area was saturated with smoke and the aroma of the Turkish coffee. The loud and excited voices of the early risers reached the opposite side of the plaza. In a reserved area, the coachmen were feeding the horses while waiting to transport some clients to the railroad station. The noisy carts of the trash collectors were on the move and so the farmers with their donkeys and cows.

Around eight o' clock, the custodian came running from the cemetery to the boulevard that led straight to downtown. His eyes were out of the orbit. He appeared disheveled. The hair was flying in all directions and he gesticulated frantically trying to catch the attention of the small groups of people that from time to time he noticed at the street corners. Those folks interrupted momentarily their business and launched fleeting glances of surprise at the running man. Their incredulity intensified while he kept on turning his head backward as if he wanted to ascertain that no one was pursuing him. At the coffee shop, he wobbled a few times and dropped on the ground. The bartender rushed over to provide him temporary care. The custodian was perspiring profusely and his frantic heart shook the entire body. The bartender grabbed a chair and helped the man to sit on, so that, he could catch his breath. A second bar attendant saw the commotion and went inside. He filled a glass of water and handed it to the custodian. The man pulled a rag from the back of his pants and wiped the sweat from his brows. A crowd, from the plaza, quickly gathered around him and queried about his health. The man alternated gestures with monosyllabic letters that he uttered with spasmodic efforts. Nobody seemed to be able to decipher neither one of them. A neighbor of the custodian offered him a cup of coffee, but he declined it with a gesture of his hand. An old man leaned over the chair and suggested him to catch his breath and relax for a while. The custodian attempted to send a message by making additional signs with his hands, but for the crowd they were parts of an unsolvable riddle. The bartender thought he had a genial idea. So, he took a pencil and a piece of paper and handed them to the man. The custodian shook his head. The people around him understood and looked at each other with dismay.

A few minutes passed by during which the people were trying to figure out what secret could hold the man who could not talk. A police officer, attracted by the excitement around in front of the coffee shop and decided to scout the area, but his intentions were thwarted by a load noise that came from behind him. A donkey had fallen on the ground on the main avenue and would not move despite the owner's repeated yelling. The traffic got snarled and the police rushed over to redirect the traffic

The crowd in the coffee shop was unaware of the outside problem or did not pay attention to it. The policeman arrived a bit late to find out what was going on. He found the inside atmosphere characterized by suspense and silence. In that moment, the custodian reacquired a nearly calm composure and began to talk in fragmented sentences, "I went to the cemetery," he said. "And I took the keys from my pocket."

"And...?" Asked the man closest to him.

"The door was locked and I had the keys."

"We heard it already," interrupted him a man of middle age.

"I opened the door."

"And, then, what?" insisted the same person.

"I saw the casket."

An old man grabbed the custodian by the shirt and pulled it.

"Ehy, you hurt me!" complained the custodian.

The policeman intervened and ordered him to release the grip.

"I am going to pull every hair of your head if you do not tell us what happened," said the old man full of rage.

"I pushed the casket on the side and it fell off the carriage."

"So, what?" The old man yelled.

The custodian made an extra effort to regain his full strength and replied, "I lost balance and fell along with it."

"Big deal!" cried out a lady.

The custodian looked around as to scrutinize the crowd before he answered. He reacquired a sense of self-assurance and said, "When I got up, I tried to raise the casket back on the carriage."

"How could you, idiot! It is too heavy for one person. We can understand if it were empty," screamed the old man.

"Exactly!" responded the custodian. "I realized that it was empty and I panicked. I left everything as it was and ran over here to tell you about it."

"You are an imbecile!" A distinguished gentleman thundered from behind. "Your head is empty, not the casket."

The sarcastic comment caused a sonorous laughter among the by-standers. The noise, slowly, abated and the same gentleman continued, "I start to believe that your head is empty."

The crowd roared. The policeman restored the order with some efforts and the custodian responded somewhat offended, "What do you mean?"

"Let us suppose that your account is not a figment of your imagination," said the gentleman, "Can you provide us with some information about the identity of the corpse?"

The custodian replied a bit confused, "What do you mean by that?"

"Whose dead body is it? That is what I mean!"

The custodian lowered his head and muttered, "It was our beloved priest."

A dreadful silence fell upon the crowd. No one dared to make any comment until a young man shouted, "To the cemetery!"

The crowd replied, "To the cemetery!"

The cemetery was about half of a mile from downtown. The general feeling was to go there and investigate. During the speedy walk, people argued about the disappearance of the priest. The mayor, heard that a march to the cemetery was in progress, dismissed the meeting he was having with the councilmen and joined the marchers.

The cemetery's mortuary hall was open. Everything was in the same place as the custodian had left it. The mayor ordered him and some young people to raise the casket from the floor up to the carriage. "There is no need, Mr. Mayor," protested the custodian. Anyone can raise it." To demonstrate the veracity of his words, he kicked the casket with his right foot. It moved. The mayor was looking with a mixture of curiosity and surprise. After a pause, he approached the casket and tried to open it. It was gratifying for him to ascertain that it was nailed. The crowd showed skepticism and urged the opening of the casket. "We will not leave this room until the custodian opens it," they demanded. The mayor submitted to their request and ordered 'operation opening." Only that would reveal the truth.

The custodian had easy time to find a screwdriver and a hammer, which he kept on top of a shelf. Under the pressure of both tools, the wood began to squeak and, at the end, the cover was removed. Everybody showed from all directions to a first sight of the deceased priest. The mass media, informed by the police, cruised over the cemetery and made numerous attempts to gain a space where they could take pictures. Those who were good enough to be the first to have a glimpse of the interior of the casket pulled back and made no comment. Their mouths were open. One journalist shouted, "There is nothing here! What happened? Where is the dead priest?"

The empty casket caused consternation among the crowd. No one was able to offer a plausible explanation. The custodian raised his right hand and asked to talk. "Maybe, the reverend resuscitated and escaped."

The mayor intervened, "How senseless is your theory! Did you ever see a dead man resuscitate? Furthermore, would you explain how he opened the casket and where would he find the hammer to close it?"

"Right there, on the shelf," responded the custodian.

"Nonsense!"

"Miracle! Miracle!" shouted the bartender who had participated at the march to the cemetery.

The crowd dispersed slowly and reconvened at the plaza to discuss the event of the day with more passion and astonishment. Being a legal matter, other than religious, the mayor reported the news to the town commissioner. In the meantime, the news spread, like a lightening all over the town and behind it. Many stories were created upon the mysterious disappearance and song writers wrote songs about it. The Altar and Rosary Club consulted with the bishop to find out if a beatification process could be initiated on behalf of their beloved priest, but he cautioned them to be patient. They had to wait first for the results of the pending investigation.

Back in the camp, the two men hardly talked to anyone for a week. The transaction of their stolen articles was postponed to a later date. The police was conducting 'Operation Recovery' and for a while they had been at their heels. Scarman took the wine chalice and scratched it at the bottom with a metal bar. It was a type of cross that he tried to impress on the gold without great success. He repeated the same act under the Eucharistic Chalice. Then, he called an old gypsy who knew how to write a bit and asked him to produce the letters "J" "C" under each one of them.

Barabbus objected to it, "Why did you make a mark underneath of them? Don't you know that it brings the value down?"

"Where did you learn those letters?"

"Somebody explained it to me."

"That's good, but what do you mean by it?"

'J' stands for 'Jesus' and 'C' stands for 'Christ.'

"Isn't the one who was on the cross behind the altar?"

"Do you believe in him?"

"I did not say that."

"What made you scratch those two letters?"

His friend looked in the empty space and said, "I do not know it."

"I hope you realize that with those scratches you made you devalued them."

"Which means?"

"The cost will go down."

"I don't think so. Those are special marks and carry a special meaning."

"Everything is special to you. If it is the way you put it, when are we going to sell it on the 'black market.'"

"Man, we have already agreed to get rid of them later around. It would be a suicide to sell all our gold at a jewelry store in Constantia, not even at the market. We get the death sentence if we get caught. Right now, we have enough money to keep us going for the next year,"

"We can't keep our goodies it for too long."

"I agree. When we go to another town we will change them in cash. And, we don't want to sell all of it, either. The value may go up next year and we will make more money."

"Man, the whole town is upside down. Let's play it safe from now on. A mistake could allow the noose to tighten its grip around our neck. It would cost us a lifetime in jail, as I said before."

Scarman had a second thought. At first, he tried to dust off the chalice with the palm of his hands. It did not work. He picked a corner of his raggedly shirt and polished it with loving care. A series of letters called his attention. He raised it with both hands and perused them. The sun's rays made the gold sparkle even more. His friend stopped checking the bountiful pillage for a moment and followed Scar's movement with the corner of his eyes. His head seemed suspended in the air. Scarman turned to him and asked, "Can you read what it says here?"

His partner swayed his head left and right to signify denial.

"What do you mean? Are you ignorant?" asked Scarman.

"Look who is talking, Mr. Knows at all."

"How are we going to find it out? Maybe, a young boy or girl from our camp will be able... They have better eyes than me."

"...Of mine too," replied Barabbus. "I would like to know what school our gypsy children attend"

"Oh, yes, I did not think of it. You are right on target."

Barabbus paused a few moments, then, he said, "We lose ownership if you do that."

"Why? Is it so important to know what is written on it?" replied imprudently Scarman

"If it is the name of an important person or church, the jeweler will recognize it and call the police and we will become jailbirds in a matter of minutes."

"I do not suppose that the jeweler is interested in causing problems. He will melt it and no trace of the chalice will ever be found."

"Excellent thinking" responded phlegmatically the other. "But not quite good."

"Why not?"

"The jeweler, to ingratiate himself with the owner, would not hesitate to betray us."

"What solution do you propose, then?"

"Let's hold on it for a while. Let's keep it for good luck."

"Good luck?" responded the other sarcastically. "Listen to you! We are in great need of money and you preach luck. You can do that when you want to foresee the future in the palm reading business, but not with something valuable like we hold in our hands."

"What do you suggest? We melt them?"

"Now, you are making sense."

"Let us meet tomorrow, then, to make the preparations."

A day went by and the two men met at an undisclosed location. Barabbus arrived a few minutes in advance and started the fire. When he realized that Scarman did not bring the chalices, he inquired, "Well, what happened to them?"

The other scratched his eyes with the back of his hands and said, "I could not sleep the whole night. There is something mysterious about them. I cannot explain it. I have the hunch that the chalices possess magic powers. If we wish to avert any disaster on us or on our clan, let us wait for better times. After all, we came here to make the arrangements. We did not agree that I had to bring the chalices too."

"Stupid!" rebutted his partner.

Back at the camp, the two men continued their arguments. Scarman wanted to write a sign on each chalice to recognize in any event, both were illiterate. He saw some 'scratches' outside of them and asked a little boy coming back from school what they meant. The letters in one chalice made up the word 'CHRISTUS." In the other, they combined in the word, "Jesus." Later, in the camp, both partners tried to gather some information on those two words, but nobody knew anything at the end, he decided that he would never give them up. His friend did not embitter their relationship and dropped the issue for the time being. Instead, he asked him, "By the way, how are the babies doing?"

"Very good!" The ladies are breast feeding them. We save money."

"Yeah, but we have to feed their big mouths."

"You can't get everything for nothing. Don't be cheap."

In the following days, the two gypsies got wind of a police possible visitation to their camp. As they suspected, they raided unexpectedly the camp at night. During the flight, Scarman dropped the Eucharistic Chalice on the ground and the police had to make a choice, either to pursue the fugitive or to take possession of the chalice. It was not hard to find out where it came from and how to give it back.

The priest's purported death had turned a quiet town into a warzone. Every governmental and public agency condemned the barbarian act. Nonetheless, there was no consensus on who might have done it. In this respect, Constantia's public opinion was divided. One half blamed the organized crime and the second half blamed the gypsies. For their part, the tribes' council did its best to dispel any doubt against them. Scarman and Barabbus went to see the chief of police and offered their cooperation. They volunteered to take part in any action that could lead to the identification and arrest of the perpetrators. The initial 'flame' of heroism quickly waned in them. The chief cautioned them of the danger of overly exposing themselves to the public eye. In such a case, anyone working for the orphanage could recognize them and the game would be over. Scarman reminded him that both had attended the funeral without any incident. Barabbus partially disproved his position. Being a standard bearer, the wind kept on blowing the banner constantly on his face, therefore, nobody recognized him.

The gypsy tribes were under tight scrutiny. Everyone was aware of it. Winds of war were blowing in their direction. A climate of mistrust and undesirability pervaded the local community. The police made many arrests at the Roma gypsy camp for alleged crimes committed by local men. The detention did not last too long. The prosecution could not substantiate the accusations with proofs and the indicted people were released shortly after. As a result of the continuous harassment and the social instability, the gypsies felt insecure. The chief smelled blood and decided to take action. To avert an open confrontation, the council voted unanimously to abandon Constantia.

One evening, the leader assembled the top men of each clan and addressed them in this way, "The sun is setting on our nation. We are considered strangers in our own land. The water that we drink is toxic. The bread we eat is spoiled and the air we breathe is polluted. Our experience in this city is over. Business is poor. We must move on. Our next step is the capital, Bucharest. Relate to your families my intentions. We will depart in three days. Prepare yourselves." He told them that he drew a map of their next journey and hoped that they would give their proper evaluation at the earliest time. He raised his right arm and said, "We will leave the city coasting the Danube River in the direction of Bucharest. From there, we follow the road to Albania where, hopefully, we will board a ship for southern Italy. Once we get there, I leave to the discretion of each tribe to establish the tents in whatever part of Europe it desires. The clans' representatives assented without objection. As the chief had ordered, they withdrew without delay to their tents to inform their relatives and friends. By the expiration date, they readily dismantled the tents and amassed on their wagons all sorts of goods from mattresses to chairs. Once the women fed the children and took a seat on the carts, the caravan moved on alongside the Danube. The new morning rose and Costantia returned to her life of stability and relaxation.

With much noise, as it was in their style, the gypsies began their exodus. To avoid any unnecessary hardship, the chief dispatched scouts ahead of them to report any inconvenience on a timely fashion.

The night before the departure, Scarman went to see the two ladies. He took the babies and placed them on the floor. One of the ladies was concerned about his intentions and watched carefully. He took out of his pocket a knife. The ladies cried out, "Don't touch them!"

"What do you think that I am going to cut their throat, you idiot? I am more interested in their safety than both of you."

The ladies covered their faces out of fear. He sharpened the knife on his pants and made a tiny incision to both of them between the index and middle finger. The babies cried. A stream of blood flowed out of the tiny hands. The ladies quickly rushed over and applied a piece of cloth on the wounds to stop the bleeding. One of them was furious, "Why did you have to do that for? That's cruelty."

Scarman replied, "Listen, who is talking about cruelty. You allowed your own mother to die without help."

CHAPTER VIII

Good-by, Motherland

The journey was arduous, long and exhaustive. The column was forced to make many stops due to the pregnant women and children. Although the weather was balmy, most of the itinerants did not wear shoes. After a while, the feet began bleeding and the dusty roads covered with sharp pebbles lacerated the skin under the feet and caused infections. The river provided water for bathing and washing, but not for drinking. The threat of dysentery was constant.

A few miles away from the capital, the chief ordered to rest for a couple of weeks. It was a peaceful spot at the foot of a mountain. The roosters were coiled in themselves in a sleepy position in their den. A rare barking of dogs broke the evening silence. It had rained. A slice of the sky was a ball of flame. The clouds were moving lazily and without a realistic aim, as if they were unconcerned about the destination. Their varied streamlines with animal or human creature's forms gave rise to many conjectures among the travelers. From above the clouds, a glowing light descended on them that gave them a surrealistic appearance. "We look like burning bushes," A young boy commented, "If this is creation, how great must be its Creator…"

The scene resembled a garden of glory in a vast ocean of darkness. When the caravan took once again the road and disappeared from the sight at the end of a long curve, the sky assumed a sullen, one-color look and was no longer fun to watch it.

The vanguard platoon reached the outskirts of the capital early in a July morning and settled on Lake Horostrau. The second column raised the tents on Lake Floreasca and the last segment on Lake Tei.

Two weeks passed and the council chief assembled the men and said, "For the time being and for obvious reasons of stability and security, some of you will do business in Plata Romana and Cale a Victoria. A second detachment will operate in Stirbei Voda and the last in Pache Protopescu. Able women and children will move around the churches of Calea 13 Septembrie and Mihail Sebastian." With no objection, the meeting was adjourned and people regrouped according to their clans to lay out their plans.

Bucharest was sleeping in her long summer days. The northern wind brushed through the city and kept the temperature sustainable. Life appeared to run its usual course, but only for a short period. Early in the afternoon, Scarman and Barabbus decided that the time was ripe to sell part of their valuables. Barabbus was in favor of selling the gold chalice, which would have rendered the most, but his partner was adamantly opposed to it, at least for the time being. With that in mind, they attended a black market meeting. The negotiations for the rest of the booty lasted for two hours. The scorching sun was having its toll on all the participants. Patience was getting thin with Scarman. "Listen men, I am selling these jewels for half price. What else do you expect us to do? Sell them at no price at all?"

"Absolutely not...!" replied one of the negotiators. "We are offering you a fair market price."

Barabbus intervened, "Man, we got to make a living. We have women and children to feed. Give us a fair share."

"I heard this nonsense before," replied the interlocutor. "We are not trading peanuts, but gold and, once the deal is over, you get out here rich, not poor." He stared at the chalice. "For this, I would offer you a substantial amount of money."

Scarman grabbed his arm. The man looked at him with surprise, "Why? You don't want to sell it?"

"Hands off of it!" responded Scarman in a firm tone.

"That's strange," said the buyer. "Some people don't know how to be good business men."

"Listen to me!" Scarman insisted, "Take it or leave it. Either you accept our price on the goodies or the sale does not take off. The chalice is not for sale. I keep it with me for protection only."

"The businessman took a pause of reflection on the proposal and thought, that, after all, the terms were advantageous to him. "It is a deal!" he exclaimed.

Around five o' clock a crowd assembled in front of the police station to demand from the chief to take action against some gypsy criminals. A lady broke down in tears, "They stole my wallet in the market."

"Did you see the thief?" asked the chief.

"How could I? People were pushing and shoving. It was impossible to find it out."

A distinguished gentleman added, "You ought to know, excellent chief, that since the invasion of these barbarian hordes of this noble Roman city, we lost peace, security and money."

"What is your accusation?"

"I had just purchased a brand new pair of shoes and a suit. I bent down to tie the laces on my old shoes and when I got up it was all gone."

"Where did it take place?" answered calmly the police chief.

"In Boulevard Regina Maria, half an hour ago."

"Very well! All of you, who have complaints, sign these documents."

The lady, still sobbing, signed it.

The gentleman, instead, banged the cane against the door and began to stir the emotions of the mob. "We want justice, not pieces of papers," he yelled.

The people sustained his appeal, "Yes, justice! Justice!"

The crowd was getting rowdy and the chief had to use threatening language and means to disperse it.

In the ensuing days, the police station got swarmed once more by enraged citizens,

who denounced extortions, robberies and lies by fortune teller that they considered as impostors. This time the police could not ignore their indignation and stationed agents in the most crucial areas of the city.

The days were sleepy and the sky changed its outlook. It dressed up with scattered clouds, black and ominous. A violent storm developed in the north and the lake swelled, like a pregnant woman, to an unprecedented high level threatening the gypsies' camps. The council chief, who always looked after his people survival, urged them to stay calm. By the evening the weather was worsening. At that point, he summoned the tribes' representative and spoke to them in these terms, "My dear friends, I am saddened to take this drastic decision. We do not feel welcomed anymore in our beloved country. Even the forces of nature are against us. We can no longer sustain a double fight. I command, with the authority given to me by you, that we must make preparations to evacuate our beloved capital. The days ahead are hard and the future uncertain. I am sure of one thing. For the sake of our children and for a better life for them, we will direct our dreams toward the capital of our past empire, Rome." He raised his right hand and shouted, "Italia!"

The gypsies responded in unison, "Italia! Italia!"

It had rained the night before. The sky showed red streaks along the north. The clouds were moving in slowly. They had like human and animal forms. Around them, there were circles of glowing fire. The rest of the cosmic picture was an ocean of darkness. As soon as the wind brushed out of sight those clouds, the dark color dominated the entire celestial vault. Everything seemed to be unstable. In the midst of such impending apocalyptic scenario, something suddenly changed. The wind stopped inexplicably its furious blasting and the air got terribly still.

The momentary pause of nature's rage did not appease completely the beech gypsies, who were the first to feel uneasy. They kept on looking at the dogs, which moved nervously their tail and sniffed the sand. An old man with mustaches and long gray hair brought the index and middle fingers on his lips and emitted a long, swirling whistle. Shortly after, many of his ethnicity clan gathered around him. Others arrived in haste as the time went by He briefed them on briefly on the weather predictions and expressed his hope for the better. The men disappeared in all directions as fast as they came. They streamlined to their habitats where they reconvened again. The chief explained to them the secrecy of the new meeting and cautioned them to be on the alert.

In a matter of an hour, the beaches became semi-desert. The unusual disappearance of the gypsies made apprehensive the vacationers and the small business operators who depended on their labor. "Who is going to bring beer, fruit juice, ice-cream and mineral water to the people," exclaimed a bartender.

"Their low wage allows us to keep the prices down and attract more tourism," echoed him his colleague.

"I agree only partially," interjected a visitor. "These people are highly unreliable."

"They are pathologically lazy," added a foreign woman. "I knew their character, but I was oblivious of their lack of respect and responsibility."

The sky got redder. A cracking noise lacerated the air. The dogs barked incessantly. The gypsies felt that an impending danger was lurking all over the camp. Suddenly, the earth shook several times in succession. The tremor made vibrate the buildings in Constantia. The sea got nasty and vomited waves after waves of foam on the beach. As the waves got swollen, they reversed in the streets. The wind reassumed his ferocious behavior and buffeted trees and houses. Some of the city streets got split in the center halting the traffic everywhere. A few old buildings of the suburb could not withstand the tremendous shock and collapsed. In less than an hour, Costantia became a ghost town, devastated and depopulated. The human loss was counted in the thousands. Bucharest was in the same predicament.

In the gypsies' camp, the scenario was slightly different. Some tents were literally sucked in by the earth, but the overwhelming majority of them survived. The chief, amid the sight of rubbish, misery and social threats, ordered the immediate evacuation of the camp. "Get your belongings!" he shouted, "And let's go!"

A couple of hours later, the earth stopped trembling and so the fume coming from its mouth. Once again, dark clouds convened above the sky and opened their cataracts. The inhabitants of that area swore that they never saw such a deluge. The streets were flooded and the caravan had to wait a bit longer before it moved sluggishly. The wagons wheels got stock repeatedly in the mud and strong men had to use all their strength to pull them out. The people were drenched to the bones. One old folk commented, "What a miserable day! Could not the chief choose a better day for traveling? At least, we could have waited until the rain subsided."

But the rain came down relentlessly for days and weeks. A young man exclaimed, "With this slush we won't go too far."

A friend of him added, "We have no choice." And, so, like a swarm of countless aunts, the Roma gypsies continued their march for survival. Behind them, the police raided their camps by surprise, but found only an overflowing lake and an immense ocean of mud and litters. Upon seeing no living soul, the police chief exclaimed, "They fooled us once again."

A group of gypsies remembered that there was a major feast in Bucharest in honor of San Nicolao. They were not going to miss it, therefore, they went back. The weather's rage abated. Dark clouds shifted from Bucharest to the north and the fortune tellers spied the sky for new signs. The Rumanian fascist government kept a constant surveillance on the gypsies' camps. Their presence in the capital was considered to be a burden, a bad omen, a black spot on their political image. The police commissioner looked up and frowned, "I have never seen before this massive flock of dark clouds. I feel a heavy weight hanging on my head. They are phantoms galloping from many directions as if they planned to gather here. The police commissioner kept his head high looking upward in an apparent state of total mental absorption. A few seconds passed by and he added, "Some slices of clouds are thin and gray and are stationary. The ones from the east have the profile of hunting dogs. Others have human forms. If I did not wear this uniform, I would be scared. "After these personal observations, he spoke no more and returned to his office more perplexed than ever.

A procession in honor of San Nicolau was in the initial stage in the empty space before the cathedral steps. The gypsies groups, who had decided to return temporarily, were watching unconcerned. Being unable to conduct their business as usual, they were swallowed up by the crowd. Only Scarman and Barabbus displayed a genuine (false) interest. They looked at the people making the sign of the cross and decided to join them in that ritual. The act did not escape the vigilant eye of a bystander, who whispered to his neighbor, "They come from rural areas. I would not be surprised if they are illiterate."

"What makes you say that?" responded the woman next to him.

"Didn't you see them? They made the sign of the cross upside down."

"How stupid can they be?"

Antonio Casale

Scarman asked his partner, "Why do they make the sign of the cross? Aren't they superstitious?"

"That does not explain anything to me," responded Barabbus with a tone of superiority.

"What can I tell you? Maybe, they don't feel good. How else can I explain it to you?" And he roared into a sonorous laughter. The people around shifted their attention to them.

"Scarman did not appreciate the sarcastic comment, "Hush up!"

The statue of the saint was being carried toward them. He asked, "Who is the man they are carrying on the shoulders?"

Barabbus was about to laugh again, but Scarman prevented him by putting the right hand on his mouth. Barabbus told him, "That is a statue, stupid."

"Christians have strange habits!" replied his partner.

The procession moved on at the pace of a turtle because the organizers stopped at every step to collect the money and pin it on the clothes of the statue. After one hour of journey, the statue was brought back to the Cathedral.

At the Central Park, a young gypsy girl, known in the whole camp, for her beauty and dancing grace, was confabulating with a local youngster. He was only fascinated by the gypsy culture, which, in his view, possessed something mysterious. He was charming and respectful and made no advance. The girl's boyfriend did not appreciate the prolonged conversation. Taken by a violent rapt, he rushed on the scene and struck his girlfriend repeatedly with a stone. The girl fell down in a pool of blood. The girl's interlocutor got petrified and was unable to assist the girl. When he, finally, realized the gravity of the situation and tried to help her, the grimness of the blood made him vomit. Some onlookers rushed to the scene and sought medical help. They summoned a middle age doctor living nearby. By the time he arrived on an old heavy bike, it was too late. She expired while he was checking her pulse. One of the eyewitnesses ran to the main square to alert the police. They apprehended the criminal, who was hiding behind the bushes and took him in custody. The gypsy clan was in turmoil. Hardly anyone slept that night. The news reached the gypsies' avantgarde camp. The chief stopped the march and ordered to go back to Bucharest to aid the tribe who remained behind.

The police quickly informed the mayor. Without consulting with the politicians of his own party, he took a drastic unilateral decision that had nothing to do with the girl's death directly, but that it was intended to avert any possible insurrection. He called on the gypsy leaders and informed them that they could not expect to settle permanently in the area. The gypsies' anger increased. They sought justice. The mayor attempted to assuage resentment by promising him to allow justice to take its course. He also emphasized that he would not tolerate insubordination and take strong action against anyone in their camp that would disturb the city's peace. He insisted that the decision was related to the government's plan to expand the city borders, which would incorporate their camp. He looked at them with outward compassion and said, "I am sorry! It is a political bipartisan agreement."

Fires of rebellion soon began to brew in the camp. The supreme chief staged another meeting which became tumultuous as it went on. It took all the persuasive power of each clan's representatives to quell down the unrest and resume the exodus for Italy. The journey, they explained, would be long and treacherous, especially for pregnant women, children and old people, but it was worth the price. The itinerary was clear. They had to march in the direction of Sofia and, from there, take the road to Kosovo and Skoder (Albania). Subsequent to that, they would do the sea crossing to Bari by renting boats from the local fishing community. Scarman and Barabbus assured the crowd that they were going to buy two boats. Encouraged by the latest promise, the people agreed. They lifted up the tents and the caravan once again began their nomadic life.

In Albania, the gypsies could not embark on a regular ship that made a weekly trip to Italy. The only ship available could not accommodate thousands of people and the rate was relatively high. Hardly anyone could afford it. The local fishermen made frequent trips to the Italian peninsula, but only when the sea was calm. The cost was not prohibitive, but gypsy leaders found a stratagem. They rented the boats; in that way, most of the passengers sailed freely. Despite the cost advantage, the crossing was not easy. Many got seasick. Those who were seating on the floor in the middle of the boat had the worst deal. They did not have a free way to the edge and vomited on other passengers. Most of them got terrorized when the boat swayed to the extreme left or right at the passage of a big ship. Old people and women, lacking swimming skills, were scared to death to fall in the water. It would have been the end of their life. Children, instead, enjoyed the jerky movements of the boat and laughed at the ladies' screams. Many women gave birth right during the crossing in extremely uncomfortable conditions. There was no space and no medical personnel to attend the birth of the newly born.

Surely, for all of them, it was the first time they saw the Italian land. The scene, before their eyes was breathtaking. The Mediterrean water was deep blue and skilled men caught some fish that they consumed raw among them. The approach to the shores was fascinating. The waves ran beach and left the foam behind. In other areas, they buffeted the stiff cliffs and tumbled back into the sea. A handful of houses hung over the hard rocks of the Gargano's hills. A similar scene appeared at the Strait of Manfredonia.

The passengers who landed there saw a line of houses that formed a crown around the golf and marveled.

At the lower part of the hills, soaring beach trees expanded their branches way out of the ordinary and almost kissed the ground. The boats gently approached the port and threw their anchor. A unison shout broke out of the ships, "Italia! Italia!" The passengers felt in delirium. Many hugged each other; others cried, while the rest sang and danced. A couple of fishermen, hanging on the tip of a peek, were casting the lines in a shallow area. The sight of that human wave made them stop. They ran over to watch those newcomers from distant lands. A few small boats glided silently by, perhaps, carrying the bounty of the nightly labor. The men on board waived the handkerchief. One of the gypsies raised the left hand and pointed to a church pinnacle. "Bari! Bari!" He shouted. The port authority director corrected the man's misconception. "It's a guess, but not the right one. Here, we are in Manfredonia's bay. And those are just a handful of houses. If it were the city of Bari, you would recognize it by the steeples of St. Nicholas' church."

Minutes later, the first migrants landed on the Italian shores. It was the year 1929. The leader knelt and kissed the ground. "We have reached the land of our forefathers. Blessed be this nation and its inhabitants," he said. The local population had never seen such a massive migration to their soil and, pressed by curiosity, came to welcome them. The chief gathered the tribes an addressed them in this way, "My children, from now on, each one of you is free to dwell in any part of the peninsula. This is a free country. You may even go to other friendly nations such as of France and Spain. The Romans came to our country and mixed with our population. We are brothers and sisters in blood, not just in words. I don't expect you to make a prompt and right choice on the location of your preferred residence. Time and experience will help you out. I am confident that with good will and your spirit of entrepreneurship you will have success in life. Good luck and live in peace."

Chapter IX

A Priestly Sermon

The sun was lazy to rise that Sunday morning. Some pinky, thick clouds hung over the gypsy camp and barred it from visiting the town with its morning rays.

The chiefs of each gypsy clan were in ferment at the frugal breakfast. The focal point of their conversation rotated around the place of settlement. Although the supreme chief did not have a preferential list of the cities, he had left it up to them to decide. The new freedom turned out to be unmanageable in a new country with different language, culture and traditions. They met to see if they could find a consensus on where to settle. A couple of tribes' representatives were in favor of remaining in the area, while the rest of them expressed the desire to move elsewhere. The debate was long and emotional. By the end of it, there was more dissent than agreement. The prevailing mood called for unity; however, there were those who were in favor of dismemberment. The end result was disheartening confusion. To avoid further division, they agreed that it would be in the best interest of all to cast a vote at a date to designate soon.

This last decision seemed to appeal to everybody and the meeting came to a halt.

On Sunday, the cathedral's bells of Alberobello were inviting the faithful to the Mass. Like a flock of scattered sheep, they left their stone houses in silence one by one or in groups of two or three. From time to time, they met friends or relatives with whom they continued to walk toward the temple.

The gypsies were lying on the sidewalks with their legs widespread. Married women had one hand stretched to the passers-by, while the other was busy feeding the babies. The young children begged for mercy to the well tailored people. Occasionally, a penny tumbled in the tin bowl next to the mothers.

Scarman and his partner were chewing nervously a straw. Human lines of people passed by them that with a mixture of pride and vanity on their way to the main square. The endless swarm of people stirred in them concern and curiosity. Without pronouncing a single word, but exchanging only a look, they got up and joined the crowd.

Inside the temple, the priest, dressed in religious robes, just finished to go over with his assistants to the last recommendations. The altar boy rang a little bell. It announced the entrance of the prelate and his entourage to the main altar. The parishioners rose to their feet. The priest bowed and sat on a high chair followed by the rest of them who took seats in different locations. The altar boys flanked the priest; the lectors sat across of them; while other assistants found accommodation at the first pews. The priest invited the congregation to sit and began to officiate the ceremony.

The church was packed. The back doors were opened to allow those standing to participate to the religious function. Many more stood up outside of the temple. It was not a convenient place to be because some occasional inconsiderate wagon drivers shouted at the animals in passing by and distracted the outside audience. A young lady with a soprano voice read the gospel. From the choir, the youngsters with their angelic voice, raised hymns to heaven. Their melody sweetened the interior of the church, and even behind it, for about five minutes. Eventually, the singing came to a halt and it was time for the homily.

The celebrant approached with an unsteady pace the staircase that led to the pulpit. He was close to eighty years old and overweight. He held in his hand a big handkerchief he used to wipe the sweat from his forehead, especially in hot days. He ascended the few steps that led to the pulpit with fatigue. Once he reached the top, he drank a half glass of water and stood in silence for half a minute, as if he were in meditation. The atmosphere was full of suspense. He set aside the script and pulled up his shirt sleeves. An aid came and placed the tiara on his head.

Outside, Scarman leaned over to Barabbus, and whispered to him, "What is going on, man?"

"I wish I knew it," responded vaguely the other.

"Maybe, we ought to investigate."

"We do not even know what they are doing inside. What is this building anyhow? What are they doing now? I can't see too well from this position," prostested his friend.

"Well, if there is action, you know what to expect. The chiefs think we are rich. The money we got from the sale of the gold is gone. Those two babies are costing us a fortune and I don't think it is a bad idea to take a peak. So, let's get in."

The priest had already begun to deliver the fiery attack on the perpetrators of the crime that occurred in the center of the city the week before. With the help of their elbows, the two gypsies, inch by inch, gained access to the interior of the church. They browsed around with their eyes and recognized some familiar scenes: the statues, the altar, the chandeliers, the chalice…Oh, yes, the chalice! They hearts began to tumble. They knew by then that they had stepped into a sacred territory. They wanted to leave, but the pressure from behind was so compelling that they could not move. Scarman, with gestures of his hand and face said to his partner, "What is this crowd doing here?"

"I wish I knew it," whispered back his partner.

"It appears that this is a sacred ground, a place of prayer. They kneel, close their hands and kneel again."

"Sch,h. Shot up! All of these people can hear you."

One of the parishioners standing in front of them turned back his head and motioned to them show reverence to the place. The two men closed their mouths in a sign of obedience.

A parishioner next to them said, "Do you realize that you are in a church?" Aren't you ashamed? You are disturbing the priest."

That word was alien to Scarman who asked, "Who is the priest?" Barabbus put a finger on his lips.

The same man replied to Scarman, "You come to church to pray and do not even recognize a priest from his religious garments?"

"Garments?" repeated Scarman with incredulity. He pointed the finger toward his friend and reprimanded him, "Don't you know who is a priest?"

"Don't you know it?" repeated the other.

"You are stupid," replied Scarman.

"Enough!" ordered a tall, big man. In saying that, he placed both hands on their shoulders and pressed them down. The two gypsies felt some pain and complained. Scarman put the index finger vertically on the point of his nose and the issue was temporarily solved.

The priest was sweating profusely. The sacristan took the high hexagonal hat from the reverend's head and placed it on the chair. The priest felt relieved and continued, "Brothers and sisters..." He paused a moment to take another sip of water.

Scarman looked at his partner and muttered, "What is he talking about? How can we be his brothers if we do not even know him? I think he drank too much wine."

"Be quiet, otherwise, the big man will squash us like two flat meatballs."

At that moment, the same big man laid his hands again on their shoulders and squeezed them down. "Auch!" The two gypsies protested. "You are hurting us."

"If you don't quit disturbing the audience, I am going to squeeze you like lemons."

The prelate continued, "I am sick and tired of counting coins of one, five and ten cents. Not even the demons are interested in them anymore."

"I take them!" shouted Scarman

The orator was surprised to hear that someone in the congregation had interrupted him and paused again for an additional sip of water. The parishioners turned around and started to laugh, yet they could not see the gypsies. The turmoil caused by Scarman and Barabbus could not be tolerated anymore. The stout, tall man grabbed both of them again and pressed them down. The pressure was so enormous and unbearable that caused Scarman to protest, "I did not do it."

Barabbus added his complaint, "Hey, this is my head!"

At that point, the reverend raised the tone of his voice, "Many women walk around with the latest fashion clothes. Their fingers are covered with brilliant rings. Golden earrings dangle down their ears and splendid necklaces adorn their necks. Gold has become so common that bracelets of rare beauty cover their pulses and even dangle down their ankles.

This is not to say that men wear poor quality clothes. Look at them! They are all around you dressed up in elegant attire. They wear shiny shoes and immaculate shirts under expensive suits. From the small pocket on the top left side of their jackets, a white handkerchief emerges like an eagle from mighty rocks. At times, you may see them coming here escorted by bodyguards. We live in a modern society, brothers and sisters." And he emphasized the last words. "Progress is good," he continued. "But we have to share this bounty."

The two gypsies applauded frantically followed by many others in the audience. When the big man realized that the prelate's words included him too, he slowly released the pressure on the gypsies.

The priest was not content with what he had said and went on, "I cannot restore your church with coins. A contractor does not want money, but bills of thousand and millions of lire. I cannot rejuvenate the statues; I cannot paint the interior of this magnificent temple if you donate coins of one, five or ten cents. If you continue doing that, I will refuse them."

The priest noticed that some malcontent brewed up division the audience and abruptly ended the homely. His assistant took off the miter back on his head. The presbyter descended the stairs with caution step by step. At the altar, he took off the eye glasses and wiped again his face.

It was time for collection. The priest looked down at the parishioners and reminded them them to be generous. Scarman turned to his friend and said, "He is right. People have to give more."

Barabbus replied, "It is always better to be generous. You never lose."

The ushers lined up with baskets at the end of the isle. Others were resting against the wall. Scarman gave a glance to his partner and moved toward the two empty baskets. It was not easy to pass by, but by shoving left and right, they made it with some difficulties. They grabbed the baskets and started to collect. The ushers had already started the collection and were unaware of what was going on their back. Some parishioners had already dropped some money in the gypsies' baskets when two hands pressed heavily on the gypsies' shoulders and pulled them backward. Those standing around them realized that the two men were impostors and surrounded them unleashing various threats on them. From words, they passed top facts and joined the big man in evicting them from the premises. On the top steps of the church, the big man kicked both of them on the butt.

The gypsies rumbled down the stairs and ended up on the grass below against a tree. "Oh, my ribs are broken," complained Scarman.

The other had hard time responding. He had hit the tree with his head and suffered a slight concussion. When he finally felt a bit relieved, he exclaimed in a low tone, "At least, only your ribs are broken. Look at me! The whole body is shattered. Poor me! Poor, my family! Does the church have any insurance? Can we get any money?"

"What are you complaining about? You didn't get hurt."

"Look who is criticizing me?"

"I don't think we can get any money out of this man who spoke from the purple."

"You mean "pulpit," corrected him his partner.

"It does not make any difference."

"Eh, remember that the babies' care is costing us a fortune. We have to raise some money. Our only prize is the chalice."

"Don't forget the heavy dues we had to pay to the chiefs for the passage to this country."

"I suppose we have to sharpen our tools to survive."

Outside of the church, a communist sympathizer commented acridly the priest's homily. 'The church is becoming too politicized. I am not sure at times where I am."

A gentleman next to him replied, "Are you hard of hearing? He was talking about revenues. When it comes to give the fair dues to the church, people still have the old mentality. They are living in the past.

What do you do with pennies? Try to change the roof at your house. You see how much they charge you!

If parishioners do not donate substantially at the weekly Mass, how are they going to keep up with the expenses?"

The parishioners debated for days on the donation issue and soon it divided the public opinion. The news reverberated all over the peninsula and the priest made some proselytes. Most of the clergy in other dioceses sided tacitly with him. One of them dared to celebrate a Mass at the feast of 'L'Unita', the Communist national newspaper organizer. Ice cream vendors decided immediately to take action and raised their price neglecting the counting of the cents. The homely made the priest famous worldwide. In Argentina, shoppers received candies for change instead of cents and banks refrained from using coins.

Further down the street, Scarman appeared nervous. He walked up and down the street engaged in a continuous monologue. Barabbus asked, "What's going on, man? What are you nervous about?"

"No, nothng."

"What do you mean 'nothing'?"

"It's, it's that. I remember a priest in Costantia that complained about the money too. So, I heard."

"Man, we all talk about money, don't we?"

"The problem is that ..." He did not finish the sentence. His friend said, "Don't be silly."

The following Sunday, the gypsies' chiefs issued a statement. The tribes were free to operate where ever they wished. No longer, they were bound to stay together. Scarman and Barabbus, along with their clan, dismantled their tents and, after innumerable vicissitudes, settled at Rotondi, near Naples.

CHAPTER X

Human Merchandise

Rotondi does not have much history behind it. It is resting at the foot of Mt. Partenio. In ancient Rome, it was known as Castrum Rotondarum and in the Thirteen Century, it belonged to various families, among them the Caracciolo's. The town's only notable monument is the church of Madonna delle Stelle, resting on the slopes next to a gorge half way the summit. It was built by monks in the sixteen century with thick rocks that make the interior impenetrable. Every year, the inhabitants of the village have a feast with all sorts of culinary delights and games. At night, everybody watches the firework that illuminates the valley and the rocks under a blue sky.

One day, it had rained torrentially. The earth was drenched. Only late in the evening, the air was getting dry. The clouds had discharged their load and acquired a transparent look. They appeared unconcerned about the speed. In fact, for a while, they dispersed lazily as if they were hanging almost immobile in the space. Later, they assumed strange, monstrous human and animal shapes and accelerated somewhat their slow movement. Around them, a glowing red flame soon developed and gave them a surrealistic frame as if they belonged to out of space. They looked like bushes surrounded by fire. Once again, the sun was giving them a coat of gold in the midst of a vast ocean of air. When they finally disappeared from the sight, the sky assumed once again a gloomy mono-color view which was no longer enjoyable to watch. This time, new threatening clouds were galloping from the east and by the time they reached the town they became pitch dark.

In the area adjacent to the church, two hooded men, aided by darkness, skimmed the fence of the field and stopped in front of the main door. They launched suspicious glances all way around them. As soon as they felt sure that no one was passing by or watching them, they laid down two baskets covered by blankets and placed themselves in front of them.

The shortest had black long hair and dark brown eyes. The forehead was swollen at the center, but showed no signs of physical altercation. A canine tooth was missing and the lips were quite prominent. The nose was elongated and the skin dark.

The taller also had dark skin and long black hair. Although he was also unshaven, on the right side of the oval face, were visible cicatrices that from the ear lobe reached the corner of the mouth. Both men were slim and dressed pants without a belt and shirts lacking buttons. By now, the reader has already identified them.

Barabbus began to bite his nails. Scarman, instead, kept on scratching his chest pulling some hair and tossing it on the ground. The wind blew it away. It was getting cool. Scarman put the index and middle fingers between the lips and emitted an acute whistle that lasted about ten seconds. He waited a minute and repeated the same ritual. At the same time, a hooded man was searching with his eyes every corner of the streets. Finally, from behind a big poplar tree, emerged a lady with a shawl covering her head. She walked unsteadily and her steps were heavy. Her eyes spied all way around her for any possible intruder. She was twenty - four years old and childless. At the first, anyone could judge her being a bit fat. In reality, she was short and stocky. Her black hair fell down aimlessly on the stout shoulders. The eyebrows were thick and dark, like coal. Her nose was distorted as if she just came out of a boxing match. She had a baritone voice that scared anyone who for the first time listened to her. The skin was rough and the hands callous. She ate garlic every day and, that alone, kept people at distance. She and her husband made their living by working on a piece of land she inherited from her late father.

A tall man with an olive skin and black hair said in a raucous and resolute voice, "How long, does it take to come here? You ought to know that this is a dangerous enterprise."

"I came late from the farm. I had to cook while my husband attended the livestock," she replied, brushing him aside. The man assured himself that no one was in the vicinity and said, "Let us close the deal right away!"

"How much?" She asked.

"We have already agreed on the price in private. Why do you want to waste time now? Remember that if you report it to the police and I end up in jail, you are going to have troubles."

"Don't be so stupid! How much?"

"I give you a cheap price that you cannot refuse. It is two thousand dollars."

"Wait a minute! I will give you two thousand punches on your face if you are not going to be reasonable. These are hard times. Do you think I am a princess? It is not easy to raise that amount. For some farmers, it takes a lifetime."

The man twisted the mandibles and replied, "Look who is talking!"

The young lady took a step backward and exclaimed, "I deserve a discount. Remember?"

"It is with discount," replied the man showing all of his annoyance.

"You people have no manners. You are greedy and act like savages!"

The man replied, "Lady, either you take it or leave it. We are not at a market where you can negotiate."

She searched for the money in her bra and, when she found it, she turned around and switched some bills in the other hand. The man was getting nervous. She looked at the basket and said, "You cost me a lot of money."

"You cost me a lot of money," repeated the man in a monotonous, monosyllabic sequence. "The next time it may be cheaper," he added.

"There won't be any 'next time,' mister."

"Come on! Hurry up!"

The lady looked at him again in his eyes, pushed the money in his hands and said, "Take you poison! May you die with it!"

The man returned to her a dirty look, shoved the money in his pocket without counting it and disappeared from her sight. Behind the bushes, he tried to count the money with the aid of a lighter. The wind dispersed a few bills. He jumped on them and recounted them. At the completion of the counting, he muttered, "You dirty pig!! You fooled me."

The young spouse grabbed the basket, covered it with her shawl and mumbled a few dirty words against him before heading home.

In her bedroom, she uncovered the bundle from the basket and saw a beautiful little girl. She covered her with kisses and fell asleep next to her. She woke up when she heard babies' cries. She realized that she had to feed her and got ready for the first milking experience.

It was the turn of the short man to act. He whistled three times. Immediately after, a second woman, about twenty-two years old, dashed out of the nearest street corner and walked toward the church. She held a crucifix in her left hand. She was tall and slender. She let her long blond hair flow mostly on one side of her head and her voice was sweet and gentle. No one could escape her blue eyes during a conversation. The teeth were crooked, but somehow white. Both, she and her husband worked on a tobacco plantation run by an American entrepreneur. At her age, she was still childless. The comare of the neighborhood whispered that her partner was impotent. One of them even went as far as to suggest him a potion of herbs that would cure his sterility within a week.

As in the case of the previous woman, nobody was ever able to confirm who possessed the impotency genes.

The young lady emerged from the bushes with a veil on her face. She was having a difficult time dealing with her emotions and kept holding tightly the Rosary in her left hand. Her blue eyes brightened and a few tears fell down her cheeks. The short man insisted, "Well, do you have the money?"

She did not reply at first. Her head was bent down. The man shook her from her thoughts and said,

"Lady, this business cannot go on the whole night."

She replied, "Friend, can you, please, assure me that…"

"Lady," he responded, "When it comes to the almighty money, there is no assurance, no friend."

"Do not raise your voice, lest, some evil person will hear you."

"Good! Then, pay me."

"How much? I beg you. Be reasonable."

"Two thousand! It's the same as the other, so that, you cannot blame us of impartiality. We conduct our business on the principle of honesty. That is why people love us."

"I bet they do. I wonder where and when you people learned the honesty values. But let us go on. I am still unhappy about the price."

The man took a step backward and said, "Lady, I cannot stay here forever. If somebody sees me, I will end up in jail for the rest of my life."

"I want to go home too, good man."

"Bless your heart! First you have to pay me." And, in saying that, he stretched his right hand. She looked at him for a while. The man threatened to leave. She made a three-hundred and sixty degree turn on her feet, pulled a bundle of money from one of her stockings and began to count it. She placed some bills in her pocket and gave the rest to him. From the distance, they heard the roaring rumbling of the motor of an old motorcycle. The man got restless. He pushed the money in the pocket of his dirty pants and away he went. She covered the basket with a blanket and moved swiftly in the direction she came from. From time to time, she stopped, murmured a prayer and continued walking.

The baby boy was still sleeping when the young spouse arrived at home. Her husband just stepped in from the backyard where he had been feeding the cows and chickens. Both husband and wife were elated. The following day, they contacted the parish priest and made the preparations for the baptism.

A week passed by and the two neighbors were unable to exchange their experiences due to their new and active motherly role. Wednesday was the market day. People from everywhere flocked the main square and engaged in making deals with the vendors. The two women met in the middle of the street in front of their houses. "How is the baby?" asked the lady with the veil on her face.

"Just adorable..."She is always hungry and do you know what? I am going to start her with semolina. It is very nutritious and is easy to digest."

"My baby boy never gets tired sucking. Maybe, I too should think of switching him to a baby formula."

"Those two men were terrible, weren't they? They charged us an exorbitant amount."

"Those people are greedy. It is better not to deal with them anymore. One child is enough for the time being."

"You are absolutely right!"

They hugged each other and went on for their business.

During the summer, a man stopped in town. He purported to be a healer and to possess supernatural powers. In a short time, he made many proselytes and opened up a clinic. Espera's and Felix's mothers paid him a visit and presented their sterility problem. His personal diagnosis showed nothing abnormal. He was a very clever individual. Without their knowledge, he prepared meals with crushed broccoli and ordered the two ladies to eat one plate a day for a month. The women were very gullible because they believed that he had prepared a special medicine for them and accepted it enthusiastically. A month later, there was a coincidence. Each one got pregnant at the same time and ever since they gave birth to too many children.

CHAPTER XI

Tragic Events

The capitulation of the axis forces in North Africa gave reason to the Germans to withdraw through the Italian peninsula. In 1943, the allied forces pursued them by landing in Sicily. The partisans, the unglorified and unrecognized occult army, hammered the Germans everywhere. The small villages were no exception. Heroic acts, in many cases have been ignored. Not enough attention has been given to the anti regime people or partisans, who took to the hills harassing, obstructing the retreat and causing heavy casualties to Hitler's army. Hardly any historian or politician has come to the open and admitted that without the continuous help of the Italian partisans, the Allies would have had an awful hard time to dislodge their enemies from the booth.

In Rotondi, the last frontier of Avellino and Caserta to the west and east, a group of local men had their day of glory. On a spring morning, a long column of German panzers were heading toward Naples when they were spotted by a handful of the irregular army. Among them, there was an eighteen year old boy, by the name of Gerry, Felix's brother. They attacked the middle section of the column with Molotov's bombs and immediately ran forward to set on fire those, which were on the front line. The plan called for quick and short strikes on many enemy positions and, then, for refuge in the hills or on the farms. The panzers burst into flames and the smoke bellowed in the sky. Respiration for the nearby residents became difficult. The soldiers, hiding behind the tanks, started to shoot indiscriminately. The fight lasted about ten minutes. The German commander would not accept the destruction of twenty-five tanks and retaliated by razing to the ground all the houses in the area. But, the human loss was even more tragic. Fifty inhabitants, mostly old men, women and children perished under the collapsing buildings.

From wood and debris rose black and nauseating streamlines of smoke. The survivors had to cover their faces with wet rags to sustain the odor. The search was frantic. The race was against the time. The rescuers screen through stones and blocks of cement for their loved ones. Someone's loud lamentations called their immediate attention. A boy, about twelve years old was in horrible pain. He could hardly control himself. He was in a state of shock and his cries went on for a while and then abated. Felix' parents were working on the farm at that time. They heard explosions and shots, but did not make much out of it; however, when the news spread that the partisans had inflicted heavy losses on the Germans retreating troops and these had retaliated killing many people, they dropped the farming tools and ran as fast as they could to the war zone.

The blood was mixed with the debris and flies were having their field days. Some human bodies were dismembered. Legs, arms and heads were littered everywhere, a grim reminder of terrible and tragic explosions. Felix' parents recognized some dead folks and made the sign of the cross. As they moved around, they tried to bring some comfort to the victims' relatives. Whenever there was a need, they helped to accommodate the inert human bodies on a cart that the custodian of the cemetery had brought in a hurry. The identification process took a long time. Family members and doctors tried to recompose as best as the different parts of the bodies and hastened for burial

At the end of the street, lamentations rose from wounded people and reached the ears of Espera's parents. The cries from the pains grew higher as the two got closer to the area. There was a moment when the woman became suddenly pale and held on her husband's upper arm. The head rotated down his chest and he understood that something dramatic had happened. He surveyed with his eyes the rocks and stones around them. He heard a voice, "Ma, ma, mom. I cannot take this pain any longer." The woman screamed, "My son! What happened to you?" She could not bear the sight of a suffering son and fainted. Her husband was quick to hold her in his arms. There was no time to waste, but he was unable to make up his mind.

He could not decide who needed more help, his wife or his son. His hesitation made him a third victim of war disastrous circumstances. Helpless as he felt, he succumbed to panic and vacillated like a pendulum. Those were moments of mental lethargy during which he was unaware of his wife's real condition or his son's whereabouts. His mind was numbed being in the grip of a terrible fear.

In the middle of the road, Felix' parents were scouting every inch of the rubbles to see if one of their children were buried.

The news of the German violent reaction woke up the spirit of unity among the local community. Old and young, male and female displayed an uncommon sense of patriotic and human participation by providing any type of assistance to the moribund and the victims' families.

A neighbor came over with a bottle of vinegar and put it under Espera's mother nostrils. Her eyes moved a bit, quivered, opened slowly and showed symptoms of revival. At the same time, her husband too snapped out of that state of mental freeze. Espera's older brother was trapped beneath the rubbles. A group of youngsters managed to free him, but he was feeble and became momentarily victim of memory loss. They pulled him in the street and waited for medical aid. A farm doctor appeared on the scene after a long bike ride. With the scarce tools he had available, he gave him an in loco surreptitious, general examination. His gloomy face did not give much hope. In fact, he diagnosed that the spinal cord was severely injured and needed immediate care. In Rotondi, there was no hospital. He gave him an injection to calm down the pain, put him on a horse wagon and sent him to Naples. Espera's parents accompanied him and so did a neighbor, who left her husband in charge of the family and farm.

The trip was tortuous. There were military roadblocks to pass through. The craters in the streets, caused by allied aerial bombardments, made the trip even more uncomfortable. The horseman was required to descend from the cart, cover the potholes with boards or dirt, as best as he could, and go on. Thieves replaced the inexistent police force and forced the horse wagons to reroute in areas where their accomplices could survey the goods and plunder them. The animals did not take a moment of rest in a twenty-mile ride. The fear of being shot was a constant danger for the exhausted passengers. Baby gangs assaulted shops in broad daylight. Jackals pried on the victims of the bombs dropped by the plains or by snipers.

The journey lasted much longer than expected. After four hours of ride, the caravan finally reached the Cardarelli's hospital in Naples and the scenario that the city offered was, at least, depressing and desolate. Wounded soldiers were lined up on the sidewalk. Carts full of people, some with the legs dangling from their bodies and others, hopelessly laying one on top of the other, blocked the main entrance. Only a few doctors were in service. Their uniforms were blood stained, their hair ruffled and their eyes half shot for lack of sleep. The overwhelming majority of them had been fighting at the front. The hospital lacked medicine, wrapping bandage and even alcohol. They used vinegar in place of it. The nurses rushed from bed to bed to assist dying soldiers. They looked chagrin and at the ebb of their physical and mental strength. The area looked more like a market than a hospital. Whenever an airplane passed by, the pandemonium broke out among those who could still move around. For the sick and wounded, there was no hope. They could not run, walk, or move. They did not even feel the impending danger. They were already dead in their minds and dying I their flesh.

Espera's mother attempted to call the attention of the doctor in front of her. He was in the seventies and had not eaten or slept in the past forty-eight hours. From time to time, he massaged his eyes as to keep them open. He did not hear the call. He turned around someone's hand pulled him by the hand. The woman cried out, "Doc, my son is in serious conditions. I beg you. He needs your help."

"Lady, are you blind? Don't you see this butcher house? We are four doctors in all. I have not slept for three days. There are patients who are dying and you expect me to pay heed to your son?" he replied in a tired voice.

"Doctor, my son is dying. If you do not help now, I will lose them," she insisted.

"I will see what I can do later." He disengaged himself from other peoples' attention and went inside the atrium. An old man stopped him, whispered a few words in his ear and placed an envelope in his hand. The doctor assented and followed him. After about half an hour, a woman, who appeared refined in her demeanor, approached the same doctor, spoke to him softly and signaled to her attendant to give a bag to him. The doctor thanked her and brought immediate care to a patient lying on the floor inside a room.

Espera's father could not believe it. He wanted to protest loudly, to expose the injustice, vent his anger, but he thought it over and concluded that under the circumstances he had to act differently. He approached the doctor; talked briefly with him, and he, too, placed an envelope in the, doctor's hand. He grabbed the envelope, nodded and followed him. A few yards away, the doctor met the same man as before, "Have the courtesy to place it in my uniform, "said the doctor. The man had a moment of hesitation in seeing the pocket smeared with blood, but followed the order. When he withdrew the hand, he noticed that it was somewhat reddish and got scared. The doctor called the assisting nurse, nearest to him, and asked her to bring the patient immediately to the operating room.

There was no space inside. The doctor requested the nurse to remove those, who were behind hope, and accommodated Espera's brother there. His mother felt immediately relieved by the doctor's changing mood and waited with her husband in trepidation for the results of the diagnosis. The checkup was rather quick. It lasted less than ten minutes. When it was over, the doctor called them on the side and said," Keep your son immobilized for a week. I am going to put a brace on his back. He has to wear it for four months."

The boy's father protested, "How can we do that with the roads full of potholes? The journey back home is long."

"Do the best you can. Let him sit up straight."

The patient's mother was not satisfied and inquired, "But, what happened, doctor?"

"He fractured a disc. It is going to be a lengthy and slow recovery, but, at the end, he should make it."

"Will he be OK., after?" She cried out.

"He will, but expects that arthritis to creep in as he gets older. He should start walking slowly in a week, but a few steps at time. You have to be extremely cautious. A jerk, a wrong move may cause a permanent injury in the spinal cord and he could be paralyzed.

Here is the prescription for pain. As I suggested earlier, if he is lucky, he will recover well... Conversely, if the back and legs do not respond well to the treatment, take him to Rome, at the Gemelli's Hospital. They have a new wing specialized in muscular therapies.

Avoid any bump on the way back home. The mode by which the horse walks is of paramount importance."

The boy's parents looked at each other stunned. They did not even have the time to thank the doctor that he was swallowed up by the sea of patients. They took extreme care in carrying the patient on the wagon. They adjusted a sack of hay in a corner and accommodated him on it. Espera's father said to his wife," Let us get out of here right now, before it is too late."

"Yes, we need to take the boy back home quickly; otherwise, he is going to be on the chair for the rest of his life."

Her husband tried to allay her fears. "Do not feel discouraged. The doctor gave us hope. At home, he can relax and you will see that the fracture will heal in no time.'

"We hope so."

"Don't worry! He is young."

They turned the horse around and made their way out of the hospital compound with extreme care. Suddenly, something unusual happened. The doctor, came out running breathlessly from the hospital's gate, holding in his left hand the envelope that Espera's father had given him. He looked around with his eyes full of ire, burning like charcoal. When he realized that Espera's parents were out of sight, he tore the envelope apart and cast it on the ground, cursing both of them.

At the outskirts of Naples, they stopped the wagon for a few minutes to take a bite and let the horse eat. It was at that point that his wife asked her husband how much money he placed in the envelope. He responded that he was not as stupid as those who fed Dr. Mangione. "Some in the medical field," he added, "Recognize only the almighty dollar, war or no war." His wife agreed with him expressing also satisfaction that they did not have to see him again. Then, she continued, "You took an awful chance. He could have killed our son if he opened the envelope before." He did not answer. He touched his wife with the elbow. On a building, there was a Latin sentence, "Memento, semper audere."

The return trip was laden with obstacles and behind any description. The allied planes were bombing the main roads and the travelers took to the hills. Besides the lamentations, hunger and fatigue, it was impossible to find the right direction because the street signs had been destroyed by the Germans during the retreat. Traveling at night was simply a nightmare. Bandits poured from the farms or mountains to pillage the deserted houses. Dead corpses were strewn on the margin of the roads and carcasses of animals were lined up on the sidewalk. Bullets were flying all over and aerial raid were frequent. The British conducted night sorties, when it was more dangerous, while the Americans chose to carry on their military activities during the day

At one check point, the partisans stopped them and checked if they were carrying arms. One of them, it must have been the leader, gave Espera's father a pass that would allow them to return undisturbed to their town. Some of the roads were covered with rubbles and dead bodies. He had to clear them with a shovel he carried along in order to open up his passage. In some towns, only vagrant dogs were visible around the streets and plazas searching for a bone. A sordid silence dominated those areas broken up occasionally by the rifles' crackling. Not even the train whistled anymore for fear of being subject to enemy's derailment or fire.

The home arrival was a triumph of patience, determination and faith. All four passengers were practically exhausted, both physically and mentally. The young man's parents accommodated their son on his bed, thanked their neighbor for having endured their plight, "We will never forget how close to us you were in times of need." Nobody had the strength to talk. They skipped the evening meal and dropped sleepy on their beds.

A week passed by and Espera's parents noticed tiny signs of vitality in their son's legs. It was not enough for them. Despite the dangers, they decided to take him to Rome for rehabilitation. The mayor had just finished building a wing on the north side of the hospital dedicated to therapy. His dream was short lived. An allied bomb fell by mistake on the added construction and demolished it. From the wreckage, Dr. Massimo Campbell, an American from Clay, NY, and his assistants tried to salvage whatever they could, but the damage was irretrievable. It was necessary to find another temporary solution for the new patient. They created a small space in the basement among other patients' improvised beds and accommodated the boy on pillows filled with corn leaves. An old nurse was placed in charge of the new patient. Three times a day, she would go there and train him onto specific exercises aimed at relaxing the back muscles. As the days marched on, she widened the repertoire with body movements whose main objective was to stretch the back muscles and make them more. Body rotations on its axis were particularly effective. As he progressed, the nurses gave him a towel to wrap around each toe of his foot He was supposed to pull the leg back and forth, always in a slow motion, three times for thirty seconds. Another exercise that proved to be helpful was the abdominals. He had to lie on the back and turn both legs left and right three times for thirty seconds. Probably, the one that produced the most dramatic results was the 'side trick.' He leaned on one side and opened and closed the legs for thirty seconds with a bike's tube tied to the legs. The program most stressful exercise consisted in bending a leg, slowly, to the point where the patient had to raise it on a chair. It was followed by alternating it with the one that required pushing the knee toward the chest. The program called for morning and afternoon training sessions. The latter agenda demanded the lifting a weight from a sitting or lying down position. The purpose was the strengthening of the muscles. The weights were wooden poles of different size. In the evening, instead, it was a short repetitive version of body-rotating movements on a table to empower the muscles to gain more elasticity. This type of routine lasted for a couple weeks. Everybody was expecting a positive prognosis, but the doctor's report froze the family's hopes. They heard the news that they would never wanted to hear. The patient's conditions had inexplicably deteriorated. The bulletin indicated a permanent back and leg paralysis. The boy would not be able to walk normally anymore, but only on crutches. Unfortunately, the hospital was not equipped with the proper therapeutical technology after the bombing and the hopes to rehabilitate locally were shattered.

There was one residual hope, a trip to America. However, the country was far away; the war was still ravaging; the dangers lie everywhere on the Atlantic Ocean and the expenses were prohibitive. Espera's mother started to cry like a baby and her husband had his work cut out to persuade her to control herself.

One day a monk came by. He dressed in brown and raggedy robes. On his shoulders, a long and wide bag oscillated back and forth when he moved through the mounds of debris. It was empty. He stopped at Espera's house. Her parents offered him a piece of bread and a glass of wine. He accepted them gladly and sat on a stone on the opposite side of the street. The moans, from the interior of the building, made him pause while he was drinking the glass of wine. He gulped the rest of it and inquired what was wrong with the patient. They informed him that his conditions were behind repairs. He said to them, "I will pray for him." A few children, curious about the monk, came around him, but did not question him. They were barefoot and wore shorts. Their noses were running like a fountain. The word 'prayer' sounded strange to their ears. They looked at each other and started to laugh. Some adults joined them. The monk did not lose his composure. He raised his head and said, "Is it easier to say a prayer or to help the sick recover from his sickness?" Nobody seemed to understand the meaning of his statement. He got up and said, "To show the power of the prayer, I will pray for him and heal him." The small crowd did not know what to make of it. "How can he heal someone that the medicine considers incurable?" said an old man to his friend.

"The ways of the Lord are infinite," responded the other.

The monk deposited the piece of bread in his bag and prayed. The children laughed a second time. The monk called the patient's parents and inquired about the nature of his infirmity. "He can never walk again. He is paralyzed from the back to the leg," they replied with a veil of sadness on their face.

The monk pulled an envelope from the robe's pocket and said, "I have the perfect recipe. The prayer and the herbs will do the trick."

The boy's parents listened to him with a mixture of interest and pessimism. "We don't believe in sorceries, but we have nothing to lose."

"You are absolutely right in stating that you have nothing to lose. One gram of faith does not cost you anything." He gave the instruction on how to prepare the potion and left. If I do not get harmed by bandits, I may come by in a couple of weeks to find out about the boy's progress." Nobody said a word. They followed him with their eyes while he tried to maintain the balance among the rubbles. The mysterious monk disappeared as silently as he had come.

CHAPTER XII

Monsieur Serafine

After Marshal Badoglio sealed a peace treaty with the Allies in 1943, the Italian army was in disarray. Everyone took the law in his own hands. Only with the arrival of the Americans, the newly created Italian government was able to restore order with many difficulties. In the cities and in the villages, the Americans were welcomed as liberators. People poured in the streets and started mingling with the soldiers, who gave chocolates and chewing gums to the haggard and hungry children. This was especially true in the southern villages. In Rotondi, as elsewhere, people searched for American relatives among the soldiers. This bond between the two nations created a euphoric sense of belongingness that was unequaled with other nations.

The war fought in the hills also came to an end. The partisans descended to the valleys and lay down their arms. Some returned to their families, while others joined the allies in the European theater. For the first time, the town folks began to come out of their houses or hideout and gathered in the main square or in the café'. The recurrent topic of discussions was the battle of Rotondi where the partisans inflicted heavy losses to the Germans, but caused also a punitive retaliation that caused many deaths and wounded. Felix's brother emerged as the undisputed hero who facilitated the allies' advance. Soon, this honor became a center of debates. Espera's mother initiated the revolt. She heartly believed that her son and others had fought with equal bravery and needed the same recognition. Her criticism, however, was mainly directed against one group of partisans and the Communist Party, the first for being unfair in assessing the acts of heroism, the second for being too gullible.

The market people sided with her. Strengthened by their support, she became the most vociferous and unleashed venomous comments towards the decision makers and left deep scars in them. When she found out about the alleged unfairness, she beat her breast a dozen of times and swore eternal hatred to Felix' family responsible, in her opinion, to have sway the judges' decision.. "I hate them from the bottom of my heart. I cannot stand them anymore. Each time I see my son trying to walk, my mind goes to this bunch of crooks. Someday, they will pay for it." All attempts by the Communist Party to calm her down failed. Her rage overpowered her and she quit the Communist Party. One day she went to the main office and threw the membership card on the table. "You can kiss your pussycat with that," she said. Her husband refused to abandon his association with the Socialist Party, "We cannot just pull both of us out of our beloved parties. At least, one has to stay in. If we need something, we can always ask for help."

"If they pay me one hundred thousand dollar of indemnity, I will think about going back to the Party. After all, they funnel to their private checking account millions of dollars that should be used for the Party and everybody keeps his mouth shot. If a militant like me reveals their wrongdoing, they deny it. In that case, nobody knows anything. How can you break the magic circle?"

The animosity between the two families reached ridiculous heights. From that day on, whenever a wife or husband stepped out of the door, the ones across street would close his or hers. If they met in the street, one would turn her face against the wall and walk by. The other would do the same.

The news of Espera's mother squabble with the party spread like fire across the town. Alarmed by the serious repercussions that it would ensue in the following elections, Monsieur Serafine, of French heritage and president of the local Communist Party, who we met before, attempted to mend their friction. First, he solicited Espera's parents to retract their anti-Communist position and make a public apology. Despite his personal involvement and charisma, she remained inflexible. The president did not give up on a peaceful solution of the case and proposed a new round of talks to be held at a date of mutual agreement hoping to find her in a better mood. He also took another step that a political analyst labeled it 'a clever party maneuvering'. He tried to enlist the support of Espera's brother and his friends. A man in the eighties summarized the community's feelings, "This used to be a peaceful place. Now, everybody pretends to be a politician and, has as soon as we touch a hot subject, their nerves flare up."

The days ran one after the other unnoticed. Only the president realized that the longer he waited, the harder it would be to settle the dispute with Espera's parents. Without sending any assistant to announce his arrival, he decided to pay them a short visit on their farm. When Felix' parents found it out, they blocked him in the street. The lady said, "Espera's parents should take their son's claim to the government, not to our Communist Party."

Her husband was infuriated, "They are crazy! I would not give them a single penny! I would rather go to jail than pay them. My son joined the partisans too. What did he get? Potatoes!"

"Well, our first aim is to cool off the tempers," responded the president. "Later, we see what we can do. Would you be willing to take the initiative and talk to them and smooth out the differences?"

"Monsieur Serafine, you try! You are a good talker. We are farmers. We hardly know how to read or write. As far as we are concerned, we are deeply hurt for what they have been saying and doing about us and will never talk to them."

"Did they tell you what they want to do now?" her husband asked. "Something unusual, unheard of," he continued. "They want to build a church next to their backyard, not out of religious motives, of course...., but as reward to their son's healing. In addition, do you know what they want to write on the façade? "Never Forget."

"Why would they wish to do that for?" inquired with curiosity the president.

"Beats me!" replied Felix' father

The president did not wish to get enmeshed in family feuds. He only cautioned them to smooth out their differences; otherwise, the party would pay the consequences. "My main concern is to go to the election with compact ranks. Any divisive issue among our comrades will ultimately hurt us."

The president proceeded to the farm and spoke with Espera's parents. He spoke in these terms, "We appreciate your son's enlistment in the partisan's ranks, his heroic act and his faithful commitment to our ideals of freedom. We did not expect harsh, cruel and virulent reaction on the part of the Nazis."

"Then, my son should get some money or an office job. Instead, what did he get? Do you realize that he can't walk anymore?"

"We deeply feel for him, but we do not have money to compensate him. Let's do this. We wait until the next elections and if we win we will sent our elected official to Rome to present his case. Is this fair enough?"

Both, husband and wife looked at each other and felt that it was a reasonable proposal. They shook hands and the president departed on the bike happy to have accomplished an impossible mission.

Ironically, the whole case did not degenerate into a court action nor it became necessary for the Party to intervene on his behalf. The monk had left an envelope with herbs at Espera's house for her brother to take a small potion every day until the herbs finished. By the end of the second week, the young man began to walk slowly, but surely. In a matter of a few days, he reacquired his full back and leg capacity. In town, they called it a miracle. The Communist Party took distance from them and claimed that it was pure coincidence.

Two weeks passed by and the solitary monk returned as he had promised. He knocked at Espera's door and the young lady leaned from the window to see who he was. She informed her parents who went down to meet him. They were watching their son to walk on his own strength without any help. When they heard that the monk was waiting for them, they rushed downstairs to pay their respect and offer their gratitude. They invited him in. He refused food and compensation. "Prayer is power," he said. They looked at him mystified. He turned around and disappeared.

On one day, both families attended the funeral of a neighbor, who had been gunned down for unknown reasons. Various rumors floated around. Some of them spoke of a vendetta; in the opinion of others, it was jealousy motivated crime.

The local church was crowded. Espera's parents and his wife took seat in the first tow while Felix' parents opted for the last pews. The priest began the rituals by blessing the casket with holy water. Some of it ended up on those who were sitting on the first rows. The people affected by it, passed the palm of their hands to wipe the water from their faces. The ceremony continued with the aspersion of incense. He poured a spoon of powder into a bronze receptacle and dwindled it left and right. A small black cloud rose in the air, but someone began to cough. At that point, Felix' mother approached the priest and whispered in his ear,"Can you, please, pray for my son Felix' return?"

"Where is he?"

"We don't know it. The Germans took him with them. We have no news of him. He must be someplace."

"I will," responded the prelate. "But this is a funeral, not a regular Mass."

"It makes no difference. You know how it works."

The reverend looked at her astonished for the inopportune request and moved on.

The homily followed shortly after it. The prelate said, "My dearest parishioners, in these times of trials, we feel more impellent the desire for love. No more bloodshed of any sort among us! No more tears, no more pains and no more hatred. What we need is love. Our departed, beloved brother leaves us a very clear message. Love is the medicine that assuages all sorts of pains. It is the panacea for all evil. Love is like the perfume of a rose. We must learn how to forgive and forget." He was unable to finish the sentence. Felix's mother, thinking that he was referring to her, interrupted him, "That's because it did not happen to you. I came here for the dead, not for your preaching. By the way, you are not going to build a new church close to somebody's backyard, aren't you?"

Espera's father could not take that abuse and responded in a loud voice, "As long as I live, the construction of the temple will go on. I am not going to block it. Neither you nor my Party can make me change my mind."

His cousin pulled him down by the jacket sleeve and whispered to him, "Sit down! Be quiet! This is not the proper place for you to discharge your feelings." His cousin, undeterred, moved away his hand and added, "I am leaving. I have had enough! My son was on a wheelchair for a long time and I had to attend to him day and night, yet, he is not being recognized."

The relatives of the deceased person were utterly confused and upset, but managed to control their anger. A family relative muttered, "Some people know no limit to their rudeness."

The priest embarrassed and nervous hastened to shorten the ceremony. The pallbearers, at a sign of the funeral director, raised the casket on their shoulders and carried it outside on the horse carriage. Felix's father touched his wife in the ribs with the elbow and both left in a hurry banging the door behind them.

In the street, the comments varied. A woman in the fifties could not hold back her feelings, "How in the world they dare to behave like that in the temple of God? They have no respect for anyone, not even for the dead. What kind of people are they?"

A man dressed up in elegant habiliments depicted the situation in these terms, "Apparently, some individuals are concerned only in causing turmoil. Why don't they choose another place? There is no more shame, no more respect for the sacred."

A distinguished man in the sixties expressed the general feelings when he remarked, "This community has not been enjoying a serene relationship since the tragic episodes of the war. We can't blame the patriots for what happened. They did their duty. We could not stand silent under the foreign yoke. The instability of this town is due to greed and families' inability to communicate."

A bearded young man in the thirties added," If they feel like arguing and hating each other, why do not they sell their property and go live on the mountains where they can settle their disputes."

Another woman with gray hair raised her arms and said, "Hear me! My perception is that beneath the ash there is still fire. These families have not been able to extinguish it, for whatever reason, and now they vent their frustrations on others. Maybe, they are casting bad luck on our town. I had some premonitions last month when the salt shaker fell on the floor and broke without being touched by anyone. Can you explain to me how it happened? The dog has been barking ever since at night and even the chickens have not hatched any egg. If this is not bad luck, what is it? All the commotion created by these two families is taking its toll."

"I am not superstitious," replied a young lady with spectacles. "Everyone us has full control of his destiny. We are what we are because of our choices. We should go o Lourdes to wash our hearts or to Padre Pio to be exorcised."

CHAPTER XIII

Felix in Nazi Uniform

The traditional feud between Felix and Espera's families dipped its roots in years of antagonism, vendettas and ignorance. The divisive line widened with the Nazi occupation of the town. When Espera's brother became a local hero, Felix followed a differed cruel destiny. General Kappler was mortally wounded during the partisans' assault on the town of Rotondi. Felix was a fourteen year boy at that time. He found himself in the middle of the action, not out of his volition, but because he was casually passing - by. He found refuge under a portico and squatted down against the wall. The bullets were whistling all around him. The Germans came there to provide care to their general who had been hit by the partisan's fire. The high ranking official was bleeding profusely through his head and chest. He needed blood transfusion and there wasn't any available. A doctor and a nurse drew a pint of blood from Felix' arm and gave it to the general. In the meantime, the building was surrounded by the partisans. Felix had to submit to a humanitarian act that saved momentarily the enemy's life. That was not all. A captain ordered him to wear a German uniform, thus, he was drafted in the German army. Felix was very weak and could not oppose the imposition of being treated as a Nazi soldier. He did not understand a word of their language and that worsened even more his position. A German reinforcement was called in and the partisans' encirclement was broken. It was then that Espera's brother was hit. The resistance fragmented and eventually died down. Felix motioned to the officers that he wanted to go back home. One of them was in favor of his release, but the general ordered to keep him. He was in pain and could hardly move or talk. He communicated in a few monosyllabic words. In one occasion, he was clear enough to be well understood. He expressed his desire to adopt the boy. The soldiers looked at each other with astonishment, but made no comment. They obeyed and treated him with respect. In the midst of this tacit arrangement, Felix was the innocent victim of a language barrier and a unilateral decision.

General Kappler was originally from Hamburg. He had a wife and a daughter at home. He had fought with Rommel in Tripoli and was highly influential in Berlin. He was rather young to occupy such a high ranking status in the German army. Hitler transferred him to Italy to organize the resistance of the axis forces. During the retreat, his conditions got better, but he was not in position to conduct military activities. He had requested to fly to Germany to complete the healing process, but Hitler, short of generals, ordered him to remain in active duty.

Felix demonstrated early a proclivity to learn the German language aided by the age and by the willingness of the soldiers to utilize him as much as they could. The general made him understand that he would process the legal adoption documents as soon as the war was going to be over. Felix did not wish to refuse the general's plan. He was afraid that any opposition to the general's wish would deteriorate the general's frail health.

At night, Felix dreamed a lot. "I may be rich soon and I could come back to town and marry Esperanza. Neither of our family could ever stop us." He turned his head toward the window and said, "If I don't take this chance, I will never be able to marry her." Never, the thought of being shipped back home in a bag or a casket passed through his mind. Every hour was fraught with dangers and life was dangling on a thin line.

As Felix' platoon retreated to the Nord, the general's conditions steadily deteriorated and at Opera, near Milan, he expired in the arms of Felix. Before he gave up his spirit, he told him, "Felix, I have a wife and a daughter back in Hamburg. Search for them and tell them how much I loved them. Tell them that I am dying with their names on my lips and their face in my heart." Felix tried to respond that he did not have any money and did not know the city. Moreover, with the war raging on, he could not carry out that responsibility. The general looked at his soldiers and wanted to say something. But, it was too late. His words never reached their ears. The soldier, who had fought for and led so gallantly the German army dropped his head in Felix's arms and gave up his spirit. The news was sent to Berlin and the flag was raised half way.

The death of their highest ranking military official brought a change in the soldiers' attitude toward the young Italian soldier and did not approach him anymore with deference. Felix sensed the mood shift and planned an escape. The occasion emerged when a small unit of partisans made an incursion in Felix' convoy. They hit and ran causing many casualties in the German platoon. The unit was running in serious difficulties. In one of those sorties, the young boy stripped himself of the German uniform and found refuge in one of the houses nearby underneath of a bed. He was terrorized and remained in that position for hours, while the military action moved about a mile away.

There was smoke and smell of blood all over the hills and towns. No one dared to leave the house during the gun battle. Later, another Nazi unit, protected by heavy guns, was able to return to the previous location to retrieve valuable material and their dead comrades. Abruptly, fire broke out in the main square. A partisan from above a bell tower of the local church shut and killed a German soldier. In retaliation, the commander ordered a sweeping raid that resulted in the capture of all the local community which was transferred to concentration camps either in Germany or in Poland.

During the search and destroy operation from house to house, a soldier apprehended a boy hiding under a bed and pulled him out at gun point. The soldier was surprised to hear him speak his native tongue and asked him, "Where did you learn to speak my language?"

"In school, sir, but I don't remember much. You know how it is."

"I see," responded the paratrooper with a high dose of skepticism. "In the meantime, follow me."

"Wait!" protested the young man. "I have to take care of my parents."

"If that's your wish, than come with me because they are on the truck."

"How can that be?" inquired the boy trying to disengage himself from the hand grip.

The soldier had no time to waste and dragged him away without responding. The soldier picked up a uniform from his military vehicle and handed it over to the boy before the prisoners were forced to climb into the vehicle.

The truck was crammed with old people and children crying aloud for being carried away and women screaming, fearing for the worst. The column slowly moved toward the Brennero Pass. The fumes emanated by the trucks created dark clouds under a blue sky. The village breathed a funereal air. It was a bunch of houses hanging on the rocks without a human soul. The only survivors were cats and dogs, a grim reminder of a section of the human race that had lost control of its own identity and the power to think rationally.

In Innsbruck, the caravan stopped at the central railroad station. The prisoners were removed from the truck and placed on wagons used to transport cattle. People were denied the opportunity to meet their physical needs outside. No food was provided. No window allowed them to breathe fresh air or look outside. Like animals in steel boxes, they were shipped to the butcher house.

General Kappler's death brought a deep feeling of discouragement within the military apparatus which was already running to his demise. The Nazi commemorated the loss by lowering the flags at half staff and observed a minute of silence in all state educational and military institutions. Three soldiers brought the news to the general's family. They rang the bell and Mrs. Kappler's wife and daughter opened the door. The presence of three soldiers was taken as an omen. The three men stood on attention and presented to them a letter from the furher and Germany's flag wrapped up in the form of a triangle.

The two women fell into each other arms and stood in silence for a while. The mother was the first to disengage from the hug. She looked straight in the soldiers'eyes, made a salute and withdrew. The messengers turned around, stood on the attention once again, and returned to their jeep.

The city mayor invited both, mother and daughter, to a commemoration ceremony at city hall, but they courteously refused the invitation. For a long time, they did not show up in public. The loss of a central figure in the family, such that of a husband and father and the depressing news coming from the front were not conducive to a relaxing mood. It took a lot of motherly love before she convinced her daughter, Fiorella, to take some steps out of her residence and take fresh air in the park.

As the war continued, it became dangerous to expose oneself in public. One night, the allies rained thousands of bombs on the city center where the general's family lived. Some historical buildings were crippled; others were razed to the ground. By the early morning, when the airplanes ceased to vomit their fire, the whole city was reduced in mountains of rubbles. The spectacle offered by Hamburg was analogous to the earthquake of the city of San Francisco in 1905. The devastation was incalculable. In every street there were destruction and death. It was impossible to travel. People's corpses were strewn everywhere. They got caught on their way home by the bombs. Many died for lack of medical assistance. Funeral homes could not carry on their services and the churches spared by the punishment were desolate. The survivors were frantically searching for their loved ones. Not even the looters had an easy time. A massive chunk of concrete fell from the top of a building trapping some of them. Three were pronounced dead on the scene, while others suffered serious injuries. The volunteer crews did their best to extract the victims from under the rubble. Some cases of assaulting food stores emerged in the suburbs, but the military presence discourage any subversive attempt. The grim scenario of one section of the city was equal to any other. The military sirens wailed and the ambulances could not take the wounded to the hospital because the traffic was paralyzed. Army units were dispatched with the sole purpose of reactivating it. The task could not be completed in a matter of hours. High cranes catapulted heavy chunks of concrete into the river to create some space. Buldozers gulped thousands of tons of concrete to fill up the main square and the football fields. Nobody expected a quick fix, but the behavior of the citizens of Hamburg was admirable.

It took a week of around the clock relentless work of the firemen, the volunteer corpse and the military presence to reopen the traffic with extreme difficulty. Despite their efforts, the boulevards could only operate on two lanes and only the main streets were free of rubble. In the following months, the allied bombardment plans shifted to other cities and Hamburg began to dedicate all her energy to the cleaning and rebuilding process.

CHAPTER **XIV**

Buchenwald and the Gypsies

The Nazi considered the gypsies non Arian, asocial, and uncultured race. This political view made them susceptible to incarceration without legal defense. Initially, the government position was a bit benevolent. The gypsies could register at the local municipal building and enjoy a limited freedom. Later, Himmler gathered them like a bunch of leaves at Buchenwald. By the end of the war, most of them perished like other fellow prisoners by malnourishment, slave labor, as a result of medical researches or ended up in the crematorium. Many gypsies volunteered in the army and were sent to Stalingrad. Out of all of them, hardly anyone ever saw Germany again. The majority of those who were kept in camps met the same fate than those of other nationalities. A few thousands survived the lagers. Some of them, Scarman and Barabbus served as 'capot' to save their skin.

At the beginning, Buchenwald was a concentration camp of small entity. At the entrance, there was a sign, "Jedem Das Sein." As the war waged on and the number of prisoners increased dramatically, the Nazi needed more space. The recovered data indicate that the lager swelled to close one hundred thousand inmates. To enlarge the prison camp, the military needed rocks and slave labor.

Scarman and Barabbus understood one law. If they wanted to avoid suffering and death they had to serve the new owner, no matter what, even at the cost of being brutal. Most of their people had been exterminated by various means. They decided, therefore, to cooperate and requested to be enlisted as 'capot.' To demonstrate their complete allegiance to their leaders, the new German guards implemented a rule that allowed each prisoner a dish of soup a day and a loaf of bread to share among eight of them. At times, to stir the prisoners' rivalry, they threw bread in the mud. Brawls ensued among themselves to get it first. As an additional act of humiliation, the two gypsies made them genuflect and, then, kicked them, causing them to end up face down in the mud. If a prisoner became vociferous, he would be tied with a chain against a cart and let him die by dehydration in the scorching sun. In some instances, the 'capot' condemned old people to the crematorium because they were no longer considered 'a profit.' Scarman kept a private list for himself. He considered them objects, names, nothing else, just like the Nazi echelon demanded.

The guards' behavior was so inhuman that they caught the attention of the commander -in-chief. He had a secret plan to submit to the Fuhrer. His focus was to increase production to modernize the camp. The approval came from Berlin on the same day. Scarman and Barabbus were elated to receive the first choice. To implement the objective, the gypsies forced the prisoners to carry huge stones from the cave to the the camp center. Whoever dissented with them or was sick, tired or tried to carry light rocks, was shot to death on the spot.

The promotion, allowed Scarman and Barabbus to run an office from a bunker where they directed the operations in a more secure and relaxed ambiance. One of their primary concerns was the coordination of medical experimentations, such as the tattooed skin. They accomplished it, first, by skinning the inmates and, secondly, by making the tattoos.

The prisoners did not remain inactive and responded on their own terms. Some of the cultured, more intellectual people devised a strategy to provide 'asylum' to some of their fellow prisoners condemned to death. This became a realistic possibility as the camp crammed with prisoners.

Death had thousand faces. In 1944, American planes bombed a nearby armament factory next to the SS compound. About eight thousand inmates tragically lost their lives. Besides this incident, prisoners died like flies every day by means of starvation, unhealthy hygiene and medical researches. The weakest did not have any strength to resist an order or to do even the lightest menial job and succumbed to the brutality of the guards who directed them mainly to the gas chamber. There were times when the soldiers did not even threaten them with the butt of the rifle. The prisoners fell down, like flies, not out of their own volition, but out of lack of energy and will to live.

This was the scenario when Fiorella was forced to enter the gates of Buchenwald.

CHAPTER XV

Fiorella

Fiorella graduated a year in advance from high school in Hamburg. She was an exceptional student with a vocation to art and medicine. She spent her free time on Saturdays in a new, local museum, which had been able to purchase a few Italian paintings, mostly from obscure individuals engaged in ambiguous deals. The well informed scholars knew that the German officials had expropriated them from private art collectors during their retreat from Italy. The scarce crowd did not distract her from her contemplative mood. She would stay there for a long time fascinated by the colors and the movements of the figures. She was particularly interested in observing Caravaggio, who, by inventing the perspective, had changed the history of painting. More than in one occasion, she manifested to her parents her desire to study in Florence as soon as the war was over. Her mother made an attempt to dissuade her, "Honey, the city of Michelangelo is too far and dangerous nowadays. Make some researches. You may be interested in a closer location with similar advantages, like Amsterdam, where I can visit you more often. To satisfy your medical vocation, go to the zoo and study the animals."

"Mama, I am seventeen year old and I cannot stay forever under your wings. I must learn to fly on my own."

"Did you expose your wishes to daddy last year?"

"Yes, he was open to my future plans. If he were here, he would confirm it."

"Knowing his fascination for the Renaissance, I am not surprised for his support to your dream," admitted unwillingly her mother.

Fiorella had no political fascination. She was not a member of the Youth Party and spent her spare time with her friends driven more by social or artistic motivations. One Saturday, the sun unexpectedly visited the city, after a long period of neglect. It was very tempting to take a walk. She stopped in front of a statue and began to analyze it in all its details. A girl passed by. She recognized her and wanted to talk to her, but Fiorella, absorbed as she was in her thoughts, did not respond to her greetings. The girl smiled and moved on. She made a few steps and stopped again. She was of a Jewish descent and acted with the most absolute caution. She was terribly afraid of being spied. If she were recognized and reported to the police, it would have been the end of it. In that moment, Fiorella finished her contemplation and gave a glance around to ascertain that she was not being an object of ridicule or considered a lunatic for observing the statue for a long period of time. She recognized her friend and hugged her. At the same time, she acted with discretion knowing the political implications if she got caught talking with a Jew. She launched a glance around the park. The presence of only a bunch of old people in the area, enjoying the warm weather, assured her that it was safe to talk. She asked her, "Why didn't you call me?"

"You were involved in a mysterious mental monolog and I did not want to disturb you."

"Not at all! As you well know, I love painting and sculpture. Those cold stones hold a special attraction for me. They speak a mysterious language that I strive to decipher."

The whole park appeared in lethargy. Nobody expected it to turn alive so suddenly. A group of old people was discussing the latest war events and how the Russians and the allies were getting closer to their motherland. A couple more women joined them as they were passing by. One old man said, "We should have attacked only Russia."

"That's for sure!" Responded another man. "But, tell me. Did you hear about the retreat on all fronts? The allies and the Russians offensives are gaining momentum"

"How do you know it? The media are depicting a different scenario."

"What else can they write? I heard it over the radio. There is a daily program transmitted in London and it is directed to all Europe."

"It won't be too long," said a short man. We should have never allied with Italy. They were not prepared.

We lost the war when we helped them in Yougoslavia and Greece."

A gardener, who was raking leaves approached the two girls and made a signal to a secret agent hiding behind the trees. He sent a second signal. In the meantime, Fiorella continued the conversation with her friend while walking. When they reached the group, the agent ordered them and the group of old people to take a seat on the military truck that was called in from a nearby street. Fiorella tried to explain her innocence, but the agent ignored her. Three guards were posted on the truck to vigil on the prisoners at gunpoint. The trip to an unspecified destination lasted four hours. When the truck finally stopped spitting fumes in the air, they had arrived at the gates of Buchenwald.

Felix had been watching the new group of inmates with interest. He noticed a girl on the other side of the fence. She was staring at him. More than the exuberant physic, her luxurious blond hair, falling from her head like a cascade, caught immediately his attention. Under those long, thin, golden threads hid two big blue eyes. On their screen, one could detect a deep feeling of sadness and anger. She was of medium stature and red freckles covered her arms and face. She did not look emaciated, which made him ponder on it for a while. Was she being transferred here from another camp? Impossible! Could she be an undercover agent? A spy? These ideas revolved in his mind and kept him on the alert. He was sure of one thing: she looked too good to be there among dying people. The internal debate made him nervous and curious. He got close to the fence and asked her why a living human being was doing among the dead. The girl was captivated by the foreign accent; nonetheless, she refused to answer. Felix insisted and, finally, she gave in. After a long pause, she told him that her name was Fiorella and that she was accused of collaborating with the Jews. It was not true. I was talking to a friend."

"That is what happens in this country. I hope we can get out here alive. With the daily air raids of the last week, I am not sure..."

"Where are you from?" she asked. Your dark hair and accent eloquently indicate your Italian nationality."

"Besides the pain of going through this hell, you add also discrimination," he replied with poignant irony.

"Oh,no,no," she hurried to rectify. "That's not true! It is a matter of fact that I love your country. When the war is over, I plan to go there to study."

"Do you really believe that the war will end soon? He inquired with skepticism.

She placed her right hand on the mouth and whispered, "I am positive."

"What prompts you to state that?"

"The American should be here in a month or so…"

"Were they the ones who bombarded us last week?"

She nodded, but did not proffer a word.

He lowered his head and said, "They killed many prisoners. The guards made a pile of them and burned them. You can still smell…. from that hole there," and pointed toward the area where the odor came from.

"They threw on the bodies a kind of chemical that made it difficult for us to breathe."

"I am sure that many inmates perished."

"Even among the guards, there were many deaths. The camp commander hired some Ukrainians and gypsies to replace them."

"Hang on a bit longer."

"You talk as if you are not part of this tragedy," he said.

Fiorella stretched her hand and reached his. Felix was taken by surprise, but did not object. He realized that the move stunned him. No one in the camp ever said a word of consolation to him and now a girl made him feel a human being again. For a few moments, both hands were tight. They were disjointed by an imperious voice, "Stay all away from the fence or I kill you," yelled a guard. The girl said to Felix, "These poor souls are unharmed and dry in their bodies like old branches ready to fall at the first passage of the wind. There is no need to be cruel."

The guard, standing a few feet away, noticed that the conversation was extending behind his order, decided to break them up. Fiorella stretched her hand through the wire and Felix did the same. The guard pulled her back. Both hands hit the wire and blood spilled on the steel. "I am going to get out of here!" She shouted. Felix remained with his hand stretched with blood dripping on the ground.

"And, how are you going to do that?" responded the guard pushing her away and gun point. It is a matter of fact; I am going to make sure that you are not going to go home again. Saying that and pulling her away was one act. Felix protested, "Don't touch her. She is my sister!"

The guard looked sternly at him and said. "One at the time! First, I take care of her, and then, of you. Be patient."

Inside an isolated barrack, Fiorella was screaming. She tried to untangle herself more than once from the guard's grip. He dragged her to a dark room where he ordered her to undress. She withdrew against the wall with rage spilling from her eyes. He unbuckled his pants and laid the rifle on the floor. She cried out, "Don't touch me!" The soldier grabbed her shirt and ripped it. The girl began to shiver and cry, "Please, do not touch me. My father was general Kappler."

"Oh, yea! First, let me take care of you." He grabbed the bra and pulled it. The girl fell violently on the floor. He started to laugh and to pull down his pants even further down. The girl grabbed a brick from a pile in a corner and hurled it at him. He dodged it. The girl kicked his right leg. He lost balance and ended up against a gasoline can. His eyes were two charcoal of fire. He tried again to submit her to is wishes. She jumped against the wall with a feline movement. The guard pulled her against him. A man, from somewhere, grabbed the guard's rifle and pulled the trigger. Fiorella heard the whistling of a bullet, but could not recognize the intruder in the darkness. The molester dropped his arms and the head fell backward. He bounced back and forth a few times and dropped dead on a pile of rags. The girl buttoned quickly the shirt and recomposed herself. The guard did not. The anonymous person disappeared underneath the tent. The noise made the guards, outside, laugh. They thought that their comrade was having fun. The shot changed somewhat their reactions. One of them asked why he had to shot her. The others said, "He had good time. Now, he no longer needs her, therefore, he is going to take her to the crematorium."

The oldest in the group smirked, "Maybe, he fired a shot to intimidate her to submit to his wishes."

The youngest guard said, "He had good time. If she were alive, she could incriminate him at the end of the war."

At the main gate, all the guards stood at the attention at the passage of a car. The passenger was a high ranking Nazi. The chauffer stopped the car. The SS official stepped out and conferred briefly with the head of the camp. He went back to the car and confabulated with his aids. He put on the black gloves and went straight to the barrack where Fiorella was fighting for her dignity and her life. The guards appeared under the influence of alcohol or drugs. They were voicing loudly their opinions about what was going on in the barrack. The SS official pointed the pistol against them. One by one fell like flies. At that point, Fiorella was even more stunned than before and did not know what to do until she was called out. The official gave her a military salute and offered her his personal and government apologies.

At the gate, a second passenger lady stepped out of the car. Fiorella recognized her and ran to her arms. The military car whisked them away to their house. Fiorella internment had lasted just the time for her mother to put in motion the political machine. It was wartime and to reach Berlin and get to the right channels was a nightmare, but she made it just on time.

CHAPTER XVI

The Escape

Felix had committed a crime and was punishable of death, but no one knew it. At least, for the moment.... The death of the guard was reported to the main branch of the camp and the wheel of justice was put to motion. A questioning process began. The young inmate felt uneasy. He knew that eventually the truth would condemn him to the gas chamber. From then on, he started to work on a plan that would assure his safety. There was only one glitch: how to implement it.

In the camp, the stench was unbearable. The guards protected themselves with masks. One day, a woman was struggling to get to the latrine for her daily physical needs. She was too weak. Her legs gave in, twisted and she fell in the mud. A young man ran over to help her. Barabbus and his partner did not appreciate the charitable act. They pointed the gun at him and took off the safety ready to shoot him. The boy said, "At my town people are kind and gentle. Not even the gypsies are capable of such cruelties. The two guards exchanged a quick glance. The boy stood there waiting to die. Barabbus whispered to his partner's ear, "Don't you recognize this voice?"

"I think I do," responded the other.

Scarman asked him, "I see that you have an accent. Are you Italian? What is your town?"

"I come from Rotondi."

That name rang in their ears like a thunder. The two pointed their guns down and confabulated on the side a minute or so. For the first time they were having doubts. To avoid any suspicion among other fellow guards, the two gypsies pointed once again the rifle at the boy and ordered him to go to their bunker.

The office offered no glimpse of hope to anyone entering the premises. Human skulls paraded the cavernous walls and blood splattered hair chunks hung from a rocky ceiling. Some coffers were full of jewels and the smell of crinoline had a nauseating effect on the boy.

"You said that you come from Rotondi," inquired the tall and slim 'capot'.

"Yes, sir!"

"Can you mention the name of the main square?"

"Freedom Square."

"Do you remember any of the peoples' names?"

"How can I?" responded the boy. "There are so many. But if you wish, I can mention the names of the pharmacist and Don Pepe, the coffee shop owner."

"Enough!" shouted Barabbus causing the boy to shiver.

The guards interrupted the interrogation. Instead, they locked themselves in their dusty and terrifying office and exchanged their views. The boy waited outside. Their strange behavior puzzled him. The door slowly opened. Felix asked them, "Do you know anyone from my town?"

"Barabbus replied, "How would we know them?" He became pensive for a short time, then, he continued, "No, after the famous battle of El Alamein, we retreated by the booth and passed by your town."

"You must have been fighting for many years."

"For too long!" responded Scarman.

Barabbus insisted, "Can you tell us your parents' names?"

"How would you know them? You just passed by my town," replied the boy with skepticism.

Barabbus got irritated, "You answer my question!"

The gypsy with the scar on his nose got up and opened the door to ascertain that no one was listening. He turned his attention to the boy, "What is your name?"

"They call me 'Felix," a Latin name, by the way."

Neither one of the guards was interested in other languages. The same man asked him, "Show me your right hand." The boy acquiesced. Scarman looked at Barabbus in disbelief. Neither one of them had the will to talk. They felt like paralyzed. A scream from the street brought both of them back to the reality of the camp. It was a fleeting slice of time. A prisoner had been shot to death. Scarman fixed his eyes on the boy again, "Who are your parents?" The boy got suspicious. He was afraid that they were conducting an investigation of the guard's death and did not respond.

The short gypsy shouted, "Do you understand that I have the power to send you to the crematorium right now?"

Felix gave indications of losing his speech control. Barabbus did not want to inflict upon him unnecessary pain. He discharged him with the understanding that they would continue the interrogation the day after.

Before he left, Barabbus pointed the finger against him and said, "Don't think that we do not know who shot the guard. We have been following you since you stepped on this ground."

Felix felt terrified. He knew that his life depended on these two mercenaries.

During the night none of them could sleep. Too many questions revolved around the computer of their minds. When the two gypsies got up they heard that Berlin had initiated an investigation that shook them from the top to the bottom of their boots. A spy from within the camp had prepared a list of accusations against them. The most prominent focused the guard's death and on the transgressions of Himmler's orders. The papers were in the hands of the camp's chief military official. He had three days to carry out the investigation. At its completion, the two gypsies were to appear in person in Berlin before a jury. In the meantime, the head investigator had to keep them under tight surveillance. The news had a devastating effect on them. They lost the initial cruelty fervor and rarely showed up in public.

Up to now, the archives on concentration camps have not revealed the truth. We do know if the rumor was an act of vendetta started from a low ranking official who tried to gain favors with his superiors.

Scarman and Barabbus realized that their end was about to come. Before then, they decided to do the unthinkable. They immediately called the boy back to their office. Scarman closed the door and locked it.

Felix looked at Barabbus. He had a chalice in close to his heart. What's that?" asked the boy.

"Don't you see it? It is a chalice."

"What are you going to do with that?"

"I tell you later."

Scarman pulled the boy toward him and said," Never mind the chalice for now. Look straight in my eyes and swear that this is going to remain among us."

The boy raised his right hand, "I swear!" he said.

Both guards felt relieved by the oath. Scarman continued, "Listen! Your life is in jeopardy. We know who shot to death the guard who was having fun with that pretty girl."

The boy started to cry. "I don't want to die. Please, don't kill me. I don't want to die."

Barabbus tried to calm him down by saying, "Stop crying and listen to us." The boy was sobbing and shaking.

Scarman addressed him in this way, "Tonight, we will bring you out of your barrack and take you in the woods. Outside, the field is mined all way around the fence. Do not touch it. It has high voltage. It will kill you instantly. There is only one safe passage you can take. Follow us. We will pretend to have killed you by firing a shot. You walk straight for about a mile until you see a sign. Once you are out of that sign, you are safe. We will provide you with a pair of pants and shirt and some money. As you reach the summit of the hill, get rid of your prisoner's garments."

"How?" responded the boy still in pray of panic.

"Bury them! We give you pants, shirts and jacket from dead people. We have plenty of them. After ten minutes, we will shot in the air. The alarm will go on and the search operation will begin. By the time they prepare the hunting with German shepherds dogs, you should be in a safety zone. If they should be at your heels, move on. Keep on going through the fields until you reach the city of Weimar. Look for the house of Cornelius. He is a Catholic priest who wears a yellow shirt. Good luck!"

The boy asked him, "Why are you doing this for me? Who are you?"

"Someday, you will recognize us, that is, if we are going to survive this hell."

"The boy hugged them and said, "I hope and pray you will come back home too."

With tears in his eyes, he added, "I can never repay you for saving my life, but if we meet again, no matter when and where I will get married, you will be my guests of honor."

"Promise?"

"Promise!" 'Felix turned around and asked them, "How will I recognize you?"

Barabbus raised the chalice and said, "This is the sign of eternal friendship between us. And now, let's hurry before it gets too late."

"Wait! I have one last favor to ask you."

"What?" pressured him Barabbus.

"I have many Juice friends in barracks 4 and 5. Get them out there before it is too late. I will be eternally grateful."

The two gypsies looked at each other wondering why he was so concerned about Jews. Barabbus put both hands firmly on his shoulders and shook them. "Tomorrow, we will do it. We will stack them in dumpsters and pretend to dump them outside the camp. They will find a way out."

Felix hugged both of them.

Scarman ordered him to get into a drum. He stuck a big sign 'Toxic Material' and rolled it in a bulldozer. He threw additional trash in it and drove away outside of the camp to dump the load in a big dumpster. The fire would incinerate it. Barabbus followed the truck on foot holding a shovel in his hand. In a couple of minutes they passed by the inspection gate. A guard climbed on the bulldozer and checked the content. Satisfied with what he had seen, descended quickly with one hand on his mouth. The two gypsies and arrived at the site without any further delay. Barabbus pulled down the barrel with the aid of the shovel and stopped it in front of him. He gestured to the rest of the crew that he was going to discharge the toxic material down the road, behind the trees. At the safe point, he opened it and let the boy out. "Go! Follow this path. Good luck and may your God be with you." The boy hugged him and could not stop crying. The gypsy told him, "Stop doing this! They may come after me and kill us both!"

"Someday, I will find out why you saved my life!" He raised his hand and bid good-by."

For the first time in his life, the gypsy cried. He dug a hole and put back the dirt. He decided that it was not necessary to fire a shot because he had changed the plan and returned to the dumpster. He winked at Scarman. The initial stage of the plan was successful.

Felix walked for miles in the darkness. Every noise he heard in the woods, regardless of their origin, gave him a heart palpitation. Even when the wind brushed the leaves in all directions, he feared the Nazi dogs were at his heels. He was not sure whether in the camp his disappearance would go unnoticed and was very cautious because the woods were heavily guarded by soldiers. One mistake could cost him his life. He ran with all the residual strength left in him to gain as much ground as possible from his imaginary pursuers. During the night, it rained torrentially in that part of the region. Felix' clothes were soaked and heavy. Under his feet, he felt a blanket of leaves that squeaked at his passage. It was slippery. He tried to run. The soles of the shoes were worn out and the small sticks on the ground pinched his feet. He slipped a couple of times and ended up with the face on the ground. Each time he got up, he had to get rid of the leaves stuck on his face. The wet hair, unruly as it was, fell down on his eyes hampering the vision. Often, he had to push them back to be able to see something in the darkness. His safety depended on minimizing the noise or averting it altogether. Any unnecessary noise would alert the enemy. He did not follow any path. He carried no flashlight. This inconvenience caused him much harm. At times, forcing his way through thick bushes, he got scratched by the sharp sticks causing bleeding on his arms and neck. A tall and old oak tree was resting on the ground for its eternal rest. Felix did not see it. He stumbled against it and fell. It was late when he realized that he ended up in a big hole filled with old leaves and brushes. He got submerged by them and became invisible by human eye. He was exhausted, hungry and cold. A whistle traveled at the speed of light through the valley. He heard human steps and dogs' barking getting closer. At one point, they were within thirty feet away. Heavy breathing reached his ears and made his brains rumble. Ten minutes passed by and he was still immobile in his position. Suddenly, he heard human voices that he could hardly decipher. Only two words became clearly audible, "Achtung" and "Jovel". Some of the words became more distinct. The dogs were pushing the soldiers near him. He was hopelessly waiting for his demise, in silence, cold, hungry, exhausted and in prey of desperation. In that very instant what seemed to be a successful search operation turned into a sudden retreat. The captain received the order to organize their units around the city's perimeter. There was no time to ask for explanations. It was an order. The Russians were gaining ground and were pressing on the outskirts of Buchenwald.

Eventually, sleep overcame Felix and he spent the rest of the night in the ditch. He woke up at the dawn. Some plains were hovering overhead, probably, in a reconnaissance mission, to test any existing defense system in the area. Felix came out of the dungeon with some efforts and stopped on top of the hill. He stretched his eyes down the valley and could see the suburb of the city of Weimar. The body was achy and often he had to pluck off some tiny animals that found refuge on his clothes and warm skin. He looked around to ascertain that no one was spying on him and started his real freedom journey. At the bottom of the hill, a pretty pond served as a resting place for birds and other animals of the area. He washed his hands and face. It was cold, terribly cold.

Apparently, in proximity of the city, it had not rained at all. The streets were clear and the trees dry. He passed by a farmhouse and noticed a pair of pants and a shirt drying on a clothesline. They had dried under the sun of the previous day. He pulled them off the line and ran toward a bush. It took him two minutes to change the clothes. A rake was idle on the ground nearby. He had an intuition. He picked it up and put it on his shoulders. The rest was relatively easy.

As he approached the city, he ran into a long column of military vehicles moving toward east. Without any plausible reason, the column stopped when Felix was within one hundred yards from the road. A general stepped down a jeep, confabulated lively with some assistants riding alongside him on motorcycles. One of them opened a map and went over some geographical points with his finger. The general nodded and argued about the best way to reach the defensive area in the shortest time. At his signal, the long column restarted the march. By the time the last vehicle passed by Felix' location, airplanes stopped roaring from above.

Felix was undecided on whether to wait a bit longer or to go on. Finally, he took the option of walking on the main road. A girl of about eighteen years old was riding a bike. She was proceeding slowly. It was hard for her to be in complete control of the steering wheel that was wiggling here and there. The rider was paying attention elsewhere. The sight of a young man distracted her even more and she hit a stone. The fall caused abrasions on both legs. Felix dropped the rake and ran over to assist her. The girl was laying down with her arms stretched out groaning from the pain. He asked her if she got hurt. Instead of answering him, she whined even more and ran into apparent convulsions. The pain was being aggressive and unbearable. Felix did his best to assure her that it was not a serious case. A closer scrutiny at the girl made him change his mind. Her upper arm had a gash of blood. He ripped part of his shirt and it over the wound to block the blood flow. That approach relieved her anxiety and, shortly after, she resumed her normal breathing. At first, she avoided any eye contact with him. His presence made her nervous. The uncomfortable condition did not last long and she started to stare at the strange face trying to define his identity somehow. The unresponsive attention of the young man brought her to a quick change of mind regrouped her strength and managed to raise herself on her feet. She stood up, got on the saddle, made a gesture of assurance and took off but only for a few meters for she stopped.

The girl had only one shoe. The long and coarse stockings arrived up to the knees. One part of the shirt fell on one side of a dilapidated gown. The woolen gloves were holed on both sides as if they had been perforated by a welding torch or a drill. Her thick and dirty blond hair covered her deep blue eyes. One cheek was smeared with grease. The skin was like a peach. The nose was small and cute. She could have been a couple years older that Felix.

She looked at the young man with detached interest as if she had a premonition of future events. That boy, all skin and bones, reminded her of the prisoners in the concentration camps from the outside. She appeared to be in a hurry to meet her destiny. Before she left for good, she made an effort to smile and opened her mouth. Her teeth were crystal like. She pulled an apple from the pocket of her jacket and offered it to him. "Here, take it!" she said. You must be hungry."

Felix accepted it and cleaned it on his side pants. He dipped the teeth in the fruit and devoured it without raising his head. He even ate the pit. The girl stared at him intensely as to unravel his most intimate feelings. Felix asked her, "I heard a rumor that a Catholic priest is aiding the Jews to escape to the West. Do you know anything about him?"

The girl bent her head on the side and looked at him with suspicion and stopped short from accusing him an enemy of the state. "Are you one of them?" she queried.

"I am not a Jew," explained Felix.

"Then, why are you looking for him?"

"Just curiosity," responded Felix, who, in the meantime, had picked up the rake and placed it on his shoulders.

The girl changed her position and said, "O.K. I will tell you. He was living in that white house next to that church with high steeples."

"What do you mean by that?" inquired apprehensively Felix.

The girl launched a glance full of surprise at him and said, "Are you the only one around here who does not know it? Where have you been?"

"I mind my business, miss."

"Your farmers never know anything. You live in a world of your own. You are not interested in the political life of the country. Then, when something happens, bang, you are shocked."

Felix tried to offer his apologies, but she said, "Never mind!"

He scrutinized her and started to like her, but he had another pressing matter to tell her, "We farmers go to town once a week for the market. We pass the rest of the days working on the field."

"O.K., O.K." she replied with a smile.

"Please, tell me. Please, tell me what happened to him," insisted Felix. "Be smart! What do you think? Didn't I tell you that he used to live there?"

"He must have been a good man," replied the young man in a pensive mood.

"He was good in saving the lives of the Jews, yes. You should know that those who become accomplices of foreigners are traitors." The girl stared deeply at him as to delve in the secrets of his heart and asked, "Why are you asking these questions about him? Did you know him?"

"How would I know him? As I said before, I rarely move from the farm."

She was unimpressed by his evasive answers, placed a foot on a pedal and was ready to press on it.

Felix' eyes were imploring her. She smiled and said, "I have a correction to make if this will satisfy you. I think you have been misinformed. The man you call a priest, in reality, was the Vatican attache' in Berlin. He came here once a week to provide false passports to the Jews. Do you know how many Jews he saved without casting a single shadow of doubt around him? Felix was expecting to hear a number and opened his mouth that meant curiosity, "How many?" he inquired.

"Thousands! The Vatican, of course, denies it, but the SS have proofs. Someday, the world will know the truth, if Rome agrees to unravel the secrets. That false priest outfoxed the SS all these years. The Nazi have been particularly embarrassed and upset because the man did not do it for the Church or his country, but for another nationality."

"But, if he was the Vatican attache', as you claim, wasn't he a priest?" insisted Felix

"That is the general rule, but there are exceptions to the case. Sometimes, to cover up secret operations, they hire ex-spy agents in Italy."

Felix remained pensive for a while. The girl looked at him intensely. She grabbed him by the collar of his shirt and pulled him toward her. Felix did not oppose any resistance. She kissed him. The kiss left a dirty mark on his cheek. It was getting late. She placed her left hand on his lips and said in a soft voice,"Danke und aufwiedersen!" She pressed on the pedals and sped away.

Felix remained speechless. She turned around and waved. He waved back at her and shouted, "Aufwiedersen!"

The allied air raids became more frequent. A bomb fell in the curve at the end of the road where the girl had arrived. Felix saw the bike fragments blown the bridge. He covered his eyes and cried.

The tragedy shook up the young man. For a while, he was unable to take any decision. In the middle of nowhere and for fear of being caught any time, he wondered aimlessly. He did not dare to get near the house of the Vatican attaché,' who, he understood, had been murdered. There was no point to look for him anymore. Even if he tried to find out something from the neighbors, he ran the risk of falling in the hands of spies that were active everywhere. He changed his plans and started to walk toward the city in the hope of finding a job. Shortly after, he met a farmer. The old man scrutinized from

Antonio Casale

head to toe and asked him if he wanted to give him a hand on the farm. In return, he would give him lodging and food until his two sons returned from war. The offer appeared to Felix like the manna from heaven and accepted it enthusiastically. The farmer looked at him once again and said, "You need a hot bath. I go to start the fire. You draw the water from the well and pour it in the big kettle on top of the tripod. Check the water temperature. When it gets hot, add cold water to make the temperature lukewarm. Use the pail that lies against the wall in the stable." Felix was ready to go when the old man added, "By the way, there are a pair of pants and a shirt in the barn. They may not fit you, but they come handy now."

Felix followed the farmer's order. He touched the water in the kettle with the hand and withdrew it immediately. "Ouch!" he yelled. He dumped a pail of cold water into it and tested the temperature. It was cold. He started to undress and shivered. He looked at his shoes. They were worn out and broken. The toes were black from the cold. They looked bluish. Dreary thoughts flashed through his mid. "They could be frozen," he thought. He felt no feeling in them. The pants and shirt were converted into the breeding ground of all sorts of bugs. There was only one way to get rid of them, the fire. He checked again the water temperature. It was getting cool fast. The quick immersion in the tub produced in him feelings of relief and self satisfaction. He could not remember the last time when he enjoyed a warm bath. On his side, he noticed a pair of scissors, a big chunk of soap and a coarse cloth that resembled a sheet. He bent over the tub and cut his hair in big chunks as best and as fast as he could. The second stage of the bath pertained to scrubbing his body with the soap. Dirt and bugs were well entrenched on the skin. The first time was not sufficient. It was necessary to repeat the operation a second time. For a few minutes, he stood there enjoying those moments of hygiene and solitude until the water temperature cooled off even more. It was cold inside the barn and he wiped up and dressed up with a lightning speed. The pants were long and the shirt wide, but it did not matter. The farmer opened the door and hollered, "I am going to milk the cow and look for some potatoes. Get inside and add some wood in the fireplace. I will be back shortly."

Felix felt reborn after the bath. Now, he needed food to satisfy his stomach. He followed the master's instruction and stood in front

120

of the flames to keep warm. The meal was rather simple. There was milk, a piece of bread and a few potatoes. Felix devoured his portion and was looking around for additional food.

He grabbed the bottle of milk and gulped it. The old man looked at him with compassion and smiled. He dropped his piece of bread in Felix's dish and watched his sons' picture on the wall. His face turned serious. For a while, he did not utter a word.

The bombardments continued in the next weeks. The Americans occupied Buchenwald on April 1945. Hitler committed suicide in his bunker along with his wife Eva Brown. The armistice was signed.

Three months later, two young men were approaching the farm house. They banged on the door as if they were in a hurry. The old man peeped through a hole in the door and got emotional. He opened it and hugged his sons. They looked malnourished and emaciated. He wanted to know the latest events of the war, but his sons were in no hurry. They asked for hot water, so that, they could take a bath. The old man informed them that a young man was living temporarily with him and that he was going to call him to get to start the fire. In the meantime, he was going to put some food on the table. The young man did not respond at his whistle and that made the old man wonder. He decided to go to the barn and see for himself what he was doing, but there was no trace him. The search went on for a few minutes without success, then, the old man gave up and started the fire on his own.

Felix arrived in the city of Weimar, where Goethe lived, without knowing anyone. The only person who could have helped him had been killed. After months of living off charity and some sporadic manual work in the area, he decided to take a train directed to Dusseldorf. Most of the passengers did not have the ticket. They hid in the bathroom or on the back of the last wagon. The controller forced his way through the various compartments packed with people from many nations. Groups of passengers formed a circle around him to slow down the ticket control. Most of the illegal passengers slipped through and avoided payment. In some instances, the travelers would not open the doors where the children were sleeping claiming that they could not be disturbed. The recently formed new government knew too well that it needed years to reorganize the national economic and industrial infrastructure and did not enforce the law to the extreme. The order was to let things flow with the tide. The popular saying was that 'people could not draw blood out of the stones if there were no jobs.'

Unfortunately, Dusseldorf too had been completely destroyed, therefore, there was no reason for Felix to remain there any longer. He made up his mind and decided to move to Hamburg. On the train, squeezed against the window, Felix took the pen and wrote to Espera.

My Dearest,

I know that you wonder why I did not write to you before. It would be too lengthy to describe all the hardship that I endured in the concentration camp at Buchenwald. Through no fault of mine, I wasted the most precious years of my life when I could have spent them with you.

I wanted to come home so badly immediately after the end of war, but I was penniless and Germany was in chaos. With the new democratic government the situation is normalizing. I just found a job and I like it. I plan to come home and marry you as soon as I save enough money.

I cannot describe how much I have missed you and still miss you. But, I promise you one thing. I will always remain true to our love.

Forever, yours,
Felix

Felix kept on writing twice a week to Espera, however, he did not receive any reply from her. He made an effort to write to his parents inquiring about her, but the answer was sibylline, "As you know, our relations were interrupted long time ago. We see her once in a while going to the farm. The family is very secretive and the mother does not allow her to speak to anyone, except with Mosca, who has been visiting them lately on a daily basis."

In the successive three months, Felix kept on writing to Espera on a regular basis. The fact that he did not receive a single letter bothered him immensely and tried to find a logic reason behind it. If his parents could not provide a credible excuse, he needed to look elsewhere for an answer. The Postal Office in Germany got restored rather quickly and efficiently. "Could it have been the Italian Postal Service the real culprit?" He asked himself. The Italian government still in its embryonic reorganizational stage, perhaps, was not in condition to respond effectively and quickly to the needs of its citizens. It was a time of political turmoil. The intergovernmental squabbles were frequent and it did not help the nation from recovering from the economic, social and financial collapse as it should have been. Additionally, the political divisiveness between Communism and the Demochristian Party discouraged foreign investment and unemployment was rampant. The Fascist heritage was still alive widening the gap between the executive and legislative branch. Among the nostalgic of the past regime, hardly anyone realized that the nemesis of the dictatorship dealt a disastrous blow to the richest sector of the Italian life: tourism. Two local politicians had been involved in a corruption scam that had links with the hierarchy of their Party in Rome. Some minor parties charged them with a chain of bribery schemes. They had dissipated one million lire with lavish banquets. The Communists accused them of unethical conduct and called for the President's resignation. Nepotism was widespread. Many senators' relatives got the lowest grades on a national contest, yet, the system awarded them with the jobs. It made news also the disregard of rich people for taxes. In the city of Cortina d'Ampezzo alone, la Finanza, after intensive investigations, found thirty of them possessing sport cars worth three hundred thousand dollar and up, but they declared one thousand dollar of annual income. The Post Office was no exception. Mail carriers took the law in their hands for the lack of inspectors. They opened letters coming from countries such as America, Germany or Australia and robbed them of dollars and marks. Some of them got caught dumping entire sacks of mail at the bottom of the mountain, but the dismissal process that the head of the department promised was lengthy and slow. At the end, they all made it with impunity.

In this climate of allegedly political frauds, bitterness and lack of moral models, mistrust increased among the citizens. Felix' suspicions were well motivated and decided to take action.

CHAPTER XVII

The Post War Hamburg

Hamburg rests on River Elba. It is intersected by a couple thousands bridges, more than Venice or Amsterdam. Prior to the war, it had one million inhabitants. The city was and is one of the most beautiful in the world. Innumerable rivers and canals divide the city which is surrounded in the North by Denmark and at the West by the Netherlands. The bountiful presence of water favors the growth of flora, grass and trees. The parks in Hamburg are always dressed in green.

Even though the British Air Force destroyed the suburb of Hammerbrook causing more than forty thousand victims, the city rose from the dust and became, once again, vibrant, cosmopolitan and industrious. Germany was reduced to rubble and needed urgently foreign labor to undertake the rebuilding process. Thousands of foreign soldiers or private citizens held captive in concentration camps refused to return to their motherland. They realized that in nowhere else in Europe the labor opportunities were so abundant and opted to remain to ameliorate their future and their children's lives. Millions more would come out of their free will in the following years. Those who had a trade had no problem either in finding a job or opening up their own business. This was the scenario that gradually unfolded before Felix's eyes.

At Dusseldorf, Felix did not feel comfortable. A truck loaded with logs was fueling at a gasoline station. Felix got closer and heard the driver telling the serviceman that he was heading for Hamburg. He was pressed by time because the Americans were expected in town any time. Felix heard the conversation and walked to the back of the truck. When he realized that no one was looking, he climbed on the back and found a hole among the logs.

During the trip, Felix remembered the last request that general Kappler had made him on his deathbed. He brushed away the idea for the time being. He was dirty, disheveled and with no decent attire. His top priorities were a job, money and a place to sleep. "Under these conditions, I am not going to look for his family," he said.

The driver was speeding and the truck was swallowing up mile after mile. But unpredictable events stopped the race against time. At a certain point, the highway was blocked. It had been devastated in previous weeks by the bombs and with the chaos reigning all over the country and Europe, it was almost impossible to carry out road reparations. But the main problem came when a gasoline truck caught fire and the whole highway for a stretch of two miles turned into a bulge of flames. He emerged from the truck without knowing the extent of the danger. The area was in smoke and respiration difficult. He ran away from the flames and found refuge in a nearby field. In the meantime, the firemen trucks arrived on the scene and tried to contain the huge balls of flames that billowed in the sky threatening the adjacent houses. It took several hours before they were able to extinguish the fire. Felix was watching the situation with great concern. He could not stay there for a long time, so, he took the chance of returning to the same place and wait for departure. The driver went back to his truck and checked if the load was still intact or was damaged by the flames. Among the logs, he noticed someone who had his face covered with the back of his hand. Upon a closer look, he found out that it was a boy. He ordered him to get out and asked him how he got there unharmed. Felix was too tired and hungry to even apologize. Upon a second look, the driver said to him. "Eh, kid, are you fasting for some religious reasons? Look at yourself in the truck mirror. You look like you are on a hunger strike."

Felix did as he was told. His face gaunt and resembled that of a skinned rabbit. He had only skin and bones. He touched his shoulders and the clavicle protruded way out. The legs were thin and the abdomen was almost inexistent. The driver opened the door and cleared the interior of the cabin. He smiled and said, "Come! Sit on the other side. Let's go." He grabbed a big sandwich he had just bought and handed it to him.

The driver put on opera music and pushed the foot on the gas. They arrived close to Hamburg and for some reasons he decided to stop the music. He turned to the passenger side and said, "Eh, are you mute or deaf? Why don't you talk? You have not said a word in all this time."

"I, I come from a concentration camp."

The driver stepped on the brakes causing the whole truck to shake. The car from behind made a sudden twist with the wheels to avoid a collision. Another vehicle following it did not make it on time to slow down, crossed the double lanes and ended up on the right shoulders of the road. The driver, who was with Felix, decided to take the extreme left lane that led to a gasoline station and restaurant. Shortly after, the traffic resumed with normality. The driver invited Felix for a cup of coffee. The smoke emitted by the parked trucks was asphyxiating and the noise deafening. The two travelers found a small table in a corner and sat. The waiter came to take the order. The driver asked him, "Do you have anything to eat? This young man is going to break down like a rotten log if he does not eat something."

The waiter looked at the boy and noticed a foreign accent. "Really, you need some flesh in your dry bones. You are a living skeleton. Unfortunately, we've hardly any food."

"Eh, do you want to feel responsible for the health of this boy you call 'living skeleton?'" protested the driver.

The waiter tried to appease him, "Let me see if I can find something. I will be back shortly."

"Now we are talking business," replied the driver. He looked at Felix and smiled.

Felix was almost closing his eyes. He felt broken physically and mentally.

The driver seemed to read his thoughts. "What are you thinking about?" He did not wait for the answer because the waiter came and asked him, "Can he be patient five minutes longer?"

The boy did not respond. "Oh, no, exclaimed the driver almost in an exasperated mood. "This guy is going to die in my company." He got up and went in search of the owner. He met him half way between their table and the kitchen. "Eh, hurry up! This man is about to drop dead and your waiter takes his sweet time."

"Here, I am" responded the waiter in a reassuring tone. "I brought cheese and bread and a cool beer."

"Eh, how is he going to eat? Asked him the owner. "He is not moving," he added.

The waiter put a cup of coffee in front of Felix. The aroma rose to his nostrils. He made an effort to open his eyes. The waiter brought the cup to Felix's lips. He sipped it once, twice, three times. The hot liquid caused an electric vibration in his stomach. He shivered for a few seconds, shook his shoulders and finished the coffee. He looked at the driver and asked him what it was. The driver looked at the waiter with a surprised look and said, "Did you hear? He doesn't know what it is."

The waiter was about to laugh, but controlled his impulses, "Where does he come from?" He asked. "Where is he going?"

"I haven't the slightest idea. I gave him a ride. He told me that he was detained in a concentration camp and that is all. I have my doubts, though, eh..."

"If he says so, why should you doubt him?" Reprimanded him the waiter.

Felix started to eat. At the beginning, it was hard to chew. The waiter looked at the driver with apprehension, "Let him finish eating. As he gets his strength back, he will be able to talk like a radio."

"Like a radio, no," protested the driver. "But to conduct a decent conversation, yes."

"That's the way it works, my friend."

"If your diagnosis is correct, it is going to take a month for him to gain a bit of weight."

"It is your problem, man. Why do you care about?"

The driver gave him a dirty look.

By the time he finished eating, Felix felt much better. He recounted, in short, his odyssey and how he was in search of general Kappler's family. This name alarmed the driver. The general was famous in Germany. The waiter shook his head, leaned over the driver and whispered to him, "He has been too long at Buchenwald."

"I don't know," responded the driver with indifference.

The waiter started to feel sorry for Felix and asked him" Would you like to work here? I will talk to the boss. We have a small spare room on the back. You may sleep there. Wait a minute. I will be right back."

Without waiting for Felix' approval, the waiter took off. He met the boss in his office. "Can you give a job to a young man?"

"Is he a cook?

"No, he claims that he was at Buchenwald. I doubt that is true."

"I see. Is he healthy?"

"I am not sure if he is going to make it tomorrow in these conditions."

"Maybe he is dehydrated."

"He hasn't eaten a decent meal in ages."

"You mean...." He did not finish his thought.

"Let's put it in this way," interjected the waiter. "At least, he survived."

The boss said, "Well, I think it is a question of food. Let's give him a chance."

A couple of minutes later, he showed up with a broad smile. "Man, you are lucky! Come with me. I will give you some clean clothes. Take a shower and come down, so that, you can start working."

The driver marveled at the swift shift of the events. He attempted to offer one last recommendation to the boss, "But, he..."

"Don't worry! He will make it. He needs a week of good food and beer."

Felix welcomed the idea of working there, at least, temporarily. The driver said, "Well, I guess I am no longer of any help. Hamburg is a few miles away from here. I have to stop there tomorrow for some business."

Felix was ready to jump at the opportunity, but he had already opted to work in the restaurant.

He hugged the driver, "So long and thank you for all you have done for me. I hope I can compensate your good heart some day."

The driver replied, "No need for it. Maybe, some day we will meet again."

Felix was dirty behind description. For health reasons, the waiter called a barber and made shave Felix' head. Felix appeared relieved by the loss of the long hair, not so much the barber who did something unusual. He put on fire the hair and the apron he had used. His strange behavior caused apprehension to the owner. The smell came to the interior of the restaurant all the way from the backyard. The waiters felt nauseated and, interpreting the feelings of the owner, locked the doors for the time being. They unlocked them when the smoke subsided and the wind had dispersed the odor. Felix stood sitting in the back yard waiting for the next course of action to take. Two waiters came to his rescue. They carried out a big pan of hot water. The steam formed a huge cloud that took different shapes as it rose in the air. The men dumped additional cold water in a wooden bath hub until the temperature reached a sustainable degree. The older waiter ordered him, "Take off your clothes and throw them on the fire. This is a bar of soap. Don't eat it. It is not a candy. The towel is hanging on the partition. Wash yourself well. Empty the bath hub and disinfect it with this liquid. Put on the new clothes and, as soon as you are ready, come to the kitchen. We know that you ate something before, but we have in store for you a nice meal. We want to perk you up and restore your health. We need you as much as you need us." He made a couple of steps forward, turned around and added, "Our clients don't like dirty waiters. If we are not presentable, they will not show up again."

Felix took longer than expected to cleanse his skin. He complied in full with the waiters' orders and showed up for the meal. At the end of a working day, he was tired and went to bed. It was the first time in years that he slept in a decent bed with fresh, clean sheets. As the time went by, he grew stronger and worked hard earning the respect of every co-worker and the administrative personnel. Considering that culinary art was not his vocation, he honored those who supported him and helped him.

One evening, a lady stopped to eat where Felix worked. More than food, she was trying to get mechanical assistance at a late hour when all the garages were closed. She appeared quite nervous. Her husband managed a car shop in Hamburg, but could not communicate with him because the telephone lines were broken. She had a flat tire and did not know how to cope with it. Worse yet, she had to lodge in the area for the night. The unexpected course of events would have caused in her husband a tremendous anxiety. Felix heard her plight and promised assistance. The lady's face brightened in an instant. "Do you know how to replace a tire? I will pay you well."

"There is no need for it, madam. I am a mechanic."

"But..." responded the lady with incredulity. "You are a waiter, a cook. Aren't you?"

"Not by choice... I am new in town and..."

"Oh, my heavens," exclaimed the lady even more surprised than before. "What made you choose this trade?"

"As I said before, I was forced by circumstances, madam."

"I see. May I ask you when you can change the spare tire? I am pressed by time," she begged him.

"I will do it right now."

"Aren't you working?"

"I am going to be in my lunchtime in five minutes."

"That's very nice of you. I really appreciate it."

"It is my pleasure."

In fifteen minutes. Felix completed the job. The lady was ecstatic. "If you ever look for a mechanic position in Hamburg, this is my business card. I will be pleased to recommend you to my husband." She handed it to him along with payment and departed.

Felix remained stunned. He put the card in his pocket. His co-workers gave sporadic glances outside and could not understand why he subjected himself to a dirty job during his lunch time.

Felix was scheduled to go on vacation the first week of July when the clientele is scarce. Most of them make reservations every year with Italian beach hotels and restaurants. The German cities look like phantoms. Nobody wants to stay here in the hottest months of the year. Felix could not afford to go back to his hometown. Not yet. He had saved some money, but was not enough for his plans to marry Espera. He rented an apartment in Hamburg near St. Nicholas Church, which boasted being the tallest building in the Nineteen Century. On n Monday morning, he made a phone call. The shop secretary conferred with the owner and invited him for an interview two days later.

"So, you helped my wife to replace the spare tire? Glad to meet you and thank for your great assistance. You do not know how much we both appreciate it."

Felix was surprised to start the conversation on a positive note and did not expect such enthusiastic commendation. "Sir," he said. "I did not consider my help a heroic act. You would have done the same in my place if another woman was desperate of help as your spouse was."

"I would have done it gladly," he replied in a broad smile.

"I happened to be in the right place at the right time."

"You are very correct. Tell me now. As I understand, you are interested in a mechanical job, right?"

"Yes, sir! I would appreciate it very much if you give me that opportunity."

"Do you have any experience? When did you learn the trade? You are so young."

"Well, I was an apprentice in Italy from an early age. When the Germans stopped in my town, they drafted me and I kept up learning from them."

"Is it how you learned the language?"

"In part, yes... the rest, I learned it in..." He did not finish the sentence.

"Go on. Don't be afraid," he encouraged him.

"Sir, I ended up at Buchenwald for no fault of mine."

"I did not mean to resuscitate a sad part of your life. Indeed, tell me. Are you capable of changing brakes? "Can you smooth the drums? Can you change the gasket in the engine?"

"Sir, with all due respect, I can do most of mechanical work related to cars. I survived the concentration camp partly because one day a week the guards allowed me to help them in the garage. Now, if in the outside world technology improved much faster, I don't know it. It depends how many innovations the car industry has absorbed while I was a prisoner during this span of time. Whatever it is, I am willing to learn anything I missed."

Felix made a great impression on his interlocutor who hired him beginning the following week.

Back at the restaurant, the head chef said to his colleagues, "Do you remember Felix the day he stepped in this place? He resembled a stalk of straw. He was susceptible to being blown apart at the first whistle of the wind."

"I surely do," confirmed one of his co-workers. "Now, he has put on some weight and is energetic."

"You are absolutely right," added a third colleague. "With all the potatoes and meat that you fed him every day, he is showing a little belly."

"Don't exaggerate! He keeps himself in shape. Let's not underestimate his dedication to work."

"He is fantastic!" commented the chief. "I won't be surprised if he replaces me when I retire in the next two years."

"He is young and clever. He invents recopies that veteran chefs don't even dream of creating," said the second chef.

"If he deserves it, why not...? More power to him," concluded the head chef

Felix spent his vacation time in the car shop and was expect to resume his duty at the restaurant on the first day of the month. He did not show up, neither he called. He lacked the courage to abandon those who had been his savior in time of extreme need. At the restaurant, they were waiting for him. His absence gave rise to all sorts of speculations. Finally, one Tuesday morning, the owner received a letter. He saw Felix's name and hurried to open it. It said the following:

Dear Mr. Wolfe:

It is with great sadness that I am writing to you these few lines. I owe you so much and I did so little for you; consequently, I do not know how to start. It is with profound pain and great chagrin that I must inform you of my decision to live in Hamburg. It has not been easy to make that choice. Since my early years in Italy, I was brought up as a mechanic and that passion has remained in me. At your restaurant I adapted myself as a waiter and cook to survive and sustain myself financially. I must confess to you that the restaurant work is not in my DNA.

Please, forgive me for any damage or disappointment that I may cause to you and to my ex-co-workers. Rest assured for my deep respect to all of you.

I wish all good health and continuous success.

Yours,
Felix.

CHAPTER XVIII

Mrs. Kappler

Felix's letter made the restaurant crew a bit bitter. They did their best to keep him alive and reshape his future. The head chef, especially, said to the owner, "I feel bad, not to mention betrayed; nonetheless, I must confess to you that I was impressed with his intelligence and never doubted that he would reshape his life in another professional field. I sensed it." His colleagues agreed.

Felix set a veil on his previous culinary experience and started working as a mechanic. On a rainy September morning, a lady brought her car for check up. The manager welcomed her, "Good morning, Mrs. Kappler, how may I assist you?"

"Last time I came here, you suggested me to bring the car for check every six months. I know that I did not make an appointment. I took my chance. If you have time, I can leave the car here, now."

"You are correct."

"How long is it going to take?"

"I am not sure. Let me check my mechanics' schedule. We are finishing another car. Do you wish to wait? We have coffee and cookies in the waiting room."

No, thank you. I prefer going back home."

"In that case, we will call you."

"Thank you, kindly."

At the sound of that name, Felix raised his head from the floor and tried to have a glimpse of the general's wife. He wanted to talk to her, but he also realized that it was neither the opportune place nor the proper time for a private conversation. He rested with his back on the floor and kept on completing his job.

For the rest of the day, Felix was absent minded. He went to the office and, with the excuse of checking a bill, he copied down Mrs. Kappler's address and slipped it in his pocket. No one in the office or on the floor got suspicious of any wrongdoing.

In the afternoon, Mrs. Kappler arrived to the garage in a taxi to pick up her car. She noticed her car parked outside and went to the office to check with the manager. The gentleman welcomed him as usual with reverence, and handed over the keys to her. Since she always paid by mail, she thanked him and wished him a good evening. He bowed and opened the car door for her. She waved good-by and drove away. Felix, from inside the garage, pretended to be working. In reality, he was following every step that she made through the mirror of the car he was fixing.

On Sunday, at three o'clock, Mrs. Kappler's bell rang. A feminine voice asked, "Who is it?"

"My name is Felix and I am here to convey to you an important message from your late husband. I would like to talk to you in private, if I may."

Her husband's name made her shiver. Many journalists had tried before to interview her, but she always refused. The accent made her think that he came from a foreign press and told him that she was not interested in meeting anyone. The abrupt end of the conversation caused disappointment in him. He never dreamed that a classy lady would offer such an impolite reaction.

Mrs. Kappler was a woman of medium stature with a petite body and big blue eyes that seemed to overpower the whole facial dimension. Her coarse, blond hair barely rested on her shoulders. She seldom smiled, but when she did it was very captivating. Her voice was thin, almost inaudible at times, unless the interlocutor was close to her. Her demeanor was gracious, but she could be firm and proud if the circumstances demanded it. Educated in a Lutheran school, she had a lot of influence on her daughter's upbringing. Her husband, a military man, adored her. The time he spent at home was dedicated to her and their child. Every morning he prepared the breakfast and in the evening took them for dinner in the most prestigious restaurants of Hamburg.

Every morning, the florist from around the corner would show up with a bunch of red roses. The general's death brought a profound change in her life. It was a love loss for her and her daughter. The double tragedy was too heavy for her to bear and, since then, she entrenched herself in her own privacy. Deprived of her husband's gentle and deep love, she changed her social attitude and lived a lonely life. It was rumored by neighbors that she had become introverted and unapproachable. She reversed all her love to her only daughter and cast her shadow on the girl in every aspect of her life. To some close friends, she revealed several times, "People can never understand how devastating can be the loss of a loved one."

Felix could not rest in peace until he accomplished his mission. Now that he found her, he wanted to keep his promise to a man on the deathbed. Each day that passed by carried an extra burden on him. He tried to digit a few telephone numbers he had written in his book, but the answer was always the same 'wrong number.' After a various attempts, he desisted from pursuing that objective. Obviously, she had an unlisted number. The idea of returning to her house began to lose ground. She could have considered his behavior a nuisance and subjected him to penal sanctions. On the other hand, he did want to cross over the boundary line of civility either. The repercussions could have detrimental consequences for his job and, so, he dropped the whole idea of searching for her phone number or going back to her house. A simple meeting, informational in nature, was causing him a mental agony. Nothing seemed to work

Perhaps a letter would do the trick. He took a pen and a sheet of paper and jotted down a few comments, nonetheless, he never mailed it.

He was convinced more than ever that a personal encounter was the best approach. He had tried and failed. One evening, he was walking through the streets of Hamburg. He was hungry. There were many Italian restaurants downtown. He chose the nearest one and walked in. A lady was all alone at a table in a corner. He noticed that the waiters paid special attention to her and treated her with respect. He asked to one of them what was so important about her and they told him that she was Mrs. Kappler, the widow of a famous German general. Felix thought that he could not miss that chance. He rushed to the floral shop and sent her a gorgeous mixture of multicolor flowers accompanied with a card. He took his seat back in the restaurant and kept on checking every move she made.

Mrs. Kappler was surprised to see the waiter bring her the flowers. She thanked him and opened the card. She read the few lines, but was unable to figure out who was the anonymous donor. Felix thought it was the right moment to act. He approached her table and introduced himself. The lady looked at him with surprise. He asked her if he could join her.

"No, you may not," was her reply. And in saying that, she got up.

"Mrs. Kappler, I come from Italy. I have a message for you."

"You are the classical Italian impostor," she answered in an irritated tone. "If my mind serves me well," she continued, "You have the same accent of that young man who rang the bell at my house the other day and now you are acting like a Casanova sending flowers and card. Who are you, anyhow? What are you seeking from me?"

"I am not looking for anything. I just beg you to listen to me."

"If your aim is to entice me in a romantic trap, you miscalculated your plan. I am not interested in any escapade with adults, let alone with a young fellows like you. I am old enough to be your mother."

Felix was patiently waiting for his turn to speak, "Mrs. Kappler!"

The lady was stunned to hear a second time her last name. "Incidentally, how do you know my last name?" She inquired. "How do you know me? If you insist to waste my time I am going to call the manager."

Felix tried to defend his case by saying, "Your husband died in Italy in the town of Rotondi. Are you willing to deny it?"

For the first time, Mrs. Kappler took a long pause before she answered. That name was familiar to her. She had read it on the military documents and on the death certificate she kept at home in a safe. For the first time, she softened her obstinacy for a dialog and asked, "What else do you know about my husband?"

"Finally!" exclaimed the intruder. "May I sit?"

"You may," she replied in an almost imperceptible voice.

The young man called the waiter, "A bottle of champagne, please."

"No," protested the lady. "You are going too far now."

Felix looked at the waiter and said, "Never mind!" Then, he turned his attention once again to her and said, "If my information is not confirmed by facts, you are in a position to disprove them or to confirm them."

"Let's hear" said the lady half way between being fastidious and curious.

Felix took the floor and said, "Mrs. Kappler! The general during the retreat, stopped at my town. His soldiers drafted me. I was only fifteen. Your husband liked me so much that he wanted to adopt me as a son. Needless to say, he needed your consent. He would have discussed the matter with you at the end of the war. Unfortunately, a communist bullet deprived him of his wish."

"Oh, my heavens!" she exclaimed with astonishment. "How many more lies are you going to forge?"

"I have no knowledge of whether his soldiers are dead or alive. They are the only witnesses who could prove or disprove my words. If you check the military archives, you may be able to find them."

"Listen! My husband never kept anything secret from me. He told me every little event that occurred in his life or any plan that he had and that concerned both of us."

"No, you would not. He revealed it to me just before he..."

"He was mortally wounded. Is that what you would like me to believe?"

Felix fell back on his chair and said, "You have a daughter. Don't you?"

"Why are you being so personal?" She inquired. "Don't you think you are transposing the limits of privacy?" she added.

Felix opened his arms in a gesture of helplessness, "I thought you wanted to know the truth. Obviosuly, I am wrong."

She did not answer. He continued, "Didn't you want to test my information?"

"Yes, but don't push your luck."

"Isn't your daughter about eighteen twenty years old by now? Isn't her name Fiorella?" he insisted.

Mrs. Kappler had a sudden moment of pride. She got up and staring at his eyes, she muttered, "Now, young man, you must tell me how you attained all this information. I demand it!" Her voice increased in intensity.

Felix invited her to sit. She did. He continued, "The general died in my arms."

At that point, the lady assumed a more cooperative attitude. "Can you elaborate?" she asked.

The doctor did his best to stop the cerebral hemorrhage. The general realized that life was sleeping away from him and said in a broken, but firm voice, "When you see my wife and daughter, tell them that I am passing away with their smiles in my heart."

Mrs. Kappler could not resist anymore. She drew a handkerchief from inside her shirt sleeve and wiped her eyes." "I am really sorry if I caused you any pain, but I had to keep a promise I did to a man on his death bed."

Mrs. Kappler was sobbing, "Now, I feel that you are being sincere. You may come and visit me and my daughter at my house. It will be a cup of coffee, maybe, not as good as your expresso, but I will try to compete."

Felix smiled. "Mr. Kappler, I regret to refuse your invitation. My initial intent was to give you a message, not to bother you. You disappointed me a lot."

Mrs. Kappler replied, "I apologize for my apparent unbecoming demeanor, but a widow has to be cautious in her social contacts, especially if her husband was an army general." She got up and called for the bill.

The waiter came and informed her that it had been paid already. "I suppose this is another act of chivalry by you. Isn't?" She said to him. Felix did not respond. He picked up the vase of flowers and said, "I will accompany you to your car.

Outside, it was getting chilly. The humidity made them shiver. The sun had gone to sleep hours before and the wind was getting nervous like an untamed horse. Felix opened the door for her. She got comfortable on her front seat and he handed her over the flowers. She found a space for them at the bottom of the passenger front seat. She took the ignition key and started the vehicle. "So, you don't wish to meet my daughter," she asked with a malicious smile.

"I already met her."

The lady drew back against her seat. The meeting had provided one surprise after another. She protested, "I feel betrayed. Why didn't you tell me that before? Under what circumstances did you meet her.?"

Felix understood that the conversation hit another big hurdle and tried to do his best not to get her more apprehensive. "You did not give me the chance. You see, Mrs. Kappler, do you really think that I wanted to waste your time when I rang the bell at your house?"

The last statement struck the lady's imagination even further. She did not know what to make of it. She took off her eyeglasses and said, "It is time that you are more explicit. Your twisted and incomplete statements hide many subterfuges that need to be brought to my attention."

"If you press me, then, I will be honest. "I met her at Buchenwald."

Mrs. Kappler sank on her seat. She could not control her poise anymore and got pale. That work drove a ridge in the bottom of her heart. That name obsessed her. It struck a painful note in her ear. She never wanted anyone to know about that episode that involved her daughter. "How did this stranger know her past? Could she trust him?

What role did he play at Buchenwald? How could he play any role at all at that young age?" These questions were spinning in the vortex of her mind and caused her a temporary state of dizziness. The car was still running. She stretched her hand and turned off the ignition key. She closed her eyes. "When will this family's sore spot ever be washed off?" She muttered.

"I really don't know," responded Felix

"Life is made up of so many unpredictable events. Look at you. You were a stranger to me and, gradually, you are invading my life. This is a horrific evening." Her head was dangling down her neck. She raised it and added, "Before I leave, tell me, under what circumstances you met my daughter. What were you doing there? Were you a guard?"

Felix frowned. "No. I was not. I was an inmate. After your husband's untimely death, the German army went in disarray during the retreat. I passed from one platoon to another. The new dog owners threw me in the concentration camp after days of traveling in a cattle box."

"Oh, my heavens! I can't believe it! You met Fiorella at Buchenwald."

"It happened more than that, Mrs. Kappler," he said scratching his head.

The adrenaline was reaching Mrs. Kapller's brains. "Oh, no! How much more is in it? This is mental abuse. This is mental harassment, young man,' stated the lady on the verge o f a mental collapse.

"If I can appease your mind..."

"Please, do so," she urged him.

"I, I, I..."

"I, what? She begged him."

"I killed a guard. I never told anyone.

"No! Tell me that you did not."

"I can't. I did it."

"Why did you kill a German soldier? You are a traitor!"

"Madam, calm down a bit! In the concentration camp, even among the capotes there were different nationalities. Our conscience speaks loudly and clearly when we are called to meet our responsibilities. Either we have to stand for the truth or we can consider ourselves a lower form of human beings."

"I can't believe that you are a murderer."

Felix could not suppress anymore his feelings, "Madam, a guard would have raped your daughter if I did not intervene.

guard who was trying to rape her." ...And, probably, he was going to ..."

The lady's head fell down as if she were dead. Felix shook her up to ascertain that she was alive. "You did that for my daughter?" She uttered those words in fragments.

"There is more to it," continued Felix.

The lady did not have the strength to answer him. She could only look at him.

"I saw you when you came to the camp to reclaim your daughter. You ran to her and hugged her."

"Yes, I took her back to the car immediately. The stench of the camp and the sight of those miserable souls made me vomit on the way back."

"There is one last thing that you ought to know."

"More?" She inquired dumbfound.

The SS official murdered four or five guards who were mocking you daughter outside of the barrack where she was dragged by a guard. When you heard the rattling of the gun... That's what it was."

"Oh, no, this is too much for me to comprehend. She took his hand and said, "I was wrong all way along. I do not know how to apologize. What you did for my husband and my daughter ...Why did you do that? You risked your life more than once for people you did not know.' She stepped out of the car and hugged him. "I pray you. Come to my house. We will talk it over in a more serene. I am deeply appreciative for all what you have done. Now, more than ever, I have the perception that you are part of my family."

"Mrs. Kappler, I am very grateful for that. I do not want to light a fire that I may not be able to extinguish. You see. I have to go back to my motherland. I have been back since 1943 Someone is waiting for me there."

"You don't need to go any further," she said. Her face turned serious. Her hands got cold. She returned in the car and started it. "If we can help you in something, let us know." She pressed the pedal on the gas drove away swallowed up by the fog.

CHAPTER XIX

Changing Moods

Mrs. Kappler did not sleep a wink the whole night. Her mind was an ocean of thoughts n a tempest tossed by the waves of doubts against cliffs of the unknown. The bed turned into a battleground of ideas.

Every position she took lasted only four or five seconds. No matter what she did, it turned sour. The pillows were restless. They ended up wherever she moved. Her feet were unusually warm. The palms of her hands were likewise. She pretended to ignore to what ascribe her mental turmoil. A noise from the street put a temporary stop to her state of restlessness. Perhaps, a wandering dog intruded in a trash can. The window was slightly open. A soft breeze filtered through it and cooled the air. In the sky, the stars appeared and disappeared in a constant game covered, at times, by vagrant clouds. The general's wife was tempted to get up and walk or keep herself busy, but she discarded that idea because her daughter was sleeping. The other alternative was to descend quietly the stairs and go out to the street. The fresh air was too inviting to refuse, but there was a glitch. Walking alone at night on the sidewalk had other comprehensible implications of dignity and self-respect other than being unsafe. She covered her head with a pillow and tried to fall asleep again if she did not want to be tired and sleepy the following day. The appearance of a foreigner on the screen of her life troubled her. During many turnovers in bed, she said, "He will always be a mechanic, a trade incompatible with her high social status."

Days, weeks and months passed by like the wind. In that span of time, she never discussed that topic with her daughter, the only one who could have helped her. Her daughter was seeing periodically a psychiatrist to deal with the aftermath of Buchenwald internment. Her mother did not dare to revive those tempestuous moments. Early in the morning, she got up and prepared breakfast for both. Fiorella got up an hour later. She ate and went to the gym.

Mrs. Kappler, for some reasons, did not like being alone and invited in her closest friend. "I am quite upset. I am a bundle of nerves," she said.

"What's bothering you?" questioned her friend. "Unlock your heart and you will feel better."

"I blame Italy for losing the war and for my husband's death."

"Fortunately, my dear, the guns don't thunder anymore. I don't think it is helpful to our soul to look retrospectively and criticize people who brought the demise of our nation. That job belongs to the historians."

"The war is over, but the wounds are still bleeding."

"Every German family lost a loved one."

Mrs. Kappler stood silent for a while. The sleepless night was having some deleterious repercussions on her. She closed and opened her eyes at intervals. Her friend filled a cup of coffee for her and said, "Drink it! It will perk you up." She waited for her to sip it and said, "Learn how to forget and forgive. That is the best medicine."

She brushed the hair with her fingers and muttered, "How can I forget that they murdered my husband in Italy. And, now, an Italian young man shows up on the threshold of my life."

"I see," replied her friend with a smirk.

"Don't get any idea. He is about twenty years old. His demeanor troubles me. It makes me uneasy."

"In what way?"

"He is another Valentino. He sent me flowers, paid for the bill in a restaurant and so on."

"What is wrong with that? I would be flattered."

"Except that he is a pack of lies. If you knew the stories that he invented... He even told me that he killed a 'capot' for Fiorella's sake."

"Did you tell her?"

"I don't dare."

Her friend raised her eyebrows, "How can you deny the discovery of truth unless you test it?"

Mrs. Kappler took a long pause of reflection and said in a low voice, "It is not that."

"I understand," her friend responded with a touch of compassion. "Maybe, he is interested in your daughter," she added."

"Honestly, that's been on the back of my mind since he appeared on the scene of our life. Who is going to corroborate now his claim that he saved my daughter's life?"

"Don't let that trouble you. Did he mention anything about the incident?"

"Not a word! Does this imply that he is an impostor? But, I have to blame myself, too. I was a fool for inviting him at my house. It was against everything I believed in. I made such a blunder that I haven't been able to rest my mind ever since."

"Don't dramatize, my dear. There are worse things than this. Relax on it for a while and talk it over with your daughter."

"Not a chance!" she responded with an irritated tone. "It would be a great disservice to her. She really underwent traumatic moments... She has been making a lot of progress with the guidance of the psychiatrist."

"You are on the right track," encouraged her her friend.

"By the same token, I haven't been able to rest. It would be better for all of us if he never tried to establish contacts at my house or at the restaurant."

"Only the future will tell."

"There is nothing to tell," replied Mrs. Kappler looking outside. "That boy is a serpent enchanter, a merchant of illusions, a mind reader, and a magic musician"

"Her friend broke into a loud laughter.

"Without waiting for her reaction, Mrs. Kapper continued, "Don't you know how Italians are? They are boastful for being Latin lovers; they eat pizza and pasta galore; they sing even on the job and they are proud of their artistic tradition. At the end, they are loafers and lack order."

"I am not sure if I want to agree with you on that. The northerners have a great sense of organization and a high degree of work ethics. You also forgot one very important thing, the church of Rome."

Mrs. Kappler kept on chewing her nails. Her friend asked her, "Is he working?"

"Yes, he is a mechanic. Do you realize the abysm that separates our social classes? I don't want anybody to step in my house with greasy hands."

Her friend could not hold back another sonorous laughter. "My dear, you are structuring an architectural future family framework that exists only in your mind. You are placing the cart before the oxen.

Mrs. Kappler took a deep breath. "This may seem crazy to you, but I have the perception that this boy will frustrate Fiorella's marriage plans. I have a feeling and a deep one, too."

"Don't get stressed up over this issue," cautioned her friend. The wind blows wherever it wants to and we cannot stop it."

"I am not a Don Quijote who sliced the empty air with his sword. I am going to do everything in my power to prevent it."

"My friend, you are obsessed over your daughter's future spouse? From what I hear, the boy is handsome, is a good worker and respectful. He may have dirty hands, but clean heart."

"Hush! Mrs. Kappler ordered her. Just promise me that you will never repeat this conversation to my daughter."

Her friend crossed her fingers and repeated, "I promise."

"My daughter's prince has to come from German blood. I don't waiver on that."

"My dear, what's all this business of blood, grease hands and whatever...Isn't an honor better than all these silly things?" She had did not wait for her answer. She added, "My dear friend, I want you to know that I don't believe not even in one thing in what you said. You lied out of rage, jealousy and what else."

Mrs. Kappler put her head down and did not respond.

Contrary to his previous stand, Felix tried to make contacts with Mrs. Kappler. He wrote her a letter in which he expressed the desire to share with her daughter the Buchenwald experience. His initiative did not fit in her agenda. She refused to read it and threw it in the trash. Obviously, the reply never came and Felix decided to ascertain that he had written the correct address. To do that end, he took the bus and stopped in front of her her house. He checked attentively the name of the street and the house number. Both were in line with what he had written. Not content of his investigation, he rang the bell. From the window, someone moved slightly the curtains and, then, let them go.

Felix returned home disconsolate. He tried again to reactivate the communication with Espera, but the result with the same, no answer. Anxiety increased in him because he put money in each letter, so that, she could spend it at will. He did not want to go back to his town, yet. He had in mind to earn more money and buy a house in Italy. All these ideas were creating a vortex in Felix mind that began to leave the toll. He spent many sleepless nights on that account and, for lack of time, ate fast food brought in by American entrepreneurs The consequences were obviously self-evident. The situation was deteriorating at a time when his job reputation rose to the highest. The department foreman increased his wage and promoted him to a more advanced technological department.

CHAPTER XX

The Party

It was carnival and the car shop-owner organized a party among the high school of his suburb and the nearby college. For a while, he had been sensing Felix's inability to cope with his private life. The rumors became more consistent at the end of the summer and tried to rescue him from romantic demises. With the help of some friends, he rounded up the local school band, 'The Silly Boys' and invited them to play at a party. As the name implied, their musical talent was very limited. They could play only waltzes and polkas, and, occasionally, a tango. In reality, nobody paid attention to their artistic deficiencies. The desire to spend a joyful evening with a charming partner prevailed over any musical inconsistency. Actually, no one knew how to dance well. There were young men, lucky to have survived the horror of the war, those who had been exiled or persecuted and those who had suffered at home the allied air strikes. Actually, no one of them knew how to dance. In the best years of their youth, they were taught how to kill, not to dance. Now, they wanted to forget, to alleviate their pains, to start all over to live, to heal their wounds. Their minds were not projected to exhibit artistic expertise, but to have good time.

The owner or acting manager informed the guests that there were two rigorous rules that everyone was expected to respect. Each one of them was asked to wear a mask and observe silence during the dance. An infraction to either rule would be sanctioned with a fine. Both rules violations would bar the participant from further dances during the evening and possibly with the expulsion from the premises. None of them objected to the rules and the party began.

The carnival was open to young girls and boys from age fifteen to twenty-five. Two female cooks were hired to provide food galore and beer in abundance.

Felix was particularly attentive in his attire. He put on his best suit and made sure that he had the deodorant underneath the armpits. He sprayed a little cologne on is hair and got ready for the party.

A girl dressed in black with a white shirt and a bow brought, from time to time, a tray of different food to those who were resting. During the pauses, a female dancer took a seat next to the main door to catch some fresh air. She was tall, blond, elegant and sweet in manners. Often, she launched provocative looks at Felix. For some reasons, that Italian boy transpired charisma and mystery to her. Earlier on, she had confided to a friend that she loved mystery books.

All the participants were supposed to wear masks of different types and colors. Felix wore a mask representing a goat. The girls were wearing all sorts of masks ranging from princess, empress, Cinderella and, so on. The band began and the first couple glided gracefully on the dancing floor. Felix looked toward the table with jars of beer on it and spotted a girl wearing a princess' mask. He approached her and extended his right hand. "May I have the honor to dance with you," he asked her.

"The honor is all mine," she replied with an ostentatious smile that evidenced all her happiness. She reached his hand and, in a couple of seconds, they joined the other couples on the floor. Among swift steps, pirouettes and bows, she whispered to his ears, "You are an excellent dancer."

"Felix felt confused, "Thank you for the compliments, but the merit is all yours."

"No, remember that the man guides the woman."

"That's very flattering of you."

In reality, no one was exempted from mistakes. In fact, either by distraction or by missing a beat, Felix, inadvertently, stepped on her right foot. She barely suppressed the pain and stopped. He apologized and drew her against his chest. She leaned her head against his. He felt her beating heart and smelled the fragrance of a red rose emerging from her hair. He wanted to continue holding that position, but she was bashful and prompted him to release the grip. He accompanied her to a chair, where she took off her shoe.

He toes were livid. She wished she could take off her mask because she was sweating. An attendant hurried with a bag of ice and applied it on her foot. She held the pack for about three minutes. The ice numbed the pain and the swelling subsided. He kissed her foot and wiped it with a handkerchief. She blushed. She wanted so badly to see the face of that gentleman, but she was forbidden by the rules. He became very apologetic through gestures of his hands. She reminded him that they were not dancing and gently scuffed his apology. It was time off for the band. The dancers took advantage of the pause and focused their attention on knowing each other. A couple approached the girl with the swollen toes and inquired about the extent of the injury. The girl downplayed her unpleasant condition and decided to move to the farthest corner to relax for a while. Felix followed her and offered her a couple of aspirins to alleviate the discomfort. The pain abated, but her facial contortions clearly indicated that she was in no condition to continue dancing. Not to spend the rest of the evening watching and taking care of her foot, she decided to call it quit. She greeted everybody, thanked the organizer and went down the street. Felix helped her and waited with her until the taxi arrived. He kissed her hand and helped her to get in the car. She said in a soft voice, "The next time I will wear better shoes. Sorry for depriving you from enjoying the evening. Danke und aufiedersen."

Felix stretched out his hands if he wanted to hold her back, but the taxi was gone.

CHAPTER XXI

The Departure.

It was a sultry Saturday. The wind stopped running as if its god Eolus had ordered it. The clouds too fell asleep and hung in the air motionless. The sun filtered only in some open spaces and reached the earth only with some rays. Even the traffic seemed paralyzed. It was a lazy day with a high degree of humidity. But this was not the reason why Felix did not close his eyes during the night. The dancing party, instead of helping him, made him feel even more isolated. What bothered him the most, at least so it appeared, was his inability to complete a relationship with the opposite gender.

The day after, he decided to pack up. "Nobody will stop me from seeing her. This time, I will go to the end of the matter. The old times have gone." He spoke to the shop manager who showed him much sympathy, but he also tried to entice him to stay by offering him a higher salary and the possibility of a future promotion. And with that promise, he was able, at least temporarily, to hold him back.

As it was noted earlier, Felix did not receive a single letter from Espera and never mentioned his personal relationship with her in public or private. As the year was about to bid good-by to the new one, he showed symptoms of impatience, restlessness and tension. It was not hard to evince that his mind was in turmoil. He spent much time in front of the mirror of his bedroom asking himself whether she had remained true to their love. Since his questions remained unanswered, he spent time reminiscing about the rare secret meetings they were able to arrange and in which she expressed her unconditional love to him, "You will always dwell in my heart. You will be my only true love. If I have to, I will wait for you until the end of the world." Those words were sealed in his soul and provided him with an immeasurable psychological support during the lonely hours. Those memories were especially a palliative in the concentration camp where he and his fellow inmates were victims of the inhumane conditions that the guards imposed. It is useless to remind the reader that the lack of communication with his loved one caused him a lot of anguish. Whenever he attempted to give a rational explanation to his tormented relationship, he would call her in the hope that from somewhere the wind, if not the postal office, would send him a message from her. Every day, he agonized when he saw the mailman passing by without delivering any letter in his mailbox; however, to the reader, it may sound surprising that he assumed that attitude. He knew too well the antagonism and animosity that divided their families since his first romantic meeting with her. Tired of trying to initiate a direct contact with Espera, he sought help from his closest friend, but he found out that he had died during the war. The effects of a lack of epistolary exchange with his sweetheart were beginning to emerge. The repercussions were sending ominous messages to his brains. Even though he had regained his health and found a remunerating job, he could not assert his identity in a social context. Wherever he went, he was plagued with suspicion. His mind wondered and, often, he was caught being absent minded. Many girls tried to let him forget his homeland and his past by inviting him to birthday parties, but he acted like a stubborn mule. He spent many hours at night with his eyes open dreaming about the love of his life.

Christmas was getting closer and the days were shorter. The cold sent shock waves through the skin of the walkers. Although he was well dressed, Felix shivered on the downtown sidewalks. Passing by an Italian pastry shop, he heard a famous Neapolitan song, "My dear mother, Christmas is approaching, and more I think of it, more I feel bitter..." He could not hold back a few tears. Someone heard him saying, "The only way I can put an end to this ordeal is to sell the car, quit the job and search for her. My main concern is the relationship between both families. Maybe, the war has healed all the past wounds. If they did not mend their ways, I will take Espera and we will elope."

As the reader noticed earlier, the shop owner was apprehensive about Felix future plans. He relied heavily on his performance and contribution for the business success. He made every attempt to dissuade him from taking the drastic action of leaving permanently and was ready to throw another party with the intention of letting him mingle with a local girl. His tactic did not prevail over the young man's determination. As a last effort, the gentleman offered to accompany him with his car to the party, but Felix remained inflexible on his determination to find out of his own terms if his relation with Espera had become tenuous over the long period of absence and, therefore, he needed to rekindle them, or were completely extinct.

His return trip was one of the most traumatic. As the reader shall see, in the search of a butterfly, he became the innocent victim of unpredictable circumstances that, somehow, twisted his future.

At the Hamburg railroad station, he asked a policeman which train was bound for Italy. He replied, "It is written up there." He made a gesture with his head to show the exact location and turned his attention to a couple of girl passengers. Felix felt dissatisfied by the policeman's information and looked for a train employee in uniform. He found one and asked him the same question. The man replied, "Do you have the ticket? Show it to me and I will indicate to you the time and the track."

"No, I did not purchase it yet," responded Felix apologetically.

"The laborer got the perception that the young man had never traveled before, so, he added, "Without the ticket, I can't help you." Then, he pointed at the box office and said, "Go there and buy a ticket for Italy." He added immediately after, "Wait! What is your destination?"

"Naples"

"Well, tell them that you want to go to Naples."

"Where will I take the train? Do I look at the signs on the railroad tracks here?" inquired Felix.

"Exactly!" responded the man. "The number of the track is written on the ticket."

Felix held him back by the hand and asked him once again, "How do I know the departure time?"

"It is written on the signs. They give you the destination, the track number and the time of departure. Don't worry about it! You won't get lost!""

Felix thanked him and followed the man's suggestion. He stood in line for five minutes before he could talk to the cashier, "A ticket for Naples, Italy, please. When does it leave and on which track?"

"Fifty marks."

"Boy!" exclaimed Felix. "I asked you about something else."

"Fifty marks, please!" replied the employee.

Felix searched for the money in his pants' pocket and paid.

The cashier put the money in the cash register and said, "Track 3, five thirty p.m."

"I really appreciate it!" responded Felix.

The cashier said, "Who is next? And where are you going?"

Felix picked up his bag and went to the railroad tracks to ascertain where he belonged. He was so excited that he bumped into another passenger. "I am very sorry, miss. I did not realize that you were passing by."

The girl had blond coarse hair and blond eyebrows. She watched him with interest, but did not say anything.

Felix noticed that she had a wristwatch and asked her the time.

"It is three thirty," she responded.

"Would you be so kind to tell me where track 9 is?"

"It is right here," she replied with a smile.

"Thank you. You are so kind."

"Kindness is part of my personality. It is nothing special." She hesitated a moment and asked him, "Are you going to Italy?"

"Yes, indeed."

"Do you mind to watch my suitcase? I have to buy a newspaper."

"Why not? We are traveling together."

The girl took two minutes and Felix was ready to ask, "Are you sure that our train will stop here?"

The girl looked at him with curiosity and said, "Don't worry! When the train arrives, follow me."

"Yes, of course," responded Felix full of excitement

"By the way, what is your destination?" asked the girl.

"I am going to Naples, but they told me that the first stop is in Milan."

"So, you are from Naples!"

"Nearby…"

"Then, you have to change train. In Italian it is called 'Coincidenza."

"I thought it was a no-stop trip," asked the young man with an innocent look.

The girl paused a few moments before responding. She realized that the boy lacked traveling experience and did not make any derogatory comment. Indeed, in an attempt to help him have a better vision of his destination, she said, "I hope you know that in Milan you have to change train."

Felix became alarmed at that information. "You mean that the train does not go directly to destination? They told me that it is a 'direct type of train," he explained.

"That is true, but the word, 'direct' means 'slow.' It is not related to destination, but to speed. We went over this before. Remember?" She explained to him.

Felix was utterly confused. He wiped the forehead with a rough cloth and sat on the cardboard suitcase. "Good heavens, I found an angel," he exclaimed.

The girl laughed for the first time since they met and, in doing so, showed a line of white denture.

Felix felt embarrassed. The girl stared at him, but did not try to alarm him, "First of all, let us hope the train will be on time."

"Why, do they come late? It is ridiculous if they do." Responded Felix very much concerned by the news.

The girl smiled. The winds of war have just abandoned Europe. It is understandable that there may be delays with the railroad system. With all the problems in the infrastructures that the belligerent countries have now, it won't hurt us to wait ten minutes longer."

"No!" responded Felix in a bewildered gesture. "It cannot be! I have been waiting here already half an hour. It is not just ten minutes. In the way things are going, I have to wait three more hours for this blessed train? That's crazy!"

"Well, I just warned you. It doesn't mean that we have to wait all that time. As I said, the transportation system needs time to recover from destruction. The delays test our patience. Are you patient?" she asked facetiously.

"I have neither patience nor desire to stay here forever," responded Felix almost annoyed by the type of question.

The girl tried to scrutinize that face covered by a light beard. He noticed it and turned around.

Felix was visibly calmer. Fortunately, the girl's patience and the authority by which she provides accurate information abated his state of uneasiness and made him feel more secure. She had a premonition of what going on in his mind and did not push the issue any longer. She pulled an apple from her purse and offered half of it to him, "Let's have a bite. This will make you feel better. It will assuage your hunger." Felix declined the offer stating that he did not have a knife to cut it. The girl surprised him by biting on one side and invited him to do the same on the opposite side. So, it took place the most unique and burlesque act in a railroad station. Both finished eating the apple suspended between their mouths without letting it fall. When it was over, only the pit divided their lips. Their noses were wet and so their mouths. A small group of people gathered around them to watch the unusual scene and applauded both of them. The girl and Felix could not stop laughing.

The clamor subsided and Felix asked her, "Are you traveling for pleasure or business."

"Actually, for neither..." responded the girl without showing any emotion.

"There has to be a reason," protested Felix.

"I am going to be an art student in Florence."

"That's great!" Felix exclaimed. "So, you like to be a professional artist in the future."

"Let's not exaggerate! Let's say that it is my wish, but I don't have the talent." answered the girl while raising her eyebrows.

"Never mind! Don't be modest! You have a lot of talent."

"Not really. It is only love for it. If it doesn't work, I will turn to medical studies. I like biology."

"Wow!" responded Felix. "That's awesome! Are you traveling alone?"

"Are you asking me this because you are interested in following the same path?"

"The only path that I am following right now is that which leads me to my town," he replied in a serious tone." He took a brief pause, then, he added, "But you seem to have an expertise in avoiding questions," he said." No answer came. Perhaps, the girl was getting annoyed with certain personal comments. He did not catch on the girl's sensitivity and insisted, "You did not tell me if you are traveling alone,"

"But, I am not alone" and accompanied her response with a smirk. "My boyfriend is walking around. That's how he kills the time while he is waiting."

Feliix uttered an exclamation of surprise and disappointment. "I don't believe it! All this time, I thought you were alone.'

"Evidently, you made an inaccurate assumption. Be cautious the next time you see a lonely girl." She accompanied the last word with another smirk.

"I guess so!" he responded with astonishment.

The whistle of an approaching train rang under the station's vaults. The passengers were amassing their belongings on the walkway next to the track. Others scrambled through the coffee shops and restrooms. They were all interested in seeking a suitable position to get first in the wagons to secure a seat by placing on their bags. The younger people positioned themselves at the edge of the track, ready to open the door, climb the stairs and reserve a compartment for their families. Once they got in, they could grab the baggage through the windows from those who remained on the sidewalk. The faster ones ran all the way back the runway to occupy the seats on the last wagons of the second class. It was a race against time and the old folks were no match for them.

The locomotive finally reached the station's outer perimeter. It was puffing black dense smoke that soon inundated the area where the passengers were located causing many of them to cough. The train was moving at a slow pace and the passengers' impatience and tension grew. It was nervous racking. Finally, the train came to a rest. Soon, arguments and scuffles began at the doorway of every wagon making more difficult for the outgoing passengers to step down the door. In many cases the railroad police had to intervene to restore order.

"It is the train we have to take," shouted the girl to Felix.

Felix grabbed the luggage and ran toward the train still in movement.

"No, wait!" yelled the girl. "It is dangerous. First the train has to stop completely, then, the passengers have to get off. And, then, it will be our turn.

"But the train stopped!" yelled Felix.

"It did, but it is moving again. Maybe, the conductor wants to warn us not to be too aggressive."

"This is crazy!" he answered.

The coolness by which the girl faced that chaotic situation surprised Felix to the point that he decided that it was wiser to hang on with her.

A second whistle interrupted their dialog. Another train was entering the railroad station's grounds to unload passengers and load others on a different track. Felix got up and held tightly the luggage's handle. The girl held him back. "It is not ours. Stay put."

Felix had no reservation in the second class either. He stood in the hallway close to his suitcase. He could not move. All compartments were already taken and there was a continuous flow of people of all ages up and down the corridor. It was too narrow for baggage and people to get by. The controller had hard time checking the tickets. Felix stood a long time in that position and felt asphyxiated. He was getting impatient, uncomfortable and exhausted. It was hot humid and the sweat smell from armpits and feet prevailed on the fresh air entering from the windows. Stressed women pushed their way through to gain the bathroom entrance. For lack of space, passengers had accommodated their luggage in each one of them. It was not uncommon that many sought refuge in the first class and occupied illegally the vacant seats.

The girl, in the meanwhile had lost contact with Felix. The first class was crammed too. It took her about fifteen minutes before she arrived at her seat. The person who occupied it refused to get up. The prompt and energetic intervention of the controller sedated the boiling tempers and brought the unruly tempers under control. The man who abusively appropriated of her seat ended up in the second class where he belonged in the first place. Since the seat next to her was vacant, she purchased the ticket for it too. It was sultry. She wiped the sweat from her forehead and went in search of the boy. She found him in the next wagon sweating profusely in discomfort. From far away, she made many attempts to catch his attention; however, the visibility was poor and the audition power was almost nil in the midst of a vociferous audience. At last, she asked a tall man, who was pressing for that direction to alert him. She raised her hand and motioned to him to go her way. The passage to the second class was horrendous and the stench, near the bathroom, unbearable. Most of the time, it was at a standstill, unless a fresh breeze came in from the windows. Passengers were cramming every space of the wagons. The controller himself felt powerless and his vexed face was emblematic of his distress to check the tickets.

Passage from one wagon to another was almost impossible except when the railroad stopped at every city to allow some passengers to get out. People created a human wall and did not allow the controller to get by, in many cases, on purpose. After a while, he gave up. He knew that many passengers did not have the ticket. The government was tacitly closing his eyes because the railroad reconstruction process had just begun.

For Felix, it was an ordeal to reach her. He was forced to lift the luggage above his head with the help of fellow passengers. When he finally arrived at destination, he was overwhelmed by the heat and stress and fell on his seat. He was still perspiring. She pulled the handkerchief out of her shirt sleeves and wiped his face. His lips were dry. She put a bottle of water on them and he drank avidly. Felix looked at her with inquisitiveness. She said to him, "The train is already late one hour. By the time it will leave, the delay will increase to two hours."

"I don't care anymore," responded Felix. "I am on the train with destination Naples. That's all it matters to me. At least, we are inside and can rest."

"You are absolutely right!" she answered. She took a magazine and began to read. Felix raised his head, as if he were waking up from a dream, "Where is your boyfriend going to sit?" he inquired.

"I am afraid he lost his chance."

"It can't be!" And he voiced his objection loudly. The passengers around him looked at him with disdain. "No, it is not fair. I am going to stand up on his behalf"

The girl pulled him down by the shirt and begged him, "Will you, please, calm down, now?"

"I will not allow you to do that to him," he protested.

"He missed the train. What can I tell you?"

"You mean you left him behind?"

"I did not!" She explained to him. "He made a choice not to come along."

"That's horrendous!"

"I wholly agree with you, but life is made up of unpredictable events."

"Look, what happens when there is lack of communication."

Ten minutes later, her eyes played a game between closing and opening. She leaned her head against his and fell asleep. Felix did not mind it. He leaned to her side and tried to rest. It was not for too long. The controller and a passenger opened up with difficulties their way and came directly where Felix was resting. He tapped him on his shoulder and said, "I regret it, but you have to get up."

Felix was stunned. He did not want to wake up his companion and took a lot of care not to disrupt her sleep. "Why?" protested Felix to the controller.

"This seat belongs to him," he explained.

"I told this girl that her boyfriend was going to come back, but she is stubborn."

The girl heard all that noise around her and woke up. Without panicking, she said calmly, "I paid for his ticket. The number 15 is right here on it. So, where is the irregularity?"

The controlled checked again the other passenger's ticket and shook his head, "You are absolutely right, miss. Nothing is irregular!" He emphasized. He turned to the passenger claiming the seat and said, "The only difference is that your seat number fifteen is for second class. This is first class."

"What does that mean?" protested the man.

"In this wagon, you pay more. In the second class, you pay less.

Felix looked at his companion. He felt ashamed to have raised unwarranted objections and lowered his head. The girl told him, "What's the matter? Do you feel troubled?"

"No, just ashamed."

"Why? Because you made a mistake? We all make mistakes. 'Errare humanum est.'"

"Felix drew back his head. The girl spoke Latin to him. He stared at her with curiosity and asked, "When did you ever learn another language?"

"In these days, we have no choice. Don't you speak German?"

"You mean I kill it."

She started to laugh. "I understand you. For me, that is the most important thing."

A feeling of tenderness crossed his whole body. He was not sure if he would be able to see her again, to thank for the assistance she gave him and for the sweet time they shared together.

Prior to the station of Florence, the whistle once again lacerated the sleepy air and traveled through the flat countryside at a light speed. Nature was still asleep. Only the barking of wondering dogs spoiled the peace. The girl opened the eyelashes, closed them and opened them again. She repositioned herself in her seat to acquire a comfortable posture. She smiled at the neighbor, but her smile turned into a bitter disappointment and dismay. She looked at him in horror and asked him in an irritated tone, "Since when were you assigned next to me? Where is my Italian companion?"

"Fraulein, I came back. The controller made mistake and so your friend. He was evicted when you had your eyes closed. This is my seat, now."

"Surely, it isn't so!" she responded with indignation. "I paid for this seat. My friend also paid before you."

"He did, but for a seat in the second. You thought you did."

"I don't believe so."

"Maybe, your Italian friend is cheap, just like the ticket."

The girl took the purse and banged it on his head, "You are a villain, rustic, arrogant person." She got up, picked up her luggage and pushed her way in search of Felix. It was a herculean effort to locate him. She did not get any cooperation from other passengers because they were crammed like sardines in a box. Her face was red from rage. The only hope for her was to see him in Florence. She thought it over and remembered that his destination was Naples. Fifteen minutes prior to the train pause in Florence, there was a tumultuous movement of people and suitcases. Everybody tried to gain a space close to the exit and patience was running thin.

Finally, the train came to a halt. Like dogs running out of a cage at dinner time, the passengers reversed themselves out of the wagons causing distress, especially to children and old women. The disembarking process lasted half an hour. The girl waited on the sidewalk to get a glimpse of Felix. She looked frantically everywhere. At times she questioned passengers to find out if they had seen a young man of medium stature, blue eyes and blond hair. The people looked at her with curiosity and compassion and walked by. She moved toward the second class wagons and provided a description of him to a policeman stationed in that area, but the reply was negative. She realized that she could not leave the suitcase behind or in trust of someone. She scuffed the idea of praying. As a last resort, she stopped the conductor, "Have you seen, by any chance a young man, alone, with a suitcase directed to Naples?"

The conductor was about to laugh. Instead, he asked her, "Did you check on the other side of the train?"

"Why would I go there for? The exit is on this side."

"No, miss, the entrance and exit are on both sides."

When she heard that, she almost fainted. She kept on searching for him all the time on one side of the train. She started to shake from the desperation. The face produced thousands little balls of sweat and tears found their way down without obstacle. She sat for a minute on a wooden bench to gain control of her emotions. Her only hope was to get back on the train and follow him to Naples.

She recomposed herself and walked quickly to track number 13. The train was scheduled to leave in ten minutes. The wagons were already filled to the brim and passengers were still coming, even though in minute groups of three or four. She headed for the first class. It took exactly the whole ten minutes to gain a seat! The loudspeaker announced the imminent departure. By the time she found a suitable space for her luggage, she felt exhausted. She sat next to a distinguished lady and closed her eyes. The situation appeared similar to the previous one. It was impossible to go to the second class, let alone visit all the wagons. She resigned to her circumstances. That Italian young man full of dynamism and mighty attractive had vanished, perhaps, forever from her dreams and from her life. She blamed herself for failing to question him on the type of ticket he had purchased. She would have paid for the first class as long as she could stay next to him. At least, she thought she did. One moment of distraction cost her hours of agonizing.

Felix, as it was pointed out, could not move from his position. When the train resumed the final stage, he was submerged by the crowd and exited from the other side losing contact with her. In vain, he waited. At last, not to miss the train, he found a fellow passenger directed to Naples too and followed him. Once he was in the second class, he could no longer move.

CHAPTER XXII

Back to Naples and the Mailman

During the last leg of the trip, Felix met others who had been in the concentration camps and shared some of their horrific experiences, but only for fleeting moments. He could not bear the internal pain that those memories carried along and passed on other topics.

When he stepped down at Piazza Garibardi Station in Naples, he knelt and kissed the ground. The sight of the Vesuvius, the fresh smell of the sea and the people's loud talk and noise had an emotional impact on him and he took a piece of cloth out of his pants pocket to wipe out his eyes. An old man reminded him to keep a hand on the suitcase handle, "Instead of crying, watch your belonging," he warned him. A boy, behind him, was already getting close to the prey. Felix did not believe to the gentleman. "In Naples, people are honest," he reminded him.

The man laughed. "Last Sunday, thieves stole ten thousand lire from the offerings of a convent not far from here. A man and a woman first robbed the few lire the monks had saved from bagging and, then, hit the prior. The unusual movement of objects alerted him, but, instead of calling for help, he ran over on his own to the site. The woman threw him on the floor. The monk was pleading for mercy. The lady dumped a pail of water on his body and apologized before she and her partner disappeared. Fortunately, the carabinieri conducted searches in the area around the convent and, based on the sketch of the thieves that the prior made to them, they recovered the meager 'trophy.' "If they rob the churches and convents, how much more they rob people in the streets?" concluded the gentleman.

Felix did not answer.

It was Advent time. The air perspired joy. The shops display windows were decorated for the occasion and mothers were busy buying gifts for their children. Fireworks were active throughout the city. An unwise young man, from the interior of his room lit some small petards and cast them out. As he exposed himself from the window, he caused a chain reaction of fires that made contact with the stove. A gas explosion ensued. The explosion distorted the rail and everything in the kitchen. These events began to open a breach in Felix mind. He asked a lady who was selling Christmas cookies, "Doesn't the law intervene?"

"What law are you talking about?" The lady protested. Then, she added, "It is impossible to live here, my friend. Are you from Naples?"

"Near…"

"Ok. A week ago, they discovered a cache of firearms. I lost a son last year. People are playing with fire. They do not understand the consequences. Down this street, at my right, a man of thirty was killed by a small fire. They took him to the hospital emergency room. They could not save his life. He had his skull fractured. Last year, I lost a son because of these stupid games."

"How can the government allow all these tragedies?"

"What government?" Yelled a senior citizen. "At the foot of the Vesuvius, young men played with fire crackers. I do not know exactly what happened. Seventy people got first degree burns."

A young lady added," There was an explosion in Piazza Plebiscito yesterday. One boy lost the right eye and another had burns in the genitals area. He may also lose his left foot function."

Felix remained astonished by the grim picture that people depicted of the firecrackers dangers.

It was time to go to his town. He approached a bystander and made inquiries about the departure time for the train to his town. One shook his shoulders. Another stared at him without replying. A third man gave him the right information.

It was two days prior Christmas and Felix was extremely emotional about seeing his family, Espera and his old friends. His adolescence had gone and that made him pensive. He sat on a bench and looked toward the crater. The war had robbed the best part of his life, of his dreams and happiness. He was sure that the concentration camp had left internal scars, but he could not identify them. "Is the post office open at this time?" he asked to a passer-by.

"It should be.

"Is it dependable?"

The man laughed, "Here, nothing and nobody can be trusted, my friend." "You look like an immigrant who wants to send money in a letter. If I were you, I would not. The Postal Office has become infamous for this reason." The man wished him a Marry Christmas and moved on.

Felix perked his ears. He was getting more convinced than ever that the money he sent to Espera had been stolen before it was delivered. He said in a voice above the normal pitch, "The government should put a stop to these illegal activities. In Germany, if a mailman did that, he would end up in jail immediately without judicial delays."

A young lady heard his soliloquy. "Excuse me! Did you say that you are coming from Germany?"

"Yes, miss, I did."

"Germany is on another planet. Everything is well organized and the law is respected because if you don't you are not going to see the daylight for a long time and no one can help you. Here the government does not exist. Everyone takes the law in his own hands with impunity."

"If you can't trust your own government…" insisted Felix and accompanied the last words with a wide gesture of his arms.

"You are right. Hopelessness is the key word. But, careful! The institutions are good; the agents are not. The human element is rotten. Do you get the idea?"

"Are you implying that the Postal Office is not a secure place to deposit money?"

"That's different!" She explained. They release you a receipt that proves the deposit. When you send money by mail without registering the letter, most likely, you kiss good-by to the money, to the letter and to your hard work."

The two spent about five minutes conversing when three carabinieri tapped on Felix's shoulders. The girl drew back waiting for their next move. Felix did not see her. He turned around and got scarred at the sight of the lawmen. The older official said, "You are under arrest."

At that order, Felix looked at them helplessly. He took courage and asked, "On what charges?"

"You are considered a deserter by the Italian law."

The girl could not hold herself back anymore and shouted, "What Italian law are you talking about? It does not exist!"

The second official faced her, "If you do not refrain from your aggressive behavior, I will be obliged to take you in custody to the nearest police station and you can spend a few nights in a dungeon."

"Arrest me, not him, you bastards!" shouted the girl.

The higher official said to Felix, "Follow us!"

The girl got stepped in again and continued to argue her point, "He is an immigrant. After years of suffering in a foreign land, he came back and you want to put him in jail? Is this just? You are barbarians! If we win the elections, we will fix you up!" One of them pushed her away to their jeep to be questioned in the office.

Felix did not oppose any resistance. He looked like a man under the influence of drugs. He could not understand why that girl was taking so viciously his defense. He did not even know who she was. The last remarks made him believe that she was a Communist sympathizer. In the meantime, a small crowd grew around the lawmen. A young girl, running from afar, opened her way and reached Felix. "Why did you leave me?" The carabinieri stopped. The girl was speaking German. Felix was amazed that she had found him. He looked at her and said, "I didn't ... I was powerless. The passengers stormed me out." His head began to spin. When he regained consciousness, he said, "It was nothing. I had memories of Buckenwald." That infamous name rang a sad note in the girl who cried out, "Felix, Felix…" At first, he heard the girl's screams and cries, then, his name. In that instant, his mind reverted to Hamburg, to Milan...

He made an effort to disengage himself from the carabinieri, but they restrained him even more. In that instant, he looked back and whispered with astonishment, "Fiorella!" The girl tried to hug him, but they blocked her. He was handcuffed and carried away. He waved with his hands in chain. The girl kept on kicking and yelling until she did not see the boy anymore.

Felix was drafted in the army and stationed at Catania, Sicily. The two officials accompanied him personally to the army depot and the draftee silently began his eighteen months of service.

Felix felt terribly demoralized. Nothing seemed to go well for him. He slept the first night in Italy in an army compound. It was common practice that veteran soldiers subjected the new recruits to the cruelest pranks. The second night, a soldier in proximity of graduation, dumped a bucket of cold water on his face in the middle of the night while he was sound asleep. Soon after, he turned the mattress upside down. All of this occurred with a lightning speed. . Felix did not even have the chance to react. He fell on the floor and, by the time he got up, the reckless soldier was in his bed. Luckly, Felix secured his money in a safe place because the army was not known for an immaculate behavior.

The first three months of military service (CAR) was tough, but it did not bother Felix too much. He had survived the holocaust. As life went on, he became friend with the Jewish comrades. Some of them were like him, simple soldiers. Others were of higher ranks. He reminisced briefly on his vicissitudes and remembered in details the ceremonies that the Jewish inmates celebrated in the camp. There was not much they could do under the watchful eyes of the SS, but they did their best to commemorate Yum Kippur and Yasha Shana. Felix was having hard time to recount his ordeal, but his comrades, realizing that it was costing him suffering, refrained from asking him further details. From then on, they held him in high respect and considered him one of them. Since that day, Felix could always count on their unconditional support in times of need.

In his spare time, Felix kept on writing to Espera, but, as usual, there was no answer. He lost his good humor and hope for the future. Life had become a maze from which he saw entrances, but no exits. He attempted to solve the puzzle that surrounded his relationship with his sweetheart. The events were greater than his own strength. "The sea waves are too high for me to float on." This is what he told his friends. His personality took a dive as he became more and more suspicious that she had another boyfriend or even got married. "I dreamed that a boy brought her a bouquet of red roses and she took her time in smelling them," he confessed to his fellow soldiers. One afternoon, he spotted a friendly mailman running his errands and stopped him. "Could you, please, cast some light on my girlfriend's lack of response?" he asked him.

"I read your conflict in this way' responded the mail deliverer. Either it is a wrong address or she lives someplace else."

Felix was dissatisfied with the mailman's logic and made an attempt to delve into the truth by contacting his sister. She responded immediately even though it took ten days for the mail before it reached him. This is what she wrote:

Dear Brother,

First of all, you cannot imagine the joy that you brought to us with your letter. We did not get your news for years and did not know whether you were dead or alive. It gave us much pain to hear your internment in the concentration camp. Thanks to God, you are alive and well.

For the other question that you asked me, your friend still lives here. A month ago, I ran into her while we were returning from the farm. She appeared tired and sad. I was able to talk to her very briefly. When I asked her if she had received any letter from you, she lowered her head, as in a state of shame, and said in a soft voice, 'never.' I asked her if she still cared for you. She turned her head on the other side and cried. At that point, I realized how disconsolate she felt. Our conversation stopped abruptly when I saw her parents appearing at the end of the road. She said, "Go now! Go! My parents will kill me if they see me talking to you." She turned for the last time toward me and said, "Tell him that he was my April flower, my first and last. I will never love anyone else in my life, no matter what. Our destiny has to go in opposite directions. So, it was written, so it will be. But, tell him for the last time, that I always loved him and he always will be in my heart." She sobbed again and ran away.

With the love of all of us, hoping to see you soon.

Your sister,
Ninnella.

Dear reader, this is what happened and this is what I am reporting to you.

Felix read the letter and sank his head between the pillows. When he lifted it up, the pillows were wet. He was unable to comprehend the absurdity of her parents' attitude. It was the beginning of a long period of solitude and depression. From then on, the conversation with his fellow soldiers became less frequent and so the visits on parks and recreational activities during his free time. In one of his moments of crisis, he wrote a second letter to his sister.

"My dear sis,

I still have a doubt in my mind that she did not spell out. I heard many foul plays on the part of the postmen, but you have to help me to see clearly in this matter. It is not going to be easy to obtain an honest answer from any of them, but if you follow my advice, you will find out the truth. Use your judgment.

Approach the mailman with tact. If you have to put something in his hand, do not hesitate to do it. That is the only way he will be willing to 'dump the basket.' I will repay you at the first opportunity. My mind continues to be bogged down by the suspicion that he stole the money and threw the letters in the garbage. We should not downplay this possibility, but it is worth to try. I have to see the end of the tunnel. I don't want to be prejudicial, but, on the other hand, I cannot stand by idle either. This is the last chance to find out the truth. I rely on you.

A big hug to all of you,
Your brother,
Felix"

The mailman in Rotondi did not show up every day at the same time in the same street. He changed routine, which was due to many factors. He had the habit of stopping in the farms to ask for material handout to people he delivered the mail. He was especially insistent with those who received a letter from a foreign country. He looked at the stamp and played his game. Often, he found himself in a bargaining position, but he did not give up unless he filled a second bag with potatoes, tomatoes or other vegetables and fruit. The ignorant farmers gave in to his requests because they feared retaliation. If his demands were not satisfied, he would hide the mail and forge distasteful apologies.

Wednesday was usually market day in town. Felix's sister casually ran into the mailman. Her first impulse was to give a glance around to ascertain that nobody was watching her. She pulled some dollar bills from her pocket and placed them in his hand. He looked at the amount and kept the other hand open. She was not pleased with his demeanor, but submitted to his silent demand by adding additional money. He appeared to be satisfied and said, "Now, we can talk business. What's the scoop?"

"If you do not cooperate, I am going to kill you."

The mailman laughed and said, "You know me. I never disappoint people."

"O.K. Tell me. Did the post office receive my brother's letters in the past years?"

"Are you referring to those destined to your family?"

"No, I mean the ones he sent to Espera"

"That changes the whole scenario." He reflected for a few moments as to remember accurately what he did and said, "I delivered her mail to her mother."

"Why not to her…?"

"She was not around."

"You are not convincing me."

"Why is that? Don't you trust me anymore?"

"I will when you tell me the whole truth."

"I have been," he responded a bit disappointed by her reaction.

"How did you deliver the mail to her mother when she was on the farm all day long? The second hypothesis is that either you or one of your co-workers violated the law by dumping the letters on the fireplace or in a precipice below the mountain. In that case, you are liable for loss of job and spend a few years behind the bars for mail fraud."

The postman's face turned reddish. The last accusations troubled him. "Listen!" he tried to explain to her. "Those unethical activities have occurred in the past."

"You define them 'unethical?' not deliberate misconduct punishable by law?

The postman put up a stiff defense line. "Let me explain to you. It is common knowledge by now that the Central Post Office has conducted rigorous and objective investigations in the area of your concern. The results have been published extensively by the media. A mailman found guilty of destroying letters will be fired instantly and will face judicial consequences without the chance of appealing. With the current job market, nobody wants to lose his job. May I inform you that we are all committed to a code of honor?"

"Good! If you adhere at the strict rules, be professional first and foremost!" replied the girl in an irritable tone.

"Thank you for reminding me of my duties."

"Don't give me this irony. Allow me to trust you, instead."

"Come on! You should not talk to me like that. Our families have known each other for a century"

"I shouldn't?" responded the girl with resentment. "Are you aware that I could put in motion the legal system and create problems for you?"

"For what?" The mailman shouted in anger.

"First of all, I would suggest you to hold down your tone. Secondly, you broke the law. Espera is an adult, not a little girl and you should not deliver to anyone else her personal mail."

"I thought that mother and daughter had agreed…"

"They agreed my eye! If on the letter it is written 'personal," you should deliver the mail to the recipient.

The mailman stood there pensive for a while. The aggressive behavior of Felix's sister shook him up to his inner core. "Perhaps, I should have used a better judgment," he admitted in a low voice. "To make up for it, I am going to reveal you a secret."

"Do you know that you destroyed the lives of two human beings? And, now, you expect me to believe in another creation of your fantasy? She admonished him.

"What I am going to tell you is not a product of my inventions. Honest…" tried to assure her the mailman apologetically, 'I did it with good intentions. Her mother is behind some architectural plans for reasons that are obscure to me. I am really sorry if I have been involuntarily responsible for any wrongdoing. What we said here must remain 'internos'. Do you hear?" The mailman closed tightly both lips with his hands.

She repeated his gesture and queried, "What do you want me to tell my brother?"

The mailman realized the seriousness of the case and was ready to back off from his promise, but the girl's threatening look made change his mind. "I was going to tell that Mo.. Mo…"

"Finish the sentence or I choke you," yelled the girl. Some people looked in their direction. The mailman cautioned her not to raise her voice; otherwise, he would be forced to drop his commitment altogether.

"Zanzara is going to arrive from Argentina tomorrow."

When she heard that name, the girl became pale. "The troublemaker is going to be here. Her second name is Mosca." She said emphatically."

"If I were you I would be concerned about her," he said by accentuating each word monosyllabically"

"Why should I?"

"She has something up to her sleeves."

"What does she have to do with us?"

"Last time she came, she started a serious conversation with Espera's mother."

"About what?"

"Her son is single. Now you know what I mean."

The girl did not answer. The mailman continued, "He is in the Argentinian army. The government gave him a special leave of absence to come here."

"What is so special?"

"The war of the Malvinas is raging. The generals are very well aware that in case of defeat, their history is over. They may lose their position and their skin."

"Is the situation so critical? Inquired the girl.

"Let me tell you. From the information I am getting, they need every single man in the fight against England. One of Zanzara's nephew died last week. The military vigilance was so strict that her son could attend the funeral because he is a soldier.

The girl was stunned by Zanzara's ability to match couples. The rest did not concern her. A couple of old ladies stood aside them curious to hear the conversation. The mailman invited Felix's sister to move next to the wall that flanked the street. "As you can see," he said, "Now, I know the magnitude of my mistake, but it was unintentional."

"Unintentional were also the bags of vegetables you received in gratitude for your favors?" responded the girl, angered by the repercussions of his irresponsible and derelict behavior.

The mailman did not respond at first. He scratched repeatedly his head. "What is done cannot be undone, but I gave you information that can reshape the present. It is up to your brother to act promptly and sagaciously. The ball is in his hands now. Besides this, I cannot help him."

The girl covered her face with both hands in a sign of resignation and despair. A friend of her recognized her and called her. She smiled and joined her without wishing good-by to the mailman.

CHAPTER XXIII

The Malvinas or Falkland

The seven hundred tiny islands gather around two main big ones called East and West Falkland that resemble two bears and are divided by the strait of Falkland Sound. They are located about three hundred miles from Buenos Aires. The land is barren and characterized by gusty winds most of the year. The agriculture is impossible. That explains the population scarcity. There are about two hundred inhabitants in all. The only activity going on is shearing. Sheep somehow are able to survive the inclement weather and they produce good wool that is shipped to England. Recently, they discovered uranium and the desire to claim ownership became urgent and controversial.

The Argentine government backs up his claim by historical events. They hypothesize that the indigenous Patagonian were the first people to arrive on the island and left artifacts that demonstrate their presence.

In the eighteen century, Great Britain occupied the islands that caused a war with Spain. At the end, The Red jackets left.

In 1833, England went back to the Falklands taking advantage of the fact that Spain had evacuated them probably as a result of the independent movements that were brewing throughout Latin America. For about one hundred and fifty years, Great Britain kept a few people there to maintain the calm.

In 1976, the military junta exiled Isabelita Peron in an undisclosed area in the interior of the country and the fascist regime. Even worse, it deprived the citizens of their freedom and took thousands of lives. In about twenty years of power, it has been reported that thirty thousand Argentineans disappeared. They came to be known as Los Desaparecidos." The women's protests against the oppressive regime soon began to shape up and caused an international uproar. They called themselves "Las Madres de la Plaza de Mayo." Every week-end mothers of every social class, but, especially, those who had lost a family member, gathered before La Casa Rosada, site of the government, and carried tacit anti-governmental posters. The marchers made an explicit plea to the military junta to provide information of their loved ones. Any delay or cover up would only exasperate them to continue their struggle to no end.

In 1982, to avert major internal strife, the junta decided to distract the public opinion by engaging in a military confrontation with Great Britain over the Malvinas(Falkland) Islands. The US tried to mediate a peace between the contestants, but Argentine rejected the overture and the US sided with Great Britain providing logistic and material aid.

The war took a brusque turn when the British navy sunk the Argentine ship Belgrano.

More than three hundred sailors lost their lives. A few more survived and among them there was Zanzara"'s son.

That same year, Zanzara's husband died in Italy. She flew over and assisted him in the last weeks of his earthly life. She asked and obtained permission from the Argentine ambassador in Rome to grant a few days of leave of absence to her son, Floris, to join her for the funerals.

Floris was a bit less than of medium stature. His brown hair was smooth like marble. The eyes' color matched the hair. The nose was a bit bumpy. The rest of his body was well built. He was one of the most social young men in town and loved life, parties and cars. He was a heavy smoker and had a proclivity to business. After years in a factory, he became a successful businessman in Mendoza. He boasted of many feminine conquests, but he hardly brought any girl to his house. More than once, his sister asked him, "Why don't you get married?"

"Why? Does it bother you if I stay single?" he responded.

"No, it is not that," she implored him. "You have just finished the military service. It is time for you to get a family."

"Listen to her! It seems that you want to get rid of me."

"You know, I cannot talk to you. As soon as I give you an advice, you go on the defensive and bring up all sorts of excuses."

"This preposterous notion of creating a family doesn't appeal to me. Is it clear? I want to enjoy life, have fun, attend parties…What is wrong with it?"

"Nothing! But you are of age. You have to think about your future."

"You sound like my mother now."

"Your mother does not say anything because you get upset. See if you can find a nice girl in Italy."

"Eveybody wants me to get married in Italy. You people sound hysterical when you touch this subject, but I do not want to marry an Italian girl. Understood?"

His sister got annoyed, dropped the subject and went on to her business.

In Italy, Zanzara and Espera's mother were close friends and neighbors. Every evening they sat in front of the house and discussed the daily events. Lately, the topic that prevailed above all others was her son's future. Both of them agreed that an Italian girl would be the most suitable for him.

Chapter XXIV

"Death of a Peacemaker"

Espera's oldest brother, was going out with Felix' cousin, but their marriage plans hit the rocks because of the traditional antagonism. The roots stretched all the way to politics. Felix' parents were stanch Communists. Espera's family shared the same political ideals; moreover, her brother was well known and esteemed in town. He had the support of the Party because he had been a partisan.

Espera had three sisters and three brothers. Everyone worked on the farm, except the younger sisters, who were destined to study. They helped the family only during the summer vacations. Besides that, they were required to study.

The local common council passed a resolution that imposed the commemoration of the partisans' resistance and their victory over the Nazi. A colorful parade was in the plan. The town mayor sent an invitation to the people who mostly distinguished themselves in advancing the socialist cause. That year, Esperanza's oldest brother, who was respected as a hero by all political parties, was on the guests' list. Each one of them was expected to deliver a speech at the culmination of the feast.

The band started the commemoration by a parade and a huge display of banners. Throughout the march, a local band kept on playing the famous communist song, "Red Banner." At the completion of it, the Communist Party chairman opened his remarks by exalting the partisans' glorious defense of the town. They had paved the way to the allied advance. He, then, went on praising the contribution put on by the local fighters, and, particularly by Espera's brother. Previous to the event, the Party hierarchy found a unanimous consensus awarding him the Medal of Honor. His name came fifth on the list. As the president called him on the stage to pin the medal on the lapel of his red shirt, he crowd went delirious. For about five minutes, there was chaos. Young people, especially, shouted slogans, played trumpets and made fists. Strangely, enough, the tumultuous standing ovation caused a bit emotion in him and a couple of tears fell on his cheeks. Someone next to him offered him his handkerchief, but he kindly refused. He pulled his own from the back pocket of his pants and wiped his face. It was the toughest test of his life. He wished he never accepted the invitation, but he was in the midst of prestigious political people and could not leave without saying a few words for the occasion.

An assistant electrician adjusted the microphone for his height. The president introduced Espera's brother. He got up and slowly approached the podium. The audience and the air, for once, stood still in the vast plaza. He took a deep breath and began to sweat. He was visibly uneasy. The Party officials were waiting for him to talk and kept on looking toward him. Finally, he raised his head and stated, "I am not worthy of this award. Thanks to the Communist Party and thank you my fellow citizens. Although I made some daring raids and took responsibility on many individual decisions that caused the destruction of many enemy tanks, it was, indeed, a Communal effort that gave us final victory." The rowdy crowd loved his remarks and went on rampage for the next half an hour. They took possession of the band's musical instruments and improvised songs. Others grabbed the chairs from the coffee shop and threw them all over. The ladies criticized the rude demeanor of the youngsters and the president had to intervene to bring order.

Espera's brother felt embarrassed by the long and unexpected tribute reserved to him, but welcomed the long interruption. It gave him an unexpected opportunity to thank the people and, who was not listening anymore, and the authorities and stepped aside. A politician shook hands and congratulated him. He staggered in his reply and he blushed. He felt he had discharged his duty, bid good-by to the authorities and ran down the stairs of the stage heading for home. A fat man exclaimed, "Look how much he loved the Party!" He pretended not to hear it and pushed his way through the crowd. A group of youngsters did not appreciate his short speech and hastily blocked his way. "We want a longer speech! We want a longer speech!" They kept on chanting. Despite their euphoric love for him, he motioned to them that the time was over and other guests had the right to speak. His apology did not placate them. They raised him on their shoulders and carried him, against his protests, around the plaza like a trophy. Everyone blessed him and made an attempt to touch his hand or a part of the body until the president requested the audience to control their emotion. Other speakers were waiting their opportunity to speak. The noisy group realized that were out of order and desisted from their improper behavior.

At home, away from the tumultuous crowd, he found his moments of glory. He grabbed a bottle of wine and a piece of cheese and sat on a rocking chair in the garden. "This is my medal of honor," he exclaimed. His justified rest lasted a brief time. A group of supporters felt disappointed by his hasty departure. Their hero was more important than the celebration itself. They followed him at home. Espera did not appreciate the presence and the clamor surrounding her brother and told them that he was on his way to Rome.

The news of the gold medal award reached every town corner in Rotondi, but not everybody was elated. The first objectors to the award ceremony were his archrival neighbors. Other old folks, too, resented it that their contribution to the cause of liberation was not duly recognized. Espera's brother did not see his girlfriend. Her brothers and sisters attended the party, but abstained from making any negative comment.

In the evening, Espera's brother decided to take his girl for a walk. Her sister, instead, followed them at every step and this bothered him immensely. There were instances when he tried to bribe the unwanted companion, but he failed. Filial obedience proved to be much stronger than money; consequently, from that time on, the couple did not show up in public anymore.

His girlfriend's father was a very respectable man. That was the impression he gave and pretended that people would address him with the well deserved title of "Don." Don Juan dressed up very neatly. He wore a blue suit that, originally, belonged to his grandfather, but it was still in good shape, and shone for having been ironed several times in the course of the years. The white shirt showed signs of overuse and the clumsy shoes showed scraped out black spots. He used to shine them with the fat of dead cows and an old rag. The soles were visibly worn out. When he walked in the streets, he kept the head high and the chest out. He swung the cane back and forth like a pendulum and that drew the attention of the children, who did not dare to get near him. An inexplicable air of dignity, of distinction, of noblesse surfaced from his manners, gestures and talk. He professed being a businessman, but hardly anyone believed him, for he never did any work. He spent the morning in the Central Bar and the office in the Communist Party conversing with his friends. He would drop in at the nearby bank a couple of times a week, but the employees raised the eyebrows knowing him as a nobleman fallen in disgrace. They surmised that the main reason for visiting the bank was to get some loans to carry on the lifestyle he purported to represent. He took the siesta in the afternoon and made a disappearing act after supper. And, there were days when nobody would see him at all. This disappearance act increased speculations that he found pasture elsewhere with high class women luring them into assisting him financially. In reality, his whereabouts where shrouded in a cloud of mystery. The only time he was visibly active in town was at the period preceding the elections. He roamed the farming areas bribing the ignorant peasants to vote for his favorite candidate. The peasants marveled at the content of the envelopes he put in their pockets and could only hypothesize that the politicians were providing him with the dough. They figured that was his only opportunity to make a kill. There was one glitch. He was not very popular with his parish priest. The dissention between the two developed a year before. Don Juan took a group of youth with him on a vacation to Bolzano. He spread the news that they were going to ski on the Alps for a week. He persuaded the Party to pay for their expenses. He confided to his closest friends that it would boost the chances of victory for his supported candidates. The boys were enthusiastic of the experience and upon their return, the day before the election, they divided the town into sections and each one marched around with political placards.

We will not divulge his political affiliation not to offend anyone of the same credo. In any public apparition, he was always flanked by his wife. He showed a high degree of chivalry. He would hold the chair before she sat; held her hand when she descended from the coach; help her take off the coat and assist her in climbing the stairs of the municipal building.

A few months later, Espera's brother and his girlfriend decided to get married. Felix parents were not particularly enthused. Indeed they did everything in their power to dissuade their niece to call off the wedding. The girl resisted the pressure and went ahead with her plans.

The church was crowded for the wedding celebration. Many uninvited guests and friends did not find space inside the temple. They were disappointed that they were going to miss the exchange of the nuptial ring ceremony. The girl was Don Juan's daughter and most of the people from the crowd came to show respect to him rather than to the spouse herself. According to the witnesses, a masked man jumped from nowhere in front of the altar preventing the clergyman from making the final remarks of the homely. The man began to blast Don Juan for being a corruptor of young minds. "There is a so called gentleman and a friend of politicians sitting right in front of me. He sows during the day and harvests at night. In those hours, many dogs roam the streets, and many immature youngsters are bitten. And that is a sin, my friends. It is against the wedding vows. It is against every norm of marital life." Don Juan looked around him and noticed that the attention had shifted from the spouses to him. He felt visibly embarrassed and hurt in his pride. He put his right hand in his jacket pocket, but his wife stopped him. She helped him to stand up and together left. The spouses were shocked. The bride fainted and the groom and the best man had their work cut out trying to revive her. The exchange of vows was called off by both parties. The audience became tumultuous because the young people clamored for Don Juan, while the old women sided with the prelate. Soon, the church looked more like a market than a place of prayer. The verbal exchanges that ensued between the opposing parties got so virulent that almost degenerated into violence. The prompt intervention of the carabinieri averted a possible physical confrontation. Outside, the young people brought Don Juan in triumph, while the women were launching venomous epithets to his regard. On the opposite side, the masked man barely managed to slip away from a group of people with aggressive intentions. He ran through the corn fields and was seen no more.

Needless to say, when the wedding ceremony came to a halt, the wedding reception was canceled causing a legitimate disappointment and protest on the part of those who had already given a gift. At home, Esperan's brother locked himself in his bedroom and refused to talk to anyone. Don Juan locked himself up in his bathroom for hours until his wife persuaded him to come out. His concierge said that he did not leave his residence for a month. Nonetheless, we, for the sake of our readers, undertook some investigations at the police station and a quite different story unfurled. Don Juan ran a renowned bordello in Bolzano, at the border with Austria. The European jet society frequented it. Most of the girls were foreigners and the fee was high. Don Juan had owned that business for twenty years under the pseudonym of "Von Put." The name of the locale was "Fraulein." It was open every day of the year. At home, he never revealed his professional activities. He maintained a low profile in terms of life style and was active only at election time when he would throw a lavish party in case his candidates were voted in. To those who thanked him, he would reply, "Thank the Party, not me." Conversely, when he traveled to the north, he dressed elegantly and his manners were very refined. They called him Dr. Von Put to which he showed every sign of his southern pride. Often, he would show in public with high-level politicians from Austria, Germany and Switzerland or with famous singers or professional soccer players. After the wedding incident, he visited for the last time Bolzano and surprised everybody when he called a real estate agent and put the building and the business for sale. Within ten days, it was sold to a Scandinavian entrepreneur, who wants to remain anonymous. He also put on sale all the furniture and mementos that brought in his coffin additional millions of marks. Reliable sources told us that from Northern Italy, he took the boat for Sicily and, later, for Malta, where he knocked at the door of every convent and orphanage, dropping an envelope in the hands of the abbots and Mothers Superiors. When he finally returned to his town, he found out that his daughter was no longer there. He locked himself in his house and fell in a deep depression.

For months, he did not show up in public where the opinion was divided in two. One side blamed the priest for the lack of security and, on the other, they blamed Don Juan or Dr. Von Put, whose moral blemishes had tarnished his daughter's marital ceremony to the point that it was called off.

Don Juan's daughter, unaware of her father's whereabouts, refused to receive any visit. Her boyfriend's efforts to see her or hear from her hit the wall. When the news of her father's activities became clearer, she packed up her clothes and took the road to a convent. Subsequent unconfirmed reports disclosed that she abandoned the monastic life. The truth is that she never came back to her village. Her parents sold the house and moved to Aosta.

The girl's boyfriend too, reached a mysterious epilogue. The fragmentation of the wedding and the news that his ex-girlfriend retired to a convent, drove him almost insane for a while. Eventually, he got better. There were rumors that one morning they saw him at the railroad station with a bag in his hand. And there were even reports from mountaineers, who swore that they had seen a corpse hanging down a tree in a state of decomposition and, therefore, hard to identify. They proceeded to bury the body, but never called the police. The truth, however, is entirely different and the reader is entitled to know it. He migrated to Chile where, for a while, he lived with the indigos. During that period, the only information that some immigrants could gather about him was rather scanty. They claimed that they saw and talked to a man with a Neapolitan accent. He had grown a beard and dressed like the indigenous population. We are certain of one thing. He moved to Santiago, the capital, and became a successful businessman. When the news reached him about his purported death in the mountain of his town, he wrote a letter to the Communist Party's President, "Please, forgive me. I am sending the letter that I wrote with my own hands to prove to malignant tongues that I am live and sound and that my disappearance was the consequence of a calumnious campaign carried on against my girlfriend's father."

The President put the letter in his private file and took this case seriously. He visited the regional bishop to whom he expressed the party's indignation for the aborted wedding. He requested the priest's transfer to a remote region of the Congo. The high prelate listened attentively and assured his interest in the matter. A week passed by and he received a letter from the bishop's office. In it, he released a statement in which he reprimanded the priest for the unwarranted and inappropriate homely remarks, but exonerated him on the ground that unruly guests initiated the interruption of the wedding ceremony.

In the aftermath of the foiled wedding, Espera's father mortified by the course of the events tried to take the law in his own hands. He took a pitchfork and ran after Don Juan's house hoping to find him. Only the quick intervention of the police averted a major incident. Espera was so deeply shaken by the turn of the events that went to the farm early in the morning and returned late in the evening not to talk to anyone.

CHAPTER XXV

Zanzara

In 1948, Bartali won the Tour de France and gave Italy an unimaginable moral boost. For a while, the Italians forgot their acrimonious political disputes and enjoyed the greatest euphoric moments since the end of the war.

The industry had been devastated by the war and the first signs of a renaissance were in the embryonic stage. Shops were struggling to open up and money was hard to come by. Hundreds of thousands of people were waiting to emigrate. It took more than one generation before Italy surged from her ashes and emigration came to a standstill.

In those years of economic and financial distress, millions flooded the American consul in Naples, Palermo, Genoa and Venice trying to escape poverty by reaching a relative in Australia or Canada, lands still unexplored in their vast natural bounties. Other opted for Argentina, Venezuela and USA. Someone immigrated to Chile, like Espera's oldest brother.

Zanzara and her family immigrated to Mendoza, Argentina, in 1950, where her cousin lived. She was well known in town not for her political acuity, artistic ability or business vocation. Like every other provincial woman, she was very introspective in peoples' affairs. The politicians were particularly interested in her service at election time. She did not do any 'dirty' work out of political aspirations. She was concerned about her chirdren's future. For the rest, she could be compensated in private. "One hand washes the other," she used to say to her friends and stuck rigorously to that policy. To carry hundreds of votes to a candidate, she had to siphon favors, some monetary, others not, to a vast section of the electorate. She organized behind the scenes lucullian parties that started in the evening and lasted until dawn. She knew that the low class looked for 'Panem et Circencem,' and through her hands passed a lot of 'dough.' She could also afford those parties because the town people were unpretentious in terms of food. They liked sausages, salami and wine accompanied by bottles of wine. She was sensitive to peoples' stomach and enjoyment and never failed in her duties.

Nepotism was widespread among politicians. Every parent knocked at the door of his trustee or legislator to find a job for his or her children and all had to do it through Zanzara's mediation. The opposition kept her in low esteem, but all marveled for the insidious and effective role she played within her Party. She was a real orquestra maestro without studying music in a scenario of Machiavellian machinations.

In the mid fifties, the desire to emigrate became impellent, almost obligatory for millions of families. Without political help a person could have waited for many years.

The Argentinian embassy was particularly helpful expediting the Visa process, but Zanzara had to promise to come home at each election time.

Zanzara's cousin had been a teacher in high school in Syracuse. He was of medium stature, blond hair, was well groomed, blue eyes and had the agility of a young man, although he had already reached the pension age. His professional career had been very successful. His only regret was the failure to get the doctoral degree in Spanish literature. He loved to recount his 'misfortune,' "The commission met to evaluate my thesis topic. It was headed by a lady who, probably, felt some sort of loving care for me. I chose a secondary Spanish literary figure, an unknown author, for my thesis. She did not like it, but promised me her help if I followed her advice. I am not sure if she did it on purpose to keep me around her a lot longer until I would feel something intimate for her. The truth is that I rejected her overture and left altogether my plan; consequently, I made up my mind to move to another city and teach in a public school system."

His success in secondary education was undeniable. His charisma, exuberance, vitality and 'savoir faire' gave him a tremendous popularity among young students. He had the geniality of making easy, difficult concepts through an incomparable sense of humor. He was not obsessed, as other colleagues, with the cognitive aspect of a topic. He was dedicated to simplicity and practicality and penetrated in the minds of his students with his typical histrionic demeanor that skimmed clownship. His exuberance was so infective that sent children into delirium and captivated the unconditional support of their parents. The administrators bowed before such an undeniable evidence of popularity and did not dare to question his skills. As long as the students considered him the top of the line, that sufficed to hold him in high esteem.

Being a bachelor until his retirement age, he could afford spending time in school for social events and enjoyed the attention of many female colleagues. During parties, he was the center of attraction for his love to dance and proclivity to socialize. He was the perfect gigolo and, upon that, he shaped the course of his life. Nonetheless, his friends claimed that he failed to realize that life reserves surprises even to the most consumed individuals.

One day, a friend called him to inquire about a Spanish-Italian dictionary that an Argentine student was looking for a long time. In the whole city, he was the only one to have it. He accepted instantly the invitation to make the dictionary available to her and the classical Cupid arrow was launched. To please her, he built a grandiose mansion, but her heart was in her homeland and the two moved to Mendoza where they had a wonderful son. He organized an Italian club and promoted various cultural activities.

When his cousin Zanzara asked him for assistance, he rented an apartment for her family on Avenida Sarmiento that crosses from east to west la Plaza de la Independencia, not distant from his house in Bartolome' Mitre.

Mendoza rests on the east side of the Andes. It is closer to Santiago de Chile than to Buenos Aires. The major products are olive and wine, but it is also a touristic passage way for skiers headed for Aconcagua, the highest peak of the Andes. The vacationers also enjoy hiking, horseback and rafting.

The irrigation system of the Huapes Indians has something in common with the Roman aqueducts. They are still functioning today. The water is transported from icy peaks to the city by different systems of irrigation. The vine-cultivators produce various types of wines at a high altitude: Chardonnai, Souvignon and Tempranello. Other types of minor importance are Criolla chica, and Negra peruana whose origin is uncertain. Some claim that it was imported from Spain, but the plant is also found in Sardinia. It would be interesting to know if the Spaniards exported it to the Mediterranean island when they occupied it or they brought to the New World from the island. To honor this great product exported all over the world, every year they have the Fiesta Nacional de la Vindimia. The organizers combine it with a Beauty Pageant similar to the one conducted in the western countries. They choose one girl for every region and, then, they elect the queen.

There were about two hundred Indian tribes in Argentina and they opposed a stiff resistance to the Conquistadores. Buenos Aires was occupied in 1560. One of the three major tribes was the Huapes.

Mendoza's first settler. De Castillo, named it, in 1561, after the governor of Santiago, Chile. Mendoza is also famous for giving the birth to Jose' de San Martin, who with Simon Bolivar, fought for the independence of South America from Spain.

Zanzara's integration in the Argertine society was never finalized. She was favored by the high number of Italians in Mendoza who dedicated their expertise to viniculture. Her mind was always in Italy. She was of middle stature, dark hair and dark eyes. Even with the modernization of hairstyles, she never allowed a stylist to color her hair. She had the great merit of not eating indiscriminately any food, but kept the weight constantly under control by eating a low quantity and high quality. She hated sugar beverages and canned food. Wine was the only drink she had at dinner time. Her highest virtue was generosity. She gave lavishly and never expected anything in return. Nonetheless, her forte was 'el movimiento.' She was constantly active all day, not working, but talking and visiting to the point that her friends called her 'Zanzara.' She was still young when her husband passed away and she had various chances of getting married, but she refused them all. Her son did not approve of her still working and let her quit.

In the course of the years, she made many transatlantic voyages. Being free from any responsibility, she had ample time to visit relatives and friends on a daily basis. During the time she spent in Italy, she enjoyed passing hours with Espera's parents talking about the old times, but she made sure that her son be the focus of their conversation.

Chapter XXVI

Espera's Brother Leaves

One evening, Espera's mother was conversing with Zanzara. "We are navigating through hard times, my good, old friend. We work all day and, at the end, we have nothing to show."

"You are not kidding. The same happens to me."

"I did not know that you were working," she replied with surprise.

Zanzara laughed loudly. "My work never ends, my dear friend. I have a double job."

"You do? Since when?"

"What I do with my sick husband is more than a job. Then, there is my son who is in war"

"What war?" she inquired with curiosity.

"You mean you are not acquainted about the Malvinas war?"

"How would I know it, my great friend? I am on the farm all day. But, tell me. Is your son sick too?"

"Are you serious?" responded Zanzara with disbelief. "He almost died. The ship on which he was serving got sunk and only half of the crew survived."

"Blessed St. Anthony!" she exclaimed. "Then, you ought to be happy."

"I should, but what about the mothers of those who died?"

"You are absolutely right. You bear a child for nine months. You raise him until he is twenty-one, then, the government calls him to go to war. Why don't they send their sons?"

"Now, you are making sense!" replied Zanzara. She raised her hands toward the heaven and said, "Padre Pio, pray for him!"

"Don't mix the saints!" She warned her. "They may get jealous, you know."

"Don't be silly! The more you pray, the better it is." She stood there silent for a few moments and started to cry.

"Why are you crying for? He is safe. When did you find it out?"

"Yesterday, I got a call."

Espera heard some cries from the other room and came to find out what was going on. "By the way" her mother said, "This is my daughter."

"I know her. I met her before. How beautiful she is. Look at her cheeks. They are nice and rosy. She must be engaged by now," she asked.

"No, she is not looking for anyone," the mother answered.

"How old is she?"

"Ask her. Don't ask me," replied the mother.

Espera said, "Twenty-five…"

"She would be perfect for my son."

Espera turned her attention to something else. He mother asked, "Did you say that your son is sick now? What was the diagnosis?"

"No, he did not get hurt from the bombs. He came out unscathed, thanks to St. Bernadette."

"From where, do you dig out all these saints?"

"Never mind! When you need help, you call on all of them."

"Yes, but now you are making a salad of saints. At any rate, before, I thought that your son had a pathology."

Zanzara raised the tone of her voice, "Just because my husband is sick, it does not mean that my son is sick too. He is as healthy as a fish. I think I was clear on it. He survived from the wreckages of a sunken ship."

Nobody made any comment and Zanzara turned toward Espera and queried, "Are you mute? You hardly said two words?"

Her mother responded for her, "My daughter is deeply depressed in these days. We all are."

"Nonsense! A gorgeous girl like her should be happy and not embroiled in psychological turbulences."

"Where did you steal those words?"

Zanzara laughed, "Once in a blue moon, I borrow a couple of them. I don't understand them, but I use them anyhow. Going back to you, what happened?"

"When someone, for no reason, spoils the happiness of your family, how would you feel? You just lay idle on the side?"

"I don't understand. I wasn't here when it happened."

Espera's mother did not know where to start. She moved many times on the chair in search of a comfortable position. When she finally felt well, she continued, "My first son fell into a deep crisis. He almost got crazy."

"How can that be possible?"

"Easy! My eldest son was supposed to get married with Felix's cousin. You know the people across street."

"Sure, sure."

"My son did the impossible, I tell you."

"You are talking in riddles. I have hard time following you. Can you go to the point without wasting time?"

"I tell you. All the newspapers are talking about it. Before the exchange of the nuptial vows and rings, the priest started to preach. Suddenly, a masked man made sarcastic and derogatory remarks about Don Juan. After the initial shock, the priest ordered him to leave the church immediately. I tell you, it was very inappropriate."

"They should have called a policeman," said her friend with emphasis.

Espera's mother appeared annoyed by her stupid remarks, "Did you ever see a policeman in a wedding party? What would he do there?"

"Arrest him?"

"The priest secured his safety in the interior of the church, but he was almost killed by a mob outside. I wonder how he escaped in the cornfields,

"As long as they got married...That is the main thing."

Espera's mother shook her head in a sign of discomfort. "Are you thick or are you an idiot?"

"If you don't tell me the rest, how do I know it?" protested Zanzara.

"After that pandemonium, as they say..."

"Oh, for good heavens! But, that's not what I heard. You are mixing everything up. There was no masked man in church."

"It does not matter. The dirty remarks were made. Nobody can argue against it."

"Oh, for heaven's sake," exclaimed Zanzara.

"Wait! When the bride saw her parents leave the church, she got up, too. My son stood there like a pepperone. You may imagine the noise and the confusion that the guests made. They demanded to be compensated for the money and time loss."

"That's ridiculous. It was not their fault. Let me ask you, instead, what are your plans now?" queried Zanzara more curious than ever.

Her friend got up. She walked a few steps forward and returned slowly to the chair as if she were counting the steps. Espera, with her head between both hands, was watching in silence. Her mother appeared to be in pain. Before sitting, she looked at her daughter and said, "We have no news of her whereabouts and we are not interested in knowing it. The game is over. We lost all the pennies that we saved to help my son to pay for the expenses."

"Good heavens!" repeated Zanzara. "I feel like being in a circus. Are you being facetious?"

"Not at all!" replied her friend in a serious tone.

"I feel so sad for all of you. It is terrible. What about your son? Where is he?"

"He immigrated to Chile."

"Oh, my good grace! Poor boy! That masked man deserves twenty years of jail."

"We have some reservation about the man or the woman. We have no idea about the identity of the individual. You heard a different account. Let's leave at that."

"Listen, my friend, we differ on the story. My point is another. We suspect that someone across street orchestrated the nuptial ceremony," and pointed to Felix house, "They must have arranged something. You know what I mean. I don't believe that somebody hired a guy to rack the marriage. That's your invention. Period."

Espera heard that name and closed her eyes, as if she were in a suffering state.

"That's awful!" she replied.

"People are so unethical! But, I tell something else. The priest racked the boat by not preventing the intruder from dishing out that incendiary language. Didn't he?" responded Zanzara with force.

"That is not the word I would use because I don't understand it."

Zanzara laughed. "If you are in contact with politicians, you learn."

"I am baffled by the whole incident. What did they gain from it? The bride was their relative too."

"Where the morals are degraded, even conscience screeches, my good friend."

For a while, all three of them observed an unusual, monastic silence, until Zanzara decided that silence was a burden too heavy for her to bear any longer and started another fire. She looked at Espera and asked her, "Are you going to get married pretty soon?"

Her mother answered for her, "She has many suitors, but as of now, there is nothing serious going on."

Her daughter laid her chin on the right hand and did not reply.

Zanzara stretched her hands forward and said, "Maybe, we can make an arrangement between your daughter and my son."

"They don't even know each other," protested her friend.

"I bet that if I show her my son's picture, she will recognize him. Of course, time blurs the memory, but I am confident she will be able to…"

Zanzara was busy searching in her purse for her son's picture. In the meantime, Espera got up. She was in no mood to talk about marriage after her brother's experience. She bid good-night and joined her older sister in another room. Her mother apologized, "You raise your children and what do you get? Once they reach the adult age, they are not going to pay attention to their parents anymore. But I am going to strangle her if she does that to me."

Zanzara laughed. "Don't get disturbed by their behavior. We are here to guide them."

Before Zanzara left, she proposed to continue the same conversation the next day. Her friend agreed.

When Zanzara reached her bedroom, she screamed.

CHAPTER XXVII

The Funeral

Floris boarded an Argentine military airline in Buenos Aires. The plane landed at Capodichino's International Airport in Naples at 9:15 A.M. on a Monday morning. Four Argentine soldiers were stationed at the bottom of the mobile ladder to remind him that his government honored him even in foreign countries. The highest ranking officials from the embassy took their time to welcome him in Italy. While the rest of them walked straight ahead outside of the compound, where a car was waiting, the police asked Floris for the passport. He read, "Floris Businissu, born in Rotondi, Italy.' He handed it back to the owner and asked him, "Is this the first time that you are returning to Italy?

"Si', señor!"

"I see, you speak Spanish."

"Bueno, my family immigrated to Argentina when I was adolescent."

"I can understand it from your accent," replied with a smile the policeman. "Is the war winding down at the Malvinas?" he asked again.

"I am coming from there."

"Are you serious?" he responded with incredulity.

"I was on the Belgrano when it got hit by a British missile. A pandemonium broke out. The ship eventually sank. Only half of the crew survived and I am one of the lucky ones."

"Good heavens! Exclaimed the policeman in a state of astonishment. "So," he added with curiosity, "Argentina lost the islands."

"I don't think so. Argentina will never give up her claim to the Malvinas. They belong to us."

Somebody yelled his name from outside. He apologized for cutting short the conversation and dashed out.

The policeman kept on looking at him until the embassy personnel whisked him away.

At the embassy, the ambassador offered a coffee and Sambuca. Floris accepted it eagerly. He had jet legs and was tired for the long trip. He needed to wake up. The living room looked like a museum. Paintings of South American artists covered the walls. At the end of a pause, the ambassador asked him, "We are embroiled in a difficult war, but our government is here to assist you at any moment in any possible way during your two weeks of leave of absence." He took a business card and gave it to him. "Use it in case of emergency." Floris was astounded by so much attention and courtesy and thanked him, "Mr. Ambassador, no words can adequately appreciate all your assistance."

"Argentina admires and is proud of you. You are an inspiration of courage and love for your country to millions of fellow citizens in our homeland and around the world," responded the ambassador. The driver was waiting outside. The ambassador made a gesture with his head. The driver picked up the suitcase and headed for the door. Floris gave the military salute to the embassy personnel and departed for his town.

Floris was rather short in stature with brown eyes and brown short hair. The eyelashes were dense and unruly. The nose was fine, but not perfect. The area in the vicinity of the nostrils presented some skin anomalies that looked like slight concave depressed spots. The face was dark and very dry. The brutal winds of the Malvinas had left a mark on him. He was twenty-five years old at that time.

The station wagon stopped in front of Zanzara's house. The four soldiers stepped outside and stood on attention. The chauffeur took care of the suitcase, while Zanzara hurried to open the door. From the window of her house, Espera was watching the scene with great interest. Floris hugged his mother and other relatives, took off his jacked and hat and went straight to the bedroom where his father was laid. He knelt and prayed for a few minutes. Only his mother stood with him. The rest of their relatives waited in the living room.

In the annals of the town, the funerals were unique 'sui generis.' It was unmatched in its opulence locally and nationally. The choreography was reminiscent of great events or death of a world personality. People of every social stratus lined up the sidewalks that led to the cemetery. They came from every corner of the region, perhaps, out of curiosity to have a glimpse and render homage to the father of one of their citizens who had obtained fame in a foreign land. They wanted to pay respect directly to one of their sons who left as an unknown boy and came back as a hero. The farmers left the machines inoperative in the fields and crowded the edge of the roads. The church was jammed since the early hours of the morning and the police de-toured the traffic of the major arteries to allow a smooth and peaceful procession.

Togni is the world most prestigious circus and the home of a renowned wild beasts' tamer. For over a century, he traveled around the globe bringing joy, entertainment and laughter. He was a close friend of the argentine ambassador in Naples. Both dined together whenever they were free from their duties right on Via Caracciolo. It was not hard, therefore, for the ambassador to make the funeral arrangements with him.

There was excitement and surprise all over the town for the presence of the animals. The farmers welcomed the idea of such a sumptuous parade of animals. The sight of hundreds of horses, giraffes and elephants, just to mention a few of them, excited the children's imagination who got more interested in them than in the funeral itself. They enjoyed the spectacle more than the adults. At times, they disentangled from the parental care to run over and pet the giant animals. The rigorous vigilance of the custodians prevented them from transforming a funeral into a game.

However, it would be unfair to claim that everybody shared the same view.

Restaurants and coffee shops managers frowned at the presence of those animals complaining that they would bring bad odor to a lugubrious atmosphere. The municipal trash collectors did not like the idea because they had to deal with the mass left behind. Many adults unleashed salacious comments to the animals' owners who did not take the proper precaution to let the animals evacuate their bowels prior to the procession. The smell that arose from the excrements left in the streets forced them to cover their nose and mouth with a cloth. For whatever reason, the major attention was focused on the animals even if there was a large representation of politicians from every region,

At ten o'clock, at the command of the master of ceremony, the funeral procession was lined up through the roads leading to the cemetery. Twelve horses led the coach carrying the casket. Twelve more followed. At the tamer's signal the long line of elephants, giraffes and more horses moved at the band musical beat and behaved like obedient school children. Aside from the inconveniences already mentioned, the spectators lined up on both sides of the streets and watched in awe the caravan of mourners and animals. Floris held his mother Zanzara by hand, while Espera walked with her mother behind them. At the very end, robust young men carried crowns of flowers.

The grandiosity of the funeral procession became the talk of the town and was reported also by the national media and by the argentine press. By the family's request, the ceremony ended without the usual political speeches and the police had the work cut out to control the traffic of animals, cars and carts.

Back at home, Espera told her mother, "I never saw a funeral of this magnitude. I am astonished. For the sake of me, it was behind my imagination."

"I can assure you that if Zanzara's son was not regarded highly in Argentina, not many people would have shown."

"I can't believe it," repeated her daughter.

"Money talks, my dear,"

"In this case, it is not a monetary matter. I don't believe her son is a millionaire. It would not hurt if he did."

"He must be well known wherever he lives, that's why I think it would be a good deal to get together with him."

"Ma, don't we have to prepare something to eat for them?"

"Yes, you are right. What should we cook?"

"Soup would be well appreciated."

"At this time of the year? We better off killing a couple of chickens. You peal a bag of potatoes from the barn and fix them with oil and other condiments. Put them in the stove at broil temperature and let them bake for twenty minutes."

"About a pie?"

"I will take care of that," assured her her mother.

CHAPTER XXVIII

The Gifts

Espera and her mother prepared a sumptuous dinner for Zanzara and her relatives. It was a good opportunity for Floris and Espera to meet, but it happened with discretion.

A week of mourning passed and Zanzara got to work on account of her son. She regained her natural style and went to Naples to visit the most renowned fashion stores. The fresh air of the golf and the vibrant vitality of the people brought her back to the new reality. She gave a glance to the Vesuvius and felt regenerated. The crater was inactive, bust still, looked majestic. Anyone, climbing the mountain and watching serenely down to the gulf, might feel an inebriating sensation. Across from the volcano, another mountain was hiding her hometown. "My son can find his happiness if he knows how to handle the wires that lead to Esperan's heart," she said to herself. "His future rests in my hands and I feel terribly responsible. Challenges never deter me from pursuing my objectives." She smirked and moved on.

Zanzara spent most of the day shopping and returned to her town late with the last train of the evening. At the railroad station, a friend helped her to unload the many boxes she carried along and to load them on the only horse carriage that operated as taxi between the railroad station and the town.. At her house, some children formed circles around the horse and tried to get on board, but the coachman drove them away with a whip. Zanzara's son heard the horse sneering and came down to help his mother. The coachman waited a while and blew a trumpet. Zanzara came out and dropped something in his hand. He looked at the amount and left the hand open. He stared at her. She turned around and closed the door. The coachman thought that she went inside to pick up additional compensation and started to feed the horse. He blew the trumpet again. Floris queried, "Ma, he is waiting for something."

"Don't pay attention to him. This taxi is never satisfied."

When the coachman realized that she would not show up to round the fee, he muttered something incomprehensible, shouted to the animal and departed in a hurry.

Zanzara was tired after a busy day, but the sight of the boxes on the table gave her the excuse not to go to bed and spent the rest of the evening wrapping the gifts with red paper. The red roses could wait for the following days; otherwise, they would have withered.

A couple of days were sufficient for Floris to overcome the jet legs and the trauma of his father's death. He caught up with his energy and sleep and was ready to move on. He went to the street to breathe the fresh air whistling from the mountains. The noise of carts, the shouts of the vendors, the barking of the dogs and a few cars passing by were sweet sounds that brought him back with his memory to his teen years.

The evening supper was quite meager at Zanzara's house. They did not get the chance to rest because someone knocked at the door. "The visitors keep on coming," commented Zanzara in a sleepy voice. Her face brightened at the sight of the newcomers. Espera, under her mother insistence, paid a respect visit to Zanzara and her son. She did not feel like going. Her mother used all her persuasive power to convince her to join her. It was a southern custom to pay a visit of courtesy to the family of the dead person. To ignore the tradition was equivalent to an insult. They fed the animals and got the supper ready for the rest of the family. Her mother yelled, "Put on the best dress and don't forget to comb your hair. You can use my comb if you don't have yours."

Zanzara's house was two blocks away from Espera's residence. They wrapped up something in a piece of cloth and walked out in the street. They knocked at the door and Zanzara jumped on her feet to open it. They hugged each other and Zanzara started to cry, "My husband left me. It is not right. He could have stayed a bit longer to see his son get married. I can't forgive him. He left me all alone. Good thing that I have a son."

Antonio Casale

Espera said, "It does no good to you to cry. Men are like that. They like to be first in everything."

While Zanzara was sobbing, Espera and her mother expressed their regrets to Floris. He looked at her straight in her eyes. She lowered her head and blushed.

Zanzara wiped her face with the dishcloth and invited the two guests in the living room. Four or five chairs were resting against the wall in the dining room. Zanzara kindly invited them to sit down while her son would make coffee. Espera's mother objected, "Don't let him do that. He is tired. My daughter can make the expresso."

Espera said, "Zanzara, don't bother! We won't stay too long."

Floris responded in a soft voice, "The fact that you are going to stay a short while should not exempt us from being hospitable."

"In that case, let my daughter help you."

"She is more than welcome. Maybe, I learn from her how to make a better expresso."

Not to argue with her mother, Espera turned around, took the coffeepot and laid it in his hand. She apologized, but he held her back, "It is OK. There is no arm into it."

She blushed. He did not wish to embarrass her and searched for the sugar.

Two minutes later, Espera exclaimed, "The coffee is ready,"

"And here are the cups, spoons and plates," added Floris feeling an unusual warmth by the presence of that strange girl. "My mother talked a lot about you and your family and we feel honored that you came to visit us," he said.

"It is our duty. When there is a death in a family, it is an obligation for a friend to show up and demonstrate solidarity. We did not do anything special."

"Your friendship has a special price for us. We value it immensely," responded Floris.

Espera blushed for the second time. She never heard such beautiful compliments. She put her hand at her mother's side and tightened it.

Espera's mother was flattered too and not to demonstrate her nervousness said, "By the way, we brought you some potatoes, a chicken and a rabbit. We are busy in the field and did not have time to look for something more valuable."

"You should not bring anything," responded Zanzara.

"Well, we could not come with our empty hands. We are poor, but with honor."

"That is very nice of you. We truly appreciate it."

"Oh, I was going to tell you. I have never seen such an elaborate funeral. It surpassed the one done for the American President" said Espera.

"Let's not exaggerate, now!" responded Zanzara. "Let's say that it was rare among us. After all, my husband was very popular, as you know."

"Indeed, but I am sure that the ambassador from Argentina played a pivotal role in the procession," said Espera.

"Either you are famous or rich because no one can explain how in the world one could come up with those ideas. And, what about the money involved…" stated Espera's mother.

Floris took a deep breath and said, "I recognize the magnitude of the event, but I do not deserve any praise.

Rich I am not. Famous I am neither."

"Humility is the mother of all virtues," intervened Zanzara.

"You have the right words at the right time," observed Espera's mother. The two senior women to the kitchen momentarily searching for a pie cutter and Floris said, "Well, let's say that my heart belongs here." When he finished sipping the coffee, he looked intensely at Espera and asked, "And your heart, where do you think it is?"

She pondered for a few moments and answered in a serious mood, "I am sure that mine belongs here too."

"Can we see each other tomorrow?" asked Floris. I have only one week left."

Espera got nervous at the invitation and began to sweat. Floris was waiting for an answer. From the kitchen, came an exclamation of joy that saved Espera from embarrassment. "It is just wonderful." It was Zanzara who was holding the pie cutter in her hand. She cut four pieces, placed them in each tray and handed them over to the rest. It did not take too long for her to finish the coffee and excused herself again, "I am going upstairs for a minute. Espera, you and your mother can keep company to my son. I will be right back." She turned around, but soon after, she stopped again, "No, Floris you go and bring down those things that are on the table. You know what I mean." Floris jumped the stairs three by three and arrived upstairs within seconds. A minute or so passed by and the ladies heard a thunderous noise of boxes falling down the stairs. Their initial suspicion was that the young man fell. To allay their fear, they got up and hurried out for his rescue. Zanzara cried out, "My son, my poor son, I come quickly. Stay there!"

The ladies rushed to the place where the noise originated and found five or six big boxes. They did not see Floris around and they thought that he dropped the boxes from upstairs. Suddenly, they noticed a movement beneath the boxes. They removed them and saw Floris who was having hard time getting up. Espera and her mother could hardly control their laughter. "You look like a skinned rabbit" exclaimed Espera.

"Don't make such stupid comments," warned her mother.

Zanzara, instead, was very much apprehensive about her son's health, "You scarred me to death! Why didn't you call for help?" Floris dusted off his clothes and apologized for the unnecessary noise and fear he had caused. Zanzara hurried to the kitchen to fill up a glass of cold water and handed it to her son, "Here, drink it. This will appease your fear. You ask the doctor. He will agree that it slows down the heart beat."

Her son drank it, not for medical motivations, but to calm her down. Espera's mother was still laughing, "I have to make a confession," she said when the excessive humor subsided. "You amaze me all the time. Every day, it seems that you change a profession. Now, you have become a doctor."

"No, doctor's assistant."

Floris smiled and said, "Let's say, doctor's assistant."

"That sounds better" corrected him his mother."

Espera excused herself and visited the bathroom. Zanzara tried to fill up her absence by proposing a second expresso. The other two assented with gusto.

The mirror did not seem friendly to Espera. She looked in it and noticed her blond hair in disarray. She grabbed a brush from her purse and tried to bring some order to it. An expression of surprise appeared on her face. The skin was dry and had many pimples. She applied promptly a cream and, to her satisfaction, they were well covered. Thoughts fumbled in her brains erratically. "I feel nervous," she said. She stretched her right hand and it was trembling. "Oh, my heavens! Will he like me?" She muttered. At that moment, she heard a voice. She looked at the shirt and the gown that belonged to her mother and made a gesture of displeasure. Her left hand was on the door knob ready to open, but, then, she locked it again. The lips did not have lipstick on. The purse was replete with beauty object, but there was no trace of the lipsticks. A couple of drops cologne in her hair would have been appropriate for the occasion, but her peasant mind did not care for things appealable to city dweller girls. Her mother called her again, and this time she joined them.

Sitting in front of those boxes was not easy for the guests. They were wondering about the content. Zanzara brought on the table the coffee and a vase of biscuits. Espera did not wait for the invitation and tasted one. It was delicious. Floris picked up the whole dish and placed it in front of her. She felt embarrassed. Floris said, "You can eat as many as you want. I bought them for you." Esperanza felt flattered. Her mother said, "If you don't want them, I eat them."

Floris answered, "They are tasty. Aren't they? You can eat them too. I have others."

Espera's mother said, "I feel uncomfortable, now. Look at all the goodies you offer us. I wanted to bring a can of coffee and I could not find it."

Zanzara was pleased in the way her son was handling the conversation and said, "Feel yourself free to eat and drink at will. Make this your house." Espera and her mother thanked her for her generous hospitality and wanted to leave, but Zanzara's mind was set elsewhere. She judged that the time was ripe to present the boxes. On each one of them, her son placed a fresh red rose. He said, "Ah, we have something here that we wish to offer you as a sign of our friendship. Please, do not take it as an offense."

Espera's mother was quick to reply, "I cannot speak for my daughter, but as for me, I don't get offended at all!"

Espera folded both arms on her chest and said to Floris, "Don't look at me. I don't want anything."

Her mother stared at the box. Occasionally, her daughter wiped the palm of her hands and cheeks. Floris picked up the first box and said, "You will like this." Espera's mother stretched her hands to grab the gift. "Please, take it!" he added. Espera's mother was inundated with a feeling of vanity and pride. Floris said, "This is for la señorita." A cloud of darkness fell on Espera's mother face. The lady did a good job in camouflaging her embarrassment and passed the box over to her daughter. Espera was hesitant. A light perfume of violet sprang from the box. She took a deep breath. The perfume invaded her lungs and made her feel dizzy. As she recovered from it, Zanzara handed her a glass of water, "Drink it," she said. "It will do you good." That comment made Espera's mother laugh again.

While Espera was sipping the water, Zanzara said, "Don't feel timid in my son's presence. I believe you attended the same elementary school."

Espera's mother reproached her, "There is only one elementary school in our town!"

Her friend responded, "I did not mean that. They should remember each other."

Her son looked at Espera and said, "I am pretty sure we were in the same class.. I still have a picture at home. I have to check it."

"Now, that I remember, maybe, we were in the same class," responded the young lady.

"Before, I could not visualize you. I had a fuzzy idea. Now, I am starting to remember. The ideas are getting clearer. I am sure we talked many times in our childhood."

Zanzara felt she a second intervention was necessary, "Things are getting better than I expected. Since you were friends, open the gift and see if you like it. He brought it from Argentina. In the pampa, they make the best wool in the world."

Espera opened it and saw a classy suit. "This is gorgeous! But, I don't want it. Give it to your girlfriend."

"He does not have any girlfriend," replied promptly Zanzara on behalf of her son. "Don't worry about that! He is single."

Espera looked down and added, "You did not have to go out of the way to celebrate our friendship."

Her son said, "Esta' bien."

The frequent use of the Sapnish language concerned Zanzara who took the floor, once again, "We take this opportunity to renew our friendship and to honor it." She turned to Espera and added, "If he uses some Spanish words, don't mind him. He has been away for years."

"There is no need for apology. I understand him very well."

Floris was waiting for his turn. As the ladies paused, he took a second box and said, "Con mucho gusto! Take this. As my mother said, it will bolster our friendship."

Espera's mother jumped at the prey, but Floris passed the box under her nose and handed it to her daughter. The lady did not appreciate the irony in the game. It was the second time that she had been fooled. She wanted to discharge her feelings, but kept her lips tight. Espera opened the box. Her eyes almost popped out of the orbit. Two pair of shoes shone under her eyes, one with high and the other with low heels. On the side, she saw four pairs of stockings well folded and from the latest fashion. "You should not do this. I cannot accept them," said Espera.

"Are you crazy, girl?" Her mother reprimanded her. "Do you know how much they cost?"

Zanzara almost caused a humorous reaction when she stated seriously, "It is offensive to return a gift."

"You gave me more than one gift," emphasized Espera.

"I did not do anything," rectified Zanzara. "It is my son who bought them for you."

Floris disregarded the girl's protestations and got another box from the table. The curiosity was mounting. Espera objected, "I hope it is destined to somebody else, otherwise, I am going to leave," Floris was holding the box near Espera's mother. This time, she pulled it and held it tightly to her bosom. It was an evening of spoiling dreams. Floris looked at Espera and said, "Now, you can try it. See if it fits well. If you don't like it..."

Espera's mother was disappointed again, but did not give up, "If you do not like it, I will take it."

Zanzara touched her friend's arm and suggested her, "Let us stay out of the business," Espera covered her face with both hands and exclaimed, "What is going on this evening?" She opened it and saw a raincoat of the ultimate fashion. It took time and efforts to try it on. Then she said, "It is out of this world." Soon after, she began to sweat from the excitement. Floris gave her his handkerchief with his name embroidered on it. She did not want to accept it, but to be polite she took "Keep it," said Floris.

She blushed and did not respond.

The last gift was resting on the table. Floris handed it to Espera's mother, "I can assure you that you will love this one." This time the old woman was not going to make a full out of herself. She refused it and passed it over to her daughter.

Zanzara said to her friend, "You are a smart woman. You had the right intuition to pass it to your daughter."

Espera could not believe that a visit to a deceased person turned into a birthday party. She showed signs of regret for having submitted to her mother's wishes. Her intentions were well motivated. She did not wish to convey a lack of sensitivity or appreciation, but the hosts' bounty was revealing to be behind her expectations and wondered if they were subject to a different interpretation. She did not want to abuse of a Her old classmate's generosity was definitely indicating a new course in their relations. Against her will, she unraveled the last gift. Her hair stood straight up and her exuberance began to explode, "I don't believe it! It's awesome! A white wool coat, two blouses and two blue shirts appeared before her in all their high quality and stylistic novelty.

"You can try them on, if you wish," Floris suggested her.

The bathroom was near. All those items were of her size. Espera wondered how he was able to guess it. He moved slightly the head toward his mother who refused to take the merit. After the few euphoric seconds, a feeling of culpability seeped through her heart. In the subsequent moments of crisis, she handed the boxes to the young man and said, "I like them all, but I cannot accept them. They are not mine. They are yours. They don't belong to me. I don't deserve them. I don't want anything. Please, take them back."

Her mother interjected, "How stupid can you be. I take them. Don't worry about that."

Zanzara stopped her from carrying out her plan. "This is a matter between the two of them. You and I are not supposed to interfere,"

"Oh, my heavens, she refuses them and I accept them. What's wrong with that?"

Floris ignored her and handed another handkerchief to Esperanza. She wiped her tears, laid her head on his shoulder and quieted down. He surrounded her body with his arms. "Don't be silly!" scorned her Zanzara. My son does not do this with any girl. Come on, now! Let's have more coffee and more biscuits."

Floris began to cultivate Espera's friendship assiduously in the days preceding his departure. He had a military obligation to honor. His leave of absence was going to expire in a week. During that time, he committed himself entirely to Espera's courtship. To stay close to her as much as possible, he even went to the farm to help her. This spontaneous attitude convinced Espera's parents that the soldier was genuine in his relationship with their daughter and invited him to join them in their daily meals. Floris used the maximum precautions to remain anonymous to the neighborhood. He visited Espera in the evening; crossed the streets when the traffic was scarce and hurried. He never entered from the front door. He used the back door from the courtyard even though the risk of getting the shoes muddy could not be discounted. As a soldier, he was instructed to care his exterior appearance. For that reason, he brought along a second pair of shoes that he would change before he entered in the house.

Zanzara did not accompany her son to Espera's house. In private, she expressed full satisfaction that she had accomplished her mission and waited for the events to unfold on their own terms. To her closest friends, she confided that her role as mediator was over. The only time she showed up was at her son's last visit. Espera invited both of them to her house to share a dinner with her family. Espera's parents offered a simple, but dignified menu. They killed a chicken, and boiled potatoes. Corn and walnuts made as a contour along with domestic wine. Even bread was homemade. Zanzara, for her part, did not wish to appear of a low class and brought a huge tray of almond biscuits and other pastry specialties. She could not resist bringing along a bottle of Sambuca liquor to use in the coffee.

The atmosphere was joyful like in the most memorable occasions. Everybody ate and drank at will. The atmosphere was euphoric. The children and the adults were restless toward the end. Their mouth was watery. They had waited too long to taste the succulent and sweet varieties of pastries that Floris had bought and wasted no time in devouring them when Espera uncovered the dishes. Zanzara was enjoying every moment of it. No one paid attention to Floris who asked permission to Espera to talk to her in private for a few minutes. Her mother motioned to the young sister to join them. Floris and Espera did not appreciate the omnipresent surveillance. Zanzara, whose eyes travelled all over, captured instantly their disapproval and used all her oratorical power to convince Espera's mother that it was fine to trust them. According to her, they needed some privacy. Considering that it was Floris' last night, Espera's mother gave in. The two young lovers walked to the adjacent room and locked the door behind them. Espera's mother, still doubtful of what was going on, winked to the other daughter. The girl placed her ear against the door to detect any unusual noise and report their conversation. Zanzara disapproved that behavior and made them known that it was unethical and uncalled for. She reiterated to the host family that it was a matter of common courtesy not to interfere with their private meeting. "Don't worry," she said. "They are not going to elope."

This last argument convinced her friend to give up the strict scrutiny. The girl was recalled to her seat and the two young lovers would plan their future.

An expression of great excitement suddenly broke out in the room where Floris and Espera were engaged in intimate talk. Everybody jumped at the opportunity to rush to the door and capture the feeling of the conversation. Only Zanzara stood still on her seat, "Leave them alone! She protested. You don't give them the air to breathe." Her friends and family ignored her latest complaint and stood there listening.

Floris pulled a small box from his inside jacket pocket and gave it to her. "Open it. It is yours," he said

"What's in it?"

"If I tell you, it won't be a surprise anymore."

"Here we go again," she responded with a smile. She stared at the box as to capture the internal secret. Her hands were sweaty. She attempted the first time to unwrap it, but failed. She tried again. She set aside the paper and opened the box. A gold necklace was shining from inside. Her face glowed with joy.

"Put it on. See how it looks on you." Espera, never had a necklace in her life. She got clumsy and could not hook it up on the back. "Help me out, please," she said.

Floris accepted with pleasure the invitation. After three trials, he was able to let the latch get into the ring.

At the end, as to reward himself, he bent over and laid his lips on her neck. She moved them away. "Don't do that," she whispered in his ear. "My family may be listening. Come on. Let's go! If we delay a bit longer, they get suspicious.

Floris held her back. "Wait! I have one last thing for you. Here it is. Open it!"

Esperanza could not wait for another surprise. She tore apart the paper in a hurry and opened it. It was a bottle of perfume. She paused for a few seconds, "I wanted to have one like this for a long time." The last words came out of her lips emphatically."

"I know. You did not have the means for it." He stared at her and added, "It puts you in a good mood. Do you like it?"

"You ask me if I like it. I love it! It is fabulous!" Espera had raised her voice and her words reached the ears of the rest of the family. The remarks, at least, reassured them that the privacy was being used in harmony with their expectations.

Espera stretched her right hand and placed it on the door knob. "We must go now," she implored him.

Floris said to her. Tomorrow, I will leave. I promise you it will take only thirty seconds. I have one last memory that I want to share with you for the rest of my life."

She looked at him with compassionate eyes. She exhorted him to hurry. Her mother would give her a piece of her mind later. The expectations were running highly. Floris pulled the last little box he had in his jacket. "Here, hold it with care."

The air was still. Even in the next room there was silence. She felt the presence of the oppressing quietness and started to shake. She decided to open the tiny box. The sight of the content made her draw back. She made a sound and fainted. Floris was quick to hold her in his arms and, with some efforts, gently helped her to sit. He took his handkerchief and used it as a ventilator on her face. It worked. Slowly, she came to her senses.

In the next room, they heard something unusual and got apprehensive. "Stay calm! They are going to show up now. Up to now, it was theater," said Zanzara.

Espera gained knowledge of her senses. She felt exhilarated. Floris took the ring with gems on top and placed it on her finger. "This is the ring of my love for you. It is the engagement ring," he said.

Espera was in a state of slight shock. It was difficult for her to speak. Her mind traveled far away. Finally, she regained her composure and said in an almost imperceptible voice, "I vow to be faithful to you I will never renege our ties." He hugged her and kissed her on the forehead. She blushed. He helped her to stand up. She took him by hand. In that moment, the door sprang right open. "Surprise!" Everyone shouted. The family noticed the ring on Espera's finger and their eyes observed time of astonishment. Nobody spoke for about a minute. At that point, Zanzara stood up. The rest of the family followed her and gave both lovers a standing ovation. Many eyes started to shed tears. Only Zanzara remained unaffected by emotions. She rushed over Esperanza's family and offered them her congratulations. Espera was emotional. Zanzara said, "Come on, now! Stop crying. This is a time of joy. Did not I assure you that everything was under control?" She hardly finished pronouncing the last word that Esperanza's sisters and brothers shouted, "Brava, Zanzara! Long life to Zanzara!"

She acknowledged wholeheartedly their appreciation and bowed.

The day of departure came. The sun rose earlier than usual and aircrafts landed and took off continually at Capodichino International Airport in Naples. Espera's family delayed a couple hours their farm labor to bid good-by to Floris. They even gave permission to Espera to accompany him to the airport. By nine o'clock in the morning, the temperature was climbing. The sky had not changed its blue face of the previous days and the gulf offered the usual scenario of boats gliding in all directions. The Vesuvius was still. Floris called Espera on the side and said, "I will write to you as soon as I arrive to Buenos Aires. Once the war is over, we make plans to get married. She hugged him. The loudspeaker was making the final call. The stewardess was ready to close the airplane's door and the airport mechanics were removing the ladder. Zanzara raised her hand and motioned them to wait. "I will always love you," whispered Floris in her ears."

"I love you too," replied Espera and looked at her ring.

The stewardess was getting impatient. Floris kissed again his girlfriend and boarded the Argentine Airline.

He took a seat next to a window and waved with both hands until the carrier moved on the runway and took the departing position.

Floris kept on waving from his seat. He pretended he was seeing them and so they did. The pilot pressed a button and the plane moved forward. It passed slowly by their window. They kept on waving at each other. The plane approached the runway. The control tower sent the 'Go ahead!" signal. The pilot pushed another button and the plane increased the speed. At one point, the plane freed itself from the asphalt. The pilot pushed a lever and the iron bird withdrew the wheels in its stomach.

A minute more and it disappeared from the sight.

. Espera followed the aircraft in the air and covered her eyes. Zanzara kept on waiving from behind the glassy window making every effort to control her emotions. She turned to Espera and said, "One of these days, you will fly too."

Chapter XXIX

The Ticket

The war for the Malvinas or Falkland Islands lasted about three months. The defeated Argentine generals were put on trial. The economy reached the ebb. There was no job anywhere and many banks went default. To keep Floris in the army, they offered him a promotion to the rank of captain although it was tempting in times of crisis; he refused it and returned to his social life.

Soon after, he found a job as a mechanic in a car company. The salary was not breathtaking, but it was sufficient to buy a car and go out in the evening. His sister did not charge him for room and board hoping that he would settle down and save some money for his future wedding. What bothered her the most was his smoking habit. Smoke caused her allergies and damaged his lungs. It seemed that he was subjugated by tobacco. In fact, he could not divorce it not even at dinner time. We would call him a chain smoker. To try to put an end to cigarettes, his sister would provoke him, "Why are you so nervous?"

"I am?" he responded with surprise. "Maybe, you are."

She did not respond at his charge. Instead, she said, "Your girlfriend has been writing to you twice a week. That is a positive sign that should keep you calm."

This time he turned his attention directly to her and snapped back, "Who told you that she writes to me frequently? Are you spying on me?"

She curved her head and stared at him, "Don't I sort out the mail every day?"

"Maybe, you should not from now on," he responded half annoyed.

"I would appreciate if you made more sense. Are you insinuating that I should wait for you at the end of the day and hand the mail to you?"

"What's wrong with that? I hope you don't open my mail," he answered in a state of light anger.

"Oh, sure, I read them all and cast them into the trash immediately after," she added with a sarcastic smile.

"That I don't believe it. You may take a pick though them and seal envelope."

"I have no interest in investigating your love stories, but you can go to the bank and buy a safety box. That will put an end to your fantasies."

"You are silly! By the way, I need to pay for the car insurance and for Espera's air ticket to Santiago." He pulled another cigarette from the pack and started to puff again.

"I would like to know where you are doing with your money," she replied in an irritated mood. "Are you sending your savings to your girlfriend?"

"I wish I did, but that is not the case. By the way, stop making personal assumptions."

"Do you mean that her parents cannot afford it?"

"What do you expect her to do?" He twisted the cigarette butt in the iron tray and said, "She cannot come here directly for immigration reasons. She has to fly to Santiago and stay with her brother for a while. Later, she will be able to join us as a tourist. Once she is here, we will get married." He paused for a couple of seconds and continued, "First, I have to save some dough."

"What are you waiting for, then? Would you like to get involved in real estate/"

"You need money for this activity."

"Not necessarily... buy apartment houses and borrow money from the bank. You will pay back with their monthly rent."

Floris lauded his sister's suggestion, but he could not conceive of doing business without a financial liquidity. The banks were not going to be too easy in approving loans. His sister was waiting for an answer. Her brother was hesitating. Finally, he asked, "What about the expenses? If a faucet breaks, you have to call a plumber. He charges dearly. If the window has to be replaced, I have to call a carpenter and I will incur in additional debts. Not to ignore the taxes... The profit would be wiped out by hiring those people."

His sister remained unperturbed. "I understand your perplexities, but you will see the light at the end of the tunnel only later. You need a lot of patience at the beginning and you must get involved personally in some menial jobs. My husband will help you."

Floris was visibly confused and took his time before responding. She got up, put her hands on both sides of his face and said, "You were foolish to invest all the money that the government gave you in gifts to your girlfriend. Now, you have to wake up. Stop smoking and start making sense."

The conversation got fragmented. Neither one of them was able to put across his, her ideas. His sister pressed for a marriage date. Her brother would and could not commit himself due to the different immigration laws in Chile and Argentina. In view of that constitutional reality, Floris insisted that there was no other alternative. His sister decided that it was in their both interest to drop the issue temporarily.

The epistolary exchange between Floris and Espera continued unabated until they reached a consensus on the marriage modalities. Her brother, in Santiago, would send her the air ticket and provide her with all the necessary assistance. That year the airline companies lowered drastically the flight prices across the board and Espera's brother took advantage of it and did as he planned. From then on, it was up to her to contact a touristic agency in a nearby town and arrange the departure.

Espera showed the first symptoms of excitement. The drawers of her chest in the bedroom were half empty, therefore, she did not have much selection to make, but whatever she had, she set it aside. Her mother told her relatives that she provided her with a substantial amount of dowry: four pillows, twelve king size sheets, two blankets, one tablecloth and three towels. The material was sufficient to fill out a big coffer. The question was who could lend it to her. No one of their relatives had one in store. Espera had saved some money her boyfriend sent her from time to time. Her mother did not approve of buying one at the market. According to her, her daughter could save the money for more important events in the future. "A luggage is not a must," she cautioned Espera. You can pack the clothes in a big bag. Besides, you do not want to make a big show. People will notice it." Her daughter did not pay heed to her and purchased one anyhow.

Her mother did not know that Espera had bought the suitcase. She stood pensive, for a while, in the kitchen and said," "Maybe, I will borrow it from a friend. On your first vacation, you will give her back."

She thought it over again and stated, "No, you don't want to do that. You become the focus of gossip in this neighborhood. Your brother will not appreciate seeing you traveling with a big bag in your hand. or with a luggage that belongs to others. Aside from feeling uncomfortable, he also would be feel humiliated. The neighbors would criticize him."

Esperanza welcomed with a relief her mother's suggestion, "Thank you, mama. Really, it does not look good for a young lady to carry a bag. But, thank you, anyhow. I have already purchased one." "You did? She queried surprised.

"What was I supposed to do? Wait until the last day to buy a luggage? Or, perhaps, not buy it at all and look like beggar?"

"I am glad that my advice pleases you" she excused herself and said, "I am going in search of the traveling agent to set up the departure for you".

Espera protested, "Why can't I do that?"

Her mother shook her head, "He would love the visit of spring chickens in his office. His sexual appetite is disgusting. He is a predator." She stepped out of the house and stopped. She went in and said, "By the way, this has to be top secret."

"How long can you keep the secret?" asked her daughter. "They won't see me for a month or two and they will question you."

"Nonsense! Once you have gone, it is O.K."

Espera's mother took off and searched for Don Luigi, the agent. He worked in a small office whose walls were covered with maps and posters of the most beautiful vacation spots in the world. On the window, he had pasted a big picture of a luxurious navigation line. He was short and had a prominent belly. His hair was gray and the skin very smooth. He dressed up with elegance every day and was exceedingly courteous with his clients.

"Good afternoon, Don Luigi. I am a lucky woman today."

"Why is that?" responded the agent dropping the eyeglasses down his nose.

The visitor said, "I came here to make a reservation for my daughter who has to go to Santiago."

"Where is that?" responded the agent with incredulity.

"In Chile, where my first son lives…. You mean…you don't know where it is? Maybe, I have to see another agent."

"Don Luigi got up instantly and held her back with an arm, "Take it easy, my wonderful lady. Be patient.

The world geography is big and it is impossible to know every place." He put back the glasses and added, "You acted properly coming here. I can let you save a lot of money. My connections…if you know what I mean; however, there are a few hurdles, but with patience and some 'dough', we will be able to reach our objective."

"I don't understand," responded the woman showing signs of nervousness.

"My dear friend, little extra things will eventually help to speed up the process," he explained with outmost calm.

"But, the ticket is paid," replied the lady more confused than ever.

"You are a woman of wisdom. You know that in order to get someplace you have to put something in someone's pocket. What do trainers put in the mouth of the dolphins during the training process? A fish!"

That's the way the social and financial wheel turns. You have to grease the wheel. Do you know what I mean?"

This is unfair! I am going to talk to the Communist Party Chairman."

"Why, he doesn't get his share?"

"The Party is uncorrupted."

The agent broke into a sonorous laughter that left the woman even more in doubt. "My dear friend, you have not traveled. Don't let anybody kid you. You can go to New York and you will find out that corruption is deeply embedded in the political and social system."

"In what kind of a world are we living?"

"I agree with you, but there is nothing we can do about it. One hand washes the other." It was humid. He grabbed a cloth from the desk drawer and wiped the forehead. He searched for the calendar and asked, "Does she have a date in mind?"

"As soon as possible," responded the confused woman.

"Does she want to travel in the first or second class?"

"I don't get it!" she responded partially annoyed. "There are social classes even when we travel? No wonder Communism wants to get rid of all these differences."

The agent smiled, "In the first class, you pay more, but you get champagne, a sofa', food and drinks galore."

"I thought that a ship or plane is a transportation vehicle, not a vessel of entertainment."

"Times have changed. Don't you realize that?"

"I guess so!"

The agent looked at the ticket and said, "This ticket is for the airplane. Does your daughter want to travel by air?"

"Can she go by boat?"

"Definitely!"

"Is the price the same?"

"Actually, by boat, it is a bit cheaper, but we can switch it over."

"How much money of difference is there" inquired the lady with curiosity.

"Not much, just a few pennies. It is a very negligent difference."

"As for me, the boat is more secure."

"Do you want the first or second class for her?"

"You said that there is not much difference?"

"Not between the plane and the boat!" emphasized the agent.

"If that is the case, let her travel in the second class by plane," assured him the woman.

"That's fine. I will make the reservation for next week, if you agree."

"Sure, sure!" agreed the lady immediately.

"I want you to know that you have to pay for the taxi."

The woman hesitated, then, said, "Why can we go by horse. I save a lot of money."

The agent fell back on his rocking chair, "I cannot travel by horse. Do you want me to get killed? There is a lot of traffic as soon as you reach the highway. The horse is good on the farm."

"How much does the chauffer charge?"

"Don't be concerned about him," reassured her agent. "He is a good man. I travel with him all the time."

"Can I pay him in potatoes? We hardly have any cash."

The agent breathed deeply. It was evident that the conversation was getting heavy. He looked at her and said, "O.K. We will see. Give me whatever money you avail. The rest we may negotiate. But, don't lose any sleep over it. We will find a way to compensate him."

Seven days passed by and Espera did not hear anything from the agent. Her mother returned to his office to complain. He polished the mustaches with a small brush and told her that all seats were taken. The lady started to sweat and looked around the room various times. She was getting nervous. Her right hand slipped in her bra. The agent was waiting avidly at the next move. The lady pulled a bunch of small bills. "This is all I have," and she handed it to him.

He got up promptly from the chair and grabbed the bills. "I am sure we are going to find a seat for your daughter," he said. "I will get in touch with you soon." The woman crossed her fingers and exclaimed, "This time we have made it."

Espera did not receive any news from the agent not even by the following week. Her parents lost their patience and rushed at the agent's office. They rang the bell, but nobody came out. The second time they knocked at the door in a rowdy manner. The noise called the attention of some tenants in the building who looked out to find out what was going on. The agent made a gesture of assent to the secretary who got up and walked to the door. She removed a piece of wood, peeped through it and reported to her boss the peoples' names. He whispered to her, "Tell them that I went to Naples trying to make a reservation for their daughter."

"Hide in the kitchen," she suggested. "You never know how they behave. They may force their way through here."

"I don't think they are going to do that."

"They are farmers and very insistent. If they see you, they will call me 'lawyer.'".

"Liar' not 'lawyer," he corrected her.

"O.K, O.K., she replied with a hand gesture of indifference."

The assistant opened the door. "Good morning! How can I serve you?"

Husband and wife looked at each other upon hearing the word, "serve.

"Communism has finally opened a hole through these thick walls," whispered the lady in her husband's ear.

"It is the agent who should serve us," responded the lady. She pushed her aside and walked straight to the office followed by her husband who was holding a fork in his hand. The secretary made a vain attempt to stop them, but they paid no attention to her. "Where is he?" asked with arrogance the lady.

"I told you that he is trying to make a reservation for your daughter. She is not the only passenger."

The lady looked at her sternly. "How many passengers can you accommodate on a boat? Thirty, fifty!"

"I am afraid that you do not have the numbers straight. A ship can carry up to two thousand passengers excluding the crew."

"What is that?" Inquired the man.

"The people, who are responsible for running the ship," she explained to him. "Then, if you fly, it is much worse.

His wife said, "Wait just a minute! Let's not mix the cards. My daughter has already the ticket. She wants to travel by air, not by boat. She needs only to make a reservation. How long does it take? Two weeks?"

The secretary replied, "I thought you said she was going by boat. Wait a minute. Do not despair. We will find a way out of the tunnel."

The lady blocked her passage and pointed the finger in a threatening mood, "Listen, buster, either you are a liar or a lawyer."

"I am neither," responded the young lady somewhat scared. "I am only an assistant. I can assure you that we have an honorable agency. Our clients are always satisfied with our service and come back to us."

"Well, I am not," shouted the lady.

The secretary drew back a step to avoid the lady's face. "We offer competitive prices and fast service."

"That's not the case with my daughter," thundered the woman.

"Maybe, the problem arose from the fact that you did not buy the ticket here. It was purchased in a foreign country."

"I don't care where it was bought. It is a ticket!"

"We do care," responded the girl with poise trying to calm down the irritated woman. "We run an honorable agency."

"Certainly, you are not showing it to me that you are honorable," shouted the lady.

Her husband grabbed a bag he had left behind the door and set it on the desk. "What is that?" asked the girl.

"It is a bag of fresh potatoes. Twenty five pounds should do it. You tell the agent that this is our front line."

"We appreciate it," said the secretary. "I am sure he will be able to do something for you."

"If he does not get busy, I am going to come back," said the lady in a belligerent posture. "And twist his neck like a chicken if he does not make the reservation," she added.

"I am sure that he would not mind them. They make good soup," replied the assistant.

The lady launched a dirty look to her. The girl's face contracted in fear and backed up a couple of steps. "I will convey the message to him on his return from Naples. We will get in touch with you in tomorrow. He is going to come back tired tonight. He has to walk from Santa Lucia's port to the railroad station."

"Wait a minute," rebutted the lady. "He told me that he drives to Naples."

"When a person cannot afford hiring a taxi, he travels alone by train to let the client save money

"The lady turned to her husband and said, "Listen to her!" Then, she looked at her and said, "Walking does good to him. He loses wait. No wonder he gets tired…"

The secretary responded, "Well, the train makes many stops before reaching our town. It is very demanding."

"How do you like that?" replied the woman. "He doesn't do it for nothing. It cost me already money and potatoes. And, if he expects a couple of chickens or rabbits, he is dead wrong." In saying that, she banged her fist on the table.

The secretary got scarred momentarily. She recomposed herself and said in a sweet manner, "It would not hurt if you did,"

"No, I am not going to give him any chicken to this turkey!" She made a head gesture to her husband and headed by the door. The assistant heard a big bang and the rooms shook. She closed her eyes and abandoned herself on the rocking chair.

Like a mouse coming out of the hideout after a cat's exit, the agent emerged with his head from underneath a bunch of boxes in the kitchen. He appeared content to have escaped the clients' rage, but he was also in bad humor for he disapproved their arrogance. "What does she think she is?" He pounded his fist against the wall and added, "If I want, their daughter will never leave this town. I could report to the government in Rome that their son is a Communist sympathizer."

"But he is already in Chile."

"Nonsense! He could be deported."

"She brought you a sack of potatoes as a gesture of good will."

"That lessens my anger." He touched the potatoes and said, "They could have made an extra effort and bring a fifty pound bag." He put the index finger on his lips and said, "I am still undecided on whether to comply with their urgent request."

"At this point, we have to rationalize our behavior. These people are rustic, tough, rough, barbarian. You got something. Be happy. You cannot stretch the rope behind the resistance line. It would backfire in terms of advertisement," cautioned him his secretary.

The agent lowered his head and walked up and down the aisle. He stopped at the end of three rounds and said, "I should not get involved with farmers. As you said, they ignore the civility code. To avoid further confrontations, I better make a reservation by next Saturday."

"Do you want me to give them the message now or tomorrow?"

"It makes more sense tomorrow. Tell them that after strenuous efforts, I was able to secure a seat in the second class. Also, say that I was exhausted and when I came home I went directly to bed."

"It will be done!"

The agent scratched his head and added, "I forgot. See if you can get a turkey or a couple of spring chickens. We have the potatoes here. We can prepare a succulent dinner."

Next evening, the secretary showed up at their house. "Hi, I am here to bring good news as I promised you yesterday. I could have come in the morning to the farm, but I did not want to spoil your day. After all, you are busy making money. I spared you time from returning to the office."

"You are learning to talk like a lawyer" responded the lady with a spicy sarcasm. "Don't go around the bush. What is the good news."

221

The secretary looked around and noticed a bunch of chickens pecking in an area near them. "We can make a deal without any problem. It is good for you and for my boss." The lady picked a fork and was about to chase her. Her husband held her back.

"Espera can leave next Saturday from Naples," says the young woman.

"At what time?" Begged her the man.

The secretary kept on looking toward the chickens. The man did not wish to exasperate the feelings. He grabbed two chickens and handed them to her. "At what time?"

"At five. All the information is written here. Keep it. And good luck!"

Espera arrived just when the deal had been locked up. By that time, she was drained of energy from waiting. She said to the secretary, "You and your fat boss are shrewd! Whatever you need to know, it is written on that paper."

The secretary thought it was far better to take off without exacerbating the matter. "Start packing up and bon voyage!" She held the animals securely against her chest and left in a hurry. Espera's mother saw the secretary leaving with the chickens and fumed with rage. She made an effort to run after her, but her husband dissuaded her. "Two chickens are not going to put us in poverty," he cautioned her.

Esperanza took the ticket and read it. She looked at her parents and said, "I am starting to pack." She ran home, locked her room door and threw herself on the bed. During the resting period, she said, "And came my last week here... It was not my intention to leave this house, but under these circumstances... The man I loved never came back to me. I have not seen him for years. He broke our relations. Why did he do that to me? I am twenty-five years old. I can't wait any longer. I want to create my own family." She laid her head on the side of the pillow and cried.

CHAPTER XXX

Espera in Chile and Argentina

Dear reader, double your energy and follow with diligence the episodes that lead to the finale. Let us keep an eye on Espera, as her marital agenda unfolds. And Felix? Where is he? Well, we need a bit more of patience before we reconnect with him.

Espera's brother cohabited with a female companion. His sister, aside the language barrier, had some difficulties of cultural character that did not allow her to mingle with his friend. She came from a rural area and had hard time adjusting to city life. She despised the maquillage and perfume that her brother's friend lavishly used and looked with suspicion to manicure and pedicure, let alone smoking cigarettes. Not being able to work for being a tourist, she spent most of the day dusting furniture, washing dishes and mopping floors. In hot, sultry days, she loved to take care of the flowers in the garden and water the grass which got dry rather quickly. In the evening, she prepared the meal for her brother and her friend. Many times, he invited her to join them in city restaurants, but she shied away. She did not trust the chefs and preferred her own cuisine. Beside these menial domestic chores, she preferred to sit on the porch and knit. At least, it was another excuse to not mingle too often with the other lady of the house. Knitting for her was not only a pastime, but also a relaxing vehicle that interrupted her daily routine. Late in the evening, she enjoyed watching the ladies go by and analyze their hair style and walking habits.

Her brother never contradicted her in her wishes, but hoped for her a stable future. After a while, she complained to Floris that she did not want to be a burden to her brother any longer. Her boyfriend, always sensitive to her feelings and needs, put in motion the political machine and, through his friends' intermediaries, expedited the VISA modalities and purchased a flight ticket at a local travel agency. According to international law agreement between Argentina and Chile, she could only travel as a tourist. The Argentine Immigration Office allowed her to stay only three months. Upon her arrival at Mendoza, her top priority was to arrange a vis a vis meeting with a priest who spoke Italian.

The flight from Santiago to Mendoza was flawless. The airplane made a smooth landing. Espera got excited and stood on her feet. The hostess gently requested her to remain seated until the aircraft reached a complete stop. Floris and his family welcomed her with big bunches of red flowers. The other passengers were astonished by the exuberant behavior of her presupposed relatives and the show of emotions that they exhibited. Floris extracted the army ID card from his wallet and the police stood immediately on the attention. The same policeman assisted Espera with the baggage at the check point. Espera was surprised that she did not have to open the suitcase. One by one, in the welcoming party, hugged and kissed the newcomer. A couple of little girls presented her flowers and boxes of chocolates. Espera was overwhelmed by such a tribute of love and sympathy. Her boyfriend saved her from additional compliments from friends and accommodated her in his car right in front of the exit. He smiled at the onlookers and whisked her away.

In the evening, Zanzara and her daughters planned a surprise party for Espera and, although, she was tired, she complied with their plan. A local band, composed of high school students, played mostly tango music. At first, Espera refused to dance, but, upon Floris' insistence, she submitted to his wishes. "You know, you make me look like a monkey. I don't know how to dance. Why did you insist?" Protested Espera.

"Just keep on moving your feet. Nobody pays attention."

"I don't know anybody here. I feel like running away."

"Don't be silly. Argentineans are good people. They mind their business. Yes, they are so passionately involved in dancing the tango that they are oblivious of what goes around them."

A long applause broke out in the crowd. Espera thought it was directed to her and blushed. Her face got red fire. She covered it with both hands and leaned over Floris. Two top tango dancers had just arrived and the guests recognized them. They made circles around them and showered them with compliments. Floris had invited them hoping to make the evening more interesting and memorable. The band started all over again and the dancers got in the center of the room to display their artistic vocation. Young waiters carried around trays of food and beverages. From time to time they yelled, "Beban el mate que te mata! Espera got scarred and withdrew in a corner. Her boyfriend reassured her that no one was going to kill her. She felt relieved and rushed to the chair next to her future sisters'-in-law. She looked around and saw about twenty empty wine bottles. The waitresses came along and cleared the table. It was midnight and many guests were a bit wobbly. Esperanza remembered that in the morning she and Floris had an appointment with the priest to make the two weeks wedding. She motioned to him to get close to her. He held a bottle of beer in his hand and his face turned luminous. "Do you remember that tomorrow we have an important meeting?"

"We do? The night is still young. Let's enjoy it."

"Be serious! It is late already. Thank everybody and close the shop."

"The shop? What shop? This is not a shop, my dear."

"You know what I mean. It is time to sleep."

"Wait a bit longer."

Espera did not like Floris' attitude. Half an hour later, she approached the light switch and began to blink it for a while. Floris tried to resist, but the professional dancers got the message and left in a hurry pretending that they had another commitment. Once they departed, the rest of the guests followed suit.

CHAPTER XXXI

The Interview

The two love birds tried their luck with the church of San Daniel. Floris was not especially interested in going there. The past week, the priest acted like the Italian clergyman. In fact, he announced that he did not like the coins in the basket. He became even more daring by stating that he would deny the absolution to those who dropped coins at Sunday collection. The parishioners considered the priestly position aggressive and counterproductive. Many of them changed parish; others, contributed whatever they could afford.

"This guy must have read the incident that occurred in Italy. I think that communication is running smoothly between them," commented Floris.

"In my modest opinion, I say that they are money hungry," commented his sister.

"Not cecessarily," interrupted her Floris. "In our modern society it is hard to survive. Workers go on strike to demand higher wages, vacations, insurances, pensions and what else. I never heard of any strike promoted or advocated by priests. Many of them live in a state of poverty. Now, I deplore the threat of denying the absolution..."

"I like money too, but let us not waste time on this subject. We need to talk to him. By the way, do not bring up that subject. If you do, I never get out of this pothole."

The secretary was expecting the future spouses on the rectory threshold. The coffee aroma reached the nostrils and made them breathe better. The secretary led them to a small waiting room and informed them that the priest was unavailable temporarily. He had to rush to the hospital.

When they heard that, the two visitors looked at each other in dismay. Espera whispered in her boy friend's ear, "I told you I am not lucky. He had to end up in the hospital right now?"

Floris contested, "Yeah, he got sick at the right time."

"If it is a serious case, he may stay there a couple of months and our plans will fly out of the window."

Floris started to scratch his bird. The secretary noticed their state of uneasiness and queries, "Is there anything I can do for you? May I offer a cup of coffee?" She asked.

"In other circumstances, I would have accepted it," replied Floris. "My girlfriend is getting nervous because we don't know when he is going to be able to officiate the mass again."

"Tomorrow, for sure" she assured them.

Espera tried to shake off her incredulity, "How can that be possible if he is in the hospital?"

"That's exactly what I would like to say," added Floris, making the secretary's assertion unsustainable.

"Oh, no, you both misunderstood," tried the secretary to reassure them.

"Not, I, maybe, she did not understand." Then, he retracted his words and said, "We both understood quite well."

The secretary put both hands on her chest and cried out, "Oh, no, he went to the hospital to visit a patient. Actually, he is there now to attend him in his final days. I am here to comply with his instructions and I will try to answer any question that you may have."

Both visitors expressed simultaneously a feeling of relief and exultation, "Urrah!" they shouted. "We misunderstood you. Now we are in business," said Floris.

Espera whispered some suggestions in Italian to Floris, but the secretary interrupted her, "You can speak your language if you wish. I spent two years in Rome."

Espera took courage and said, "We would like to get married as soon as possible without making any announcement in the church bulletin."

"What's the rush?" was her spontaneous response. Then, she looked at Floris and smiled.

"No, it is not what you are thinking," was Floris' reply. "You are thinking about vagabond hormones rattling my mind, but it is not so, not in my case. I exercise self- control."

The secretary did not insist. She pulled a document from the drawer and said, "Before we stretch the conversation even further, you should fill this questionnaire and sign it at the bottom. It is written in Spanish and Italian."

Half way down, Floris stopped and exclaimed, "Oh, oh, we hit a hurdle."

The secretary jumped next to him and asked, "What do you mean?"

He pointed at his girlfriend and stated, "She is a tourist. As I stated earlier, we prefer not to make any public announcement. Someone may call the immigration office and expatriate her."

The secretary looked concerned. "At the beginning, I wasn't sure what your intentions were."

Espera whispered in Floris'ear in Neapolitan dialect, "Should we take the chance?"

"Definitely not!" he responded in a defiant tone. "If a spy among the community informs the immigration office about your current status and what you are up to, they will deport you immediately. Do you realize the consequences? They may never allow you to step on this soil again because you violated their law."

Espera shivered in hearing the word 'deportation.'. To return to Italy it would have meant failure. She would have felt the brunt of the romantic debacle for the rest of her life. Her family would not have forgiven her. They would have cursed, rejected and repudiated her. She stood silent for a while waiting on Floris next move. He looked at the secretary and inquired if she could contact the priest.

"What would you want me to ask him?" She replied in a compassionate tone.

"Maybe we can circumvent the hurdles around us by marrying in the sacristy. We would kill a couple of birds with one stone"

In that moment, the priest opened the door and greeted them, "Good morning! I apologize for the tardiness."

Espera and Floris got up and bowed. They felt relieved that he came back. The priest took a seat at his chair and exclaimed, "What can I do for you?"

The secretary got close to his desk and reported to him in a nutshell their intentions. He was about to take the floor when Floris prevented him by saying, "Father, we would like to avoid an elaborate public ceremony. It is not in our style. If we marry in the sacristy, we could cut the expenses and the malicious tongues."

"Father, I am a farmer," added Espera. "I am short of money. I cannot afford a costly wedding. And, then, we do not wish to bother the law."

The priest covered his eyes with both hands and immersed in what appeared to be a long, endless meditation. Eventually, he snapped out of it with a sigh of relief on the part of everybody and said, "You have known each other for a year and one half, which is in your favor. The church has no qualms about it even though it prefers a longer period of acquaintance."

Floris looked at his girlfriend and made a gesture of satisfaction. She did the same.

The priest continued, "I love to unite you in the holy matrimony, but I am bound by the canon law of the Church and the law of the country..." He got up and started to walk back and forth in his office. After a couple of rounds, he stopped and fixed his eyes on Floris, "If my mind serves me well, I have seen your picture on the newspaper. You are national hero. Am I correct?"

Floris gave him a stern look, grabbed Espera by the arm and led her in a hurry out of the rectory. The priest followed them up to the entrance steps and stretched his arms forward in a vain attempt to change their minds. "Eh, wait a minute!" he hollered, but the wind blew those words in the infinite space.

At home, Floris manifested a euphoric mood that that made Esperanza wonder about his state of mind. She laid her head on the kitchen table and refused to eat. "If I knew what I was going through, I would have never left my town. I do not understand the church or the government," she said emphatically.

"It is not the government, my dear," responded Floris. "Some laws are flawed. I am not going to call anybody on this private matter. The public is not entitled to know my marital plans."

"What am I supposed to do now? Pack up again? I feel exhausted," said a disgruntled Espera.

Antonio Casale

"Stay calm, darling! My only worry is that the priest may contact the immigration office."

"If it is for that, I don't think that he is going to lower himself to that level."

"For him, it is not a question of piety, my dear, but of justice. He may be reprimanded by the bishop if he does not report us to the government, assuming that a deep throat will send the message." He paused a few seconds and his face got bright. "I have an idea! If I stay here listening to you, I may lose the initial enthusiasm that I felt on the way back from the church."

"What do you propose?" she inquired with curiosity.

"There is only one way out of this jungle. We must act secretly and expeditiously." He picked up the phone and dialed a few numbers. A young voice, at the other end of the line, answered. "Floris, how in the world are you? I fought with you side to side at the Malvinas. How can I help you?"

"I need a favor from, my old jackass," and explained to him his drama.

His friend felt sorry to hear his problem, but he was also excited to hear from him. He assured Floris that he was honored to refer it to his dad. "I will get back to you as soon as I talk to him. I will take care of it.

"Thanks a million, bud,' replied Floris.

It was dark when Floris and Espera left their abode. He was dressed in a white suite with red tie, while she wore a pink dress with a white rose in her hair. A group of family members and a selected small number of close friends accompanied them. The justice of peace invited the bride and groom to line up in front of him. From then on, everybody observed a strict silence.

The judge made some preliminary comments, added his observation of the law abiding on the spouses and proceeded directly to the central core of the ceremony. "Floris, do you take Espera for your wife for better and for worse, in poverty and richness, in health and sickness until death will take you apart?"

Floris plunged his eyes in those of Espera and answered, "Yes, I do."

"Espera, are you going to be faithful to your husband for the rest of your life without questioning him on his week-end card games and beer party?"

The guests burst into a roaring laughter and for a couple of minutes the ceremony was stalled. The Justice of Peace appeared serious as ever. Espera felt utterly embarrassed and, turning her attention to Floris, asked him, "Did you tell him to say that? What kind of questions are these?"

Floris denied it with his head, but could not stop laughing. Espera got bold and asked the judge, "How come you changed the language? How come you did not ask him the same thing you asked me?"

At that point, the judge could not hold back his humor anymore and laughed wholeheartedly. The audience, eventually, exhausted its exuberance and everything normalized.

the judge took the control of the ceremony once again and said, "Do you Mr. ciga....(He was going to say 'cigarette', but refrained just on time. Had he finished the word, he would have interrupted the ceremony for the second time and he would have created a ridiculous atmosphere. He repeated. "You, Mr. Floris, do you wish to bind in the holy matrimony with Espera?"

"I do," a confused bride replied.

"By the authority invested in me by the city of Mendoza, I pronounce you husband and wife," stated the lawman. At the request of the guests, the groom tried to kiss again the bride, but she pulled away and said, "What's going on here? What strange costumes do you have? I means, don't you have a bit of shame to do these things in the presence of strangers?"

Floris' relatives did not appreciate her comments and expressed some doubt about the validity of the ceremony, but the judge assured them that it was perfectly valid. To put to rest unnecessary arguments, the newlywed kissed each other and the guests launched flowers and confetti on them. Someone from the outside window shouted, "I don't believe that she is ready for marriage." The intruder caused some havoc among the wedding party, but he got chased away quickly. As soon as order was restored, the judge addressed the bride and groom for the last time, "Sign both documents. Tomorrow, my secretary will take them to the courthouse and you will be legally recorded. You, Espera, are a citizen of your adopted country."

Everybody applauded. "Champagne! Champagne!" shouted everybody.

"We will have an official party very shortly. Tomorrow, I will send the invitations. And now, let's celebrate!"

His wife said to him. "Why do you want the party for? Don't you think that this is enough?"

"We have overcome many obstacles. What we are going to have in a month is something we longed for a long time. We deserve it. Don't you think so? A month is not far away. After all, guests need time to prepare themselves for the great event. They have to make arrangements, plans, buy gifts... You will see. The reception should be a blockbuster."

His wife did not have the time to respond that their older brother-in-law with a beer can in his hands shouted, "You didn't even kiss your bride."

"Yes, I did. Ask her.!"

"On the cheek!"

Espera rebuked him "Aren't you ashamed to talk like that in public? Show some moderation."

The youngest brother-in-law remarked, "If I were in your place, I would have smooched with her to no end. I don't like cold fish."

"Knock it off," reproached him Floris. "You sound like a crow. We have just made the knot. Give us time to know each other better."

Espera got irritated by their invasion of privacy and answered them with a rough tone, "Why don't both of you mind your business." Floris intervened and brought the boiling minds to cool off.

The wedding party went on as scheduled. The news reached St. Daniel's rectory, and the priest was deeply disappointed. "We have lost two more sheep and we will lose many more in the future. I wonder if this is real love." He scratched his head and sank on his chair.

The weeks went by and there was no sign of pregnancy on the part of Espera. Her mother-in-law and her daughters did a lot of shopping in the department stores and amassed an incredible amount of baby's clothes. The news did not come and they started to twist their lips in a gesture of disappointment. Soon, the gestures turned into words and words became swords. A relative said, "One of them has to be sterile, otherwise, it is hard to explain this deadlock."

The rumors intensified and Espera, against her will, decided to see an oncologist who concluded that there was no chromosome imbalance in her blood. Floris too underwent a medical checkup and the results were the same. Both medical reports indicated that stress blocked the fertility process. Nine months later a baby girl arrived and a jubilation mood hung over the family.

The family grew and Floris discovered inner business qualities. His first activities centered on car wash.

His wife gave him all her support and joined him in his work. They bought apartments houses that required around the clock vigil. When the drains clogged up, she put on high boots, lowered herself in the hole and cleared it from all sorts of debris. In the afternoon, she rushed home to prepare supper for the family. In winter months, the job was much more demanding due to the adverse weather conditions. Water solidified on the floor, where the cars stood to be washed, and created hills of ice. Soon, it became a safety issue. Car washers had the most difficult time to stand up. Many opted to hold on balance on a flat spot or two and did their best to rinse the vehicles. Even the walls left nothing to imagination. Huge chunks of ice, reminiscent of spectacles seen only in the North Pole, hung from the side walls and prevented any one from seeking protection in case of a fall. There was an additional reason why Espera was so active in keeping the system under control.

"Floris," she said to her husband, "If someone slips and breaks his back, he will sue us in a court of law. We will end up paying for medical expenses, work liability and we may lose our shirt too." This was her main concern. To relieve pressure on her, he made some contacts to purchase a bar or liquor store. A close friend of him had this to say about it, "If he wants to pursue that goal, it is fine, but it is an insidious effort to expand his personal preferences. Espera is the real wind behind his wings."

The car wash business was exhausting in time and energy. She suggested to her husband to switch to an ice cream parlor. The positions of both of them were wide apart. The real cause, as it was evidenced later, came from his debilitating physical conditions.

A dark cloud appeared on the horizon of their future and they dropped the project altogether. Floris underwent a check- up and was diagnosed with an intestinal pathology that worsened in the course of the years making him irritable and inapproachable, at times. To avoid any internal dispute that would have eroded their marriage,

Espera found a job in a nearby factory. To those who questioned her real motivations, she replied that the financial burden had become unbearable.

To ease the pain of what appeared to be a long and agonizing fight with his health problems. Floris resorted to card and bocce games with his friends during the week-ends. Espera complained consistently that he neglected her too often, but to no avail. Finally, she tried to gain support from her mother-in-law, "He goes out to enjoy two days a week with those fish heads of his friends playing and drinking. He comes home late wobbling and I have to put him in bed because he is incapable of taking off his clothes and shoes."

"What do you want him to do? He is a man. He has the right to have good time. Don't you understand that it is a valve to discharge his frustrations? Why do you want to take that away from him?" tried to defend him her mother-in-law.

"His brothers-in-law are the primary culprits," insisted Espera. If they do not invite him or if they don't go, my husband will stay home."

"Don't dramatize" responded resentfully the old woman. "My son works hard the whole week. Do you wish to take away from him even that little enjoyment that he has. Does he deprive you of anything?"

"I need help at home with these four children. If he doesn't, I am going to quit working next month."

"Don't get out of hand. I am helping you. Don't I?"

"I don't need your help. I need him to stay home."

"Think of what you come from and where you are now. Stop complaining," insisted visibly annoyed the old woman.

To avoid further antagonism with her mother-in-law, Espera moved elsewhere in the house to attend to the omnipresent domestic chores.

Floris's business kept on flourishing. He purchased a farm and a movie theater. At the beginning, to make the income equate to the outcome, he got up early in the morning and worked up to very late at night. One evening, he came home exhausted. In the driveway, he called on his wife for help. Thinking that it was an emergency case, she rushed out. The sight of boxes alarmed her. "Why in the world you hide in these boxes?" she inquired. She opened them and found cases of beer. "What do you need them for?" she asked with apprehension.

"If we have guests, we should have something to offer. Don't you agree?"

"Oh, my heaven, this husband of mine is addicted and addiction of anything is the antechamber of destruction."

Floris made another attempt to win over her favor, "They were on sale and when beer is on sale, I don't hesitate to jump on it."

"Last night, you finished a case by yourself. Can you change a bit your lifestyle/?" she implored him.

"Why should I? I am happy in the way I am. Unhappy people have to make a change."

"Yeah, but you let others pay the consequences of your behavior."

"Knock it off! I don't bother anybody."

"One of these days, I am going to disappear from this house and your life and then you see how you deal with your happiness."

Floris got upset and said, "You are not the only woman around. Do you realize that?"

His wife looked at him in a challenging posture and took off.

A proverb states, "Lucky with money, unlucky with love." The business kept on thriving and Floris was elected president of the local Entrepreneur Chapter. To celebrate the occasion, he invited a few friends at his residence. At the agreed time, Floris welcomed them with a white towel on the shoulders and a high turban on the head. After the preliminaries, he called their attention and said, "This evening we wish to celebrate not just success, but friendship." He filled a glass of beer from a keg, raised it above his head and exclaimed, "To the blond beauty."

The guests looked at each other a bit in disarray and asked, "What about us?"

He smiled and said, "This beauty is inexhaustible. Drink from her beauty. She will be available the whole night"

"Urrah! Long life to the blond lady! Long life to the president!" They shouted. A cluster of people soon surrounded the keg and the foam rose to the brim of every glass. Floris filled a huge mug and sat on the porch bench. A friend followed him, took a pack of cigarettes out of his pants pocket and offered him one. He accepted it and began to smoke. Espera approached her husband in an aggressive mood, "How many times I have to repeat myself?"

"On what?" he queried.

"You are not supposed to drink or smoke. The doctor told me that you have liver problems."

"He did not tell me that. He spoke of intestinal problems."

"That was before. Now he has finished the tests."

"You know more than I do," he stated with a fastidious gesture. "He allows me to drink moderately."

"Drinking a case of beer is not equivalent to using moderation," she replied with force.

Another guest arrived. He pulled a cigarette from his shirt pocket and offered one to Floris. Espera begged him to refuse it, but he ignored her. "Leave me alone! I need my good time."

Espera felt desperate. She ran to her bedroom and locked the door. It was graduation time for their oldest daughter. Floris prepared a lavish party in her honor. He rented a tent and set on the front lawn of his house. About two- hundred guests showed up. Espera disapproved the unusual high number of guests, but contained her chagrin. She did not want to spoil her daughter's happiness. Her husband sat next and was cracking jokes. His wife leaned over him and said, "Why do we need all this beer for? Not everybody drinks it."

"Honey, baby, it is better an abundance than a lack of it. It is impossible to predict the peoples' thirst for this blond lady. Let me take care of it. You take charge of the cooking."

Espera was a great cook. She had prepared eggplants, sausages, peppers and meatballs for the great occasion and did not want to appear stingy to relatives and guests coming all the way from Canada and Italy. What made her even more upset was a lady that her husband hired to make tattoos on anyone who wished to have them on their skin. Espera considered it wasted money and made no bones about it. In the midst of so many misunderstanding and disputes, there was one more left. Floris hired a local band that played rock and roll and jazz music so loudly that the neighbors called on the police to curb down the volume. Unfortunately, no police car showed up and the tribulation lasted until the first hours of the morning.

Espera had amassed a huge amount of food and beverages for the graduation party; however, it did not seem to be sufficient. Hoards of young people, pretending to be the graduate's friends, attracted by the inviting food flavors and the rumors they heard about the beer availability, invaded the party space and joined the crowd. Espera was ready to lock the door at them, but her daughter intervened on their behalf. Her father backed her up and asked his wife to cook more for the hungry youth. Boys and girls, like a swarm of aunts, plundered the food supplies and satisfied their thirst by emptying the kegs of beer. Espera warned her husband to close the doors for the night. She was afraid that if they got drunk and caused problems, they would be responsible before the law. Floris showed signs of vacillation on his legs. His eyes were half closed. He stuttered, "There is nothing wrong into it," he answered.

Espera's reaction was vehement. She grabbed a dish and smashed it against the wall. The intervention of family members avoided a displeasing end. The crowd outside was unaware of the dispute. Indeed, one of them approached Floris and asked him, "Show us that you can stand on one foot and we will believe that you are not inebriated." Floris was oblivious to their request and sank on a chair. The dead weight that fell quickly on it almost broke the seat. He raised one foot and kept the other on the ground. "As you can see, I am not drunk," he assured them. The crowd saw him in good humor and cracked jokes. That was the last time Floris spoke during the evening. Beer and wine were too powerful for him and he submitted tacitly to their sedative, destructive force. He fell asleep and woke up very late the following morning. When his wife reminded him of how he made a fool of himself the previous night, he replied with a "No comment."

With the fumes of the party over, Espera's friends gathered at her house to gossip over the past event. The author is bound by promise not to reveal all the secrets that emerged from the conversations, but something, I believe, the reader can and should find out. One of the neighbors wasted no time in decrying the behavior of the youth, "They were shouting and played so loudly that almost burst my glass windows."

A lady, sitting next to her, added, "Floris could have stopped their vulgar language too, but he was having good time and was in no condition to stop them."

Espera lowered her head and replied in a low voice that, at times, appeared inaudible to human ear, "I had the chance to marry my first love, but I blew it." She stared each one in their eyes and said, "Please, keep this secret, otherwise, our friendship is over."

"Why didn't you marry him?" asked one of them.

"Our families were constantly feuding. They were killing each other for no apparent reason. At the end, we paid the consequences."

"I hope you don't mind my daring, but your husband claims that you are unapproachable. You are an excellent housewife; a great mother, you keep the house neat, cook three times a day, you helped him in his business, but as a wife you lack ability to love."

"He is full of baloney," responded Espera. Men are all the same. They want their wives to work like slaves all day long and, then, they expect them to be romantic.

"It is not just that," replied the woman. "He considers your manners inadequate for a modern wife."

"In your opinion, is it acceptable to drink a case of beer, wobble around and have a breath that smells of liquor?"

A lady who had been listening up to that moment said, "Espera, he made no bones about it during the party. In several occasions he claimed that you don't kiss him."

"It is very honorable for him to make those comments in public, isn't? Would you kiss your husband if he smells of smoke and beer?"

"I tell him to brush his teeth."

Everybody laughed for a while without restriction. The youngest among them called their undivided attention and said, "Let us be serious for a moment. You cannot expect that a man brushes his teeth if sits on a keg of beer every night and smokes a pack of cigarettes a day. It is unrealistic. The foul smell that he carries around is enough to kill a horse. He should quit altogether drinking and smoking. I am surprised that his doctor has not ordered him to do so."

Espera replied, "My husband makes his own rules."

The days passed by slowly and Floris was feeling uncomfortably. This time, he had no choice, but to see a specialist because his health was deteriorating. At a specified date, he brought along a close friend. In case of a bad news, he did not wish to scare his wife. The physical examination lasted more than an hour. At the end, the medical examiner discharged him recommending him to avoid stress. As soon as the results were going to be available, he would send them to his family doctor. The elevator was crowded. Floris managed to get in, while his friend remained out. Instead of waiting for another elevator, he went back to the doctor's office and asked him, "Doc, is there anything serious?"

"Are you his brother or relative?"

"No, we are buddies since childhood."

"Well, I cannot provide a diagnosis at the moment. As I said previously, we have to wait for the clinical analysis."

"I understand that, but could you give me a professional opinion."

The doctor took off his spectacles and wiped his eyes with a white handkerchief he kept in the interior of his jacket. "My guess is that a liver condition is developing at an alarming speed. The medicine that I will prescribe him, pending on the results, could very well slow down the pathology."

"What do you think can deteriorate his condition?"

"Alcohol and smoke are the principal culprits."

"You mean they are so fundamental in the liver's survival?"

The doctor twisted the lips and said, "I am afraid they are. It all depends on the extent of the existing damage." The nurse arrived and said, "Other patients are waiting for you." The doctor apologized and left. Floris' friend remained immobile for a couple of minutes. He remembered that Floris was waiting for him and rushed to the elevator. When he finally got out of the elevator, he stopped and got engaged in a brief soliloquy. Floris, instead of asking him the reason for not boarding the elevator with him, said, "Do you have money in the bank?"

"I wish I did."

The return trip was characterized by gloomy remarks, depressive mood and feelings of doom on the part of Floris. His friend tried to encourage him by depicting a scenario of hope and healing. "How nice it is for a person who is out of serious problem," He paused a moment and added, "How good it is for a survivor to express his sympathy to a wife whose husband just passed away." He got pensive and said, "It is human nature. There is nothing you can do about it. You go to a hospital to visit a man on the verge of death and you try to encourage him, but in your heart you feel good that you are not in his place. I don't blame anyone. That's the way we are."

His close friend reprimanded him, "These are not reflections that are conducive to good health!"

With winter approaching, Floris spent most of the evenings with his two close friends. Floris made no bones about it in public and when his favorite guests did not show up on their own volition he called them. Espera knew that her friend's husband had a sweet tooth and placed on the table always a plate of cookies. At their arrival, Floris used to go to the cellar in search of a few bottles of beer that he kept in the refrigerator ridge ready to extinguish his never ending thirst. Before he took off the top, he touched them. The touch resembled a caress to someone dear. The cold liquor gave him a soothing effect. He felt elated as if he were communicating with a mysterious world. His wife hollered at him."One bottle is not enough?" Her husband did not respond. He cleaned the bottle with the napkin, twisted the cap slowly with his rough fingers and sipped it. "How good it is! It is delicious! You and I are going to have fun," he remarked. He took a few steps and sank in the reclining chair. For each bottle, the ritual was the same. However, after a while, his belly looked bloated. The ashtray in front of him was full. His friend said, "I am glad you are happy."

"It is going to be better later," responded Floris.

"Your wife will make sure it will be at your satisfaction"

"If it was up to her, forget it. She is a cold fish."

His wife got tired and answered, "You should be ashamed of yourself. If you had another wife, I wonder where you would be. I do everything for you. I even shine your shoes, polish your gun prior to the hunting season; I prepare your food; and I take care of your children. What else do you expect me to do? You should have married an American woman... She would have taught you a great lesson."

"You don't understand," replied her husband with both eyes half closed. "American women belong to another hemisphere."

His friend interrupted him. "Listen to me. I lived in the State of Nevada for ten years and I can tell you that those women are great workers. Their only debility is that when they finish working they go for the "already made". They disdain cooking and love restaurants. They invented the immediate gratification way of life."

Floris made another attempt to talk, "There is nothing wrong with it. I go for it."

His wife looked at him sternly and said, "You should be ashamed of yourself!"

"Is it all you know how to say?" responded her husband in a sudden moment of lucidity.

Her female friend kept on raising her right hand hoping that her turn to talk would come soon. Finally, she spoke, "I saw a lot of wrong things in America."

Immediately after, it was her friend's turn to call attention. She continued, "Once, I attended a party. I saw two men at the center of the stage. One of them, turned to his companion and declared, "I like to introduce you my husband."

"Is there a law for gay marriage?" inquired Floris.

Espera interjected, "Nothing surprises me anymore. First they push for contraceptives and now they promote same sex marriage. The other day in New York Park a boy and a girl were caught in intimate posture. What a broth!"

Floris had a surge of revival and said,"Go for the gold!" He tried to turn a dim light on his side, but did not succeed. "There is nothing wrong with it," he kept on. "There are a lot worse things than intimate behavior. How should I put it? Maybe, they did not choose the proper place. Look at what goes on in the streets of the major cities. They are flooded with beggars, drug dealers, mafiosi and peddlers. Isn't better that young people love each other? We would have a peaceful society without violence and materialism."

His close friend interrupted him, "Your rationale is valid to a certain extent. For the rest, you are going to the extremes. The truth is that our society has become a factory, a machine that produces products based on false ideologies. For years, we have been selling to the public relativistic trash. We have been witnessing to the decay of social fabric everywhere. People protest in every street, in every corner, in every plaza, in every city about freedom of anything. You never see them demanding respect,decency and honor."

"Now, you make sense," Espera responded.

"Thank you," he said, "But there is more. Look at the ever changing world of fashion. If a girl does not meet the new guidelines, she is considered an old egg."

His wife followed up, "I agree. That type of girl is looked upon as an outsider, a gypsy, an anti-modernist and anti-progressivist."

"Morality emerges only at certain times and at certain places," emphasized her husband. "We use morality only to criticize or defend ourselves."

"What does all of this has to do with those two young people you mentioned before?" protested Floris.

His friend replied, "We are producing a hedonistic generation. We have nothing to be proud of.

The basic, fundamental notion of civic, religious and professional values is missing. People have an empty head and a drowsy mind. Nothing seems to challenge them anymore."

Espera said, "I agree with you. Even the animals behave better. We should take lessons from them.

"Let's not exaggerate," responded Floris while he was trying to find a better posture on the reclining chair. As he got comfortable, he turned to his wife and said, "Honey, baby, do you want to go to sleep now?"

"You are crazy! I am going to sleep on the couch tonight."

Espera did not wait too long to externalize her feelings to her best friend, "My husband was very sloppy during the graduation party. One part of the shirt was hanging down the pants. On the right hand, he held a pack of cigarettes, in the other, a can of beer. I am disappointed and ashamed at times."

Her friend made some hilarious remarks that instead of alleviating the tension, contributed to increase it, "Listen! Your husband loves beer. It is common knowledge. He is a champion. There is nothing you can do about it."

"Why, your husband doesn't drink?" responded resentfully Espera.

"Definitely not! He has only occasional drink and only if he is in good company."

"Well, then, he has other defects. Nobody is immune from them."

Her friend decided with good reason to drop the issue to avoid any unnecessary confrontation.

Espera cultivated her friendship only with two ladies. They were born in the same town where they had frequent contacts during the week. Their friendship continued uninterrupted when they moved to Mendoza where they both a house in the same block. Indeed, through the years, one of Espera's close friends married a teacher. The other, instead, joined knots with a prominent local politician. They visited each others' house on a daily basis and shared the evening meals or coffee quite often. It was not uncommon that during the moments of solitude Espera would turn to them to open her heart," I made a big mistake. I should have waited a bit longer."

"What's going on?" inquired the teacher's wife. "Are you having second thoughts?"

"I don't mean that. Felix truly loved me."

"Do you have any contact with him?"

"The last I heard he is married in Brazil, but he may have moved to California. I have scanty news of him."

Her friend placed her hand on Esperanza's shoulders and murmured, "It is too late now. You cannot undo what you have done."

"I am a married woman and I have a great respect for the ring I wear," she concluded.

September came. It was vintage month. Floris made wine and drank enough during and after the fermentation process. His older brother-in-law cautioned him not to exceed the limits. The wine was not seasoned yet and it could cause him harm. "It is better to wait until February when it is time to pour wine into another barrel and get rid of the deposit."

Floris replied with a traditional saying, "At St. Martin a bottle with wine." In the course of testing it, his eyesight got a bit blurry. To those who criticized him for overdrinking, he said, "I can see very clearly that this wine is excellent."

A harsh voice from behind him ordered him to stop. "You had more than enough," thundered Espera.

"I can see you," replied Floris in a tenuous voice. His wife was furious.

He took a glass of wine and handed it to her. "Take it. This is my wine."

"I can see it. You are the only one who is drinking it. Now, if you don't quit, I am going to leave this house," she replied enraged. She ran upstairs and paused in front of the mirror. She looked disheveled. The hair was in disarray. The wrinkles had caused deep furrows on her forehead. Her lips were livid. She backed up a few feet and fell on the bed.

Below, Floris looked at the teacher and said, "She wants to go see her ex- boyfriend, but I have news for him. He blew it. I stole her from him. He thought he had everything figured out, but I outsmarted him."

Espera did not hear him. After a while, she did not think it was proper to leave her closest friends abruptly and returned to converse with them. In the kitchen, she placed a big dish of sweets and the teacher's eyes glowed. Five minutes passed and Espera looked at the dish almost empty and went to the freezer to take out more cookies. The conversation suddenly changed course and the mood too. "I would love to visit Italy," said Espera. "I have not seen my family for fifteen years. I wonder about my father's well being. He is old and still works on the farm. I hear that my mother doesn't know how to operate the wash machine. My sisters have finished college and got a government's job. Next week, I am going to set aside some clothes for them. I want to pack up little by little. I do not want to be unprepared by the time I have to fly."

"You have a year of time," protested the teacher.

"Not really...I am going to look for air ticket discounts. Next days, I will call the travel agency."

"Remember not to overload the suitcase. They charge you for overweight."

"Well, I have to bring salt, pepper and cereals. It is not a bad idea to bring also toilet paper."

"I would not be concerned with such items. Times have changed. Italy has the best quality food in the world. If you give them cheap clothes, they are going to throw them in the garbage can. They find an abundance of it in the market each Wednesday. Not to mention the ... In your place, I would go to Plaza del Libertador. There are good department stores. You can buy Bisquick with 'Just add water.' " They love pancakes with syrup. Don't bring American coffee. They drink Expresso."

"Wow!" She exclaimed. "All of a sudden, America is there... Do you realize that I am unemployed and my husband is sick?'"

Espera's claim that she was poor did not convince her friends at all. They did not display any gesture of disapproval or made any derogatory comment in her presence. The news, however, spread at light speed and travelled to other countries as well. Some of her relatives and friends disputed her claim and debated on whether or not they were going to make a collection. When the rumor reached Espera's ears, she disdained the whole concept and stated that people were jealous of her and threatened false friends to carry on that ridiculous campaign. Since then, no one dared to carry on the plan new series of tests. The results came after two weeks and he was diagnosed with a terrible disease. He was affected by cirrhosis of the liver. Transplants were in the embryonic stage and the patient who ventured in the operation inevitably succumbed after a few weeks or months. Espera appeared devastated by the news. She lost appetite and, consequently, she kept on urging her husband to abandon completely the use of liquor and cigarettes. Whenever she confronted him on those issues, he would reply that the impact they had on the liver was insignificant. To sustain his claim, he would stretch his right arm and say, "See? I don't shake." In other instances, he changed his defensive language and stated, "I am not a drunk and, as far as smoking is concerned, it affects the lungs not the liver." His wife was livid. She called the doctors and asked them to reprimand her husband, who in the face of such a danger, was acting recklessly." To allay her apprehension, the doctors decided to keep him under observation at St. Gerolamus' Hospital.

Floris spent the first week on the second floor of the hospital, room 114. Across from him, his cousin was also fighting for her life. Floris' room day by day assumed the aspect of a sanctuary and friends and relatives from of all walks of life came in as pilgrims and stood in line to pay him homage. His wife got annoyed from the immense popularity that her husband enjoyed, but could do nothing to slow down the flux of the visitors. In the midst of such public support, Floris felt optimistic and ventured to state that he was undergoing additional tests and expected to be home in a matter of days. A moral boost came in the following days by the chief surgeon who explained to him that a surgery was not conceived in the immediate future. Instead, he changed his previous position by stating that, due to the most recent progress in transplant research in California, he would consider him as a serious candidate. For that reason, he suggested the patient to remain in the hospital until further notice.

The longer Floris stayed in the hospital, the more it dimmed Espera's hopes. She began to show symptoms of fatigue. She spent most of the time at her husband's side, even at night. She disliked hospital's food and skimmed many meals. As a result, she looked pale and emaciated. Her personal care suffered. Her hair looked disheveled and she wore the same clothes for days. Relatives and friends suggested her to take time off and rest, but to no avail.

Floris was getting restless. Time was flying and no decision was taken. In view of a lack of a donor, the doctors had one alternative, but to inject chemo to slow down and destroy the cancerous cells. Espera was utterly concerned. Chemo in the bloodstream would destroy also the healthy cells. The chief doctor offered his position, "We cannot wait anymore for a donor. We have no idea when or if it comes. Initially, there was one available, but for some unexplainable causes, it was considered inefficient. The only solution, right now, is chemo. If the body resists, we will win the battle."

"What is the guarantee?" asked Espera.

"I cannot give any guarantee. It all depends on the immune system and how the body reacts."

There was no other choice. With the daily dosage of chemo, Floris' body got weaker and the stomach was incapable of digesting the food. His best friend, the teacher, did his best during the three months of visitation and tried to inject in him another vision of life, "I don't mean to preach to you at this stage of your life. Nobody told me, but I am sold on faith. Without it, there is no salvation. He noticed Floris' progressive parabolic descent and increased the religious language. The sick man maintained a cognitive exuberance despite his body did not respond anymore effectively to the various functions. The specialist, however, was cognizant of the medical limitations and stopped visiting him. Espera got suspicious and fell into a depressive mood.

Espera and her two best friends were attending at Floris needs. He was exceptionally pensive and hardly talked. Actually, he could not talk. His wife, by every means, tried to open his mouth. When she realized that the efforts were useless, she turned around and suppressed the tears in a handkerchief. Not to show that she was experiencing an emotional crisis, she returned to the previous position. It was in that instant that she observed his hands and realized that they were swollen. He must have read his wife's thoughts and raised one hand to make a slight gesture. What followed was rather pathetic.

Espera and her two best friends, three visitors could not agree on the interpretation of the patient's wishes. By some obscure reasons, they finally came to the conclusion that what he really meant was a priestly visit. Later, this reading proved to be fallacious. What Floris really wanted to say was, "Go home. There is more hope."

In those sad circumstances, the two women sent the only able man available there to go in search of Father Gambito. Without delay, he descended in a hurry the stairs trying to save time and ran to the car. On the way to the church's rectory, he ran through many yellow lights. To his chagrin, the pastor did not appear at all happy at the urgent message just delivered to him and bluntly told the messenger that he had seen the patient before and there was nothing he could do about it. "After all, I have company," he added. There was a lot of noise in the kitchen. The man insisted, "Father, this is urgent. It is a question of life and death."

"I am sorry! I have guests here."

The messenger's eyes got clogged with tears. He turned around in silence and reported the gloomy message to the ladies. The news travelled on the wings of the wind throughout the city and behind it.

The media spared no time to attack the clergy with spicy headlines and most of the readers decried the event. Even the clergyman's closest friend took stand against him

Unfortunately, his parishioners began to question his behavior. According to them, he fell victim of bad habits and lost all his personal savings and money he borrowed from people. The church authorities miscalculated the prelate's ability to generate surprises. The parishioners, nonetheless, clamored for a change. The bishop finally took action. He first ordered the secrete installment of surveillance cameras in the rectory and the results came immediately after it. In one incident, one could see a lady carrying a suitcase. The pastor opened it and saw it packed up with twenty dollar bills. His eye balls bulged. He hurried to close the suitcase and brought to an undisclosed location in the cellar. A few weeks later, he was removed from his parish and placed in a health institution. A year passed by and everyone was sure that the pastor had come to the end of his race. At least, they thought that he got rid of his self-destructive habits. One morning, he went outside of the building to take fresh air. A brand new red car was waiting for him. He opened the door, sat and locked it.

That same day he got married and was seen no more. He had the last word on his private life.

The messenger, in the meantime, returned to the hospital without good news. It was only the following evening that the situation reached a point of no return. All of Floris' relatives rushed to the hospital. In the intensive care room, he was agonizing; yet, nobody heard a single lamentation or a word of discomfort. He suffered bravely on his deathbed. His best friend, to keep alive his hopes, held a rosary high in the air. Floris stared at it as much as he could. He also noticed his friend's eyes full of tears. Espera made a last attempt to encourage her husband to hold on, to hope, to resist, but his swollen hands remained static. Floris' lungs stopped breathing and the heart ceased beating. His brother-in-law announced that the battle against death was over. A long veil of silence descended on Mendoza's streets and plazas. The flag was lowered in sign of respect for their hero.

CHAPTER XXXII

Post Death Period

As we said, Floris' death had a local and national resonance. To render homage to one of the Malvinas' last survivors, the government dispatched a platoon of honor guards dressed in black suits and white shirts with black tie. The musicians wore blue pants with white jackets and gold and blue stripes. The horses were covered with a light, white mantle during the funeral cart. The band followed them. Espera chose a black dress, while her mother-in-law opted for a white gown and orange sweater. Floris' native town was represented by the Communist Party President. He wore a tricolor band around his neck and a sickle and hammer on the front of his hat. It was a monumental ceremony that lasted more than three hours. The military positioned themselves laterally to the wagon carrying the casket. Every ten feet or so someone from the crowd, that lined up the streets leading to the church, dashed out of the line and threw flowers in the direction of the casket. The band played funereal music through the half hour procession. The procession stopped at the entrance of the church where a long applause welcomed the casket. Camera operators were busy filming and snapping pictures, while the reporters made some attempts to interview relatives and friends.

The road that led to the cemetery was lined up with people many of whom stood at attention or raised their arm forward. After the closing ceremony, the honor guards fired one hundred rounds of cannon. A local man, expert in fireworks, blasted the sky with a cornucopia of different shapes and colors of them that lasted about ten minutes.

Espera stood over the casket surrounded by relatives and close friends. Suddenly, her mother-in-law cried out, "My son, my son, why have you left me? I am a widow and orphan of my only son." Someone tried to allay her sorrow, "Stay calm. We all have to go there." The mortuary hall was adorned with a large assortment of flowers, all with a huge array of hues. One displayed the names of Espera's parents; others bore the names of her sisters and brothers. One was anonymous.

Espera leaned over the casket and did not want to move despite the custodian's appeal to pay the last respects because the time was up. The military group stood on attention for the last time and boarded their vehicles to return to their base. One of Espera's young nieces began to read aloud the names of the people printed on the garlands. When she arrived at the anonymous one, she read "prisoner." Everybody thought it was one of the soldiers who had been prisoner of the British navy during the battle of the Malvinas. The whispering soon reached Espera's ears. She opened her eyes as if she had a vision and fainted in her children's arms. It took well about a quarter of an hour before she began to snap out of it. The custodian announced that he was about to close the gate. He had just finished the announcement that screams and cries burst in the chamber. Chaos ensued. No one knew exactly what was going on. Espera fainted for the second time. The pallbearers ran to the nearest road. The custodian became frantic and did not know what course of action to take. Eventually, the clamor subsided and calm returned. What actually caused so much commotion was the tremor of the casket that occurred for a few seconds due to some electrical shortages underneath of it.

The funeral had been exhausting for Espera and her family. The house became a zoo. It was practically invaded by neighbors and strangers. The neighbors continued to flock at Espera's house to console the widow. Soldiers who had served in the Malvinas' passed by with the military uniform on.

They stopped for a moment in front of Floris' house, made a salute and went on. Soon, the house became like a museum or a sanctuary. People stopped for a few moments to murmur a prayer or send a salute of respect in passing by. The reporters tried to delve in the identity of the anonymous flower sender. They even approached the florist who could only remember that a lady had paid in cash and was unable to identify her name.

Espera spent a sleepless night. She tossed on all sides on the couch unable to close a wink. Only in the morning, she fell asleep by exhaustion. In the meantime, the major local newspaper ran a headline like this, "Argentina and Mendoza pay homage and bid good-by to one of his bravest sons."

The time passed by desperately slowly for Espera. The mail had piled up. She did not have the time to read all the letters and cards of condolences. While she was shuffling them at random, one of them caught her attention. The envelope had the stamp of Sao Paulo. She opened it and read it. When she finished reading it, she put it in her pocket. No one asked her the reason for it. In her spare time, she tried to unfold it. It was sealed very tightly. A stroke of scissors cut the superior part and she was able to extract the interior sheet. The message was brief, "In these days of solitude and sadness, more than ever I am close to you. Please, let me know if I can be of any assistance.

CHAPTER XXXIII

Felix's Odyssey and the Postman

Dear reader, we left Felix behind, but we did not forget him. I know that you are eager to find out what happened to him. Here I am.

The morning after Felix completed his military obligations, the sun was half asleep and fatigued to get up... Dark, sparse clouds gathered on the city's sky and stood there immobile for hours impeding the sun from filtering through them. For Felix often scrutinized the sky, like the ancient oracle interpreters. Nature gave him premonitions about future events. That day somehow, he saw in the darkness of the clouds something singular, strange. For him, it was an ominous sign, but he felt undeterred. He did not spend any time partying with his soldiers friends. His sister's letter alarmed him immensely, therefore, he rushed to the railroad station where got on the first morning train for Naples.

The locomotive was crammed with passengers directed to the North of the peninsula seeking job opportunities. Many purchased the ticket for Germany or Luxemburg. The heavy suitcases brought along the usual odors of salami, cheese and pepperoni. The wine bottle was kept in the carry-on-bag. The departure was extremely emotional for the immigrants' families who flocked the railroad station to bid good-by to their fathers or brothers. While they waived the handkerchief from the windows of the wagons, their women or relatives screamed and wailed as if they were at a funeral. The whistle divided the loved ones for many months or even years to come. Some never came back to their homeland. Either they got married or died in countries that adopted them.

Felix, still in the military uniform, took a seat in the second class next to a window. He looked at the other passengers across and around him and noticed many eyes in tears. Men covered their face with a rough small cloth. Women were not so repressive in their emotions and displayed their feelings openly. After the ritual acquaintance and questions, related to their whereabouts with the compartment passengers, Felix considered appropriate to let them relax while he looked outside. In front of him, the poplar trees and the fields rich in vegetable and wheat ran away from his sight. They appeared headed to a distant, opposite destiny. The wind brushed violently the wagons and it made almost impossible to stick the head out of the window. Occasionally, Felix spotted a herd of cows or horses grazing pacifically in shaded areas surrounded by barbed wires and guardian dogs. The train passed by a couple of lakes. Their silvery surfaces were surrounded by amorphous contours and appeared dormant under new blue skies. Many women suffered mostly from the heat and the crammed conditions. Most of them and old people puffed, showed impatience and emanated a foul odor the sweat under their armpits. The corridors were congested and it was utterly difficult to get by. It would have been easier penetrating a thick jungle than passing through the packed mass of human beings. The bathrooms were open to the public... Those who needed to use it had to ask permission to the 'insiders' to evacuate temporarily the premises. The return trip was even more chaotic. In some cases, they had to walk over the bodies of the people lying on the floor.

Aside from the humidity, the unsanitary conditions and the overpopulation, other traveling aspects made the trip unsustainable. The poor migrants brought along all sorts of cheeses, salami, eggplants in oil jars and sardines in paper boxes .....And, who knows what else. For many passengers, the smell spurred their hunger because they could not even buy a sandwich at the stations where the train stopped periodically. To others, it gave a vomiting sensation and put their hands on the mouth to lessen the odor.

Felix was immersed in his thoughts when the ticket controller opened the door and urged the military man to give up his seat for a pregnant woman. Felix had a brusque reaction of irritation, He looked at the man and said, "Listen! With or without this uniform, which I have honored for almost two years and it cost me invisible wounds in my mind, I would gladly give it up to her, but you are an irresponsible pig. You cannot go around expecting passengers to comply with your demands, I have immense respect for women, especially those in a state of pregnancy, but you showed no respect for the uniform I am wearing. Many young people are occupying seats in the various compartments, but you decided to come to solicit me to give up my." He picked up his suitcase and pushed his way through the corridor. No one dared to say a word. A parent elbowed his son and asked him if he would get up and offer his seat to the serviceman, but he kindly declined. A mature man told Felix, "I really appreciate your sense of civility. I, too, do not tolerate that in our modern society. There are still people who act with arrogance and lack of gratitude for those who defend our motherland. This is the status of the new generation. They are insensitive to human needs. They lack a sense of civility. Parents don't affirm anymore their authority."

An older woman added, "I fully agree with you. Relations between parents and children have become so friendly that parental authority has profoundly changed its status. Parents ask and implore many times, but do not demand for fear of creating and hostile environment. They tend to appease the children rather than teaching them an education."

The first man responded, "Since women entered the labor force, they neglected the family values, mostly for lack of time and for tiredness. The natural feminine habitat for a woman is the house. Where there is lack of parental education, one can see the absence of social values. All the rest is cultural relativism."

A lot of people came out of their lethargy and applauded, but a man close to thirty turned around and said, "The soldiers are fascists. They carry on the ex-dictator's policy."

A woman, around twenty years old, addressed Felix in this way, "Don't pay attention to him. He is ignorant." Her comment upset the man who responded with verbal abuses.

Soon, a scuffle brewed up. The young man grabbed the girl by the throat and pushed her against the compartment door. The girl was on the verge of suffocation, when Felix intervened and released the girl from the grip. The young man turned around and stuck the elbow in Felix ribs. A loud cry gushed out of Felix's mouth. The pain abated soon after and Felix hit him with a powerful hook. His rival staggered. Felix lifted him up in the air and was about to launch him through the window, but there was no room to move. The ticket controller, alerted by the passengers, arrived with much difficulty, and re-established the order. He found for Felix an accommodation in the first class and assigned the other two in two separate wagons.

Felix stood next to the window and exposed his head out. The wind buffeted his sweaty face, resulted from the previous physical engagement and brought some relief to it. The exposure lasted a few minutes. The wind seemed to carry blades on its wings and he withdrew his head to wipe it with a rough cloth he kept in the pocket of his pants. He got up and went to the aisle. A young girl, with the pretense of going by, pressed her body against his. He disengaged from the pressure and returned to his seat. He stuck out his head out of the window again. The wind whipped his face with more violence until the train reduced its speed and the wind felt like a breeze. Felix noticed the fields of wheat ondulating under the passage of the wagons. Sparse clouds never made an effort to reconvene and unleash a storm on the dry land. They decided to rest for the time being. The houses alongside the railroad track multiplied and more people appeared on the roads. Then, the loudspeaker announced that the train was in proximity of Naples. That name sounded like a bell in the ears of many of them and pandemonium broke out. They moved from one class to another, grabbed their belonging and crammed the aisle like sardines. Only the heads were visible. The train slowed down the speed even more and many passengers looked out of the windows searching for familiar faces. The train finally stopped coughing smoke and parked at Naples' Central Station. The doors opened and excitement broke out. Those, who were about to get off, fought every inch of the way to get teach the exit, first. Felix looked out. His parents could not afford going to the city and stayed in town waiting in trepidation for they had not seen him since the war raged in Italy and in Europe.

The rest of the passengers watched unmoved their fellow travelers. Their minds were elsewhere. They were continuing the race to Milan, Luxemburg or Germany in search of a better life for themselves and their families. Unloading the luggage became a struggle. Eventually, the long line slimmed down and Felix was one of the last one to step down. By the time the train departed, half an hour had passed.

For those who continued the race, the waiting time seemed endless, eternal. The iron horse started to smoke again; turned its wheels and moved sluggishly. Once it warmed up, it resumed its natural speed and disappeared behind the tall oak trees.

"Felix, Felix," cried out a lady in the thirties. "I am your sister! Remember?" Felix heard his name and looked around ignoring the location where the name came from. The young lady pressed forward and opened up her way through the crowd. Felix recognized her and ran toward her and they fell in each other's arms. It took a while before both where recomposed under the curious attention of the crowd. His sister did not want to waste any time. She leaned over and whispered in his ear, "She is leaving."

"When?" He inquired with trepidation.

"Right now."

"From where?" he insisted.

"From the port of Santa Lucia. You may still make it on time. I will take care of your luggage."

"Wait for me here. I take a taxi and come right back. Don't go away."

"Go! Don't worry!"

He distanced himself from the crowd and asked to the first man he met in the street, "How far is Santa Lucia?"

"A few blocks, my good soldier."

"In terms of time, how long it would take me walking?"

"A good twenty minutes, my soldier."

A taxi man tried to call his attention, but Felix had already crossed the road and started to run toward the port.

A local vendor asked Felix's sister the reasons for her brother's excitement, "What's going on with him?"

"He had to run to meet some dear to him at the port."

"He could take the taxi. It will take him a long time walking."

"No, he is running," she rectified her.

"Granted that he is running, it is going to take him ten, fifteen minutes. You know. Time is gold. One minute may make a difference."

"I agree with you."

"For a few dollars, he may miss the love of his life."

Felix's sister looked at her with suspicion and said, "How do you know it?"

The lady laughed and said, "I am old my friend. I am old."

"What else do you know?"

The vendor let her head oscillate like a pendulum and said, "For a few dollars..."

Felix's sister got irritated and said, "He is only a soldier. Would you have paid for him?"

"If the government gave me a decent pension..."

Felix's sister looked at her with indifference and moved a bit away from her stand.

Felix kept on running frantically, crossing roads and dashing through cars and pedestrians until he reached the seacoast. People who came from the stores stopped walking and followed him with their eyes as far as they could. They thought he was a fugitive. The military uniform gave them the reason to believe that he was a deserter escaping from his military duty.

The port of Santa Lucia was jammed with the emigrants and relatives. Most of them held a handkerchief in their hands ready to use them to wipe out tears. From the deck of the third floor, Espera was waiving to her family. Suddenly, a thunderous whistle shook the gulf. The boat was about to make another Atlantic crossing. Many of its inhabitants would never see again their birth place again. Felix pushed his way through the port authorities' guards in the hope of gaining a spot where he could see her. By the time he arrived, all the passengers had boarded the boat. The laborers rolled the rope and pulled the bridge. The boat roared for the last time and coughed slightly. The commander gave the approval and the sea giant monster slowly glided on the water. Finally, Felix spotted Espera in the midst of thousands of people waiving good-by. He yelled her name once, two, three times, but she did not see him. His face became pale. The blood flux increased to the brains. His head was spinning and was on the verge of dropping on the deck. He made a last, strenuous effort to stand up, but was exhausted and lost consciousness. Some onlookers rushed over to help him to revive. He got up and followed her as much as he could. Shortly after, the moon appeared in the sky. Her appearance coincided with the disappearance of the boat from the bay of Naples and Felix bent his knees and cried. He remained there until the boat disappeared completely from his view. A port employee approached him and placed a hand on his shoulder."Soldier, get up.

I know how you feel. It happened to me, too. I know how you feel," he repeated. "If they are rose buds, early or later, they will blossom. Life is made up of unpredictable events. We must learn to react to them with patience and dignity."

Felix wiped his eyes. The man put a hand on his shoulders and hugged him.

Nearby, Espera's family was watching the scene with extreme attention. Felix passed by them without raising his head and reached the main road. He was sweating abundantly. From a taxi, a voice called his name. He was not sure if it was his imagination and looked in the direction of the car. He turned around and kept on looking in the direction of the gulf. He stood there motionless for a while until his sister came out of the taxi and helped him to get back.

The trip to Felix' hometown was marred with depression. He hardly spoke a word to his sister who was trying to console him. At home, the meeting with the rest of his family was emotional. Later, he decided to go to bed. His parents begged him to eat, but he his stomach was not up to eat. For a few days, he did not leave the house. His family did not even inform the relatives or friends right away to allow him more time to recollect his thoughts and energies. They did their best to protect his privacy; however, the news of his arrival somehow spread and his residence became swarmed with all sorts of people including reporters.

The preponderant attention by the local and national media and by his friends and neighbors suggested Felix to step out of the domestic walls to avoid his family being under constant pressure. He did it in a very discreet way. Not to be recognized by many people, he got up early in the morning and took a tour of the town trying to figure it out where he was with his mind. "Do I still remember the plaza, the elementary school he attended and the streets I, once, crossed on a daily basis?" He noticed that traffic lights were hanging in the main intersections of the village center. He observed many signs, ostentatiously displayed in the main boulevard, which urged citizens to recycle. Big dumpsters were posted on street corners. The town had done away with the traditional trash bags resting outside of the house doors. To Felix, they were expressions of civility and progress. The only drawback with those iron boxes was the stench. The inhabitants of each neighborhood, sectioned by the government, discharged a disproportionate amount of garbage that overflowed and fell on the ground. Needless to say, it became prey of rodents and other vagrant animals that littered the trash in the adjacent areas. In summer time, the odor was unbearable. Those who were accustomed to take a walk to the café', in view of them, had to accelerate the pace, while the drivers closed the windows in their vicinity.

If the central part of the town had remained somewhat untouched because of its artistic value, the same could not be said about the outskirts which had been invaded by the cement. Apartment houses and new villas sprawled all way around the geographical limits creating a sort of defensive line to the inner section of the town. The fruit industry had gained a foothold that stretched their roots all way to the Americas. Restaurants offered local cuisine and some well off immigrants started to bring their own culinary innovations. A few banks emerged in the main arteries and one of them was German. It was here that Felix began to make some contacts and transactions. None of its employees knew him, so, he felt at ease. On the way back, he passed by the foot of the mountain. The scent of the chestnut trees and junipers alongside the road gave him a sense of belongingness. He stopped and looked intensely at the bark of a trunk. Something unusual caught his attention. He saw an inscription on the side of the tree, "Espera and Felix in love forever. 1943." He analyzed the writing and admitted that it was his. He even remembered the day and the time when it occurred. It happened during a school excursion in that area. The wound of not having been able to see her in Naples was still open in his heart. He closed his eyes and stood there dreaming for a while. The past resurfaced in his memory and he felt intimately connected to it. He wanted to enjoy reliving those idyllic moments even longer, but the memories brought along pain too. A couple of birds squabbling on the tree top brought him back to reality.

He resumed his return trip to his house walking backward for a couple hundred yards staring at the tree. The children's shout nearby reminded him that he was close to town. By that time, he had lost the geographical orientation and asked to an old man how to get back to the main road. The man looked at him with curiosity and passed on. Felix had to cross the main square to return to his house. The area was not particularly crowded. He felt uncomfortable by their suffocating investigative looks and accelerated the pace. His strategy did not succeed because it intensified their attention. One person said, "I think I know who he is, but I cannot place him on the screen of my mind." From then on, it became a guessing game about his identity. Felix reached his house with a deep sense of relief. He went straight to his bedroom, took off his shoes and rested.

The following day, he woke up late. He took a cup of coffee and strolled down the street. He met the mailman along the way and exchanged greetings with him. The postman stared at him. Somehow, that face was familiar to him. He lowered his head in a pensive attitude, but when he realized that he could remember his name, he mounted on the bike and continued the mail delivery. He pedaled about fifty yards and stopped. He mumbled something, "It was not....my....fau...lt. I expl-ain..ed to your sis..ster." He was in that mood for a minute or so and then he resumed his usual work. Felix too wanted to talk to him, to discharge his rage, but decided to postpone his case to another encounter because Espera's house was within reach and he did not wish to be heard by her family. One evening, while he was in a depressive mood, he was determined to engage her mother in an explanatory debate, but his sister dissuaded him at the last minute. The new generation was no longer receptive anymore for a revival of old family feuds. "Felix," she said to her brother, "We have not spoken with her family since you were taken away from the Germans. Now that Espera is married you have in mind to mend our relations?"

As the time went by, Felix' return did not pass unobserved not even in rural areas where he went for occasional visits to his farm and met old and new acquaintances. One evening, the sun had already transferred its abode to the horizon and Felix was heading to a friend's house. On the side of the street, a woman was discharging all her irritation to the bicycle by kicking the front wheel. Once in a while, she launched glances left and right to see if someone passed by to inflate the tire. Felix directed his steps toward her ready to help her. By the time he arrived, the lady was still trying to figure out what to do with the tire. At the sound of steps, she raised her head and met Felix' eyes. The visual contact lasted a short time, but it seemed eternal. She appeared disoriented. Something clicked in her memory and became nervous. She drew back, pulled up the bicycle and dragged it away in a hurry. Felix remained speechless. After a few seconds, he regained his composure and shouted, "Where are you going, viper? Where are all the letters that I mailed to your daughter? You robbed her and me of our happiness. You may run away from me, but not from your conscience. Like Cain, you will wonder all over in search of peace." He kept on talking, but she was a bit too far to hear him. The wind sucked his words in its bosom and dispersed them forever through the adjoining farms.

Even before the war winded down, many Nazi official fled to South America. In the successive years, Felix heard successful stories about a new Eldorado in Brazil. A wave of German business entrepreneurs moved to that giant country and thrived. Felix was still young and did not wish to perish in a stagnant political society. He called the touristic agency and bought a ticket for Sao Paolo. Either out of despite or out of self -satisfaction, Espera's mother hosted a big party in her backyard. Some guests asked her the reason for the celebration. She responded that it was in honor of the president of the local Communist Party.

The best band in town was invited to perform and special chefs intervened to make the occasion memorable with all sorts of culinary delicacies. Felix, in the meantime, locked the doors and windows of his house and spent a sleepless night during which he laid the plans for his future life. His family was very opposed to his idea, but he was inflexible, "At my age," he said, "I can fly on my own. I don't need anymore to stay under parental wings. I lived alone for many years and now I should be afraid to leave again? I don't understand why all of a sudden I have become the center of attention." His firmness demonstrated a strong personality that they ignored and broke down the last and feeble resistance of his family members.

During the transatlantic crossing, Felix heard many stories about Brazil. Some of them dealt with gold available everywhere along the Amazon River; others described the squalid conditions in the 'favelas'. The most respected account depicted a giant country rich in opportunities for those who are willing to work hard. By the time he disembarked at Rio de Janeiro, Felix had his mind made up. With the mechanical background, he would gain a foothold in business in the area of Sao Paolo.

CHAPTER XXXIV

Sao Paolo and Fiorella's Vicissitudes

Sao Paolo is located between Buenos Aires and the Caribes and it is the most bustling city in Latin America. Jesuit missionaries first visited the countryside in 1554 with the intent of converting to Christianity the indigenous population. By 1711, the coffee shipments from nearby Santos made it very popular. Attracted by economic possibilities, the various ethnic immigrant groups swarmed Sao Paolo and in a short time, they transformed it in a prosperous industrial city. The boom lasted until the American Depression of 1928 when the demand for coffee hit the ebb and, in order to keep the economy flourishing, the entrepreneurs resorted to the sugar and alcohol commerce. As the number of immigrants, especially from Italy, multiplied in successive decades, the city experienced an unpredictable progress. At first, the small and medium shops began to give impulse to the local economy. The subsequent emergence of the automobile and textile industries in the district of Mooco created a new image of the city of 'green." Even the language lived moments of flexibility. The vast majority of the population spoke Portuguese, but the heavy immigration from Naples and Venice gave many variations to the national language.

Felix' permanency in Buenos Aires did not last long. The stories he heard on the boat captivated his imagination. Due to the massive Italian presence in Sao Paolo, he decided to move his residence in the district of Mooco, near the Museu de Arte, Memoria do imigrante. For a couple of years, he worked as a mechanic in a car dealership. At the owner's death, he made the move of his life. With the money borrowed from a local Genovese bank, he purchased all the company's shares. It was the first, giant financial venture that he took as a young man and profound repercussions to the rest of his life.

At this point, the reader lost track of Fiorella, but don't despair my fellow traveler. We switch channel and follow her in her wonderings.

Fiorella could not find peace since Felix was inducted in the army at Naples' railroad station. She could not forgive herself for not recognizing him quicker. Without the command of the language and of a friend or relative, she was at the mercy of unpredictable events. First of all, she looked for a bathroom in the station to relieve her physical need. She looked at the train time schedule and purchased a ticket once again for Florence scheduled at two o' clock in the afternoon. Two hours elapsed between then and the departure time. Not to stay idle, she scouted the station and noticed the information office with employees speaking different foreign languages. The German interpreter confirmed her that the train for Florence would depart from track number 5. She walked around a little longer and, then, she took a seat on the bench where she consumed a lunch and waited patiently for the train.

As usual, the station was bubbling with action. The trains arrived and departed from and to all over Italy and Europe. It was rare to see someone alone. A shoeshine boy addressed Fiorella with the characteristic Neapolitan savoir-faire, "Miss, do you want a shoe shine operation? It's cheap and lustrous. I am an expert in this business. By the time I get done, your shoes will look like new. You can trust me. I won the World Shining shoes Competition in Montreal. You can ask all these ladies around me." The people started to laugh. Fiorella responded, "Nine, nine."

"Body of thousand lizards!" exclaimed the boy. "This beauty wants me to shine her shoes nine times. As long as I get paid, I can shine them even twenty times." He set the tools on the floor and approached her right foot ready to start. The girl withdrew the foot and made him a gesture to stop. The boy looked around for assistance. One of them, who was on his way to Germany, told him, "You got it all wrong. The word 'nine' in German means' no.' The boy cleaned the nose with the back of his hand, picked up the tool box and sought customers elsewhere.

For Fiorella, Florence was an earthly paradise. During the daily classes, she was exposed to all art treasures of the city. She marveled at the spirit of the Renaissance and the monumental body of work that it generated. From every painting and carved stone, transpired a sense of excellence unmatched in human history. The museums made a profound impression on her. She remained ecstatic before Botticelli's 'Venere 'and stood in meditation in front of it for five long minutes. She did not like David's nudity and said that covering certain anatomical parts with a veil would have not harmed the sculpture.

As the time went by, however, a sense of loneliness took hold of her. At first, she ignored the extracurricular activities and, later, she started to miss classes and the initial enthusiasm in art vanished altogether. To make matters worse, she got news that her mother got diagnosed with breast cancer in advanced stage and the prognosis did not leave much hope for survival. As a result of it, Fiorella cut short her studies and rushed to her mother's side.

For two weeks, her mother battled the insidious enemy and the doctors kept her alive with the oxygen. Her daughter refused to go back to Florence and slept with her mother to keep her company. The nurses, along with the doctors, were extremely affable and offered to the general's wife the best medical assistance. Fiorella was deeply touched by their professionalism and the attention they reserved to her agonizing mother. Despite the valiant fight, her mother succumbed to the deadly disease and left her daughter alone.

After the funeral, Fiorella spent many days between the lake and the restaurants. She was extremely attracted by the dolphins dashing out of the water and diving again. A girl, next to her, kept her company by playing with the fish. One afternoon, lost balance and fell into the water. Her little arms splashed the water surface. She did not know how to swim and was about to sink. Fiorella did not realize that she was in danger. The crowd's clamor called her immediate attention. She bent down and stretched her hand to bring the girl to safety, but she missed the grip and the girl soon got swallowed by the water. At that point, Fiorella jumped in the lake with her clothes on. The efforts to recover the girl lasted a few seconds. She brought the inert body to the surface and with short strokes she reached land. The crowd quickly gathered around them, but no one knew how to apply the mouth to mouth resuscitation. The girl lay on the ground, apparently, lifeless. Fiorella was exhausted. Someone panicked; others searched for a paramedic who lived nearby. He rushed over. The girl lay with the head backward. Her lips were purple. The eyes were closed. The respiration was absent. He set a pillow under her head and placed both hands on her chest. He exerted pressure on and off for about a minute waiting for life signs. The seconds on the clock were ticking. The man was breathing heavily. The sweat was streaming down his brow. Suddenly, a cough broke the funereal silence. The crowd's hopes were heightened. The girl started to sob. The sobs and coughs alternated until her eyes slowly began to open. Fiorella regained her energy and got up to take part at the event. The girl's parents alerted by the police arrived at the scene. A long ovation followed the girl in the act of standing up. Although she still felt in a state of mental confusion, she hugged and thanked the paramedic and Fiorella. The girl's parents offered Fiorella a monetary compensation for her efforts, but she refused it.

It took a week before Fiorella resumed her regular life. She changed her professional plans and decided to become a nurse. Near the main university, there stood a tall building. It was a hospital. Next to it, there was a nursing school. She stepped in the main lobby and stopped at the main desk, "What can I do for you?" inquired the secretary in a sweet tone.

"Actually, I would like to pursue a nursing career."

"You are at the right place," she responded gently.

"That's just wonderful!"

"Please, sit down. I will be right with you." The secretary took out a document from a box and handed it to her, "Fill out this application and sign it at the bottom. There is a one hundred dollar fee."

"Can I pay with the credit card?"

"As you wish,"

During parents' week, thousand of adults and students walked in and out of the campus buildings. That day, an indecent and detestable episode occurred. Down the main street in front of the art and science building, a woman started to attack a student who had exposed herself before a transparent wall that divided two different rooms. Evidently, the lady deemed the verbal abuse insufficient punishment and passed to attack her physically. The nude student's screams called the attention of a small crowd that promptly rushed to the area. A senior student intervened to protect the girl, but the

Antonio Casale

lady launched injurious epithets to him, as well, and then pushed him outside where he fell on the lawn. The lady's husband started to kick the boy on his back. The student reacted by hitting the man on his leg causing him to fall. Being the parents' visitation week, several adults sided with the lady and manhandled the student causing him various excoriations on the body. The janitors, the students and the guards watched the spectacle without interfering. An older person, who took no side in the scuffle, called the ambulance, but the conductor refused to show up on the scene considering the case too "light.' A second call was made, this time to the Red Cross. They responded immediately. The leader examined the student's wounds and decided that they were too serious to be treated in loco and transported the young man to the nearest hospital where he received medical help and was discharged three days later. With much delay, the city police finally arrived and took the lady in custody. She defended herself asserting that she wanted to protect the students' dignity. Fiorella was disgusted by the students and parents who reacted indifferently to the scene without taking a stand on the issue. "Hear me honorable people!" She shouted. "I do not condone physical abuse, but moral degradation is worse. Remember! A participant may lose or win, but a spectator has already lost." Slowly the students' body dispersed while a surveillance camera was taping the scene.

Two years of studies allowed Fiorella to graduate from nursing school. At that time, a neurologist from the same school where Fiorella studied was invited to a conference in Rio de Janeiro. He asked Fiorella if she wished to make some introductory remarks prior to his intervention. Before accepting, she asked about the temperature. The famous doctor informed her that the coldest day in winter doesn't go below 52 degrees. The zest for living reemerged in her and she jumped at the opportunity. The following Sunday they flew South America.

Following the conference, Fiorella decided to remain in the capital for further studies. This time she applied at the veterinarian school where she was admitted with a blink of an eye. It took her four more years of studies to become a veterinarian.

Just before her medical graduation, a lab incident almost cost her life and changed the course of her future. A scientist opened a cage where he kept a family of rodents. He picked up one for an experimental demonstration and forgot to close the gate. A cat nearby jumped at the occasion and caught one of them. Fiorella ran after the feline to free the rodent, but the cat was in no mood to give up his prey. Somehow, Fiorella attempted to free the mouse by widening the cat's mouth and got bitten. Shortly after, her armpits got swollen and she felt atrocious pains in the stomach. Soon, those symptoms spread rapidly to the liver, pancreas and bladder, followed by multiple bleedings. A couple of surgeons rushed on the scene to provide their expertise. The first said to the second one, "She contracted an epidemic. It is similar to the one that caused over thirty million of victims in Europe from 1348 to1352."

A medical student whispered to the ear of a colleague, "It was called the Black Death. Boccaccio has left us a detailed account of those infamous years," responded the second.

"Thank heaven, a Jew stopped the plague by ordering the citizens to burn all their belongings in the streets," responded the other.

"Fortunately, medicine has made giant leaps and we are able to control it now."

While the doctors searched for the medicine, Fiorella was under the spell of convulsions. It took about ten minutes before the surgeons found it. In a matter of an hour, the pains subsided and in the following days she resumed her routine work.

The graduation from medical school opened new professional opportunities to Fiorella. Everything looked rosy to her, but a strange destiny seemed to wait for her. A local newspaper advertised a veterinarian position at the local animal hospital in Sao Paolo. Without reflecting too long on it, she jumped at the new job perspective. She sent a cover letter and her curriculum vitae and two weeks later she was informed that she was the top finalist. They invited her for an interview and she got the job.

At the beginning, she lived in a hotel. In the upcoming months, she rented an apartment in proximity of "O Museu de Arte." Every week-end, she spent her spare time analyzing every painting hanging down the walls of the prestigious museums. She planned to write a book on comparative art, but the project never materialized because the hospital work was very demanding.

In the same department, a doctor of affable manners offered all his assistance to Fiorella. If she wished, she could ride with him to and from the hospital. She kindly declined the invitation and rode a bus for the first few months. She loved her independence and did not expect to depend on anyone, especially male colleagues. In her apartment, there was a mirror in front of her closet. She used to look at her face and, when the eyes rested on the waist line, she frowned. She needed a remedy. For a long time, she had been a strong advocate of exercises, even though she was not a steady practitioner. Walking exercised a strange fascination in her. It acted like a balsam, both physically and psychologically. After all, strolling down the main avenues and parks would allow her to get acquainted with the city and discharge her unwarranted worries. Above all, stopping at the traffic light, crossing the streets, dodging cars and pedestrians, mingling with the human sea she met on her way out, gave her a sense of belongingness and it made her forget her loneliness. More than once, her male colleague veterinarian felt disappointed and offended by her refusal, but she insisted that walking had a medical effect on her health; however, as the time went by, the pressure for conferences and work related needs became intense and she began to get interested in purchasing a small car.

On a Saturday morning, she visited many car dealers located on the Avenida Blanca Grotta. A Ferrari car stood on the floor of a building in all her red splendor. No one passed by without being touched by her beauty. Fiorella too fell under her spell and stood there inspecting every detail of it. A salesman approached Fiorella and exclaimed, "What a beauty! Isn't? What man would not long to have a girl sitting next to him in this car?"

Fiorella did not reply. She was immersed in her own world. The sales person repeated, "More you look at her and more you fall in love with her. It is normal. I commend you for trusting this car that only Italy can produce. Art and creativity are there." He was about to add some extra compliments to the car when her eyes moved aimlessly inside the building. The man blocked her visual and said, "You like that doll, don't you? How would you like to try it? I make an exception. Only a charming girl like you will have that privilege."

Not even this time Fiorella responded. Instead, she tried to gain access to the entrance by circumventing him.

It was hot and sultry that day. People perspired easily. Fiorella took the handkerchief from her pocket book and wiped her forehead.

In that moment, she spotted someone inside going to his office. She waited a while to see if he would come out. Her curiosity faded rather quickly because he closed the door behind him and left a note outside, 'Do not disturb!" She did not want to be imprudent, but to restore her confidence she made an attempt to force her way through the door, but a security man was quick to jump ahead of her. "Miss," he said, "Don't you know how to read? May I announce you to the president when he is free?"

She looked at him and replied with a distracted smile. The man shook his head and responded to the queries of other clients. Fiorella felt an irresistible desire to see him, to talk to him. She knocked at the door once, but no one replied. She insisted again. Instead of seeing the door open, she heard the same man saying, "Miss, the transaction will last a while. Be patient. When your turn comes, you will be admitted to his office. That if you do not wish to leave now and try later." Fiorella did not understand him. She turned around and headed toward the sidewalk. The first salesman smiled and redoubled his efforts. His impertinent behavior bothered her and she crossed street. He followed her and promised her a big discount if she only sat down and listened to him. She gave him a dirty look and dashed away from his sight. Convinced that he could not catch his prey, the salesman went back to his business.

At home, Fiorella could not find peace. She turned on the TV, but did not pay heed to anything being said or seen. A migraine headache soon developed and she had to recur to aspirins to allay the pain. The night did not bring the desired sleep. Her head tossed left and right without finding a stable position. She got up and walked up and down her rooms hoping to get tired and go back to bed. That car dealer was tormenting her.

Daylight finally came without dispelling her anxiety. She showered, but refused to eat breakfast. A hot cup of coffee was sufficient to get her going. A coffee shop was not distant from her apartment and in two minutes she was there. It was Sunday, but the streets were already jammed with people going to church or to family restaurants. Fiorella sipped the coffee in a hurry and returned to the same car dealership. The same salesman welcomed her at the entrance. "I knew you would come back," he said. "Nobody can resist to the attraction of this jewel," and pointed at the Ferrari. "Once again, I renew my offer at a special price that you cannot refuse." She avoided him and proceeded straight to the main office. A short, stocky man in elegant attire smiled at her and said, "Your beauty can only be matched by another beauty. Why don't we sit down in my office and discuss the opportunities that I offer you?" He turned to an assistant and said, "Two coffees, please, with sugar for both of us."

"Right away," responded a feminine voice, thin and acute.

"No, bring only one cup of coffee for him," said Fiorella.

The man was perturbed and surprised by the negative response. He looked at her with a forced smile and said, "I am doing it for you."

Fiorella replied, "I came back here for one reason"

"I agree with you," responded the man encouraged by her reply. "In my office you will be more comfortable."

She did not budge. "I came here for one specific reason and I hope you will cooperate."

"And if I don't?" replied the man in a serious tone.

"You and I are going to lose."

"Why is that?"

"I am here to find out if you know a man by the name of Felix."

"The gentleman touched his inferior lip with the index of his right hand and said, "He was..."

"What do you mean by that? He no longer works here?"

"I am sorry, miss. Yesterday, he bade good-by to us?

"But, I saw him last night going to his office," and she pointed the direction with her finger."

"That is correct. My assistant has just taken off his name from the door. If you wish to go there and check for yourself, suit yourself."

"Where is he now?" she implored him.

"Miss, I do not know why you are asking me all these sorts of questions, but I can only tell you that I treated him like a gentleman. When he came from Itlay, first, I gave him a job as a mechanic and, later, as a salesman. He was so sharp that in a short time he became the operation manager. Last night, was his last."

When Fiorella heard that, her eyes widened and her curiosity increased. "Tell me more about him," she begged him.

"What can I tell you," said the man opening his arms. He is really a shrewd man. I liked him. Don't give me wrong. I even helped him to get an insight of the business. What hurts me the most is the aloe of secrecy that surrounds him. He refused to reveal to me his whereabouts and what he had up his sleeves. It is going to take some time before I recover from this shock." He lowered his head and added, "People are what they are, ungrateful."

"Maybe, if you treated him better, he would not have quit. Don't you think so?"

The car dealer got visibly irritated, "How can you talk to me like that? Who are you? I taught him every trick of the business. Without experience, he surged to the highest ranking position in a short time."

"Why did you treat him so favorably?"

The man launched glances left and right as to assure himself that no one would hear him. He was on the verge of talking, but stopped unexplainably. For no apparent reason, he began to cough and rushed to the bathroom. He could be heard from a distance discharging thick phlegm. Upon his return, he appeared in a more serene attitude. He stared at her and muttered, "I promised him my daughter in spouse. Oh, she is a darling! She is the pupil of my eye. She is a fresh flower, a rose full of scent. My business would have been his at my retirement for she is my only child. Now, we have both lost."

"Do you hold a grudge against him?"

"No, but he betrayed my expectations. It is a matter of fact that I wish him success in whatever honest activity he gets involved." He shook his head and concluded, "If you find him, tell him that I am still waiting for him." Fiorella shook hands and left through another door to avoid stumbling again into the same salesman who seemed to be more interested in her than in selling cars. By that time, the traffic became less chaotic and she was able to reach her apartment rather quicker.

At home, Fiorella had left a pile of dishes in the sink. The lavatory was in a mess and the bedroom in disarray. The untidiness did not bother her. Slowly, she began to bring some order out of the chaos. Being in a happy mood, she began to sing. The window was open and her voice travelled freely to the street. The passers-by raised their head to capture a gleam of the female singer. She exposed her head outside of the window to shake a small rug and realized that she had become the center of attention. She closed immediately the window and threw herself on the couch. She closed her eyes and murmured, "I am pretty sure that this time my treasure hunt will come to a close.

The air in the apartment was humid. She got up and opened the refrigerator. She grabbed a beer and gulped it without breathing. The bottle stood there empty in front of her. She drank it so fast that her head was spinning. Eventually, her head cleared and she was tempted to call some female acquaintances for advice. The temptation lasted a short while. It was a personal matter and she did not want it to become a topic for gossip. Two telephone book directories were resting underneath the telephone. She opened one and searched the page for car dealers. No name evoked interest and she was about to close it when an ad made her eyes bulge. The advertisement rested on the background of the Amalfitan Coast and read, "Under new owner, cars and motorcycles, Monday through Saturday from 9:00am to 9:00pm.

That day, she skipped the meal and did not close her eyes during the night. At the hospital, her colleague redoubled his efforts to engage her in a conversation, "Eh, baby, would you want to honor me this evening?"

"Doing what?" she responded somewhat distracted.

"We have dinner in the best restaurant in Mooco. It does not have to be necessarily Italian. It can be German. "La Comida Alemana is a fantastic place to eat. Their cuisine is exquisite. You will enjoy it. I guarantee you."

Fiorella looked at him straight in the eyes and said, "You can't even imagine what I long for right now."

"Well, tell me. I will do whatever you desire. I will make you happy. You know how much I value having you on my side."

"I am on your side, now, so what does it do to you?" She said and threw her arms upward.

"I don't mean that, my darling. I want our relationship to develop on a higher, more intimate sphere.

She became very serious and said, "From now on, please, do not address me with 'darling." I do not appreciate it."

"Would you like me to call you 'honeybone'?" And he laughed.

"No, I expect that our relations be strictly professional. Is it clear?"

"But, I care for you immensely," he insisted. "You mean everything to me, the sky, the heavens, the stars and the sea. My existence is empty without you."

She placed her hand on his mouth and said between her teeth, "Stop it! As a lover, you are not in my cards and as a poet you are mediocre."

He put his arms around her and said, "I can be more than that for you."

She disengaged quickly from his grip and distanced herself. "From now on, I am Dr. Fiorella Kappler for you. Understood?"

He remained speechless for a while, then, he said, "Go on, marry your sweet heart, your Italian pizza pie boyfriend, your ravioli maker and kiss his greasy hands. Do you want to tarnish your reputation? Be my guest! Remember that you are going to repent yourself!"

Fiorella's face got red. She got close to him and said in rage, "What I do with my private life is my business and if I want to marry an Italian and I meatball maker, I do not have to report it to you. I would be honored to have as a spouse a man whose hands are dirty after a hard, long, honest day of work. Your hands may be clean, but your heart is not. I begin to wonder how many researches you have conducted recently to pry on my privacy. You surely have hired some European investigators. Now, I know who you are Dr. Loser."

After work, Fiorella went to a beauty shop and returned home. The wardrobe was full of new dresses. She put on the most elegant black gown and a white shirt. A gold necklace sprawled around her neck and fell down her chest. She sprayed a few drops of cologne and smiled. Her teeth resembled pearls of snow. She looked at the shoes and opted for a pair with low heels that she had purchased in Florence. The long, blond hair did not need any brushing, but she did it anyhow. Down below the street, a taxi was waiting.

The car dealership was rather small, but arranged with decorum. In the interior, colorful balloons, attached on the cars doors, were hardly moving. Outside, pushed by the force of the wind, they were in perpetual motion in all directions. She stared at them for a while and entered. A salesman did not waste the time in welcoming her, "How may I help you, miss."

"I would like to speak with the owner or manager, if you don't mind."

"I am the manager. How can I help you?"

Fiorella was hesitant. "I wish to speak to the owner, then."

"He is temporarily occupied. Is there anything I can help?" In saying that, he lowered the upper part of the body in a clumsy way that made him almost trip.

"No, it is very kind of you, but I would rather wait."

The manager did his best to put on a polite demeanor." Do you care to sit down? I will bring you a nice cup of coffee."

"No, thank you. I am not a coffee drinker. I take it occasionally."

"Would you like to make an exception now?"

"No, really, I am fine."

"May I ask with whom I have the honor to speak with? I will announce you to him as soon as his consultation is over."

"Thanks you, I prefer to maintain my identity, anonymous"

"As you wish, miss."

Five minutes passed by. Fiorella was still resting on a chair. The manager bowed before her and announced that the owner was waiting for her. She got up instantly and rushed to the office. The door was half open. Her hand touched the knob and slowly pushed it. The eyes of both met and stared at each other in an interminable search. Each one of them was reading in the soul of the other. It was an identity search. For a while, neither one of them uttered a single word. He made no effort to get up. Maybe, he could not. He felt paralyzed by that girl standing before him. She closed the door with her heel, but never taking her eyes off of him. He blubbered something and tried to stand up. The strength had left him. Both hands rested on the armchair on a forty five degree angle. She kept on staring at him. Silence had taken over. Finally, she broke the impasse and moved in a slow motion, step by step, around the table until she stood right in front of him. The eyes of both of them never stopped asking questions. Her hand touched his almost by inertia.

The other hand made contact with his arm. She helped him to get up. Their noses skimmed each other. Two big tears ran down her cheeks. Their arms opened in a semicircle and closed in a tight circle. Her hand touched the light switch and the whole room got dark."

Dear reader, I imagine that your curiosity is extremely high, but the author cannot help you in this matter. He signed a document previous to the book promising not to disclose whatever they said to each other behind what he has already done. Needless to say, he does not wish to violate their privacy or the contract.

The manager was getting anxious. The meeting lasted much longer than what he expected. He knocked at the boss's office door and, without opening it, he informed him that a long line of clients was waiting for him. Felix and Fiorella were emotionally shaken. Fiorella cried most of the time. Felix too was deeply moved for whatever they shared in his office. She did not want to leave, but Felix begged her to go home, "Darling, I am very busy now. Go home and rest. You need it. I will call you as soon as I can. She held him tightly and said, "No, my love. I can't. I have been separated from you for years. I am not going to let you go anymore."

"But, darling," he insisted "Don't you want to celebrate this event with a glamorous dinner in the most elegant restaurant in Mooco?

"Of course!" she replied with enthusiasm.

"Good! Go home, rest and get ready by nine. I will pick you up."

"In that case, I will submit to the king's will," she said triumphantly. There was one more detail that remained open. She wrote on a paper her address and phone number and handed it to him. She had already moved away when she stopped, took a key and gave it to him. "Take it. In case I fall asleep..."

"No, I can't do that," he protested. "The area is inhabited by Germans. If they see me coming to your apartment, they may spread malicious rumors."

"Don't be so provincial, Felix. The world has changed. Look at the skyscrapers at Sao Paulo, the cars, life, people. Everything is different and will continue to do so. Nothing is stale anymore. We are no longer separated by language, culture or traditions. And, who cares about the Germans, the Portuguese and the Italians. Our love is better than all of them."

Felix walked to an assistant and spoke briefly with him. Fiorella was waiting. He kissed her and went on with meetings.

Outside, Fiorella waited for the light to turn green so she could cross the road. A gentleman from behind her said, "No, miss, you will ride with me in this Mercedes. Don Felix does not appreciate you walking alone in this busy area."

At those words, she looked backward and saw Felix who approved with a gesture of his hand.

It was hot by the time she entered in her apartment. The joy for having finally met his sweet heart was overwhelming. She took off the shoes and threw herself backward on the bed. It was impossible to rest.

"I have two hours. There is no hurry." Her eyes were wide open while she was dreaming, but gradually they blinked and, finally closed.

She was still sleeping when the door squeaked under the pressure of the key. Felix had called her before, but she did not hear the phone. The bedroom door was open. He did not hear any activity or noise going on. He looked at his shoes and took them off. Slowly, he proceeded toward the bedroom. She was laid with her arms stretched. He was tempted to kiss her. The fear that she would panic won over the temptation. He forgot he was carrying a large bouquet of red roses. Without generating any unnecessary noise, he placed it next to her right side and withdrew gently. He closed silently the door and left the apartment.

Ten minutes passed by and Fiorella began to toss left and right. She stretched her arms and her hand touched a rose and the thorn beneath of it. She got pinched and felt a pain. She brought both hands on her face and rubbed it. "I fell asleep! It must be late!" she exclaimed. She opened her eyes and smelled a perfume of roses. She turned her sight on the side and noticed a magnificent bouquet. She could not refrain her surprise and emitted a shout of joy. A drop of blood appeared on her finger. She got up and put a band aid on it. "Where are you?" she asked. The lack of response prompted her to search all over, but of her lover there was no trace. "Could it have been my colleague?" she questioned herself. She discarded quickly that hypothesis because he did not have the key to the apartment. Someone blew the car horn from below the street. The clock counted up to nine. She ran to the window and saw Felix waiving from a Mercedes. She waived back and motioned to him to wait five minutes. In that short lapse of time, she washed up, brushed her teeth, put a bit of make up on and selected the best dress.

Looking in the mirror, she said, "I am sorry, my darling. In the first, great night out, I overslept and I did not feel like sleeping. I can see he is punctual. I hope he will not hold it against me. It took years to win him over me and now I act like a derelict."

Fiorella locked the door with so much force that scarred other residents who appeared in front of their apartments to find out if something serious had happened. The appearance of Fiorella in the corridor generated exclamations of admiration in them. They followed her with their eyes while she descended the stairs in a hurry. When they couldn't see her anymore, they withdrew in their own rooms. Fiorella refused to wait for the elevator and arrived outside a bit breathless. Felix was waiting for her on the sidewalk. He complimented her on her attire. It was splendid! She wore an elegant pink gown with a red shirt. The shoes were black with high heels. Her blond hair flowed on one side of the face and emanated a soft perfume of violets. On the side of her hair, she pinned a rose she took from the bouquet her boyfriend brought her. Her lips had a light red color. He kissed her on her cheeks and opened the door for her and closed it as soon as he ascertained that she was comfortable."

She waited for him to take his seat and said, "The Italians are classy people. They have art and elegance in their DNA," and she smiled.

Felix accepted the compliments and replied, "They say that you cannot buy virtues."

"That's for sure!" she replied.

Before Felix ignited the motor, she asked him,""How do I look? Presentable?"

"You are just stunning!" he said.

"Do you like the rose?"

"Of course, I do. I gave it to you."

They both laughed, then, she said, "Thank you for the roses. They are just marvelous. Incidentally, why didn't you stay?"

"I did not want to scare you with my presence."

"But if I gave you the key."

"I was not sure of your reaction. I was afraid you would overreact at the beginning ignoring who was in front of you. I played it safe and left. I could have called you."

"Why didn't you?"

"I did not want to spoil your dreams."

A small card was overlapping her purse. It was the one found in the bouquet. She opened it, "To the one who made me smile again and returned to me the happiness that life robbed me."

She flung her arms around him and kissed him. "You are my happiness, darling. Let's forget the past. Today, we begin a new chapter in our life."

Not too far from them, a young man, well dressed was watching them intensely and spied every move they made. He did that until the car sped away.

Felix was getting impatient. The traffic was chaotic. His fingers moved nervously around the driving wheel. They were getting sweaty. At the beginning of the Avenida Alcantara Machado, he felt relieved. Two blocks away, at the famous restaurant, "O Vesuvius." The waiters were waiting for them. He parked the car on the back of the building and the two were welcomed by a button at the entrance. Another assistant accommodated them in a small separate, private room surrounded by glass windows. High vases of flowers from each corner gave a naturalistic feeling to the ambiance. The waiter swore white gloves and a smug. One of them opened a bottle of champagne and poured it into two glasses. He made a polite bow and returned shortly after with a big vase of red roses that he placed at the center of the table. Fiorella was overwhelmed by so much elegance and special attention. "Open the card," asked her Felix. She followed his request and read it, "To my sweet heart, may she be always beautiful and fragrant as these roses and may happiness smile on her forever." Fiorella smiled and put the card on her heart. Felix got up and kissed her. She drew the roses close to her and breathed in the scent. It was breathtaking. The privacy was not strictly observed by everyone. An intruder, from behind the glass windows, was watching the sequence of the events. Fiorella turned her head and noticed him. The smile disappeared from her lips. Felix caught the change and inquired if she were not pleased either with the gift or the service. She whispered something in his ears. The gentleman moved from his table and sat on another across from Fiorella. From that position he could face her better. His persistent and asphyxiating looks made her uncomfortable and she asked her boyfriend to exchange seat. She was visibly upset. Felix said, What is going on, here?"

"My colleague is a nuisance. I don't want to give him any opportunity to think that I am corresponding any of his illusions."

"This is interesting," exclaimed Felix in a gesture of protest. "Why didn't you disclose to me from the beginning that you were romantically involved with another man. I feel betrayed."

"Felix," she responded calmly "Your Italian proclivity to jealousy is inappropriate. I forbid you to make any innuendo of intimate relationship between him and me. Maybe, this is your pretext to impugn a sort of excuse to get rid of me. I will not allow your unfound suspicions to alter the course of our lives. You know that I love you to death. Any other insinuation on your part is destined to fail. He is a neurotic colleague, a romantic insane, a failure. What can I do? If it bothers you so much, I will quit the hospital. I do anything to remove from your mind any trace of unjustified rivalry." She picked up a rose from the vase and placed it on his nose. "How is this perfume?" she asked.

"I can't find words to describe it."

"Good! I can't describe my love for you either. It is greater than this perfume." She put the rose back in the vase and kissed him.

Felix was abundantly reassured of her love and did not extrapolate any further the issue.

The dinner continued without any further scratch and both enjoyed the exquisite food that the waiters brought throughout the evening on a wheeled carriage. "You know, this is super delicious. It reminds me of the food I had in Florence," she said.

"Wait a minute!" he objected. "Florence is not the only Italian city that provides an excellent cuisine.

Every city has its culinary specialty."

Fiorella laughed and said, "Honey, I beg your indulgence if with other highly respectable culinary traditions in your country, in our country. How do you like that?" she asked.

"Fabulous!"

The succulent dinner was wrapped up at midnight. The parking lot custodian handed the keys to Felix and rewarded him with a generous tip. A few minutes later, they were driving to a dancing hall in another district of the city.

They requested a private table and the manager complied with it immediately. While drinking a glass of cognac, Felix began to review his past since he left the army. Fiorella placed both hands under her chin and listened attentively. When he finished, she took him by the hand and led him to dance. She placed her arms around his neck and whispered to him, "I will never let you go again."

"You already told me that," he replied and accompanied his last word with laughter.

"It is a woman's prerogative to repeat."

Fiorella thought that she was enjoying her time in absolute privacy, but among the dancers there was one recognized her and greeted her, "Doctor, what are you doing here? You surely are a superb dancer."

She blushed, thanked her and complimented her too. "You are sensational!"

The two exchanged a smile and continued their dance. The music was deafening, but the dancers did not seem to mind it even if their sweet words got gulped by the loud noise. Many more people, mostly older, came in. One of them made a gesture to the band leader to lower the volume and he did. Felix did not feel comfortable being mingled with older folks and at the end of the song he led his dame away.

Outside, the temperature was balmy, a drastic contrast with the cold air that the air conditioner generated inside the dancing hall. Neither of the two lovers appeared to be tired and in common agreement decided to walk. They enjoyed strolling. Fiorella was perspiring happiness in the course of the ten blocks that separated them from the public park. A bench, behind a high bush, was empty. Felix pulled the handkerchief out of his pocked and placed it on the area where she was going to sit. Fiorella appreciated that exquisite act of courtesy and stretched her legs. Her head rested on his legs. A high street lamp distributed light on a wide area. The girl was not particularly delighted by the illumination and closed her eyes. The soft breeze brushed her hair and cooled her face.

Not too distant from them, an intermittent giggling confirmed the presence of other young couples. The laughter prompted Fiorella to move to a sitting position. Her hand soon reached her boyfriend's neck. He whispered, "What do you have up your sleeves, my dear?"

She smiled and said, "My love, don't you think that the time is ripe for us to think seriously about marriage?"

That question must have astonished Felix because he made a feeble attempt to free himself from her grip and said, "Are you for real? We have just met." The tone was so forceful, even though in a loving vein, that some of the neighbors turned their attention to them, at least, temporarily.

Fiorella, instead of getting upset or offended by the firm reply, looked straight at him, "Don't be silly! Our love story has deep roots that extend all the way to the infamous Buchenwald. Don't you agree, sweet heart?"

Felix took time before responding. Fiorella's look became serious. The answer was in the incubation process. Finally, he said, "My darling, our marriage will crumble in a few months if we do not get to know each other. We have different languages, different cultures, different traditions and different history. We don't even know if we share the same political ideals or pastime. At the present time, a sea separates us. The time will tell us whether we can cross the ocean together."

Fiorella, as if stung by in her most vulnerable inner being, had a quick reaction of self assertiveness and responded with pride, "No more of this...! Your excuses are puerile. How much do I have to do to prove my unconditional love for you? Probably, you have a labile mind. If you remembered only what I did in Naples to get you free from the carabinieri when they accused you of deserting the army. If you just thought about the pain that I suffered and the hallucinations of the concentration camp that I lived with you..." She laid her head down against the bench. A profound silence fell between them that lasted a while. Felix realized that she was very serious and said, "I did not mean to hurt you." He took her hand in his and added, "You know, more I reflect on it, more I am convinced that my remarks were inappropriate and egoistic. You are right. We shared so much suffering that should not be any more proof of our love." He waited to recompose his thoughts and said, "If you feel so serious about it..."

Fiorella could not have welcomed a better reaction from him. She leaned against his arm and said, "Please, darling, don't use that language to me again. Don't let me suffer another setback. It could be fatal."

He held her close to his heart and said, "I won't stand in your way. I share your dream."

She jumped from the bench and hugged him. "I love you! I love you! I love you!"

"Take it easy, darling! In that case, we must plan it for next year."

"Definitely not...! It is too far. I want an earlier date," she responded in a joyful defiant tone.

"Baby, I have just started a business. What do you want me to do, drop it and go bankrupt? I have to pay the bank. I have to see if it prospers. And, don't you know that the preparations have to be done a year in advance? We have to set up an appointment with the restaurant manager, with the priest, the band, the pastry maker..."

She controlled her euphoric attitude and said, "I agree with you." She paused a moment and added, "If you need financial assistance, I can support you from now on."

Felix appreciated her availability in money matters and said, "You are really giving me proof of your unconditional love. I am deeply moved."

"I have been telling you in so many different ways!" she responded with emphasis.

Felix reiterated his firm belief in the organizational aspect, "Don't you have to search for a wedding dress, prepare a list of guests, make the honey moon reservations, etc. We cannot rush, darling."

"You are absolutely right my sweet pie."

The following days were replete of activities. Felix and Fiorella met each day for several hours to try to fill in the gap created by the past. He took her to dine in the most celebrated restaurants of Mooco. Each day, their relationship intensified to the point that he introduced in his business valuable ideas that she suggested him. The car sale thrived and he bit his direct rivals in the daily stiff competition for market supremacy. At the end of the semester, Felix reported to her in a spirit of exuberance," Our income has surpassed any expectation. We paid our bank debts and we are starting with a considerable surplus.

Fiorella, responded triumphantly, "Behind a great man, there is always a great woman."

"I grant you that," he answered with a smirk. His voice waivered and said, "Next week, I will be out of town."

"And why is it?" she responded with apprehensiveness.

"I have to travel to Belo Horizonte for business and, later, to Brasilia."

"You will call me. Won't you?"

"Of course! In my free time or in the evening, I will give you a buzz."

"Will you bring me something good from Brasilia?

"I surely will."

She hung on his neck for a minute and said, "Don't forget. Promise is promise and I will be waiting."

Felix returned from his business trip and invited Fiorella to his apartment. She gently declined the invitation indicating that temporary health problems were at the basis of her refusal. He abruptly closed the phone call causing in her much dismay. Her body was achy and she did not have the strength to call him back and assure him of her love.

Ten minutes later, the bell of her apartment rang. A feeble voice barely reached his ears. He did not wait for her to open the door. "It's me!" He said. At first, the noise produced by the key scarred her, but her fear quickly turned into a joyful feeling when she recognized him, "Hi, honey, how are you doing?"

She was lying on her bed in a night gown. Her face looked pale. He handed her a small box of chocolates and touched her forehead. "The temperature is high," he commented. The kitchen was full of medical herbs. He managed to prepare a hot beverage and urged her to drink it. It was not easy. She made some efforts to push herself against the head bed. A pillow on her back alleviated her uncomfortable position. Herbal concussion acted like a tranquillizer and soon after her eyes started to get close. Felix placed a blanket on her and took a seat on the armchair. "I was concerned about the tone of your voice," she muttered.

"No, I realized immediately that you did not feel well and I came right over."

"It is so sweet of you," she answered.

During the night, her body temperature increased. Fortunately, she started to sweat and he assisted her by providing her clean towels and clothes.

In the morning, Fiorella woke up free of fever symptoms. The nostril felt the fresh aroma of coffee, while the noise of dishes and utensils arrived at her ears. She smiled. "Is there anyone violating my privacy?" Her question did not receive any answer. The slippers were down the bed where she left them.

In the act of bending down, she saw a bouquet of flowers that Felix had bought the previous day. "Good morning, darling!" He stated in a vigorous voice. "How are you doing?"

She drew back for a moment in a state of surprise and rested the right hand on her heart. Her face looked weary. The sweet perfume inundated her nostrils and lungs and she closed her eyes. "What a scare! I feel much better, thanks to you," she said.

Felix stood there watching with curiosity. A minute or so passed, during which both appeared to be absorbed in deep thought. Nearby her, a small box, well decorated, called immediately her attention. "Go on, open it!" he urged her. Her hand moved slowly toward the object. She unrevealed it and opened it. The diamonds lights of a ring struck her face. A sense of awe and profound happiness overwhelmed her. In the effort of reaching the box, her whole body slowly slipped downward. Felix's quick reaction prevented her from the further downward descent. He promptly grabbed a chair and let her sit. Her eyes reacquired the normal brightness and her strength returned like by miracle. "Go on, put it on. See if it fits. It is a gift that I brought from Brasilia." "It fits perfectly," she exclaimed with a profound feeling of gratitude and joy.

"You asked me to bring you something from my business trip," he said.

"Oh, I love it! Oh, my darling, this ring make me feel part of you." She surrounded his neck with her arms and hugged him. He pressed her against him.

"Don't press so hard," she cautioned him. "Remember that I was sick last night and I am still weak."

"Don't worry, my sunrise. I am elated just by looking at your face."

"We should celebrate the event with a bottle of champagne," she suggested.

"Great idea! But, early in the morning? It is not the proper time of the day," he protested.

"No, it is going to be now." She got up and walked around the room. When she realized that he was following her, she asked him, "Where are going?"

"I was afraid you were going to fall. I was behind you for protection.

"Exactly! She said and accompanied the exclamation with a smirk. "May I remind you" she added, "A host serves the guests, but as long as you are so sweet, I will limit my work in sharing with you this bottle of champagne with a piece of pie."

Felix jumped at the opportunity and grabbed the first bottle that lay across from him. She slapped his hand gently and reproached him, "Don't put your hand in the wrong place. You chose a bottle of Strega, which is too sharp for me."

Felix put back the Strega bottle and pulled out the right one. The glasses were already there. He filled them with the sweet liquor and crossed arms with her. The chin-chin exchange was a bit clumsy and part of her beverage fell on him. Both laughed wholeheartedly when Felix finished his glass and grabbed hers too. "Don't get drunk!" She warned him. Felix was unable to finish drinking her glass. His cellular rang. It was the general manager of his business who requested his immediate presence at his office. Fiorella expressed the desire to join him, but he cautioned her to stay put and rest.

The car building was surrounded by police cars. Felix groaned. He parked the vehicle and inquired to his manager about the urgent call and the police presence. The administrator explained to him briefly how two thieves dug a hole on the roof and made their way through the attic. They lowered a ladder and stepped in the main room close to the central door where the alarm system went off. The police, alerted by the loud sound, arrived on the scene in a short time and blocked the exit. The thieves felt like two trapped mice and opposed no resistance. Felix and his entourage met for a quick meeting and got busy to repair the damage.

At the veterinarian hospital, Fiorella's colleagues noticed the engagement ring on her finger and lavished on her extravagant, congratulatory remarks. Only one abstained. He looked livid. His eyes became fiery and his face red. The festive atmosphere overpowered him and he withdrew in a corner where a lab technician was making some tests. In the evening, he did not respond to an invitation from the president to attend a party in Fiorella's honor.

Something unusual occurred in the weeks that followed. Felix showed signs of amnesia and locked himself in an unexplained silence. This preoccupied Fiorella to the point that she was getting sick over it.

"If you are not going to cooperate with me and start talking, I am going to take you to a psychologist, an old friend of mine from Berlin. It is a matter of fact that he was a family acquaintance."

Felix blubbered something. His lips moved nervously up and down. She was standing there eager to hear from him. "I dream .. ed, I dream ... ed," he fumbled.

"About what?" she kept on pressing him.

"I dreamed about two gypsies."

"What significance do they have in your life?" she inquired. "Because you dreamed about two gypsies, you lost your tongue? Not to mention the apprehension that you caused in me."

"Felix lowered his head and said in a submissive voice, "It is more than that."

Fiorella's eyes opened up unnaturally and she stared at him. Her ears perked up and her mind became extremely attentive.

"At Buchenwald, before I escaped, "he continued, "They talked about a chalice that they brought from their homeland. Somehow, they were able to bring it in the camp. Don't ask me how. Later, they rose to the rank of 'capot' and had a better opportunity to hide it."

"May I ask the importance of that chalice?"

"It was gold."

"Is it all? All chalices, especially in Catholic churches, are made of gold. Are you concerned about the worth of it?"

"The monetary value is irrelevant here. There is something more important attached to it that makes it utterly special."

"Don't be so gullible!" she reprimanded him. "Gypsies make their living by telling tales, among other things. They are masters at it, my sweetheart. I live in a scientific environment. Remember that."

"It is not that they attribute to it miraculous powers," rebutted her boyfriend.

"Then, what is it? A gold metal? Is that what you want to remind me? And, for what purpose? I don't understand how a chalice turns you into a mute person."

Felix passed his right hand over the forehead and said, "It is all my fault. I should not have mentioned it. Don't mind me. It has no value to you."

Fiorella did not think that it was necessary to push the issue any further. She obtained her initial objective. Her boyfriend started to talk again. Later, she returned to the same subject, "If it has value for you, the chalice must have a value for me too."

This time the provocation had its effect. "Somehow, there is something mysterious in the chalice and the story of both gypsies has yet to be unfolded."

"Now, I am getting really curious. It sounds like a fascinating story. Tell me more about it."

"If I only knew what's beneath the ashes..."

"Does it still bother you their story?"

"I swore that I would invite them at my wedding, but where am I going to find them? Probably, they died in the concentration camp."

Fiorella looked at Felix with empathy and said," If it is meant, you will find them, if not now, later."

CHAPTER XXXV

Fiorella's Preparations and Wedding

A year passed by and Fiorella was getting impatient. She wanted to get married. Felix, to please her, set up an appointment with the priest of Sao Jacinto's church. Both arrived on time and took seat in the rectory's waiting room.

The priest was a short man with gray hair combed toward the forehead. His chin was the depository of a long, triangular bird. It was so prominent that it became the focus of attention of any interlocutor. He was an extremely reserved clergyman who disliked going around the bush on religious matters. He was also very strict in his religious views and never accepted compromises when theological issues were under criticism. He never allowed liturgical celebrations were tainted with what he considered blasphemous material. On other matters of secondary importance, he did not hesitate to be lenient.

The secretary announced him to the couple and sat on the armchair behind his desk. After a brief introduction, he said, "So, you want to get married."

"Yes, Father," responded immediately Fiorella.

"Have you thought of the church decoration?"

"Yes, I want the exterior isles decorated with red ribbons. All the altar steps have to be covered with white flowers, except a space for passing by. I have already contacted a German pianist who will execute Beethoven and Mozart's music. Outside of the church, I want flowers on both sides of the entrance. Of course, the red carpet has to cover the entire isle from the front to the end. A friend of mine will sing the Ave Maria of Shubert."

The secretary was taking notes all way along. When the priest heard 'Shubert', he intervened, "My dear," he said, "I run my church on sobriety. The red carpet, the flowers, the ribbons are integral parts of the decorative aspect of the ceremony, but I do have some reservations."

"What? My dress?" queried Fiorella in distress.

"Not really. If you can afford twenty million cruzeiros for the wedding dress, that is fine."

"Who told you that my dress is very expensive?" Inquired Fiorella with curiosity.

"I do not want to send a wrong message on that even though I don't consider sober sign. Again, I do not control your pocketbook. If I had a say in someone's bank account, I would devolve a few millions to the 'favellas." But, that's not the case here. I do object, however, to the music."

Felix felt that it was his responsibility to ask for clarifications. "I do not understand the relevance of a social issue with a private, religious celebration."

The priest looked very poised. "The contentious issue here is that Shubert's Ave Maria is the main contention glamorizes two young people who live in a state of sin, ergo, it is in contrast with the Church's canonical law and it violates the spirit of your wedding."

Felix looked like a boiling pot. The irritation was quite visible on his face. "If I gave you a million of cruzeiros, you would allow our singer to sing even five of those Ave Maria."

The prelate, in a rare display of his natural hot temperament, rose on his feet, hit the table with the fist and said, "Enough with blasphemies!"

"They sang it in other churches," protested Felix.

"There may very well be," responded the pastor. "There may be some priests who are part of that circle. They presume to achieve sanctity by pleasing man instead of God, but remember that they represent a minority. In our church, we have had witnesses of God who devoted their lives to mankind for the sake of Christ throughout history. I do not wish to betray Christ's teaching."

Fiorella made an attempt to bring some common sense in the debate or, at the least, to reconcile both parties, but the priest's position was irremovable, "Many of you are being too superficial toward the sacrament of marriage and wish to turn it into a carnival, an affront to dignity, civility and piety, not to mention sacredness of the ceremony itself."

"You are exaggerating now," responded Fiorella.

"I do?" replied the priest. "Last year, a couple approached me and asked if they could bring their cat and dog as witnesses. Another couple asked me if they could carry a pet pig to the altar. Lastly, two future spouses asked permission to bring a goat to their wedding."

"This is ridiculous," snapped Fiorella.

"Would you like to know another one?"

Fiorella did not respond and the priest continued, "I refused to bless a marriage of a couple who wanted to come to church on horses."

"I imagine that they would leave the animals outside," remarked the young lady.

"You should understand that the excrements stink and that is totally inappropriate with the romantic atmosphere and the religious spirit of the event," explained the priest.

The secretary had been listening anxiously up to that moment. Obviously, she was concerned about the priest's health too. He was under doctor's care for his heart. She looked at the two future spouses and said, "You may not believe it, but a girl and her boyfriend requested if they could have had a party in the sacristy immediately after the nuptial knot. You won't believe the requests we get."

"But, in other churches, they allow it," replied Fiorella.

"As our beloved Father pointed out earlier, the church, like any other institution, is infested with wolves that are incoherent with the vow that they gave at the time of the ordination. They get along and submit to every demand urged by our spoiled youth.

Faith and morality are not fashions. They are flames that keep alive our Christian doctrine." The secretary could not take any more the brunt of that conversation. She got up and told the priest that she was going to be absent temporarily. The rectory's door opened and closed.

Fiorella felt relieved, and turning toward the priest, said, "Father, let us be realistic. The church's attendance has been gradually and drastically diminishing. It is an acute crisis. Let's not widen the wound.

We would like to break the tradition and bring fresh air in a stale ceremony."

"By doing what?" Responded quickly the prelate

"Don't you realize that you are being old fashioned? It is still an Ave Maria. At the completion of the ceremony, we could have a pizza party in the courtyard."

Felix, who had been silent for a while, took the floor, "I agree. It would bring in originality."

"Always along that line," added Fiorella, "I should inform you that my white dress goes above the knees. Does it bother you?"

The priest reacquired his calm poise and answered, "If you wish to be the object of derision, go right ahead. Your originality is a reflection of bad taste and the culmination of vulgarity. In that case, it is my responsibility to preserve the religious ceremony on a rank of spiritual purity. Let's be clear about it! Nothing less is acceptable. I give you one week to reflect on it."

The two visitors shook their heads and got up. Both made a half bow simultaneously and left.

Once in the street, Felix exploded, "I do not want to come back to the place, ever." He expressed his feelings in such excited manner that Fiorella had to hold him back and remind him that patience is a virtue

"Did you like what he said," he inquired in a nervous tone.

"My dear, I have witnessed an unprecedented exhibition of narcissism. More people will not go to church. You will see."

"Nobody has the intention of robbing a religious ceremony from the spiritual connotation. If some individuals have in mind to turn a temple into a zoology exposition, it goes out of hand and, in that case, I share his views."

Fiorella face became suddenly like wax. Felix noticed it. Many ideas were running through his head. "Don't worry about it," he whispered to her ear. He helped her in the car and whisked her away.

The evening was calm. The wind had stopped brushing the leaves of the city trees. There was no breeze and the humidity was unnaturally absent. Felix and Fiorella walked hand in hand at the central park. After a while, a lazy cloud began to shape up above their heads. A soft wind suddenly showed up and dissolved it. The same wind disappeared with a higher speed. The cloud fragments quickly recomposed, as if attracted by an internal magnetic force and hung over the park watching life beneath it.

Then, it became erratic again and moved to a more suitable location.

Strolling inside the public park, Fiorella pulled Felix on the side and invited him to take a sit on a nearby bench. His hands were slightly cool. She held them in hers and warmed them up. Her face was radiant with joy. He looked at her and said, "What would you like to tell me?"

Without hesitation, she replied, "I would like to get married."

He smiled and said, "Do you know what?"

"What?" she inquired.

"You have to wait a while."

"I know it. I know it. I just want to be with you all the time." In saying that, she raised her voice and other couples going by turned their attention to them for a few seconds.

Felix placed the index of his right hand on the tip of the nose and cautioned her to whisper. "Sh-h-h. Don't disturb people."

She jumped on her feet and shouted, "I don't care! I am happy. I am the happiest woman in the world," and hugged him.

Felix tried to disengage gently from her grip and said, "Are you out of your mind? We have become the center of attraction."

"Let it be! What is wrong with that?" she thought of having made an inappropriate remark and put her head down.

Felix raised her chin and said, "I have a confession to make. I don't know how you are going to take this news."

Fiorella's face got livid. Those words seemed to be the prelude of a rupture. She looked intensely in his eyes and waited for the worst. "Tell me whatever you want, but don't leave me," she said in a soft tone.

He pulled a small box from the inside pocket of his jacket and handed it to her. "Here, it is yours. Open it."

Fiorella's hands began to tremble. Without removing her eyes from his, she ripped the paper with a small twitch on her nose. She uncovered the box and unrevealed the paper with the message on it. As she touched something solid, she was unable to suppress a feeling of overwhelming joy and fell in his arms. At that point, some couples really got concerned and asked them if they needed any help. Felix smiled and they got the message. Fiorella was ecstatic and began to sweat. Felix wiped her forehead and brow and suggested her to take control of her emotions. She picked the ring with diamonds and said, "It is simply gorgeous. I can't believe it! You are and going to be always my first and last love.

Fiorella passed a stormy night mixed with joy and apprehension. The daylight came as a liberator. Her first objective on the agenda for that day was to call the parish secretary at Santo Jacopo church and set up an appointment with the priest. At the designated date, Fiorella dressed up in a white shirt and black pants. The shoes had low and thin heels. A red rose in the hair summarized all her feelings. The make-up was much elaborated.

Felix did not oppose any resistance to Fiorella's decision He put on a pair of blue slacks and a black and went to her apartment to pick her up. The fifteen minutes car ride came to a quick end and the two promised spouses took a seat in the waiting room. About thirty seconds passed and the door slowly opened. The guests stood up. The secretary offered them a faint smile and an apology for the absence of the priest who was summoned by the bishop for an urgent meeting.

On the way out, Fiorella and Felix ran into a group of people arguing with animosity. At the sight of Fiorella and Felix sight, they resorted to a temporary lull. One of them looked at Felix and queried, "I don't mean to intrude in you private affairs, but by any chance, did you talk to Father?"

"Of course, not," responded Felix in an irritated tone.

"He is on vacation."

A lady pulled a newspaper from her pocket book and showed it to him. Felix saw the picture of Don Gallino and yawned. The lady did not seem to appreciate his disinterest and grabbed the paper from him. "This article is contrary to John Paul II. 1988 Encyclical on "Mulieres Dignitatem." Don Gallino should be more pragmatic and be concerned with the church's internal issues rather than politicize women's attire."

"What did he do?" inquired Fiorella still ignoring their main concern.

"Last week, he exposed a big sign on the steps of the church warning ladies to adhere to a dress code in church because it represents a provocation for men..."

A gentleman behind her intervened, "You should explain to these two young people the real issue of the sign. Father argues that man's aggressive behavior, even when it reaches a level of seduction and violence, is defendable because of women's deliberate exposition of certain anatomical parts of the body."

"This is untrue," responded the lady. "The pope exalts woman's dignity, but this priest denigrates it."

Fiorella interjected, "Don Gallino is right to criticize a questionable feminine attire; however, violence is always inexcusable."

Felix exposed his position in these terms, "In my view, the priest threw a pebble in the pond of both genders."

A young man said, "I don't mind watching girls in mini gowns, but I disapprove vulgarity and exhibitions of nudity and gay parades."

An adult of about thirty-five years of age added, "I don't agree with those who are exerting pressure of resignation on Father. It is better that he remains here; at least, the bishop can control him. He can't control him when he is on vacation."

Felix asked him, "Did you say that he went on vacation?"

"Yes, everybody knows that."

A man with spectacles opened his way to the center of the group and shouted, "Priests are and should be the custodians of morality. They have to be vigilant. The problem is elsewhere. Money, drugs and power put woman's dignity on the social market, on the merchandize market."

A man with mustaches concluded, "It is unjustifiable to consider women's attire as provocation acts. The chronicle of every day talks about men who kill their wives or girlfriends without physical innuendos."

While the group was dispersing, a young man said, "If a woman walks around with jewels, whose fault is it? It is the same when they do not observe the limits of good taste in attire."

The weather was changing. The sky got dark. Drops of water wetted the dry pavement. Felix looked at his hands. They were getting wet. He raised his right hand and bid good-by to the group, "Hata maña!"

The priest's forced vacation became a national issue in the church. The mass media picked any bone they found to increment the debate. Felix and Fiorella were stunned. They were in a limbo.

At the end, they decided not to wait for the reintegration of Don Gallino and looked elsewhere for marriage. They heard about Don Vito, a priest of a small parish suburb. He built a gigantic church for a small community. The neighbors were not too happy about it, but he became especially unpopular when, during a homely, threatened to withhold absolution on those parishioners who dropped coins in the basket. Felix leaned over his girlfriend and whispered, "I don't believe it. Let's get out of here. This is not for us."

The following Sunday, Felix and Fiorella attended a mass service in a slum area of the city. The church was crowded as usual. At the end of the homely, the priest made an announcement that left everybody astonished. He stretched his arms wide open and exclaimed, "Dear brothers and sisters, "I have a confession to make." Nobody gave too much emphasis to that remark. He continued, "This is my last celebration." The parishioners looked at each other thinking at a possible reassignment to a different parish as part of the bishop's periodical priestly reshuffling. If that were the case, some parishioners resented it that they were not informed ahead of time. Not that it made any difference in their lives, but many were emotionally attached to him. The priest waited for the noise to abate, then he added, "My dear sons and daughters, it is not what you may be thinking. No, I am leaving the church because my girlfriend is pregnant and I am going to marry her." The initial uproar of the parishioners was followed by a deep, religious silence. No one dared to make any remark. Their minds were frozen. The celebrant lowered his head and continued the rite. Fiorella and Felix got up and walked out on their tiptoes. As soon as they reached the street, Felix said, "It looks like that there is no more priest to marry us."

Fiorella protested, "Do not despair, my dear. One door closes and another opens. There are one hundred cathedrals in the whole country. Patience will conquer all."

"Yes, but I am about to lose it."

Fiorella put an arm around him and said, "This time, I will choose the church even if you may not like it."

"On the other hand, I sympathize with the priest. He cannot take anymore the heat and he got out of the kitchen. That's the way it should be. You cannot enjoy the love of God and the love of a woman. The two do not coincide."

"Why? A man cannot love a woman and serve God?"

"It is not that. A Married priest has to share his love. A woman is going to be forced to carry the brunt of the family. Many times, it is like being a widow.

"Certainly, there are limitations to a married priest."

Fiorella got busy and invited her sweet heart to attend a wedding celebration in a different denomination's church. Maybe, they could have availed of a new experience. It was not going to be a communal marriage where many couples would be married together as they did the previous month. Prior to the scheduled event, on the rehearsal evening, the minister summoned briefly the bride and groom and urged them to be very attentive during the ceremony. Any distraction could cause delays in the rite. He also recommended the photographers not to distract the future newlyweds with their cameras glares.

The wedding protagonists were going to be a local singer star and a baron, famous for his wealth. The minister asked them to verify if the red carpet, the flower arrangements on the altar and the readings were to their likings. At the end of it, he addressed them in this way, "Make sure that besides brushing your teeth before the ceremony, you chew a licorice to sweeten your breath. Politeness does not cost anything and it won't do any harm to the groom if he sprinkles a couple of drops of perfume on his suit. Remember that people are funny. You want to leave a good impression on them." The last remarks caused all those standing by to crack jokes. An old discolored mirror hanged on one of the walls. The priest approached it and combed his hair. "This is not an act of vanity, my friends, but of neatness. A quick review of your head will ensure your impeccable grooming."

As scheduled, the bride left their house at eleven o'clock sharp of the next day. They were riding a horse and buggy cart. The bride was sitting on a throne installed on the very top. Her body was a cornucopia of flowers of various colors. The carriage stopped a short distance from the church precinct and four poll bearers took over the carrying of the throne. The groom had opted to ride a white horse alongside the same road.

The bridal party and the spouses families followed on a carriage decorated with red and white balloons.

The coachman himself dressed in a light multicolor shirt, white pants and white shoes. Traditionally, the family members threw confetti or rice to the crowd. This time, they changed the tradition and distributed dollars alongside the way. The money bills caused an aggressive participation on the part of the young people lining up the street. It was not a rare event to see many of them rolling on the ground and fighting for the prize.

The band was composed by twenty musicians who submitted to a special competition to be part of the group. The bride and groom asked them to play popular songs rather than religious hymns. When they arrived at the central door of the temple, the musicians divided into two sections. Each formed a protective barrier to the guests.

Being a wedding of rich and famous man and woman, the family called on the police presence to maintain order on the road and inside the church.

In the meantime, the four young men supporting the throne stopped at the center of the main altar and gently lowered the bride. The temple was filled to the brim. At a signal of the minister, the choir began to play "Ciao, Bella, Ciao." The ushers took on established positions to ensure that the guests felt comfortably. The groom descended from the horse and with a military cadence proceeded toward the main altar to join his bride. The bridal party flanked the altar. Felix and Fiorella found a seat close by the altar.

The minister, accompanied by two assistants, walked toward the altar and took the central position. After the usual homily on the meaning of family unity, the minister called on the ring bearer for the exchange ceremony. The bride was chewing a gum in a relaxed position. Seeing the girl carrying the box, she said, "Honey, come here to take the ring because I don't want to get up." The groom, who was not sitting next to her, but a few feet away, complied with her desire. The minister felt offended, but to avoid any distasteful twist to the ceremony, did not step in to assert his authority. The crowd enjoyed every bit of it, especially, when the minister asked the bride and groom to exchange the kiss. The bride pulled the chewing gum from her mouth and stuck it on the bride's lip. The reaction of the guests was hilarious and tumultuous. The minister hurried to finish the ceremony and asked both the bride and the groom to stand up and present them to the guests as husband and wife.

In the act of getting up, all the flowers from the bride's body fell on the floor. The minister's mouth opened up in dismay and his eyes came out of the sockets. He raised his arms, made some incoherent sounds and fell backward, dragging along his assistants on the floor. The guests stood up to capture a glimpse of the twisting events. The bridal party members hurried to surround the body of the spouse because underneath of the nuptial veil there was hardly anything. The astonishment turned soon into disgust for many. Never before they had witnessed a sacred rite turned into a sacrilegious exhibition. They got up and left. For others, it was an unforgettable moment of hilarity. The baron took off his jacket and covered his wife's body. With the help of the assistants, he hushed her out of the temple. The newly-wed car did the rest.

The appetite of the mass media saw no end to it and created a Spanish style 'telenovela.' The minister was demoted by ministry, but his poor health played in his favor and he was, finally, restored to his rank.

Felix and his sweetheart were still reflecting on next step. They walked for a couple blocks to the parking lot they had parked the car. The car rolled past Vila Ema and stopped at the Avenida Paes de Barros where went for shopping. At the exit, they noticed a pinnacle of a church whose inferior section portrayed a neoclassical style while the top was reminiscent of the Baroque period. Felix and Fiorella decided to make an impromptu visit to the interior of the temple. They entered with a superficial reverence. He wetted his forefingers in the holy water and made the sign of the cross.

She did not echo his gesture. The columns were clearly Ionic, while the vaults were roman. The altar had a geometrical, circular configuration with an angel on the lateral wing and the image of Christ with his Mother on the main wall. The painting had been executed by an unknown Italian artist. At least, he did not sign it. In the middle of the church, a woman was scrubbing a small area of the marble floor. An idea flashed through Fiorella's mind. She approached the worker and asked her if she could speak with the reverend.

"Monsignor Mingol? He may be busy at this moment." She dropped the mop on the pail and said, "Wait a moment. I am going to look for him. If he is available, he will be happy to talk to you."

She made a few steps and stopped. She turned her head backward and said, "May I ask the reason?"

"Marriage preparations, if you know what I mean."

"Very well, I will see what I can do for you."

Shortly after, the lady came back and said, "I am so sorry! I can't help you in this matter. Monsignor has a long list of meetings today."

"When do you think we can meet with him? Tomorrow?" inquired Felix with impatience."

"My dear, "replied the woman, I am the janitress. You should go to the rectory and make an appointment with the secretary. She is nice and may fit you in his schedule."

"Is he that busy?" Fiorella queried with incredulity.

The lady laughed and replied with a mixture of understanding and compassion, "My dear, it takes weeks, even months, at times to lock in a meeting with him. So, if the secretary can get you in tomorrow, you are fortunate."

Felix and his girlfriend stared at each other without making any further comment. They thanked the lady and withdrew to the last pew next to the exit. They sat for about five minutes trying to find an answer to their dilemma, but could not in the midst of that oppressing silence. Suddenly, Fiorella noticed some movement going on around a confessional. She tapped on Felix's shoulder and, without pronouncing a word; she motioned to him to look in that direction. They got up and approached the confessional. The name on it was very visible, "Monsignor Mingol." Felix waited for a lady to get up and leave, and quickly rushed over to replace her. The people who were waiting in line did not appreciate the intruder's bad manners and many of them shook their heads that clearly reflected their disappointment.

Monsignor opened the small door that separated him from Felix and asked him what sins he had committed. Felix responded, "Father, I am deeply sorry, but I am not here to confess my sins."

"Then, what is your motive for being here? This place is reserved to confession. Obviously, you are in the wrong place."

"I understand that, Father," Felix tried to defend himself. Indeed, I am in the right place. It is urgent that I talk to you. My girlfriend is pregnant and we want to get married as soon as possible. If you know what I am."

"I suggest you to make an appointment with the secretary. We need time to prepare a marriage."

Monsignor was getting nervous, then, he added, "OK. Come on Tuesday. I can allow you no more than ten minutes. If you miss the ten o'clock appointment, you have to deal with my secretary. Now, leave immediately. This is not the place for you to be." He closed the door and turned his attention on the other side of the confessional.

Felix came out of the confessional smiling. He genuflected before the main altar, took his girlfriend by hand and led her outside. On the front steps he appeared elated. "What happened?" She asked.

"I was able to squeeze a promise from his mouth."

Which is?"

"We have an appointment with him next Tuesday."

"You were able to extract that from his lips? That's terrific!" She responded in a euphoric mood.

One of the church attendants, who were appointed to screen the flow of people in and out of the church, cautioned her to be more discreet and control her excitement in a place where silence has a primary importance.

On Tuesday, Felix and Fiorella arrived at the rectory with punctuality. The secretary announced their presence to Monsignor and asked them to enter in his office. Monsignor shook hands with both of them and asked them to have a seat. He also reminded them that had only ten minutes to discuss their case.

Before sitting, Felix placed a 'swollen' envelope in the hands of the prelate who launched a rapid, but attentive glance to it and said, "I appreciate this tangible gesture of generosity on your part." He adjusted his position on the armchair and opened his arms as when delivering a homely. His voice was soft and delicate, "My dear friends, what's in your mind? I am here to serve you."

Fiorella shared a half smile with her boyfriend and began, "Monsignor, we are going to take less time that the one you allotted to us. We would like to get married and have invited a singer, a friend of us, to sing the Ave Maria of Shubert."

The prelate first hurried to place the envelope in his vest pocket, then, he said, "Your generosity is sufficient to grant you permission. What is the date of your planned wedding?"Felix and Fiorella looked at each other in dismay and held their hands tightly from the joy. The game was over.

CHAPTER XXXVI

The Deadly Wedding Reception

Fiorella did not look at the expenses. After all, her future husband was already getting rich and she was a doctor. She was determined to have one of the most glamorous weddings ever seen in Sao Paolo. Felix hesitated on the exorbitant expenses of the reception. "A bit of moderation would not hurt," he commented. Although his girlfriend agreed with him, her wedding was the culmination of a long sought dream with the man who shared the concentration camp and other vicissitudes. Many losses had characterized her life and stigmatized her interior being. "For too long, I longed to marry you. It is not going to be a second class wedding, either. Listen, if you don't wish to participate in the payment, I am willing to bear all the expenses with my savings."

Felix responded briefly, "That is not the point. Anyway, I am not going to spoil your dream day. Do whatever makes you happy."

She hugged him and said, "Thank you, my darling."

The nuptial ceremony was postponed twice due to Fiorella's religious beliefs. She was a Lutheran and did not believe in confession. "I confess my sins only to God," she said. At the last moment, an agreement was reached between the two parties. For the love she had for Felix, Fiorella agreed to submit herself to the reconciliation sacrament. In exchange, he would respect her faith.

At the 'Pizzaria do Angelo,' the future bride and groom began to compile a list of guests. Their desire was to keep a low profile on the number, but raise the quality of the reception.

Felix opened the newspaper and the heading article called his attention. A Ukrainian man, who lived in the state of Maryland, was under the accusation of having been a capot' in the concentration camp at Buchenwald. He was also under heavy suspicion for the death of three Italian prisoners, two of them priests.

A more devastating accusation came from other sources who claimed that he committed additional atrocities at the expenses of other nationalities even though two gypsies tried to dissuade him. The word, "gypsies' sounded a bell in Felix's mind and he read avidly the whole article. He stood there pensive for a long time until Fiorella woke him up from his thoughts, "What happened, honey? Did you read something sad?"

"No, not really," he tried to cover up his feelings by placing the newspaper in his jacket packet. He spent the whole night tossing on each side of the bed. He kept on repeating, "The two gypsies, where are they?"

The hospital, where Fiorella was in service, got the news of the grandiosity of the wedding plan and made all sorts of comments. The doctor, who was secretly in love with her, suggested his colleagues to throw a party in her honor to help her defray the expenses of the onerous reception. He quelled any dissent by proposing to bear all the expenses if they did not get along with his plan Although, the idea was palatable to most of them, the director thought it wise not to get engaged in a massive party on the animal hospital grounds. The sanitary reasons played the primary role in his rejection. The dynamic doctor, however, did not give up and, shortly after, started to elaborate another more diabolic project.

"Restaurants' Uniform" was a renown shop in the suburb of Sao Paulo. It was popular for being the first to offer the latest fashion uniforms at an affordable price. The veterinarian doctor arrived in an early afternoon and began scouting around the different styles. A lady employee approached him with a smile, "How can I serve you, sir?"

"I am browsing around, madam."

"May I help you in choosing the right uniform?"

"Well, I guess I am at the mercy of you assistance. What would you suggest me?"

"Is the uniform for your wife?"

Oh, yes, indeed," responded in a hurry the doctor who barely hid a sense of discomfort

"May I ask you the size?" Inquired politely the assistant.

"She has a body almost like mine."

"Which is?" responded the employee in an interrogative tone. The veterinarian felt uneasy about it. "Do you mind to measure my size?"

"Not at all," replied the woman with a courteous gesture. When she finished, she went to the rack at the right and pulled out a uniform, "This would fit perfectly to your wife."

"Could I try it on?" he asked her.

"Absolutely! The fitting room is straight ahead of us."

The man tried the uniform and he saw that it fit impeccably well. "I buy it."

The lady said, "Very well! Your wife will be happy with your choice. Please, follow me at the cash register where I will pack it up for you.

"How can I pay?" inquired the client.

"As you wish, with the credit card or in cash."

The man paid the bill and left. The saleswoman followed him with her eyes until he stopped in front of a beauty shop supply and, after launching a few glances around, entered. He perused some hair pieces and tried some of them. The mirror in front of him allowed him to see how he looked. He picked one and proceeded toward a glassy box containing various types of lipstick. His preference went for the red color. Further down, there was an array of earrings. Five minutes later, he left with one bag one on each hand.

In the meantime, Fiorella arranged the wedding reception in every detail. On that same Saturday evening, a waitress with long blond hair approached the huge, rectangular table of the wedding party. She gave a glance around her and brought in some champagne bottles from cases resting at the nearby entrance. She placed them on the table one by one. She opened a few and filled the glasses half way. The names of the bridal party and those of the guests had already been prepared by the manager and were laid on the table.

The appearance on the scene of an apparently strange waitress did not throw the kitchen personnel into chaos. Those who noticed her were working feverishly and did not bother questioning anyone. By the time the reception was over, exhaustion played a vital role in putting to dormancy the entire episode. Her quick disappearance from the kitchen put to rest the whole issue.

The waitress in the reception room did her best to camouflage her identity. She dropped some powder in Fiorella's glass, checked the silverware and gained in the exit door in a hurry. The manager came in to oversee the reception hall and noticed that the glasses had already been filled half way with champagne.

He launched a glance toward the exit and barely saw a string of long blond hair. There were two blond ladies among the personnel in service that evening, but both of them swore that they had nothing to do with the champagne bottles although one of them admitted that she had brought the cases next to the entrance. The manager grew suspicious with the passing minutes. To dispel any doubt from her mind, she tasted three different glasses, but she did not find any anomalous taste in them. The waitress, in the meantime, escaped the premises undisturbed.

The guests began to show up in pairs and in groups. The bride and the groom arrived with ten minutes of delay. In the midst of such an excitement, the master of the ceremony grabbed a bell and called the participants to her attention. He announced the official opening of the reception and received a standing ovation. He, then, invited them to raise their glass and cheer to the future spouses. Fiorella and Felix crossed their right arm and drank the glasses content. Soon after, Fiorella experienced frequent symptoms of sleepiness. They brought her a coffee to keep her awake. The result was null. A dame from the wedding party debited the condition to the heavy engagement in the wedding preparations. Another one claimed that it was the normal consequence of a nuptial tension. Soon, this idea spread around the guests and obtained a major consensus. In a latter confession, Felix admitted that during the first honeymoon night his wife did not sleep a wink. Another indiscretion that became food for speculation was Fiorella's precocious pregnancy. Those moments of disorientation lasted about an hour at the end of which she started to feel a sense of relief and the reception continued without interruption with everybody's satisfaction.

In reality, Fiorella had a tumultuous honeymoon night. She experienced sporadic hot flash sensation followed by drowsiness. She attributed restlessness to exhaustion and tried to sleep, but it was not that easy. In the following days, she was hoping to get better. Her husband attributed her condition to tension. As soon as they got back home, Fiorella's first act was to arrange an appointment with the pediatrician. The first medical test revealed the presence of foreign chemicals in the body that caused a 'conflict' in the ovarian organs. Fiorella read the verdict through the lines and cried. She was sterile.

Felix arranged other visits with the best specialists of the area, but subsequent tests confirmed the initial diagnosis. She could not bear any children. Fiorella was on the brink of a deep depressive state, "But, doctor, isn't there anything that can be done? In America, don't they have special clinics where they are working on staminal cells?" She implored.

"My dear, it is true that they are conducting many researches, but we are in the embryonic stage of what I consider to be the medicine of the future."

"Conceding that the process is at a sunrise stage, can they reverse the condition?" she insisted.

"I agree with you that the American medical field is effervescent in all sectors of medicine and they made tremendous strides in area of your concern, but they have not solved a tiny, but tough enigma."

"If they are on the front line," interjected Felix "They ought to be able to give some answers."

"Not only....." smiled the doctor moving his head half way up and down. "As I said, they are within an arm's reach. Lab researches need patience, determination and money, a lot of it." Fiorella could not find peace. The doctor raised his head and tried to look at her eyes, "Listen to what I am going to say now. There is a second option you can evaluate. They are experimenting a new fecundity method. It is called 'In vitro.' Your husband could choose to be the initiator of a creation process with another woman volunteer and the creature will be yours."

"What do you mean exactly, doctor?" objected Fiorella.

"Any woman would provide her chromosomes without getting pregnant."

"The baby would never be mine," she responded in a low tone.

"Biologically? Of course, not! But, it would be your husband's child.

"What about the legal implications?" Felix objected without hesitation. "The mother could appeal in court and claim the newly born to belong to her. The law, in these cases, can be ambiguous."

Felix made an attempt to give a response. He was unsure of his position and gave a glance to his wife for assistance. Every second seemed to last a long time. He and the doctor were waiting. Finally, the doctor suggested them to discuss the matter in private at home. And if they decided to go ahead, he was going to address them to a clinic in California. Fiorella did not respond.

Her face was a mask of dejection. Felix responded that they were going to consider his suggestion.

Fiorella lost the will to live. Her husband tried to console her and took her on frequent excursions to the mountains to let her recoup her peace of mind., but his attempts resulted futile because she fell even more into a depressive state from which she never recovered.

"Honey, don't feel depressed," he told her. "Life goes on."

She shook her head and said, "No, life has rubbed me of the joy of being mother. It has lost all its meaning for me."

"But we can adopt a baby. We donate happiness to someone who does not have it. That should make you feel better," insisted her husband.

Fiorella made an attempt to shake her head. "I feel that I am not going to pass this test," she stated in a disconsolate tone.

He husband reprimanded her, "Don't be so pessimistic,"

"I eagerly waited for the fruit of the only man I ever loved in my life. There is no sense anymore to live."

Her husband was losing his patience, "Stop talking like this! First, I heard the news that you cannot bear children and now I hear all these ominous arguments from you." And each word was accompanied by a sob.

In the following days, Fiorella hardly spoke at home even though her husband tried to revamp the same topic. She became moody. She refused to supper and before going to bed she said in tears, "I am not interested in the hypothesis advanced by the pediatrician."

"I don't think it is a bad idea. After all, we can adopt a baby or two or three."

"Or, nothing!" she replied very annoyed. Her husband followed her with his eyes until she closed the door on her way to the bedroom.

The following days, weeks and months were monotonous. Fiorella withdrew to her private life and renounced even to stroll down the street in the evening or to go out to a restaurant during the week-end as she was accustomed. Her husband confided to his inner circle of friends that his wife had lost the zest for life.

One evening, the sun brushed the windows of their house and hurried away leaving a yellowish streak of light. Fiorella was resting on a rocking chair. She watched the sun setting. Her husband was at her side.

Suddenly, she thrust her body forward and hugged him. Felix did not understand the motive. The grip lasted a minute or so. When it loosened up, she fell backward on the rocking chair. She reclined her head on his chest, gave him a last passionate look and closed her eyes forever. Her husband quickly applied a mouth to mouth resuscitation for about five minutes. His face was covered with sweat. He touched her face. It was cold, cold like ice. He touched her pulse, but heard no pulsation. He placed his ear on her heart. Tears began to stream down his face. There was no hissing sound around. A thunderous noise from the street below brought him back to reality. A trailer's tire had blown up. He called the ambulance and returned to his wife's side. The telephone rang, but he did not pick it up. The paramedics arrived within a blink of an eye. They transported her immediately to the hospital where she was pronounced dead. Felix never left her a moment. He came back home alone and dejected. He had no more tear to cry, no more time to sleep, no more happiness to share. The terrifying mood of the concentration camp came back to haunt him for years to come.

One early morning, the police knocked at the door of the veterinarian. He was half asleep. A policeman, in civilian clothes said, "You are under arrest."

The doctor opened his eyes and began to tremble. "On what charges?"

"On manslaughter...You are being charged for the death of Fiorella Kappler."

"No!" he protested. "I am innocent. I did not kill anyone. This is a day of infamy."

"You have to prove it in court. Right now, dress up and let's go." The same policeman stopped and added, "Incidentally, you have the right to remain silent until you request legal assistance. Any statement you make may be damaging to your position."

The doctor dressed up in a hurry and was handcuffed. A small crowd gathered on the sidewalk. He covered his face with the jacket and got in the car.

CHAPTER XXXVII

Floris' Death

As it was mentioned earlier, Floris experienced severe health problems. He submitted to a new series of tests hoping to come to grip with the hidden problem. The results came after two weeks and he was diagnosed with a terrible disease: cirrhosis of liver. Transplants were in the embryonic stage at that time and the patient, who dared to venture in the surgery inevitably succumbed a few weeks or months later. Espera appeared devastated by the news and lost appetite and weight. Nonetheless, she kept on urging her husband to abandon completely the use of cigarettes and liquor. Whenever she confronted him on those issues, he would invariably put up a defensive mechanism and say, "See? I don't shake. So, what's all this concern?" In other instances, he changed his defensive language and stated, "I am not drunk and, as far as smoking is concerned, it affects lungs not the liver." His wife was livid. She called the doctors and asked them to reprimand her husband, who in the face of the danger, was still acting irresponsibly, according to her. To allay her apprehension, the doctors decided to keep under observation at St. Gerolamus Hospital.

Floris spent the first week on the first floor in room 111. Across from him, his friend was fighting for her life. Floris' room assumed the aspect of a pilgrimage. People from all walks of life stood in line to pay him homage. His wife got annoyed by the immense popularity that he enjoyed, but could not do anything to slow down the flux of visitors. In the midst of such public support, Floris felt optimistic and ventured to state that he was undergoing additional tests and expected to be home in a matter of days. A moral boost came in the following days by the chief general surgeon who explained to him that a surgery was not conceived in the immediate future. Instead, he changed his previous position by stating that, due to the most recent progress in transplant research in California, he would consider him a serious candidate for a transplant. For that reason, he suggested the patient to remain in the hospital until further notice.

The longer Floris stayed in the hospital, the more it dimmed Espera's hopes. She began to show symptoms of fatigue and spent most of her time at her husband's side, even at night. She disliked hospital's food and skipped many meals. As a result, she looked pale and emaciated. Her personal care suffered. Her hair looked disheveled and she wore the same clothes for days. Relatives and friends suggested her to take time off and rest, but their suggestions fell on deaf ears.

Floris was getting restless. Time was flying and no decision was yet taken. In view of the lack of a donor, the doctors had one alternative, inject chemo to destroy cancerous cells. Espera was utterly concerned about the new medical methodology. Chemo in the bloodstream would destroy also healthy cells. The chief doctor presented his position in the following terms, "We cannot wait anymore for a donor and we have no idea when it could be available. Initially, there was a possibility, but for some unexplainable causes, it was considered to be inefficient. The only solution is chemo. If the body resists, we will win the battle."

"What is the guarantee? Espera asked.

"I cannot give you any guarantee," responded the doctor. "It all depends on how the body responds."

There was no other choice. Due to the chemo daily dosage, Floris' body got weaker and the stomach was incapable of digesting the food. His best friend did his best during those three months of visitation and tried to inject in him another vision of life, "I didn't mean to preach to you at this stage of your life. Nobody told me to do this, but I am sold on faith. Without it, there is no salvation. "He noticed Floris' progressive parabolic descent and increased his religious language. The sick man maintained a cognitive exuberance despite his body did not respond anymore effectively to the various function. The specialist, however, was cognizant of the medical truth and stopped visiting him. Espera got suspicious and fell into a depressive mood.

Espera and her best friends were attending at Floris' needs. He was exceptionally pensive and hardly talked. Actually, he could not talk. His wife, by every means, tried to open his mouth. When she realized that her efforts were futile, she turned around and suppressed the tears in a handkerchief. Not to show that she was experiencing an emotional crisis, she returned to her previous position. It was in that instant she observed his hands and realized that they were quite swollen. He must have read her mind because he made a gesture with his hand. What followed was rather pathetic. The three visitors could not agree on the interpretation of the hand gesture. By some obscure reasons, they finally come to the conclusion that what he really meant was a priestly visit. Later, this reading proved to be fallacious and what Floris really meant was, "go home. There is no more hope."

In those circumstances, the two women sent the only man available to go in search of Father Gambito. Without delay, he descended he ran to the car and passed through many yellow lights. The rectory was full of smoke and food odors. To his chagrin, the pastor did not welcome the urgent message and bluntly told him that he had seen the patient already and that there was nothing he could do about it. "I have company, after all," he said.

The messenger insisted, "Father, this is a question of life and death. It is urgent."

"I am sorry! I have guests here."

The messenger's eyes clogged with tears. He turned around in silence and reported the gloomy message to the two ladies. The news travelled on the wings of the wind throughout the city and behind it. The media spared no time to attack the clergyman with spicy headlines and most of the readers decried the pastor's behavior. Even the clergyman's closest friend took a stand against him. Later, he fell victim of bad habits and lost all his savings and money borrowed by people. The church authorities miscalculated the prelate's ability to generate surprises. The parishioners clamored for a change. The bishop ordered the secret installment of surveillance cameras in the rectory which brought its first fruit. A lady was caught carrying a suitcase there. The pastor opened it. It was packed with twenty dollar bills. His eyes bulged out. He hurried to close the suitcase and hurried to hide it in an undisclosed location of the cellar. A few weeks later, he was removed from his office and placed in a care institution. But neither the parishioners nor the bishop knew him well. The pastor still had a surprise in his sleeves. One morning, he went out to the garden to take fresh air. A brand new car was waiting for him. He opened the door, sat on the front seat and away he went. The same day, he got married and was seen no more. He had the last word on his private life.

The messenger, in the meantime, returned to the hospital without good news. It was only the following evening that the situation reached a point of no return and realized the inconvenience of bothering the pastor. All of Floris' relatives rushed to the hospital. In the intensive care room, he was agonizing; yet, nobody heard a lamentation o a word of discomfort from him. He was fighting the last battle of his life as a gallant man. His best friend, to keep his hopes alive, held a rosary high in the air, so that, he could see it. Floris stared at it as much as he could. He also noticed his friend's eyes covered with tears. Espera made a last attempt to encourage her husband to hold on, to hope, to resist, but the swollen hands remained static. Floris' lungs stopped breathing and his heart ceased beating. His brother-in-law announced that the battle against death was over. A long veil of silence descended on Mendoza's streets and plazas. The flag was lowered in sign of respect to their home hero.

As we said, Floris' death had a local and national resonance. To render homage to one of the Malvinas' last survivors, the government dispatched a platoon of honor guards dressed in black suit and white shirt with black tie. The musicians wore blue pants and with jackets with gold and blue stripes.

The horses were all white and lead the funeral cart. The band followed. Espera chose a black dress while her mother-in-law opted for a white gown and an orange sweater. Floris' native town was represented by the Communist Party President. He wore the Argentine flag wrapped around his neck and a sickle and hammer cloth on his chest. It was a monumental ceremony that lasted more than three hours. The military positioned themselves laterally to the wagon carrying the casket. Every ten feet someone from the crowd dashed out of the crowd that lined up the street leading to church and threw flowers in the direction of the casket. The band played funeral music through the whole time. The procession stopped at the entrance of the church where a long applause welcomed the casket. Camera operators were busy filming and snapping pictures for the event, while the reporters made some attempts to interview relatives and friends.

The road that led to the cemetery was lined up with people, who stood at attention or stretched out their right arm at the passage of the funerary carriage. After the closure of the ceremony in the cemetery, the honor guards fired one hundred rounds of cannon. A local man, expert in fireworks added up his own by firing a cornucopia of different bombs in shapes and colors that lasted about ten minutes.

Espera leaned over the casket and did not want to move despite the custodian's appeal to pay the last respect because the time was up. The military group stood on attention and boarded their vehicle to return to their base. One of Espera's young nieces began to read aloud the names of the people printed on the garlands. When she arrived at the anonymous one, she read, "prisoner.' Everybody thought he was one of the soldiers who had been prisoners of the British navy during the battle of the Malvinas. The whispering soon reached Espera's ears. She opened her eyes as if she had a vision and fainted in her children's arms. It took well a quarter of an hour before she snapped out of it. The custodian announced that he was about to close the gates. He had just finished the announcement that screams and cries burst in the chamber. Chaos ensued. No one knew exactly what was going on. Espera fainted for the second time. The pallbearers took to the nearest exist. The custodian was getting frantic and wasn't sure what course of action to take. Actually, an electric shortage had caused a tremor around the casket for a few second. Eventually, the clamor subsided and calm reasserted its role.

The funeral had been exhaustive for Espera and her family. The house became a zoo. It was practically impossible to walk due to the invasion of neighbors and friends. A group of soldiers stopped at Floris' house, paid their tribute and went on. Soon, the house converted into a museum. People stopped to analyze the war pictures or murmured a prayer. The reporters came back hunting for the anonymous flower sender, but to no avail. They even approached the florist, but he only remembered that a lady paid in cash for the flowers.

Espera spent a sleepless night. She tossed left and right on the couch unable to close a wink. Only in the morning, she fell asleep. In the meantime, the major local newspaper ran a headline like this, "Argentina and Mendoza pay homage and bid good-by to one of his bravest sons."

The time passed by desperately slowly for Espera. The mail had piled up. She did not have time to read all the letters and condolences cards. While she was shuffling them at random, one of them caught her attention. She opened it and read it. When she finished reading it, she folded it and put it in her pocket. No one asked her the reason for it. In her spare time, she tried to unfold the letter, but did not read it. She showed it to her best friend only later. She opened it and read this message, "In this time of solitude and sadness, more than ever, I am closer to you. Please, let me know if I can be of any assistance."

Chapter XXXVIII

Felix

Years after Fiorella's death, Felix decided to sell his business and return to his homeland. In his town, he owned an old decrepit house. Despite the strong structure, he decided that it was in his best interest to demolish it and built a custom house with all the modern accessories, rather than remodel it.

On the upper level, he built a long balcony from which he had a stupendous view of the mountains. He knew that Espera was a widow and he also got the news that she would come on vacation for a couple of weeks, but nobody was able to tell him the date. Every evening, therefore, at sunset, he sat on the balcony and perused her house across from him. Some gossipers claimed that he owned other land where he could have built his house in an exclusive area, but he preferred to lived, as before, across from Espera's house.

As long as he stayed stuck on his balcony every evening, the old ladies passing by began to whisper, "He is a depressed widower."

"I bet he still loves Espera,"

"How can you make that assumption?"

"Look! He is glued like a statue up there and keeps on watching her house almost constantly."

"Constantly, no," reproached her friend. "Let us say that he alternates glances at the street and at her window."

"No, I believe that he is still metabolizing his wife's loss."

"Eh!" protested her friend. "Many years have passed by, now."

"Let me tell you something," responded the other with emphasis. "For someone, it may take a few years; for others, it may take even a lifetime."

"I will not argue that point," said the woman after taking a deep breath. "But if the flame of his ex-love is still running deep in his veins, he is ready for an unconditional relationship with her."

Most of the year at sunset, children convened in the area adjacent to Felix house to play soccer or many other games. One evening, a dark cloud appeared on the summit of the mountain and the children's mother took it as a warning of an imminent storm and warned them to return home. The children ignored their concern and went on having good time. Felix followed them for a short while with nonchalance. His face got suddenly bright when from Espera's window appeared a feminine silhouette. He perked his eyes and remained motionless. The lady had an angelic figure and, in her movements, seemed to walk lightly above the floor. Her brown hair, under the influence of the last pale sun rays, looked golden. She wore a deep blue house coat. Felix' eyes were fixed on hers. She disappeared for a moment. Felix was still watching motionless at the window. When she returned, she held a red rose in her right hand. She raised it to smell it. Felix' eyes were glued on her. That figure had hypnotized him. In a moment of reawakening, he jumped from his chair and threw his right arm forward in the unrealistic attempt to touch her, to feel her, to pull her toward him. But dreams belong to the realm of mind and his arm remained outstretched for sometimes until he got tired and it fell downward in its natural position. Slowly, a couple of tears rushed down her cheeks. She made the motion of handing the rose to him and left. Once again, Felix thrust his body forward to catch the rose, but he grabbed only air.

Felix passed the whole night in a profound turmoil. At two o'clock in the morning he saw the light on in her room. He went down to the street and stood against the wall in the hope of feeling her breath. A motor scooter passed by and the driver honked the horn. Felix made a gesture of disapproval and ran back to his house for fear the 'comare' of his neighborhood would see him and have a new item for gossip in the next weeks.

Felix got up early in the morning and walked down the street and stopped at the door of the milkman. "Good morning. I came for a liter of fresh milk," he said.

"It is a matter of fact, we have just milked the first cow," replied the milkman's wife. "Please, come in."

"Thank you."

"What's going on, my friend? You have a worried look this morning. Did you sleep well last night?"

"Not really! I do not know how to explain it."

"I bet I can."

Felix looked at her with suspicion, "Why are you asking me these questions?"

"Come on, baby! We all know what you are up to. Nothing escapes our scrutiny in this neighborhood."

"That is self-evident," explained Felix somewhat annoyed.

"Don't get offended, baby. We look after your safety. You should appreciate it."

"What I don't appreciate is your investigative eye. You people are nosy."

"Look who is talking." And she followed her comment with a sonorous and prolonged laughter.

"Well, I do not have any time to waste," said Felix and excused for cutting the conversation short.

"Since when are you in a hurry? I suppose you have to go back on your balcony, but do not worry. She is going to be there for a couple more days. Don't rush."

"You seem to be very much acquainted with peoples' lives," said Felix with a half smile.

"Save your irony, babe. I have serious questions and you treat me like a child."

"Stop being facetious, I have so many problems to solve."

"And the biggest one is right here in the corner," she boasted by pushing even more forward her prominent chest.

"As long as you are the information office, tell me on what day she arrived and how long she is going to be here."

The lady launched an arrogant scrutiny around him and said, "Now you are talking business. Now you are approaching me like a real lady, an important lady."

"Avoid this nonsense and let's go to the crux of the matter."

"O.K. I will tell you. She arrived yesterday morning and she will depart in two weeks."

"Two weeks?" he responded with dismay. "A traveler pays so much money for the ticket to stay here only two weeks?"

"That's not all, my friend. She has to spend some time in Rome where her brother lives and in Milan where she has two more brothers. Do I deserve a compliment now?"

Felix dodged her question. "This means that she may leave anytime," he answered with anxiety.

"For once, you are on target."

"I can't believe it."

The lady came forward, walked a couple of times in a circular formation and raised her head, "You still love her, don't you?"

Felix did not answer right away and stood there pensive in front of the counter. The lady, noticing that he was absorbed in his thoughts, murmured, "Men are weak and stupid. I knew it before, but now I have a confirmation."

Felix turned around and left. The rumor of a revived Felix's interest in Espera spread like wild fire in the neighborhood at first and in the whole village later. At every sunset, the 'comare' formed a knitting group in front of one's house. Some of them started a new project from the beginning, while others engaged in mending old jackets and pants. They touched about every aspect of the neighborhood, but, at the end, the topic geared inevitably around Felix and his old love flame. The most senior of them even suggested hiring a songwriter to compose a lyric. The initiative quickly generated a general consensus, but due to Felix' lukewarm support, it failed to get off the ground. He let the ladies know that, although the idea was based on a valid premise, he had no intention of becoming the talk of the town. In reality, he was determined at all costs to protect Espera's privacy.

Felix was perturbed and restless. He departed from the 'comare'and decided to make a brief visit to the coffee shop. He had just turned around when a female gypsy blocked his way. "Again?" he exclaimed.

The young gypsy held him by the arm and said, "Good man, give me just a minute. I have a wonderful news for you."

Felix tried to disengage himself from the grip, but she would not give up. "Open your hand, generous gentleman." He resisted for a moment the invitation, but the girl stretched it for him. Felix attempted to roll back his hand, but to no avail. The fortune teller scrutinized the lines on the palm and said, "You will climb many mountains. You will cross many waters and walk many roads."

317

Felix interrupted her, "I have been doing that all my life, my dear lady. Your words are no news to me."

The gypsy insisted, "Despite the pains that you will suffer, you will see the sun at the end of the tunnel."

Felix stood deeply pensive in the middle of the street. The gypsy stretched her hand. There was no response on his part. She tried to shake him up, "Handsome man, are you OK.?"

Felix replied with a feeble voice, "Yes, I am fine."

"Well, you don't answer me. I was getting very concerned."

From the corner, a car emerged at high speed. The gypsy pulled Felix toward her. The two touched each other. The group of ladies, who were closely watching the scene, started to gag. Felix complained to the young lady for the rough jerk she gave him. She replied, "Most generous man, if I did not pull you over, you would have been killed by those 'hot rods.' Felix wobbled while he moved to the side of the road. The gypsy followed him. Felix dropped some money in her basket and moved on. She begged him to let her accompany him wherever he went. He declined the offer, "I had in mind to stop at the coffee shop, but now I think I am going to go buy a bottle of milk. Good -by and good luck," he told her. The gypsy followed him for a while and, then, she yelled, "If you don't want the bottle of milk, you can give it to me. I will not refuse it. My stomach is empty. The street noise did not allow him to hear her. The gypsy girl turned around and joined her clan streamlining in front of her. A neighbor was spying from behind the window. As soon as the scene was over, she shook her head and stated, "How can man be so imbecile? He could have made a pious act by paying me; instead, he gave the money to the gypsy girl. I could have foretold his future even better."

As it was mentioned earlier, Felix's romantic life had the effect of a thunder. In every street corner, in every coffee shop in the main plaza and even in the weekly open market, it became a major topic of gossip.

What everybody asked was very simple. Would the fugacious glimpses of Espera represented a straw fire, an isolated idyllic parenthesis or the rekindling of an old, juvenile love suppressed by family feuds, but ready to sprout for a full bloom? The customers of the coffee shop started something unusual. Between an expresso and a shot of cognac, they invented a new game, called FE, A'roulette.' It was divided in two parts. On one side, it was written 'yes' and on the opposite side, 'no.' Players bet on either word. Those who thought that the romance would have a happy conclusion would bet on 'yes,' while the opponents would choose the 'no' side. Soon, the game became very popular on a regional and national level.

Two days passed by and Felix had to resign to the loss of a dream, too good to be true. As one of the 'comare' preannounced to him, Espera's presence in her hometown would last very briefly. In fact, her sisters showed up and drove her to their houses in Rome.

As the result of Espera's sudden disappearance, Felix demeanor changed drastically. He became vexed and inapproachable. The same lady that predicted his amorous adventure asked him. "What's going on, my dear? Your face has lost luster. You look like a bird in a cage."

Felix replied in a desperate tone, "It took a lifetime to see her and now the wind blew her away."

The lady shook her head, "It was not the wind, but her sisters who took her away.

"I am asking myself if it was a dream or what?"

"I alerted you, my friend," reminded him the lady. "I warned you that her visit would be short lived. You did not pay heed at me. Instead of acting, you stood on top of that pinnacle, like an owl, and expected that a generous soul would bring you the 'prey' to your mouth."

"Don't be facetious" scorned her Felix. "What could I have done under those circumstances? I was waiting for the magic moment to strike a conversation with her."

"Are you positive that she is committed to re-evaluate your juvenile fire by exchanging with you a couple of glances?"

"If I did not believe in my dream, "I would not be seeking your precious advice."

The last statement swelled up with pride the old lady's ego who said, "It is very kind of you to express such honorable feeling in my regard. On the other hand, I am inclined to revamp the past based on conjectures, rather than facts."

Felix changed his mood and got irritated, "At my age, I have a firm grip on my feelings. If it were not so, I would not be wasting my time, energy and brains."

"And, mine, too..." she added.

Felix did not appreciate her latest comment. He was aware that he was fighting against time and unpredictable events already spoiled his plans. The lady looked at him straight in his eyes and said, "I know exactly what you are thinking."

"What? Felix implored her.

"You are contemplating in going to Rome and press your luck before she departs. I warn you. It is a senseless, futile attempt without her consensus."

"How am I going to obtain her permission unless I see her?" Protested Felix.

"You should have acted promptly before. Nonetheless, I believe that you should try to get in touch with her first. The main problem consists in the mobility of the family members. Because she came here for a short time, her family's members are on a moving trail. It is going to be hard to track her down."Felix looked disconsolate. "What do you expect me to do?" He begged her.

"My good friend, time is gold. Each moment that goes by, it is equivalent to a drop of gold tat slides away from you. I could act as an intermediary in this utterly difficult situation."

Felix jumped at the opportunity and expected quick action.

The lady said, "I am not looking for any pecuniary compensation, even though, I don't think you will be disrespectful."

Felix was listening attentively.

The lady continued, "Drop your present plan and pay a visit at Mendoza. There, you stand a better chance to rebuild your past."

Felix protested, "I don't know anybody there."

The neighbor replied, "Take you time to make some researches. I am confident that someone will set you on the right track."

Felix accepted the advice, but before he left, his friend said, "I am sure that at mission accomplished you will remember me."

In Mendoza, lived a couple very close to Espera. Every evening they met to sip a cup of coffee and discuss the daily events. It was inevitable that in some occasions the conversation would slide on her future plans. In one of her rarest moments of candid confessions, she said, "Since I saw my ex-boyfriend from my house window in my hometown, my life has not been the same. He has been calling me on a daily basis." She looked at the teacher and said, "I wonder who gave him my phone number."

"You mean you had another love story with someone else before you got married?" Her close friend inquired in a state of surprise.

Espera blushed and, after a long pause, responded, "We were teenagers when love struck us. We were innocent, you know, but very serious in our commitment."

Her friend pointed the finger against her and said, "You never mentioned to me your romantic past, you stinker!

"That's too long and painful to repeat. The new one started last year when I paid a visit to my family in my hometown. I repent myself. I should not have gone there." She scratched her head and shook her head.

"Did you know that he went back to live in town after his wife's death?"

"Surely, we knew it. My husband called his parents all the time." Espera took a few moments of pause. She was enjoying watching two birds resting on a branch of a tree in the backyard.

Her friend said, "Woo, what's happening?"

"Espera leaned forward and covered he face with both hands. "I saw him from my window for about thirty seconds," she recalled. It was the spark that ignited our innocent, young love when everything we did was a dream and each act or move or word seemed limitless and heavenly. Now, that I have seen him after many years, I cannot forget him anymore."

"Did you reveal this secret to anyone?" Asked her friend.

She uncovered her face and said, "No, it was too dangerous for my self-esteem and for the dream I was recreating."

"Not even to your in-laws?"

"How could I?"

"Do you wish to keep it between us?"

"Of course! People would not understand anyhow. The new generation lives in a technological world where the word 'love' has been replaced by 'computer." Their hearts doesn't pump anymore with genuine love. People have become as cold as the machines, their daily intimate companions."

Her friend said, "I wholeheartedly agree with you. I sense that we live in another planet among aliens. We lost touch with our feelings, our friend and our family."

"You are not kidding! We have lost touch with ourselves," emphasized her close friend.

"Once, man used to yearn for a kiss. Now, they seek immediate gratification. The flowers that the young men buy for their loved ones don't have scent and a boy does not write a poem to his girl. Love is like fast food."

Her friend laughed so hard that she touched her belly for fear that it would explode. Espera took advantage of it to relax a bit, then, she continued, "Unfortunately, our immaculate love, as it was through the years, was not matched by our families' respect for each other."

"didn't they get along?" Her friend questioned her.

Espera shook her head in a sign of denial, "They carried on a brutal feud that reverberated on their children.

They lived by 'lex talionis,' eye for eye and tooth for tooth."

"Without the gardners'attention, the flowers dried out. Is that your message?"

"Exactly!" replied Espera. "Let's say that they made it impossible for us to live our love story." She looked outside of the window and said, "I can't even begin to tell you the negative repercussions that affected us."

"Do you hate them or hold any grudge against them?"

Espera made a gesture of disapproval with her hand. "It is even late to think about their errors. Many years have elapsed since I was a little girl. Now, they are in the world of truth. Let them rest in peace."

"I am sure they acted in your best interest ignoring that they were hurting you. They were sons and daughters of another culture that kept them blind from the truth. Thank the Lord that your story did not end up in a tragedy."

Espera attempted a half smile and said, "At times, I question myself on that."

Espera felt she was in debt with history and wanted to discharge all her anger. Her juvenile love had been aborted and unjustly suppressed for too long. "I paid a high price," she said raising her head. "What else life can offer me?"

"I am sure that you were devastated by your parental attitude and the impossibility to get news of your love."

"It was wartime," continued Espera in a submissive tome. "He got drafted in the army by the Nazi"

"I don't understand that," apologized her friend.

"They forced him to go with them. It is all I know. I did not hear from him for years even after the war ended. I did not know if he were dead or alive. What would you have done in similar circumstances? My mother got together with a neighbor and made me marry a boy who had emigrated in Argentina."

"Couldn't you find out anything from your neighbors?"

"How? We were kept like animals in a cage. We worked all day, the whole week. My family was so wrapped up in itself that I was unable to gather any information about Felix. The few times I was able to seek information to neighbors, nobody seemed to know if he were dead or alive"

"So, you got married."

"What could you do? Run away? Where? When you reached a certain age...but I had a knot in my throat all the time."

"Not even after marriage you got any news about him?"

"Much later,.. yes. By that time I was married and he was too."

Her friend got a bit daring and asked," This is none of my business and if you don't wish to answer I am not going to be offended. Did you love your husband?"

"Well, yes and no."

"This is an ambiguous statement."

"I loved him in a way. He was an excellent provider, but some aspects of his personality raised my concern. For instance, he raised too much his elbow. To worsen our relations was his strong commitment to week-end games. He succumbed too easily to his friends' pressure."

"We know that."

"Then, you know very well that he smoked," insisted Espera.

"Well, smoke does not have any relevance in marital relationship," objected gently her friend.

"I am surprised that you defend him on that. Smoke was deleterious to his health and affected us also."

"I had in mind something else," insinuated her friend.

"I got it!" responded quickly Espera. "He left the butts all over and the kitchen looked like a chimney with black clouds hanging down the ceiling. This is true!" And she raised her right hand. "Now, I understand a bit. Yes, it was hard to sleep next to him because he had a foul smell. Between the beer and the smoke I am not sure which one was worse. When you combine them, they are a deterrent even for skunks."

Her friend laughed for a couple for minutes. When she resumed her natural demeanor, she said, "I don't mean to defend anyone, but you do not know how blessed you were. You admitted that he was a great provider; yet, you spelled out more negative than positive traits. You didn't mention that he was a family man. He was very devoted to you and to the children. He gave you freedom on financial matters and he considered you the queen of the house. He even built a house for you and you had your own car.

What else did you expect from a working man? You have no idea how many husbands behave with their wives and children. Read the papers!

Chapter XXXIX

Espera First Return Trip and the Truth

Fifteen years passed by lazily. Espera was nostalgic about her homeland and family. She missed them dearly, especially her parents. She used two suitcases to pack up pillow cases, sheets, hand cotton aprons and children's clothes. There was also enough room for flour, sugar, pancake mix, nuts and chocolates. Her son had hard time closing them. A leg of a pants and half shirt hung out of a suitcase. He reopened it and made a gesture of surprise, "Wow! No wonder I could not close it. What did you put in here? Look at the soap, hygienic paper, matches, long underwear, cereals..."

"Oh, shut up! "Clothes the suitcases and keep your mouth shut."

"Do you think that you are going to Africa?"

"Nobody told you to scrutinize what I packed. I asked to close and lock the suitcases."

He pulled some items out and pressed them in a plastic bag that looked like a pregnant woman.

At the airport, Espera's suitcases were receiving special attention from the custom service department. The weight was way behind the limit and only one suitcase per passenger was allowed. Espera was getting extremely irritated. She approached a man in uniform, told him her name and dropped something in his hand. The officer was quick to empty his hand in the jacket pocket. He made a signal to a police and the suitcases rolled on the belt. Espera made a deep sigh of relief. She turned on the side and said, "If they gave me problems,

I would have raised hell in broad day time." Then, she realized that her public behavior was unbecoming of a hero's wife.

The first part of the flight was partially insidious. Gusty winds whipped the aircraft almost constantly. They made it bounce left and right increasing the passengers' fear each time the wings flipped up or down.

A thunder of immense proportions shook violently the airspace and caused panic among them. The aircraft vibrated for a minute or so and, then, fell into an air pocket losing about two-thousand feet of height. Most of the women screamed, followed by children and disabled. Married girls in time of expectations fainted; others held their children tightly to their breast. Black clouds appeared on the horizon and formed an interminable barrier through which the airplane vanished for a while that seemed to be eternal. The same clouds burst into a vicious rain that blasted against the aircraft. Despite the very precarious weather conditions, the pilot maintained his proverbial calm. He warned the passengers to secure their seat belt and refrain from walking in the aisle until further notice. Even the aviation personnel were requested to hold on their sitting positions. Finally, the pilot steered to the right of the air course for about ten miles. It was a dangerous maneuver that could have caused an air collision with the approaching aircraft. He got out of the storm space and soon after was able to return to his air route unscathed.

The plane was at that geographical space in the vicinity of Great Britain.

As the plane approached Europe's mainland, the passengers sitting next to the windows, could have a glimpse of a wide magnitude of the Alps' front side and, once upon them, admire the summit which looked like a flat glassy dish. The glacial outposts were absent at that time of the year. The sun had melted down to feed the rivers and lakes below the valley. Some vagrant clouds were spinning above the empty vault of heaven. As the aircraft bid good-by to the last peak of the mountain range, an idyllic scene appeared before them. A bunch of goats were climbing easily through a tortuous path of rocks, while an endless line of sheep flock grazed on the lower plane. The flight was an hour away from the Italian capital, but Espera felt a strong feeling of intimacy with the Alps because it reminded her of her village mountains.

Espera admired the majestic scenario with aw. She remained speechless until that picture of untouched beauty slowly vanished from her sight. Her face was dark and covered with sweat. She could not hear anybody, not even the lady sitting at her side. She was visibly shaken by emotions. With a strenuous effort, she recuperated the power of speech when the speaker announced that the plane was landing at Rome's airport. "What a strange destiny. I put my family's life and mine in jeopardy just to see my parents, brothers and sisters. I should have never left Italy in the first place," she whispered to her neighbor.

The sky was getting clear, the landing near. She closed her eyes and reopened them when the aircraft touched the ground at Leonardo da Vinci's runway.

Espera looked through the window and noticed the airmobiles (the airport vehicles) dashing from one place to another among the numerous aircrafts stationed there. All passengers stood up and applauded the pilot. They were hugging each other and crying. Big tears were running down Espera's cheeks. A lady took a handkerchief from her purse and handed it to her. Espera thanked her. The cabin opened and the mobile staircase was connected to the aircraft. The caravan of the passengers slowly and meekly proceeded toward the gate of freedom.

At the airport, the passport rituals were expedited by three policemen who looked at the Italian passports with unusual speed, almost wit superficiality. On the other side, of the barricade, Espera's brother was waiting for her. The encounter was very emotional as the reader can imagine. She hung on his shoulders for quite a while wiping her eyes occasionally. Eventually, she recomposed herself and he carried the suitcases into the car. The traffic was intense and to get out of the airport grounds, it took about ten minutes.

Throughout the trip, Espera did not stop talking a moment. The wind was whistling through the open windows, but it did not deter her from emptying her memory reservoir. Soon, the wavy hills, that preceded the town mountain range, seemed to chase clouds that appeared along the line of the horizon. The hills' shoulders were protected by a blanket of straight chestnut trees that hugged both flanks of the mountain up to the shimmering waters of Caserta's royal park. From then on, the rich hues, mainly green and blue, broke down and were no longer inspiring. New colors coming from rocks, lime caves and burned charcoal piles dominated with some sorts of sporadic interruptions.

Espera stretched her eyes outside the window and a perfume of violets and petunia soared from the cliffs of the hills. In the background, loomed spectacular, tall, modern buildings. "Oh, my Lord," she said. "This unspoiled breath of nature brings me back many years ago when I gazed the mountains from my farm during the midday pauses." Her brother tried to capture the meaning of her words, but the wind had carried them away already.

The car stopped smoking. Espera was amazed at the changes in her old neighborhood. Old houses had been demolished. New architecturally inspiring constructions mushroomed everywhere. The facades of the houses, in relatively good shape, had been restructured and painted with lively new colors. She hardly recognized her old adobe. "Oh, for heaven sake, what have you done with it?" she questioned her brother. At that moment, she heard a loud, intermittent barking. She wiped her face and stretched her ears. The dog, she had left as a puppy, now was in age. His mouth drooled and he opened it to catch occasional flies that passed by. Its long hanging ears did not have anymore the strength to perk up. The discolored, yellowish hair were fluffy and lifeless. He languished in a state of torpor in the shed on a straw bed. He sensed the presence of his old owner and forced his way out running toward the car. Espera had hard time getting out of the vehicle. The dog was jumping all over her trying to lick her cheeks. The display of so much affection overwhelmed her and she broke down in tears. Her brother pulled the animal away, but he escaped his grip and ran back to the old owner moaning constantly. Espera, who had momentarily wiped the tears, fell once again victim of her emotions. Finally, to control his excitement and her own feelings, she walked with him to the house.

Espera's father had grown older and ran some health risk factors before meeting his daughter. He was a bit unstable on his feet, but managed to move toward her. His wife provided him with adequate emotional support. When father and daughter met, they fell in each other arms and it took a while before the relatives pulled them apart gently. One of them remarked, "Do you want her all for you. Don't you think that you should share her with us too?"

The vacation proceeded quite well in town. Espera tried to catch up with the past by asking all sorts of questions to family and relatives, while she was quiet reluctant to reminisce on her own life stories in South America. She offered an apology which was not quite well received, "The discomfort of the jet leg is still present," she complained. Her older sister was aware of it and invited her to stroll down the main avenue, "It will loosen up your blood circulation."

A long line of giant oak trees flanked both sides of the boulevard like soldiers on the attention. A harmonious, colorful mixture of flower in shape and size, among them roses, violets and petunias, surrounded the trees in a circular form and inundated the nostrils of the walkers. The perfume gave them the sensation of being on the Elysian Fields.

Across from them, a bunch of girls was laughing and walking. One of them was Felix youngest sister. Espera caught a glimpse of her at the same time she was looking toward her. The eyes of both of them met for an instant. Neither one of them made an attempt to stop and converse. Espera's sister touched her sister's arm. Espera muttered, "I can't believe it. She changed altogether. I almost did not recognize her."

"Do you remember her?"

Espera did not reply and continued walking absent mind for the rest of the time. She ran into some old friends with whom she chatted briefly. Then, her voice got dimmer and lost luster. She showed signs of fatigue and said, If you don't mind, I would like to go back home."

Her sister reproached her, "All of a sudden? "What is the matter with you? You have just arrived."

"Oh, I am tired, that's all."

Espera's response was not totally satisfactory to her sister and, although she was perplexed by her attitude, did not insist anymore.

Further up, a rose vendor was shouting his merchandise, "I chopped the prices. They are unbeatable. I want to be crazy today. My roses are the most beautiful in the world and I give you a big break in your pocket. No one can afford selling them at this retailer's price. Bit by bit, a small crowd gathered around his stand. His unique way of advertising was having a positive impact on the onlookers, attracted many his curious word choice. Espera and her sister stopped to give a glance to the variety of roses. In a blink of an eye, the crow got bigger and rowdy. A young man and his girlfriend were shoving to gain first access to the front row. A couple of old folks were almost thrown off balance. A woman in the eighties said, "Look, he has reduced the price drastically because the weather is going to be hot like an oven tomorrow. If he does not sell them quickly, they get withered and he is going to suffer a big loss."

"I agree," replied her husband. "You know what? We both gain. So, I am going to buy a bunch of roses for your birthday."

"You are very kind. I love you immensely," replied his spouse boasting her chest. She kissed him and said, "You forgot something."

"What?" Her husband responded in an evident state of embarrassment.

"You always forget. My birthday is next week and by that time the roses are going to be as dry as your eyelashes."

He spouse smiled and said, "What count is the good intention."

"I forgive you because on that day you will buy some fresh ones."

Her husband shook his head in dismay. "I can't ever win with this lady."

The people around them waited patiently for the romantic dispute to end, when another began. A girl, in his twenties, ordered tulips and petunias.

Her boyfriend objected, "For what purpose?"

"I would like to go to the cemetery."

"Now?" he responded with incredulity.

"Not at sunset," she responded. "Tomorrow, I am not in a hurry."

Espera could not take her eyes off the girl. Her sister grabbed her by the arm and dragged her away. As they gained some distance from the vendor, her sister said, "What is the matter with you? You gave me the impression that you were hypnotized. Not even the aliens act like you. They don't stare at people for a long time."

"I think I recognize that girl," she answered with disinterest.

"After many years of absence?"

"Some people do not change much not even after thirty years."

"If you asked me, I would have given you all the information you desired. That girl you left here in the childhood is now a full blossomed young lady."

"Married?"

"She was supposed to a couple of years ago."

"Who is she, anyhow?"

"She is Zanzara's niece."

"Well, what happened?" queried Espera more curious than ever. Her sister lowered her voice and began, "It was her birthday and her boyfriend took her for a motorcycle ride to buy a bouquet of roses for her. It was raining torrentially. The visibility was low and the streets got flooded in a matter of minutes. We never saw so much rain in our town." She shook her head and continued, "The boy lost control of the vehicle and fell with the head on the pavement."

"Didn't he wear the helmet?"

"He did, but it fell off. The ambulance promptly arrived at the location. A paramedic applied mouth to mouth resuscitation inside a house, but he did not respond. The crew exhausted all the options and when they realized that their efforts were futile, they transported him with urgency to the nearest hospital. The boy fell into coma for a week, but, then, he did not make it anymore."

By the time Esperan's sister finished her account, they arrived home. The mountain evening breeze replaced the day heat and made humidity more bearable.

The following day, Espera decided to go to the cemetery and bring some flowers on the tombs of her relatives. At one point, she turned around and noticed a group of people, well dressed up, in a mourning mood. They seemed to be profoundly embedded in a religious silence around a tomb. From the front of the cemetery arrived the agonizing pains of a dying motorcycle. The rider decided to put an end to the moribund motors last notes by turning off the key. He was a friend of the dead motorcyclist and had stopped to give him their final good-by. On the back seat, rode a young girl. He stretched his hand and helped her to descend from the vehicle. She held tightly a bunch of flowers in her right hand. They entered the cemetery grounds and walked straight ahead. The sight of the family around the tomb where they were directed to made them interrupt their walk. It was enough that one of them detected the couple's presence that everybody's attention was diverted toward them. The two youngsters felt a bit intimidated and waited for their next move. It did not take too long to realize that they were in a hostile environment. Every member of the group manifested with gestures that the two intruders were 'persone non grate." Their unqualified behavior did not deter the girl from proceeding forward to lay the bouquet of roses on the tomb of her ex-boyfriend. The relatives of the dead boy did not appreciate the girl's imprudence and started to unleash profanities toward her. The girl remained defiant and a tumultuous confrontation ensued.

Espera, from a discreet distance, stopped attending to her business and watched the scene which was unrevealing at fast speed. The boy thought it was his responsibility to defend his girlfriend and joined her.

His arrival did not subdue the people's anger. Indeed, he increased it. They accused her of having caused their relative's death. The girl tried to explain to them that it was an accident and that she came there to pay respect to him. They would not hear of it and abused her verbally. Someone even pushed her, while others shoved her. Her boyfriend intervened on her behalf and expressed his indignation that a peaceful visit degenerated into a stormy violence.

"If my cousin Flelix would be here, you would not have dared to mistreat me."

Espera shivered upon hearing that name. "Oh, mother of mine, it cannot be. She made an effort to divert her attention to something else, but it was useless. "People have become insensitive to the voice of civility," she murmured. She stayed in a pensive mood for a minute or so, then, she raised her head. The people grabbed vases of flowers from other tombs and began to throw them to the girl and her friend. At first, thery were able to dodge a few of them, but others ended up on his backs. Two adult ladies jumped on the girl and pulled her hair. The atmosphere became incandescent. The custodian saw that the tempers were flaring up, took a shortcut to get to the opposite side of the cemetery and avoid the brawl. Espera exclaimed, "I don't believe it!" She went after him, grabbed him by the neck and led him back to the scene. His voice meant nothing to the litigants. Infuriated by their lack of respect, he took a water hose and began to shower them. Four of them ran after him, grabbed him by the feet and arms and grabbed him and threw him in an empty grave about ten feet deep. One middle aged man wrote on a paper, 'Requiescam in pace' and dropped it on his body. Espera covered her face with both hands in a sign of disbelief and clamored, "That's incredible!" She rushed over the empty tomb to provide assistance to the custodian and saw him bouncing from one side to another of the ditch. He kept on crying, "Help! Help! I broke my bones. I cannot move. I am paralyzed."

Espera felt disgusted. She put up a brave act and ran out to alert the police. The people, hearing the police sirens crying out desperately, set aside their vengeance and dispersed in all directions. The young couple bandaged their wounds and the lawmen escorted them to the motorcycle.

Espera returned home in a state of shock. She abhorred violence. Her family pressed her to hear what had happened. She said in a low voice, "I went to the cemetery to pay respect to our dead relatives, but what I saw makes me want to go back home as soon as possible."

Her oldest sister replied, "Unfortunately, the wind of hatred continues to blow over uncultured people and fuels even more the fire of their family feuds. It is a shame at this time of history that people are incapable or unable to extinguish it. Vendetta still is the protagonist in their daily lives. Unless people change their mind and hearts, there will be no hope for our young generation."

The youngest sister said, "I am completely stunned. I thought that our families had banned the stupid rivalry that has characterized their existence from time immemorial."

Espera got next to her and said, "Call the travel agent. It is not the town that I dislike, it is the people."

"This is your home, my dear," responded her sister.

"How can it be if nothing has changed since I left?"

Their parents had their eyes closed, their heads bending down. They did not say a single word.

In her bedroom, Espera could not sleep. The name 'Felix' had regenerated new anxiety in her. She tossed throughout the night left and right never finding a comfortable position. The following morning she got up very late.

The day prior to departure, Espera met for the second and last time with Felix's sister.

The years did not dim their memories. Espera recounted what she had witnessed in the cemetery. Felix' sister said, "I heard about it. It was my cousin. By the way, did you know that my brother searched for you all over? On the day of his military discharge, he came straight here and when he did not find you he ran to Naples. He saw the boat leaving, but not you."

Espera's face became pale. She was completely oblivious of his attempt to reach her did not have. Nobody ever mentioned anything to her prior or after her departure. A sort of a suspicion began to grow in her heart. It was the tip of iceberg against which hit many inner questions and came back unanswered. It would have been better if her old classmate never revealed that truth. It was very painful for her. Not to disappoint her friend, she queried, "Where was he in the previous years? All of a sudden, he came out of the darkness on my last day? I don't want to hear his name again. I am married and have children. You may imagine that I have no desire to see him. He is no longer part of my life. I erased his name from my heart forever."

"You really did?" asked Felix' sister.

"What makes you doubt it?"

"It is not that I doubt it..." she commented and, without waiting for an answer, she took a couple of steps back and forth as if she were pondering on some thoughts. She felt in discomfort. She wanted to open the gates of Felix past and flood her whole being, but hesitated. Espera kept on scrutinizing her. Her interlocutor got impatient and broke the silence, "He desperately tried to get in touch with you even from the concentration camp."

Upon hearing that word Espera got visibly shaken. Her hand fell on a pole and held it tightly for protection

Her mind got flooded with doubts. For the first time, conscience rebelled and asked, "What did you say?"

Felix' sister did not answer. She just nodded. A long silence followed. "I bet that they didn't even tell you about the many letters he mailed to you and that, the mailman did not deliver them because..."

Espera placed a hand on her mouth. She muttered a few monosyllabic words that sounded more like fragmented prayers than comments. A veil of sadness fell on her face. Her mind was pray of confusion

She unfolded both arms toward her and said in a soft, fine voice, "No more, I pray you. I feel like dying. My whole life is in turmoil. Why did you tell me that?" After other moments of unbearable silence, she apologized, "No, no, it is not your fault. You are a carrier of truth. Who could ever criticize or curse you? You should be praised for you honesty. Woo to those who kept me in the darkness."

"You want to know the truth, don't you?

Espera lowered her head. Two big tears fell on her hands. Her friend threw her arms around her. Five long, endless minutes passed by in that moving position. Espera could no longer resist, "It is over, but not over," she said. It was getting late. She touched her face and slowly walked home, never raising her head from looking down.

Her friend raised a bit her voice, "Maybe, he still loves you." Espera stopped, turned toward her without looking at her, "Sometimes, the truth is too powerful, too much for us human beings to bear. Perhaps, it would be better if I never heard of it, but then we can't hush it under the ashes."

"If you do, it would suffocate you. I would hunt you for the rest of your life. Those individuals who alienated you from knowing the truth are responsible. You have paid the price already, a high one."

"I guess I did not have the right to be free." She waved and walked away.

At home, Espera did not even look at her mother. Her sisters and brothers felt her uneasiness and thought that it was due to her departure. She put their anxiety to rest by saying," It took almost three decades before I found out part of the truth."

"What truth?" The youngest brother pressed on her.

"The truth that concerns me."

"What truth are you referring to?" inquired her sisters.

"I cannot tell you now."

"Why not?"

"It would be too heavy of a burden for someone. When someone hides the truth, he or she should pay the consequences and not the victim. It is too late to repair the wrongdoing now."

Espera's sisters and brothers felt vexed. They did not know what to make of her accusations. Her mother was the only one not to raise any objection. Indeed, she invited the rest of the family to get down the kitchen, "Espera is very busy packing."

Espera postponed for two days her departure for Argentina. The urge to share her feelings with her brother and sisters became impellent, almost unbearable. It was not an easy task, but she felt even more urgent the wish to speak to her mother. The temperature was unsustainable. Outside, it was breezy. They went out and waited for their mother. The eldest sister got right on a subject of remarriage. "Did you inform m?"

"Not yet....She will be back soon."

"I have no intention of talking about my second marriage. It would be nice for all of you to go for an ice-cream when she arrives. I prefer to talk alone with her."

Espera's mother came in and looked at her daughter. The atmosphere was tense. The other daughters did as Espera wished. Their mother cut it short without being drawn in the topic, "If I were you, I would hang on your independence. Tell him that you have no intention of restarting an extinguished fire."

"I would, but my heart speaks a different language."

"Well, keep your heart under control. Don't let your feelings for him overpower you. Do you have any commitment with the man?

"Not yet..., but my children are married and I live alone."

"I don't care. At this stage of your life, you should be concerned with your soul and not with carnal pleasures."

Espera began to show signs of discomfort, "Ma, he was my first love, the one that you deliberately kept away from me."

Her mother remained motionless. Lugubrious memories surfaced on the monitor of her mental computer. She made an attempt to deviate the crux of the conversation. It was impossible. The past was rushing back by waves in full strength. The thought of just thinking about Felix made her shiver. Finally, she raised herself on the chair and said, "Don't be disrespectful to your mother. Remember that I raised you and I married you to a gentleman."

Espera pushed back her long hair and said, "If you were so concerned about my well being, answer me. Did you ever think that my happiness is more important than anything else?"

"This is your appreciation," she said in a low cadence. Having said that, she fell backward on the chair and looked bewildered. She blubbered a few monosyllabic words and hit the head against the wall. Her eyes wondered around and she placed her hand on the left side of the chest.

Espera did not see her and continued, "Even adopted children get a better deal."

Those words must have hurt her mother from the innermost of her soul, "Who? Who? Who told you that? Who was the Judas that did that?"

Espera did not expect that reaction and got highly suspicious, but felt unable to respond on the spot. Drops of sweat appeared on her forehead. She grabbed a cloth nearby and dried her face. Her life appeared at a turning point and she was no longer in control of her feelings. "Ma," she said, "I know that you raised me, but you treated me like a slave. Even at this stage of my life you are trying to impose on me your authority. You have decided everything for me including my marriage. Don't you think that you have exceeded your motherly mission? You should have guided me, not forced me. I am your daughter, not your dog."

Her mother took some deep breaths and said, "Don't accuse me of such ridiculous things."

"You have exercised your power over me to the point where I question..."

"You question what?" Her mother stated with disdain.

"A Neapolitan song says that children are pieces of heart."

Why? Did we mistreat you? Your father and I have treated all of you in the same way.

We worked on the farm all day to raise you. We are honorable people."

"Oh, yeah? You have a misguided concept of parental justice. You have missed it all way along."

"Listen to you with those fancy words. Just because you live in a city it does not entitle you to talk to me like a stranger. I do not accept any moral judgment from you. Keep your sermons for yourself," her mother stated resentfully.

"I know. You are right. You don't like to listen to the fact that you aborted my first love and now you are ready to place obstacles on my happiness again."

Why? Weren't you happy with your husband? He left you rich and comfortable and you have the indecency to complain."

"This is not the point protested Espera.

"Oh, no! Tell me! How many women wished to marry a man who would allow them to live a decent life, full of comfort and money?"

Espera got extremely irritated and responded, "Ma, will you stop? we are talking about happiness and free choice." Her mother did not grasp the real meaning of her statement and replied, "You are the same and you will never change."

Espera hurled a dish against the wall. The crash left many pieces all over the floor. "Did you hear them?" Screamed Espera. "That's how my heart was broken when you kept me away from my Felix."

"If you really loved him, why didn't he search for you?" answered her mother in a furious tone.

Espera resented the statement and replied, "How do you dare to bluff at your age?"

"What are you insinuating?" Responded her mother in defiance. "You are offending your mother's dignity now."

"Oh, no? Her daughter reacted in a sharp tone. "I suppose you never did anything wrong."

Her mother did not respond immediately. She fumbled some monosyllabic sounds that lasted about thirty seconds. She stuck her bust out and continued, "I have nothing to hide. Whatever your father and I did, it was for your own good."

Espera had difficulty in answering quickly. Finally, she said in a low voice as if she did not wish to be heard, "Not even the letters that you concealed from me?"

Her mother's eyes wondered around the orbits. It was the most unpleasant and stunning news of the entire argument. She coughed once, twice, then, she answered, "Whoever gave you that information is a licensed liar."

"Nobody told me that, ma. I did not even mention it to Felix."

"You are making accusations without witnesses. For this reason, you are not credible. You are fishing for something that does not exist. Isn't?"

"No, it is a secret that I swore not to break it."

"So, you are hiding behind the wall of secrecy. Don't you? You know that it is false. Not even the mailman would side with you."

Espera assumed a more composed posture and replied, "You are absolutely right. He is dead now."

Her mother hit the table with her right fist and shouted, "Even if you had those letters in your hands, what could you prove?"

"They belong to me. They are part of my history," screamed Espera.

"I am sorry to disappoint you. That mail is the fruit of that man's imagination."

"Ma, his name is Felix," reminded her.

Esopera put on a forced smile. She pulled a letter from her pocketbook. Her mother's face became pale. Her body began to tremble; yet, she took the time to shout, "It is a forgery!" Don't you see that his real objective is to divide us? Discharge him! He does not belong to you. It is a matter of fact that he does not belong to this house. He is a counterfeiter. By the sacred cows of India I am going to sue him," she shouted.

"Ma, stop being a hypocrite," exploded her daughter.

"It's not true! It is a false letter!" responded angrily her mother.

"How can you prove it?" Espera answered in a lower tone of her voice.

"Some tears began to stream down her mother's cheeks. She shook her head and added, "It is not possible! And, in a candid gesture of honesty she admitted, "I burned them all."

Espera's face changed color. It became like wax. She stood there in silence not knowing what would be her next step. The air was tense and the argument had reached the climax. Espera showed her the letter again and whispered in her ear, "This letter was right in this house. I found it accidentally among papers. Do you need more proofs?

Her mother reclined her head on the right side and appeared in a resting position. In the meanwhile, the rest of the family came back and thought that everything was normal.

Two months later, their mother died. Their father joined her in the tomb a month later.

Espera's departure left her family in despair. Nobody could find any explanation to her vague accusatory innuendos. During the return flight, she could not find peace and tossed constantly left and right on her seat during the entire trip that took her to Buenos Aires and, later, to Mendoza. The passengers next to her attempted to converse, but she would not respond. Even the food that the hostess brought with punctuality lost appeal to her. Coffee was the only beverage she did not refuse and she got up only once to use the rest room. Before making the connection to her hometown, she spent six hours at the airport. She sat on a chair in the vicinity of the boarding gate and slept most of the time. The announcement for the departure came. A passenger touched Espera on the arm and said, "Don't you want to board?" She looked with surprise at the stranger and thanked her. The line was getting longer. She made an effort to get up, but fell back on the chair. On the second attempt, she was able to stand up. She dragged herself on the aircraft and sank on the seat.

Time was running frantically on both sides of the ocean. The phone calls between Espera and Felix multiplied and became more intimate. Espera's immediate family appeared oblivious of the romantic telephone and epistolary correspondence. Espera's sisters-in-law never made any comment that could go behind the family limits. Even when later when they got tacitly informed by a deep throat, they opted to maintain the most rigorous reservation. Only in one occasion a breech. One of them was heard sayings "She never loved my brother."

The following year, under Felix' pressure, Espera returned to Italy. She met with Felix in an undisclosed location in Rome With the excuse of needing fresh air, she took the dog for a walk, while her sisters were busy with domestic chores. The dog's company reassured her sisters of her safety. A short distance from her residence, there was an area, small in diameter, but dense with trees and shrubs. He was waiting for her at the entrance with a big bunch of red roses. The dog barked at the sight of a stranger, but she kept him quiet by giving her a bone. At the beginning, neither one made the first step. They stared at each other intensely as if each wanted to ascertain of the other's identity, then, they fell in each other's arms. "These are for you, my love," whispered Felix.

She laughed and said, "What am I going to do with them?" She protested. "I can't take them home. If my sisters see them, they are going to question me."

"It was a way to welcome you in the sweetest way, my sweet heart."

Espera reclined on his shoulder and said, "Dear, do you remember, so many years ago, when I was playing on the river and you scarred me by placing your hands on my eyes?"

"I remember too well when your mother cracked a pole on my back."

"All these years wasted." She placed her hands on his shoulders and asked him, "Why?"

Felix shook his head and looked upward toward the sky. "It was written up there."

"Tel me, how are you doing?"

"Now, very well financially! You can recall that I was going to the mechanic shop. The Nazi forced me to join their ranks."

Espera put her fingers on his lips and said, "No more of this. It pains me to hear it. Your sister told me all about it. When I found out the truth, I became furious and I discharged all my rage on my mother. As you know, she and my father died a few months later."

Felix's face got serious. "My dear, my parents had their share of complicity in this foiled romance. Let's set a veil of forgiveness on the past and let's start living again."

"But, we cannot forget the past. It destroyed our happiness, our lives."

"I understand, but unless we forget, we cannot start living in harmony with our conscience."

Espera hugged him. She looked at the watch and got startled, "Oh, my gosh, I have to go back. They get worried if I delay too long. Listen! Tomorrow, we will go to Florence. Come there and we will talk more."

"How? With your family around?" Objected Felix.

"Show up and we will find a way."

She was leaving when he grabbed by the arm and said, "Oh, no, you have to wait." He took a small box and handed it to her.

She opened it and saw a splendid gold necklace. "Here, let me help you to put it on."

A cry of joy came out of her lungs, "That' just incredible! It fits me beautifully." She hugged him and said, "I love you so much." He kissed her on the forehead and watched her disappear on the road ahead of him.

Florence was and is busy even in the evenings. The mass of tourists reversed in the streets in search of new artistic adventures that the Mother of the Renaissance seemed to offer at every street corner and square. Espera and her sisters, with their respective husbands, were enjoying a delicious gelato in a prestigious ice cream parlor of the city center. A man caught sight of her and motioned to her to follow him. She excused herself pretending to use the restroom. The man took her by the hand and led her to the banks of the Arno River. It was not easy. The streets were jammed with tourists from all over the world. They had to push their way through the sea of people not to waste time. Espera gave a glance to the sky. The moon was showing up in her full dimension and brightness. Espera turned her attention to Felix and said, "You are just crazy."

Felix did not answer. He surrounded her with his arms and kissed her on her forehead.

"I waited a lifetime for these moments," he said. "Please, tell me that we will never separate again."

"Felix, my love, this is not the proper time to reminisce about the past and talk about separation. It hurts me just to think about it."

Even on the river banks young and old people pressed to get by. After a couple of minutes, Espera said, "Felix, my darling, I have to go now. I have to rush back; otherwise, they get suspicious and will go to the bathroom."

"My darling, I had to see you. I had to tell you that I love you forever and nobody will separate us." He loosened the grip and continued, "Look at the moon mirroring in the water and at the stars more splendid than ever. The whole universe is watching us."

Espera gave a glance at the water below that looked like a sheet of glass and said, "Remember that I came back to see you, to share with you these fleeting moments and to renew our vows of eternal love as we did so long ago." She turned aside and said, "And, now, I must go. If they don't see me, they may think that I got lost and will call the police for help." She stopped a few steps further and said, "Oh, I forgot. Why don't you come to Santiago next year? A friend of mine has invited me at her daughter's wedding."

Felix replied, "He invited me too."

"Great! I will call you from home."

"Good-by, my first rose of April." He escorted her up to a block from the ice- cream parlor and disappeared among the crowd. In the meantime, Espera's family entourage got apprehensive about her tardiness and had initiated a search in the immediate area.

"Where did you go?" inquired her younger sister.

"After the bathroom, I took a stroll to the river. Florence is fascinating in every aspect."

"You could have mentioned to us. We would have been happy to accompany you."

"Don't do that again," added another sister. "We got scared. If you are not familiar with the city, you can get easily lost."

The evening breeze made more tolerable the heat wave unleashed by mother's nature during the day. The mass of tourists appreciated the lower temperature and preferred to dine in front of the restaurants rather than inside. Espera's family reached the main door of Santa Maria del Fiore. Espera observed moments of silent reflection. The rest of the family was respectfully waiting for her next to the station wagon.

In Italy, many drivers prefer to travel at night for long trips. The rationale is simple and applies everywhere. The traffic is scarce. The only real problem may originate in discos. Young people get inebriated with too much alcohol or other toxic substances and drive at impossible speed. Espera's brother-in-law was just thing about them when he noticed that a car was following him. He brought it to the attention of the passengers, who, one by one, looked backward trying to identify the driver. It was a futile attempt in the middle of the night with gleaming lights resembling stars on the highway. Espera was the only one not to turn back. She closed her eyes and pretended to sleep. Her younger sister said, "This is a singular situation. When we speed up, he accelerates and when we slow down, he does the same. Either he just came out of the disco or he is up to something. Another sister was able to identify the license plate, but it did not serve any purpose because the car could have been stolen. The apprehension evaporated at Rome's toll station. The unknown driver took the road to Naples.

Espera postponed for two days her return trip to Argentina. The urge to share her feelings with her brothers and sisters became impellent, almost unbearable.

CHAPTER XL

Trial Time

Espera returned to Mendoza in a state of mental turbulence. Her friends tried to find out what was behind her nervous condition, but to no avail. Not even her children's frequent visitations at her house eased up her frustration and restlessness. They realized that their mother was stretching the moaning time behind the ordinary, but did not wish to interfere with her personal feelings and made no further attempts to bring her to reality. A couple months later her behavior had hardly changed and her family started to wonder how longer she would be willing to go on like that. Felix was very sensitive to the issue and, even though he was eager to open some sort of communication, decided to be prudent and stay on the sideline for a bit longer. The memories of Rome and Florence were like flames under the ash and made many pressures on him. Finally, he made up his mind and broke the ice.

October came and Felix thought that the time was ripe to act. Both of them had been invited to a wedding in Santiago. The date was getting closer and he was unsure how to approach the event. Like the morning dew that liquefies slowly under the sunrise, Espera too began to shorten the social distance between her and her friends. Life acquired a pristine savor and she began to get ready for the wedding Felix increased his phone calls and the expectations for their meeting in Santiago were steadily climbing. The mood kept on oscillating up and down and Felix finally told her, "I bet your in-laws are holding you back. As long as we meet at the wedding in Santiago, I can wait without any problem."

Before taking a final decision, Espera thought that it would be necessary to take a couple important steps. First, she sounded out her children before the news broke out. She approached them individually in separate occasions and their response was astonishing. Her daughter encouraged her, "Ma, I am favorable to a second marriage. Make sure that the property be divided among us children prior to such event."

"Don't talk to me in those terms," responded her mother with an irate accent. I was in love with this man before I met your father. Love is not a financial enterprise. It is the union of two hearts."

"I beg your pardon," responded her daughter in an ironic tone.

"Of course, I will take the necessary steps to guarantee you the heredity, but that is not the reason why I want to marry him."

"Did you inquire about his financial status?" insisted her daughter.

"If it is for that, he is loaded."

"Then, what are you waiting for?"

"I want to discuss the matter with your brothers also."

"That's a good idea. I am sure they will share my same feelings."

"What about your grandmother and the rest of them?"

"Who cares? It's your life, not theirs."

"You know how they are."

"Don't let them bother you. You are not extorting anything from their money account. It is your happiness. Go for it. You are taking anything away from us. He owns lots of property. Go for the gold."

Espera shook her head and said, "You never change. You are just like your father."

"I learned from the best," her daughter replied.

In the early evening the oldest son stopped by. "Ma, I got the news that you want to remarry."

His mother blushed. "Well, as I was explaining to your sister, I knew this man since I was a teenager, long before I met your father."

"Do it! You are still young and you deserve to have a second chance. Happiness may not come around a second time."

"Son, one of these days, I will tell all of you in details what happened to me when I was a child, probably, you will support me even more."

"Ma, I support you without knowing your past," insisted her son.

As it was expected, sometime later, her youngest son stopped by and she brought her concern to his attention as well. "Son, perhaps your brother or sister have already mentioned to you on a new step that I would like to take in my private life."

"Yes, they did." He looked straight in her eyes and said, "Ma, this is your life. No one of us has the right to impose on you our view. You don't need our counsel. We need yours. You have enough experience to make the right choice on your own.

"Yes, but the course of action I am about to take is not one that deals with buying groceries."

"You got to be happy."

"I know and I appreciate it. This is a life time decision, son, that would affect me deeply and, possibly, you too."

"I don't see it in that way," responded her son. I understand he got money and business. You have nothing to lose. Our own concern is that your marriage may affect your relations with our aunts and uncles. They will be terrified at the news and the repercussion will be unpredictable. You know how they are."

His mother got irritated, "What's matter with your people. We are not in medieval times when marriages were arranged."

"Look who is talking," replied her son.

Espera face became serious, "I forbid you to address me in these terms." She lowered her head and said, "Those were other times."

"Suit yourself. I would have no qualms to marry a rich woman."

His mother covered her face with both hands in a state of dismay. "I think that the crux of the matter, at this point, is another."

"I know it, I know it," he repeated twice. Your sisters-in-law would hold a grudge against you. Is that what you would like to say?"

"Exactly!" replied his mother.

"What about grandmother?"

"She would never forgive me."

"If you feel so sensitive about their reaction, move out of town.'

"That would not be a bad idea," and stopped talking for a while until her son tried to wake her up from her lethargy and said, "Well, I don't think you need me anymore."

A fly rested on her forehead and she drove her away with a newspaper. She turned her attention back to her son and said, "I will always need all of you, not financially..."

Her son opened his arms and hugged her, "Ma, we will see each other even if you go to live out of town."

Espera showed signs of agitation. "Son, there is a big problem, as big as a rock."

"What is it? Ma?" inquired with great concern her son.

"He told me that if I wish we can spend six months here and six months in Italy. I made it clear that I would rather live here."

"Ma, what do you care? We take the plain and in a few hours we are at your house during your semester abroad. That will give us the chance to visit Italy even more closely."

Espera seemed relieved by that latest statement. Both opened their arms and hugged each other.

Espera appeared to have put behind her the frictions that still existed with her sisters and brothers. What she heard from Felix' sister, put additional strains on their relations. A glacial wind descended between them and, eventually, the weekly telephone conversations came to a halt. A neighbor made an attempt to pacify them, but neither side showed any interest. Time, which is a well known healer, in this occasion did alleviate their alienation. A wall of suspicions and accusations was erected between both sides of the ocean and Espera did not mention them anymore not even in her family conversations.

Felix was oblivious of the family diatribe and continued to make the trip preparations. He was quite embedded in his wardrobe and brought along a list of items he needed each time he went shopping. One evening, he exclaimed, "Am I stupid? I forgot. I go there without bringing a gift to her? What am I going to buy for her? Chocolates?" He discarded that idea. The chocolates would melt in the suitcase during the trip. It could also damage the suits and money. "He discarded the idea of using plastic paper around the box, despite the fact it offered a major protective guarantee. He feared that atmospheric turbulences and landing could cause violent bumping among suitcases and it could cause the rupture of the plastic and the subsequent melting of the chocolates. At the end, Felix discarded all those ideas flying through his mind and interrupted his preparations.

A few minutes later, a neighbor of Felix stopped in front of a jewelry store. She launched a curious glance at some gold medallions exhibited in the small display window and recognized Felix sorting out rings and necklaces. She smiled and departed quickly.

CHAPTER XLI

Meeting at Santiago

The death of Esperanza's parents caused a rift between her and the rest of her family. From then on, a glacial wind kept them apart. Relations soon cooled off and ended their weekly conversations. Initially, Espera felt visibly shaken and got tense as soon as a family member or a friend would touch that subject. Later, she became completely disinterested and alienated to the point that she would not participate in a conversation which dealt with parental or brotherly family relations.

Felix, in the meantime, was restless like an unbridled horse. He started to pack up the suitcase being meticulous at every minor detail regarding his wardrobe. At the end, he checked the list of items he needed and exclaimed, "Ah, I missed the most important thing. How could I be so absent minded? O.K. but, what gift can I buy for her? Chocolates always express a nobility of the soul, but they melt during the flight and all my clothes will need to go to the laundry." He paused a moment. He shook his head and added, "I can use a plastic bag, but it does not offer a guarantee. If it bursts, it will damage documents, money and the rest." He discarded that idea and put in motion another.

In Mendoza, time seemed to fall asleep. It was afternoon and Espera lie down on her couch and put her eyes to rest. The bridal shop image was ever present in her mind. She saw a train going by mountains, rivers and over gorges. The images stopped suddenly and she saw herself walking by a bridal shop. A woman mannequin wore a white dress. Her face was covered by a pink veil.

Darkness soon faded leaving behind a trail of fatigue and dreams. A feeling of dormancy spread over her eyes. Different thoughts were flying around in her mind each trying to take supremacy over the other. The minutes were passing by. To put an end to that assault, she got up and drank coffee. On the table, a pen and a sheet of paper were laying aside. She taught of writing to Felix for an advice. At first, it seemed to be the appropriate step to take, then, she changed her mind. After all, a wedding arrangement was a woman's prerogative and the best action was to visit the bridal shop and ask the owner's opinion. It was not hard to do that. The lady inquired about the date, the religious ceremony, the reception and personal preferences, then, she showed her various options. With this frame of mind, Espera took additional time to make further examinations. It was not easy to choose among highly fashionable wedding dresses. The owner was waiting patiently for her to make up her mind. Espera walked sluggishly to the table. The pen and the paper were in front of her. The temptation was increasing in intensity. It was a hamletic decision whose repercussion would affect the rest of her life. The name of her boyfriend resounded in her mind. The fear that he would be calling her in the street made her shiver. She ran to the door to see if someone was calling her. She reassured herself and returned to the table. Her mandibles looked tense. A couple of tears ran down the cheeks. The boutique was not equipped with air conditioner. It was easy to sweat in the sultry temperature. Now, the pen was on the paper. She looked at the lady and said, "I know what I want, but I am going to postpone my signature at a later date.

The new day saw the sun wake up early from the mountaintop. A bright light illuminated the bedroom.

The telephone rang, "Good morning, my love. How are you?" Someone said from the other side of the telephone line. Espera recognized the voice and answered, "A bit tired, my joy."

"What are you up to?"

"Oh, not much. I just woke up."

"Have you given any thought on our future?"

"Well, yes and no... Yesterday, I shopped around for the bridal gown. Being on the planning stage, I did not go behind the date and the place. Right now, I am sure on one item."

"What is that?" inquired readily Felix who did not like to have surprises.

"If we get married, I don't want to celebrate the ceremony in our hometown."

"Did you change your mind already?"

"Yes, I want to go to Alberobello."

"Why all way down to the south? Felix inquired in a surprise mood.

"Remember! It is a woman's prerogative. Tomorrow, I will stop at another boutique for a wedding gown."

"With all these beautiful wedding shops in Italy, you want to buy the dress in there?"

"Honey, do not interfere with my personal choice."

Felix did not wish to cause any fracture in their relations on the account of a dress and answered, "Not at all. I was just curious."

The new day approached and Espera had on top of her agenda the visit of some other city's bridal boutiques. Past the cathedral, she noticed a display window where they had exposed a center piece, a head piece and a bouquet next to a wedding dress. A young bridal consultant greeted her and invited her in to watch the wide selection that they had on all sorts of bridal dresses at the lowest prices. "Moreover, "she added, "We offer free consultation on the reception. It does not seem an important issue, but our past clients have saved thousands of dollars. We offer also custom designed shoes with no extra obligation on your part."

"I am just browsing around. I have no personal interest." explained Espera.

"If I am not too indiscreet, may I ask if you are engaged," insisted the consultant.

Espera drew a step back and said, "At my age?"

"Why? You are still young and look like being in love."

"Yes and no," defended herself Espera.

"I knew that something is going on in your personal life, something positive of course. I can read it in your eyes."

"Well, yes," apologized Espera. I am planning a simple wedding, but I am not sure."

"Miss," continued the shop employee, "We are different from other nuptial shops. We do everything customized and our dresses are reasonably priced in comparison to others."

Finally, Espera accepted the invitation of the young lady and entered the premises. The array of bridal gowns made her blush. The shop she visited the day earlier was a midget in comparison of this one. After a short visit, she stopped in front of a dress and said "Two thousand dollars for this gown does not seem a reasonable price at all." "No, miss," responded the vendor. "Here, we are committed to the clients' happiness. We take pride in investing in your joy on the wedding day and always take a step backward to satisfy you. We even take a loss at times with well off people like you."

"How do you know me?" queried Espera.

"My, dear, did you forget that we live in a technological era? We know each other's business?"

We know where your banking deposits are and where you live."

Espera protested, "I don't believe it. When did you ever come to my house?" asked Espera.

"Never!"

"So, you don't know where I live."

"You just wrote it down on the paper I gave you."

"But you have never been there."

"I don't have to be there, my dear lady. The computer will show it to me."

"How?" responded curiously Espera.

"By satellite...We can even put your wedding picture on the computer. You can see them whenever you wish. The computers are transforming our way of life. And if you want to find out how much money I have in the bank, you can search on the computer. You will find it. I don't get offended. That's the way of life. Everybody knows everybody's business."

"I prefer the traditional life."

Espera did not wish to carry on that conversation and said, "I prefer the traditional life."

"Wishful thinking! There is no way we can go back anymore, my friend." The young lady noticed that Espera was deeply disturbed by the news on over the banking accounts and said, "Listen, dear, how many guests are you planning to have?"

"I have to narrow down the invitation list."

"Why?"

"I plan to wed in Italy."

"That is nice. By the dress here and take it to your hometown because it is much more expensive there."

"I agree with you, but you got to give me a discount."

"Don't worry about that," responded the vendor. Then, she queried, "Do you plan to walk to the church?"

"I have already hired a photographer and a coachman."

"A coachmen?" Inquired the salesgirl in an interrogative tone. "Why do you need him for?"

"I have opted for horses and carriage to take me to church. I dislike the limo."

"Are you crazy?" interrupted her the girl. "If the horses fall, you can break your neck."

"There is nothing to worry," responded Espera. "The distance between the church and our future house is within a short distance."

The saleswoman took a long pause. Espera inquired, "What's wrong?"

"Nothing, I just thought that the horses may not be the best means of transportation for a wedding, not in the present time.... not to take into account the traffic. The carriage belongs to another world, to another era."

Espera rubbed her eyes as if she were trying to wake up. "Maybe...I am an old fashion duck."

The young lady added, "Did you apply for the wedding license? It may not have immediate urgency, but you don't want to forget because it takes time."

The cell phone rang. Espera excused herself and returned to the sidewalk to answer the call. It was Felix. "Ciao, my love... I am getting ready for departure."

"Listen, do we need to take the blood test prior to marriage?"

"I am not sure. Much time has elapsed since we got married in different ways. It may not be necessary."

"That's a law."

"Well, if we have to, we take it."

"Are we going to have music?"

"Everything is under control. I need a confirmation on that date."

"Not yet. As I said, when I come back, we will finalize some residual features, like the menu at the restaurant, the publications in church, and so on."

She had just finished talking that he intervened briskly, "Incidentally, honey, we have not planned for the honeymoon, yet. We have not set up any date."

Espera was not in a mood to touch a subject which for her represented a mined field. "Don't you think that it would be better to stay home? We have bills to pay, you know. After all, we have to buy a house in Alberobello. We have a lot of expenses ahead of us, so don't rush.."

Felix murmured in a state of utter surprise, "No honeymoon?"

What are you saying?" inquired Espera. "I cannot hear you too well."

Felix spelled out his thoughts very slowly, "We have enough funds to purchase a house.

Don't worry about it."

Espera quickly replied, "Honey, baby, don't count on me. I cannot afford it."

"I don't expect that... As I said, I will take care of it. I cannot renounce to the honeymoon," he stressed out.

Espera cut him short. "Call me on Sunday at three o' clock. My brother is out at that time. Love you, happiness."

"Wait!" Pressed on Felix. "You were cutting me short."

"No, the long phone calls are very expensive. Remember?"

"Don't be concerned with it, flower of my joy. I am paying the bill."

Espera did not appreciate his posture, but ignored it for the moment. "You would not expect me to pay it. Would you? If it were not for my husband's pension, I would be begging down the bridges in the city center."

"I will never let you do that," protested promptly Felix.

"Thank you. You are very kind. "She paused a few moments, then, she added, "How is your trip preparation? Are you still in the planning stage?

"No, I have been working on quite steadily. The last hurdle is a gift for you. I have been running all over to find something that it pleases you immensely. I am still exploring some possibilities. I think I have placed my eyes on something that you will enjoy very much."

"Don't bother, honey baby. You know that I am not a materialistic person."

"Oh, I know it, but my heart is set on it and when we meet I want you to put it on you."

"Blueberry pie, you know I love you even without gifts. Before I forget it," she added, "do not raise any suspicion at the wedding in Santiago. I do not want anyone know about our relations."

"Early or later, they will find it out anyhow?" responded Felix with ingenuity.

"Right, but as of now, I expect you to assure the secrecy of it. Promise?"

"Promise!"

"I will see you shortly. By the way, promise me that you will not touch any liquor during the wedding."

"Not even a drop?" inquired Felix with curiosity.

"Not even a drop."

"Yes, mom!" responded Felix.

"She threw him a kiss before she bid him "Good- by."

Felix cast his hand foreword to catch the kiss. When he opened his hand and realized that there was nothing in it, he smacked it on the table and yelled, "How long shall I wait?"

After the phone conversation, Espera went back home. The air was humid. A multitude of pinkish clouds ran on each other forming a mountain chain. Rain was not in the plans of the weather and people enjoyed the afternoon sun. Espera felt devoid of energy and felt that it was time to enjoy a siesta. When she finally woke up, the sun was bidding 'adios' to the day. She felt impellent the desire to discharge her day emotions with her close friend and crossed the street to visit her. "You know, today I visited a bridal shop and talked to Felix. I tell you, those dresses are very expensive."

What do you care? Let him pay. If he really wants to marry you... He has the bacon, Espera."

I can't do that. It is very improper, although you are right. He should pay if he is so hard the issue."

Espera lowered her head and said in a low tone, "At times, I feel so undecided. Felix did not even meet my children and we are talking about marriage. It is very awkward. Then, there is my mother-in-law who is a very royal pain. At times, I feel like dropping all wedding plans, all my relations with him."

"Don't be silly," responded her friend. "Don't allow external interferences to wipe out your dreams."

"Early this morning, she paid me a brief visit. And you know what she said?"

"What did she say?" responded her friend with a pinch of curiosity.

"She told me that since her husband's death, she never went out with another man."

"She still holds on the marital vows. It is admirable. She still shows a juvenile beauty."

"Let's not exaggerate!" The windows were open and her words were flying around in the street below. Fortunately no one was listening. "Don't give me wrong. I am criticizing her face, but at her age who would be interested in her?"

"Eh, she can go to a beauty parlor and have her hair fixed up."

"Are you joking? She never washes her hair.

"Don't go to the extremes now," protested her friend. Her appearance needs a radical renovation.

"Don't tell her that," warned her Espera. "You could become her worst enemy, not to mention her daughters."

"I know that," reassured her her friend. "Let us be realistic. This is not fantasy. Anybody, in her presence, would observe the dress she wears reaching the floor almost. The apron is her most inseparable apron. The only time she does not wear it is during s wedding. So, if you do not like the apron, invite her to your wedding."

Espera did not appreciate the language frivolity. Her countenance turned serious. "She is opposed to any romantic involvement between a widow and the opposite gender."

"She can't compare herself with you," she said with a veil of annoyance on her face. "She is very old, while you are still in the mature stage. You still look young and attractive."

"Don't say that. You are pulling my leg now," said Espera in self defense.

"Not at all," insisted her friend.

"Look yourself in the mirror. At the age of fifty-two, you look better than younger ladies."

"Please, do not butter me up."

"Am I?" responded her friend touching her chest with both arms. "In terms of dynamism, you are second to none."

A broad smile lighted Espera's face. "I agree with you on that."

"When he stops here," inquired her friend, "Will he lodge in your house?"

Espera was unable to refrain from laughing for a while. As soon as she was able to control it, she said, "Well, I fixed up the bedroom. It is not too big, but it is sufficient to accommodate both of us."

"Wow!" exclaimed in astonishment her friend, "You did that?" she asked.

Espera was taken by surprise and did not respond immediately. A red color appeared on her face. She had revealed too much of her intimacy. "This is meant for the wedding, if it is meant and only when we live here. I do not like to spend the whole year in Italy. I have my children here," she explained. "If he does stop here, which I doubt, he should lodge in a hotel or motel nearby us."

Not to embarrass any further, her friend changed topic and said, "I heard that in Santiago wedding receptions are restricted only to family members of the bride and groom."

"Who provided you with such a misinformation?" exclaimed Espera. "In the Italian community, nothing is small or restrictive. My sisters-in-law can vouch for it. They have been there." Immediately after, a veil of sadness covered Espera's face.

"Quit losing your good humor when you mention them," stated her friend with firmness. "If they were all responsive to human understanding, we would live in a better world."

Espera remained pensive for a while, then, she said, "The world is made up of all types of human beings.

Some are kind; others are unkind."

"So, stop letting them control your life," responded her friend by raising the volume of her voice.

"It is not as easy as you imagine..." The conversation stalled abruptly. The telephone rang and Espera went to her bedroom to answer it. Her friend got up and silently dashed away.

Espera seemed to be unable to cope with the events. The wedding reception in Santiago was approaching. There she would meet Felix and lay the grounds for the wedding and iron out some additional differences. As it was in her style, she did not want to be unprepared.

In the afternoon, she returned to the bridal shop to sound out the owner on the price. Despite two hours of arguing back and forth, they found no apparent agreement and Espera left everything suspended. She postponed the final decision to her boyfriend's meeting.

The evening news began at eight o' clock in Italy and Felix was watching it from the sofa. They were showing a clip on Nazi war criminals. A judge accused Himmler of organizing the Buchenwald concentration camp. At that moment, Felix's eyes became blurry; his mind numbed and his lips dry. He drew back and reclined on the couch. He stood in that position until the mind cleared up and his heart restored its normal beating.

All his efforts to forget the past became useless. On the monitor of his mind, he kept on seeing scenes of his life with Fiorella. A couple of times, he covered his face with both hands trying to stop the memories. Suddenly, he jumped on his feet. He was recalling the escape planned for him by the gypsies. His forehead soon got wet with sweat. Hi wiped it with a handkerchief, but the sweat reappeared again. He called Espera. "What is the matter, my dear?" She asked.

"I have been experiencing mental confusion."

"How is that?" she inquired.

"I can't shake off my mind a dream."

"About what?" She insisted.

"It is not so pleasant to reminisce about it."

"Don't you think that I ought to know if we are going to be husband and wife?"

This time, Felix wiped his forehead with the back of his right hand. "Mon amour," he started saying, "I made an oath when I fled from the concentration camp."

Espera did not respond. She was waiting for him to continue.

"A couple gypsies helped me to escape."

"It was very noble of them."

"I know. That's why I told them that I would invite them to my wedding some day."

"Did you say "Gyspsies?" Are you out of your mind? Wherever they go, they leave a bad odor. They don't; don't shave; don't comb their hair; their clothes are splattered with oil..."

Felix interrupted her, "Hold it, hold it! Hold it! It's not their fault if they live this kind of life."

"Oh, come on!" rebutted Espera. "You are defending the scum of human race. They have nothing to offer.

Every ethnic group has come out of its den in Argentina. They are the only ones who won't make a step to improve their lot."

"What did they do to you that you are so antagonistic." "Nothing personal... I distaste lazy people who, like parasites, live on social welfares. They refuse to be productive. Do you understand that they slow down the economy? It is in their DNA to be loafers.

People don't want to work. They would never do what I do. Tenants leave the apartments filthy and I have to scrap stoves, cabinets, disinfect bathrooms, paint and other chores. A person's dignity is seen in their willingness to get out of the ghetto.'

Felix started to shiver. He became pale and turned his ears away from the receiver. He was in no mood to cause any friction in their relations over an ethnic issue and decided to listen. His silence became heavy, very heavy and Espera suddenly felt uncomfortable. When she realized that her interlocutor no longer participated in the conversation, she lowered the tone of her, voice, which had been high up to that point, and said, "You may not like where I stand for, but this is my position."

Felix made some efforts to conceal his disapproval and cautiously moved the conversational topic to their private concerns and the bitterness soon evaporated.

Felix took an Alitalia direct flight from Rome and arrived at the Chilean capital early in the morning. The airport police scrutinized his passport, but did not bother checking the suitcase. He took a taxi and went directly to the hotel. He experienced the 'jet legs' and did not move from his room. He lay down on the couch and soon closed his eyes. When he reopened them, he felt drowsy. The clock sounded five o' clock in the afternoon. "Oh, my head," he exclaimed. Pretty soon, I have to attend the wedding where I will meet the love of my life. I hope that the time together is not going to be that short. We have to be careful not to give any sign of romanticism between us. I am pretty sure that someone will be scrutinizing us. Espera was seating with her children at the south side of the ballroom.

Across from her, Felix was in a state of tension. He felt the impulse of going there and hug her. Too many eyes were fixed on them and did not want to appear indiscreet. The time to act came with the second dance. His forehead began to pour out copious sweat and he had to make frequent use of handkerchief. If he waited a few seconds more, he would have lost the great chance. A man in the fifties got up and slowly directed his steps toward her. Every moment was precious for Felix. He got up and, while the pretender was bowing before Espera, he took her by hand and asked permission to dance. The man raised his eyes in the hope that Espera was going to accept his invitation, but, to his great surprise, she had left already.

The couple did not escape the scrutiny of a fat lady who, in the process of moving forward and whispering something to the ear of a friend, went too far bending over and fell among the chairs. The chaos that followed gave Felix and Espera the opportunity to get mingled in the middle among dancers.

It was then that Felix leaned over Espera. His lips were trembling. He made a strenuous effort and said, "I love you. I love you forever. You will not be able to escape anymore from my sight. I will follow you wherever you go."

"Love me without bounds," she replied.

A lady overheard him and leaned backward to inform her sister-in-law. Her husband prompt intervention prevented another big mess. The lady soon reacquired her usual posture and said to her neighbor," Aren't they the farmers who lived in our neighborhood?" "Surely, they are! I saw him in my latest trip to Italy. He is well liked, but there are persistent rumors that He became rich through connections with the gypsy mafia."

"That's how he made his money? That explains it," said the woman.

In the meantime, order was reestablished in the area where the fat lady had fallen down. The band played another dancing music. The lady around Espera did not cease or desist speaking about her or Felix even though she used all her ability to not participate in their conversation. An old lady, with plenty of make up around her eyes and a long gold chain around her neck, tried to revive the topic of her concern, "By the way, did you attend the funeral of Espera's parents?"

Felix silence in the matter did not quell down the desire to gossip. So, a man in the eighties, sitting across from him, raised his hands, a gesture that called the attention of the neighbors, said, "Strange things happened lately. I could mention two events that took place prematurely one from another."

A fat lady, right behind him, overheard him and leaned backward to add her opinion, but almost fell. It took all of her husband strength to hold back that mass of human flesh. Once she gained her previous stable position, she turned around something inaudible even to those who were sitting in her vicinity. When she realized that no one reacted to her statement, she got up, not without difficulties, and whispered to someone's ear, "I heard that one of Espera's sister raised a pandemonium on a matter of family concern and caused an internal division hard to heal." The lady did not know personally Espera and kept on voicing her presupposed veritable information.

Espera's cousins got tired and criticized the ill manners of the lady and her imprudence to intrude in someone's family life. A man got up and said, "Mom, the lady who got up is the one you accused before; therefore, don't spit in the air if you do not wish that it falls on your face." Espera's cousin got livid, She got up and said in an imperious tone of voice, "I did not accuse anyone of anything and before you talk about me wash your mouth otherwise I bang this purse on your head." And she did exactly that. The man who got hit yelled, "Eh, this is my head. Are you crazy?"

"No, I am in a good state mind." Saying that and hitting him again was one act. The intervention of the relatives prevented the worsening of the situation.

Felix was following the scenario with a visible concern He gave a hand signal to Espera, who excused herself and went to the bathroom. Felix expressed the desire to breathe some fresh air and dashed out of his company.

Two minutes later, Espera joined Felix outside, It was dark. Some guests were smoking; others were finishing their drinks. Only a few were taking deep breath as to replenish their lungs with oxygen. Felix took quickly Espera by hand and led away from the sight of anyone. Behind a bush, Felix hugged her and kissed her on her forehead, "I waited a long time for these moments, my darling."

Espera extended her hug longer than usual and said, "Finally, we are able to be together after the short parenthesis in Florence. Each time we meet our freedom expands." She disengaged herself from the tight embrace and added, "Those ignorant ladies inside the hall really got me upset."

"Don't pay attention to those peasants. They are rough and tough. They don't have a measure of kindness and courtesy. I told you, they are rough."

"They are vulgar, that is what they are."

"You are absolutely, right, "responded Felix and drawing Espera to his chest.

Espera cut him short, "I don't want to talk about those gypsies. We have to finalize our wedding plans. We did not even mention the reception, the church, the guests, the restaurants, the band, nothing. Do you realize that the time is not our friend?"

"You make the decision, my love. It is a matter of fact that we did not even discuss the honeymoon."

"What about that?" she inquired with naivete'.

"I mean we have to choose a location, book a hotel reservation..."

"Don't you think it would be better staying home? After all, we will have to cover many bills."

"It comes once in a lifetime, my dear. If we need to take a loan from the bank, we will. Later, we pay back, but I don't think we are in that position. We have the means to sustain the expenses."

"Maybe, you do. I don't."

"Don't worry, honey. I will take care of it."

"I am sure on one thing. I do not want a gypsy type of wedding."

"There is nothing wrong with gypsies, my dear," tried to appease her Felix.

Espera bowed her head. "My darling, what happened?"

"No, nothing..." responded Espera in a thin tone of voice. "There is one last thing we did not mention," she said.

"What my darling," implored her Felix.

"Where are we going to live?"

"Where, where?" responded Felix in an obvious state of nervousness. "I transferred all my assets to Italy. I purchased land and other types of properties."

"No, I want to live in Argentina."

"But, my love, how can I supervise what I own from far away?"

"Hire a manager," she suggested.

"They are crook. Nobody is honest anymore. You cannot trust anyone."

"By the way, who is going to control the finances? Who is going to wash the dishes? Who is going to pass the vacuum cleaner?" inquired a proud Espera.

"Well, we divide the activities. In certain matters, I have to be the dominant figure."

I would not use the word 'dominant' in marital relations. And if as you say, I should play the victim, then, you are on the wrong side of the road. I don't think that is the right way to go. You still live in the past. The old times have gone forever. Time for you has stopped. What happened to you Felix? What happened to the unconditional love that you promised me when we were just teenagers?"

In the sky, the moon looked like a slice of melon in the midst of millions of brilliant lights.

Espera looked at them and said, "At times, I doubt that our dream will ever come true." Felix drew back at that statement. She continued, "Too many things have happened recently."

"But, no..." a tense Felix tried to reassure her. "Let's make a compromise. We live six months in Argentina and six months in Italy. In that way, you don't miss too much your children and I can control my business."

Espera remained silent. Felix took advantage of it by charging even more his ideas. When you go back to Mendoza after the wedding, I stop by to see you before I continue for Buenos Aires and take the plain for Italy. Wait for me at the bus station. Do you know where it is?"

"Yes, I do. It is across from university, on the main boulevard. If you don't mind, I can come for a short while to your house and meet your children. This is a wonderful opportunity to get acquainted with them."

"Absolutely,not!" Responded Espera. "I think it is high time to get in before they get involved in another scuffle. Let me go first. You follow me in a couple of minutes."

Felix held her back. "You can't leave just like that," begged her Felix.

"What is happening this evening confirms all of my fears. Maybe, we should abandon our plans and wait for better future times."

Felix face became dark even though the moon's light was shining on it. "My love," he protested, "We cannot postpone anymore our union. It would be a disaster"

Espera placed her index finger on his lips and said, "I forbid you to mention that word for the time being."

Felix remained speechless. He tried to unravel the mass of ideas brewing in his mind, but had no time. He was stunned by the sudden turn of the events. "But, my darling, do you realize how hard it would be for me not to accomplish our dream? All of a sudden, you have changed altogether your state of mind. I do not recognize you anymore. I came from the other side of the earth to meet with you, to smell your breath, to hear your voice, to feel your emotions."

She became deadly serious and said, "Felix, don't be a fool. I can't never marry you. We are too different, too incompatible to each other. We live too distant from each other." She abruptly disengaged herself from his arms and returned to her table. Felix tried to stop her and remained with both arms stretched outward in a gesture of stopping her. He stood there frozen like a statue

Darkness descended slowly and inexorably. Inside the wedding hall, the party continued with all its colorful features. Espera returned to her table with a grim face. She was welcomed by eye movements and whisperings. No one dared to revamp the previous gossips, because some of the old ladies who had sparkled the polemics, begged their husbands to go back home. The cutting of the cake was accomplished and the groom began the casting of the bow. Many young people chose to stand up ready to grasp the prize. Unfortunately, the piece of cloth landed on Espera's head and everybody applauded. Espera did not exalt. She threw the bow back to the groom, who repeated the same activity. One gentleman approached Espera's table and, looking at her, said, "Young lady, you are the next candidate for marriage."

"She is not young," responded a lady from the floor.

Espera gave her a dirty look and said, "Look at yourself! You look like an old maid." The message did not reach destination and the comment which could have degenerated into another poignant argument, died out. Espera turned to her cousin and whispered something to her ear. Her relative got up immediately and dispensed kisses and good-by to her friends. The bride, their cousin, begged them to stay longer, but Espera was in evident bad humor. He told them that he would see them after the honeymoon. The two women hurried to exit and waked to the car not far away.

All alone outside, near the bush where Espera had been, Felix was a bundle of nerves. He could not find any logical explanation to Espera's sudden change of mind. Contrarily to Espera, he did not go back to the wedding hall to bid good-by to some old friends and to express his best wishes to the bride and groom. With the head hanging down his body, he slowly returned to the hotel where he stayed two extra days to recuperate from the deep romantic trauma. It was early in the morning when he took the bus that would take him back to Mendoza and, later to Buenos Aires, where he was scheduled to board the flight for Italy.

At Mendoza, in Calle de la Caridad, the bus station was ebullient with activities. Buses arrived and departed every five minutes. Passengers struggled with their luggage and long lines of prospective passengers were disorderly massed up in front of the ticket box. Nobody paid attention to a bus coming from Santiago. The chauffeur parked it in the space provided and announced the arrival in the city. The passengers were visibly tired after hours of traveling. Some of them hurried down to pick their suitcases, while other, who had a handbag, rushed to the bathroom already flooded with people. Only one man decided to walk directly to the telephone cabin. He sat to look at a phone number. When he finally found it, he launched a glance to the sky and closed his eyes. He stood in that position for a while until an old man tapped on the door and asked him if he were fine. "Are you all right?" he inquired. "Do you need a glass of water? There is a water fountain inside. Go there, take a sip of water. You will feel refreshened."

The man looked at him like a puzzle and smiled. Time was running out. He dialed a few numbers, but the line seemed to be busy. His cellular did not have an international program and, therefore, he could not use it. But, it would not have made any difference. The other line was constantly busy. "Maybe, she disconnected the phone knowing that I would call her," he said. No one needed to make a phone call and he remained pensive for a while.

Most of the passengers took care of their hunger pranks and were walking around the hall. The sound of a bus horn alerted many of them who lined up to board the bus. One passenger recognized the man in the cabin and tipped on the door, "Come on! Let's go!" The man did not respond. His mind seemed numbed.

The other got suspicious, opened the door and grabbed the man by the arm. "Come on! You miss the bus!"

Espera's house was a few miles away from the train station.

Chapter **XLII**

Santiago's Aftermath

Espera unplugged the phone and cut all types of communication with the world. She dedicated her time and energies to the garden. That summer had been unusually dry. Flowers and plants needed water. One evening, suddenly, the sky opened its gates and it rained for several hours. The dirt softened up and vegetation put on a smiley face again. Later, the news of an imminent hurricane scared people to death and everyone took refuge in the most remote corners of the cellar. The dreaded storm devastated adjacent farming areas and fell dormant as quickly as it came. Calm was soon restored among the inhabitants and life resumed its normal activities.

The escaped danger animated Espera's close friend to pay her a brief visit. She knocked at the door, but received no answer. Espera peeped through a small hole in the door and recognized the visitor. She invited her in and offered a cup of mate. Espera looked emaciated, vexed and displayed symptoms of depression. Her face had lost the luster of the previous weeks. The wrinkles on her forehead appeared more prominent and her look was gloomy. Even her voice was tarnished with raucousness. The glamour that characterized the guests' visits lost its splendor. "What's the matter, Espera? You look like a phantom. What's bothering you?"

Espera did not respond. She shook her head. "Are you sick? May I help you in something?" inquired her friend. Espera entrenched herself in a rigorous silence. Her friend put her arm around Espera's shoulders and in a gentle tone asked, "Are you sick? You are not being yourself! Stop being stubborn! Talk to me! You can trust me. We know each other for forty years."

Espera made an effort to turn her head toward her. After various attempts, she said in a low voice, "I blew it."

"You blew what? The horn? The candle? What?" She insisted. "What else?"

Her close friend caught the underlying meaning and replied, "Tell me. Things did not turn out in the way you expected with him, right?"

Espera confirmed it with a gesture of her head. "How is it possible," continued her friend. "You enjoyed a wonderful relationship with him. You were making wedding plans..."

Espera shook her head once again and said, "It was not meant to be. It was too good to be true."

"Where is he now? Is he still in Santiago?"

Espera straightened up her body and said, "There would be no reason for him to stay there. The ones who remained behind are the old ladies who were interested in gossip."

"This is a terrible blow to your dream, but do not despair."

Espera felt a bit energized and said, "He stopped here, downtown on his way to Buenos Aires and I ignored him. I did not have the heart to invite him to my house or even to bid good-by to him. Everything happened so fast."

Espera's friends opened her mouth at that news, "You mean, he stopped downtown and you invite him for a coffee? Do you realize the macroscopic error that you committed?"

Espera looked at her friend for the first time and replied, "How could I? Our relations were already strained."

"It would have been an act of courtesy, Espera, to meet him at the bus station. You missed a wonderful opportunity to mend your ways."

Espera took her time to answer, "It's useless! We departed in different ways. It was destiny that..." She paused a few moments, then, she continued, "If I accepted him at home, it would have become of public dominion."

"So, what? What's stopping you from freeing yourself from these old tales? This 'telenovela' is dragging on for too long."

"I disagree. When all the obstacles will be removed, then, I will consider."

"What if he finds another woman?" queried her friend.

"I doubt it. Our love has been tested in many fires."

"You mean, it is fireproof?"

"If you say so."

"Did you tell him that?"

"Not yet. Everything has to follow its course. When the time is ripe I will."

"You still love him, don't you?"

"That does not mean that we cannot live separately and respect each other. You do not have to live with someone if you love him. Love has so many different facets."

Her friend interrupted her, "Don't be silly. Don't drag on this internal conflict for too long. Call him and apologize. First, restore communication and, later,

You start all over again."

Espera showed chagrin at the suggestion. "There is no sense. Each time I move around, I see a mountain to climb. At my age, my legs are getting weaker."

"Quit being a bird of bad omen. You are still young and attractive. I bet a lot of bees dance around you when you appear in public."

Espera found the comment very amusing and laughed. "Good thing you came. You brought a breath of fresh air in my life. I felt miserable until now. I must admit that I am feeling better."

Her friend felt relieved. Her efforts to restore confidence and hope in Espera were paying off. She turned her eyes on the floor and noticed the telephone line unplugged. She looked at her and said, "How could you do that? It is very imprudent and dangerous. In an emergency situation, we can't even get in touch with you."

Espera felt amiss and culpable," I admit it. I was wrong."

"I know that you're confused mind stalled your reason. It made it incapable of using the rational process."

"Exactly!"

"Good girl! Now that you rightly acknowledge the gravity of your behavior, plug back the telephone and get back to your act."

As soon as Espera restored the communication, the telephone rang. Espera's friend got up and proceeded toward the door. "Where are you going?" protested Espera.

"I will come back this evening for an expresso coffee."

"Promise?"

Her friend smiled and closed the door behind her. It had been a sunny day until that time. She looked up and said, "Oh, boy, we are going to have another storm." Dark clouds convened above her head as if they were headed for a meeting. Shortly after, they discharged all their water content from their bellies on to the town.

The sun was still sleeping behind a curtain of mountain range. It woke up just on time to greet Felix on his return home. The traveler did not even pay attention to the late sunrise. He appeared to be under shock.

His pace was slow and uncertain. He dragged a luggage which moved off balance, especially when it found potholes on its way. At that time, a clan of gypsies was marauding around his neighborhood and some ladies insisted on foretelling his future. The most attractive among them, offered him to ease his tension by looking at the palm of his hand. Felix stopped. His eyes were glazed. He lazily put the right hand in his pants' pocket and drew out some changes. He dropped it in their hard wood baskets and wished them good day. The gypsies reciprocated by showering him with blessings, but remained in the area.

Suddenly, a new group of gypsies emerged from behind the street corner and, solicited by the females of the first detachment, began to raise their supplications to Felix' house. The rumor called the attention of the residents and one by one showed up in the street. It took a good ten minutes of persuasion before the wondering gypsies moved someplace else. One, two three windows opened up one after the other. The 'comare' heard about Felix presence and raised their heads trying to get a glimpse of him. At one point, a window of his house opened. He waived briefly and withdrew.

The ladies felt disappointed by Felix. They looked upward and got terrified by what they saw. They murmured something and rushed back to their kitchen. A strong wind brushed the streets and the sky became pitch black in a short while. For three days, it rained uninterruptedly. The streets got flooded by the time the sky decided to lock its gates. The children quickly crowded the streets barefoot and improvised paper boats that floated everywhere drawn by the water currents.

By late afternoon, the water had already receded in rivulets which became small tributaries of a river below. The ladies, again, reversed themselves outside to clear the front doors from the debris that the violent storm had left behind.

Felix returned to Italy as a confused man. He did not show up in the coffee shop every morning as it was his custom. He even renounced to the evening cards games or to the sharing of some daily anecdotes. His seclusion did not pass unobserved to the 'comare' of the street below who provided fuel to all sorts of speculations from the most banal to the most serious. Like scavengers, they were ready to devour the left over carcasses of a defeated man. While some of them swore to have seen his face hiding behind the curtains, feeble and on the verge of collapse; others claimed that he was love sick. At that point the conversation got hot and one suggested that his girlfriend was pregnant. Felix himself fueled the gossip that circulated in the neighborhood. In the evening, the kitchen light was extinguished. A dim and thin column of a pale flame interrupted the funereal atmosphere of the dining room. The usual 'comare' stretched the neck upward and commented in this way, "His house looks like a mortuary chamber.'

"I hope his mind did not go astray," suggested another.

"A third lady shook slightly her head and said, "Up there, someone is preparing a funeral."

"Why?" objected the first one.

"His girlfriend must have given him the discharge papers."

"Do you really think so?"

"He turned into a hermit. How else could you interpret his monk behavior?"

"In a way, I can understand his inner drama?" she said in a serious tone. "Have you ever been rejected from a friend, a club, a relationship, and socially marginalized by a friend?"

Last comment brought everyone to a deep reflection and the issue stopped there.

Days later, Felix took the first steps to come out of his shell. He exchange brief greetings with his neighbors and tried to speed up his pace in the direction of the main square. His move was quickly interpreted by his neighbors as to avoid questions related to his personal life. So, two ladies got bold and blocked his passage. The first asked abruptly, "Hi, stranger! Are you still in search of happiness?"

Felix was disturbed by the intrusion of his privacy and pretended not to hear, but when he realized that the lady was still waiting for an answer, he said, "Well, happiness is the aim of every human being, not just mine. Nobody can hide it.

"Listen to him!" responded the second lady, "Since you came back, you have turned to philosophy." She put up a broad smile and added, "You are not going to fool us, baby. We are not spring chickens."

"We know right away when somebody is lies," added the first lady.

"I don't understand your insinuations," rebutted Felix.

"Listen to him! He makes believe that he is indifferent to love. What a faker!"

"Friends, I appreciate your concern, but I have some commitments. Please, excuse me." And, in saying this, he departed.

A week passed by and Felix was able to make a contact with Espera. He begged her to commit herself once for all to his ideals. He left her the option of getting married in a monastery if she so wished. Her replies to him appeared always morbid, "I don't have time to devout myself to married life. I changed my future plans."

Felix felt desperate, "Women are mysterious," he muttered in one of the frequent moments of depressive mood. He spent sleepless nights wondering on what possibly brought her to a change her heart from a dream which was within reach.

A month passed by and Espera's mother-in-law became severely sick. She lost control of her physical functions and in many instances she messed up the bed. According to the nurses, the bathroom was in a horrible state of stench and they had to clean with some special chemicals. Espera, often, cared for her and spent many hours in her company.

Chapter **XLIII**

The Dream

During the long period of self-confinement, Felix decided that the time was long overdue for him to really try to locate the two gypsies who helped him to evade from the concentration camp. Were they still alive? How could he locate them? He remembered that he promised them to invite them to his wedding. Now, he did not stand a chance to marry the woman of his tender years love, nor he knew where they were living or if they died during the bombardments. In his life, he had never failed to be faithful to his word. He honored it with general Kessler, who on his death bed asked him to take a message to his family. And, he did it even in adverse circumstances. He reminisced on the numerous occasions he tried to renew the contacts with Espera, even though they failed one after the other. Not being able to find an answer, he laid the head on the table and fell into an obsessive muteness. For a while, he stood motionless and would have remained like that longer if it were not for the children's shouts from below the streets. He set himself up and assumed an erect position. "Life goes on," he murmured. He opened slightly the curtains and smiled at the children playing soccer. "If I were as young as they," he said. He closed the curtains and was on the verge of going down the street and making some attempts with the local gypsies to locate his benefactors, but the sudden sound of rain slipping on the glassy windows, made him change his mind. He rolled up the curtains for a moment to check the weather. It was raining hard and the festive mood of the children no longer filled the streets. At the sight of the rain, the mothers called them quickly inside.

The laptop lay idle on the table. A thin layer of dust covered it. It was a sign of inactivity. Felix gave a glance to it; grabbed a cloth and dusted it. He turned it on, but the mouse did not cooperate. After a few shakes, he was able to reactivate it. He went online and searched for the two gypsies. His efforts resulted futile because the first name was insufficient to even start the search. He was about to give up when on the screen appeared a gypsy community living in Alberobello, in the Puglie region.

For the moment, Felix dropped his project since Espera was unwilling to mend off their relations he felt it was a waste of time. Their lack of communication drew him even deeper into a state of loneliness. The rare times he showed up at the store or at the market, he bought necessities and rushed back home leaving the 'comare' disappointed because they could not 'squeeze' him like a lemon with their private investigations. The communicative distance led them to believe that he had lost control of his mind. The suspicion was validated even further by the fact that he cut off the telephone line and he relied only on the cellular.

What raised further the neighbors' eyebrows was Felix's new initiative that to them appeared preposterous. One of their sons, through a link on the computer, found out that Felix was ready to get married. He was unable to get the last name, but that was sufficient to put on in motion another round of the gossip machine. At the end, they tried to get an answer from Espera, but the voice mail kept on repeating that she was unavailable.

The 'comare's' avid appetite in wedding scoops got their satisfaction a couple of weeks later. A double wedding ceremony was scheduled at their church, called Madonna delle Stelle. It was built almost on a cliff surrounded by enormous rocks at the foot of the mountain. On foot, it took half an hour. Of course, people no longer were willing to sweat a few pounds off and relied on transportation to reach the area. When Felix's neighbors found out from reliable sources that Felix was going to assist at the ceremony, they did not want to miss any chance and flocked the church. Some of them even suggested that he could be one of the grooms.

The pews were all taken. The front seats showed a sign that read, 'reserved' and one of them was for Felix. He dressed up for the occasion and arrived on time. The priest, an old man with gray hair and eyeglasses, gave a peak from behind the altar to ascertain that the future newlyweds were at the front steps of the church. His assistant motioned to him that indeed they were and the music began. A bride, accompanied by her father, appeared at the entrance and walked slowly in the isle. A big roar rose through the crowd. In front of the altar, the bride's father raised the veil from her face and deposited a kiss on her cheek and let the veil fall back on her face. He turned around and took his seat in on the reserved section of the pews. The priest showed up in all his glamorous religious garments followed by the deacon and the altar boys.

Shortly after, another bride (this one pregnant) appeared at the entrance of the church and walked slowly down the aisle. She stopped at the left side of the previous bride. They smiled at each other and waited for their future spouses. The inhabitants of the local town swore that they never witnessed to a double wedding at their church. It was a unique and unforgettable evening.

After about ten minutes of waiting, the crowd began to feel restless and made known their disappointment with loud critical comments. Suddenly, silence returned. A groom appeared at the entrance. Everybody stood up and an explosion of joy ripped the silence. "Hurrah, to the groom! One is here!" Felix appeared at the end of the hall. He looked disoriented by so much attention. The people at both winds of the isle started to pat him on the arms and voiced their best wishes. By the time he reached the front row and took place in the designated seat, he felt like a fearful sparrow. The 'comare' looked at each other. The pores of their skin perspired by satisfaction. For once, they thought, they had guessed right and gave Felix with a standing ovation. They exuberance turned quickly into dismal disappointment. Someone spread the rumor that Felix was only a guest; therefore, many old ladies got up and were ready to leave. The priest motioned them to sit down. The word was passed around like a lightning that the real groom had just stepped out of the limousine and the second one was scheduled to arrive too. The groom accelerated the pace to reach the altar fast. Being between two brides, it made him uncomfortable. He looked at the first and, then, at the second and realized that he was in deep trouble. Both brides were waiting for another groom. After a moment of confusion, the pregnant bride grabbed the cushion and began to hit the groom.

The other bride covered her mouth with both hands and fainted. The groom tried to gain the way out, but the family of the pregnant girl blocked him and began a fist fight. The relatives of the fainted groom accused the man of being a cheater and a womanizer. They grabbed the chairs and hit him from all sides.

The priest ran to the sacristy and called the police intervention

Women were pulling hair to each other. Some of them, seeing Felix dressed in high attire, pulled the candle stick from their place and threw them at him. Felix shouted his innocence and made various attempts to gain the exit. One young man yelled that Felix was sitting on a reserved seat and, therefore, he was a traitor. They surrounded him and started to pull his clothes off. The public excitement rose gradually and made them lose control of their sense of civility. They unbelted his pants and were about to pulled down. Luckily a policeman used the baton to drive them away.

Outside of the church, the opposing relatives, oblivious of the police presence, started to kick each other again. Across from the main door, there was a fruit and vegetable stand. The vendor, a fat man with a big Panama hat, was having enjoying the street theater going on and launched some acoustic epithets now to one side and later to another. Soon, his good time turned sour. Women and youngsters joined their strength in grabbing the boxes of tomatoes and throwing them at whoever happened to be in front of them.

The merchant's reaction was rather quick. He pulled out a pole from the stand and began to chase the vandals. He was able to make only a few gains in front of him. The people from the back quickly overpowered him and lodged him in a big trash can standing nearby. Additional police force arrived and, with some difficulties, put an end to the deplorable scene.

Felix arrived home unrecognizable. His face was a mask of tomato paste and his clothes were dirty and ripped. The children, who saw him in those conditions, thought he was a beggar and, instead of having pity for him, they derided him.

The church melee left a deep scar in Felix's heart and mind. Even the closest neighbors began to wonder about his mental and physical well being. He lowered the Italian flag at a low staff and closed the curtains of his house windows. His disappearance from social life augmented the suspicion among the 'comare' that love was the culprit of his malaise. Some of them proposed to arrange a meeting between him and a local lady, but the major obstacle consisted in getting in contact with him. He had cut the telephone line, put a stop to his daily promenades and drove out from his garage whenever he had to go out to shop. Gossip increased when he disappeared from the scene for a couple of weeks. During that time, he screened the meanders of the gypsies' district in Alberobello in search of his benefactors.

Chapter XLIV

Alberobello

This unique town is a short distance from Bari and rests on a calcareous hill from which the inhabitants draw the material to build their adobes. The name originates from the Greek word 'truolloi', which means 'dome.' Olive groves, almonds and vine trees flourish on the hills which are adaptable particularly to that type of viticulture. The trulli are conical structures covered by the rocky material which was considered to be too fragile to sustain the weather. In fact in the seventeen century, a royal degree prohibited the construction of the 'trulli' with the calcareous material and replaced it with stones. A subsequent degree by Ferdinand IV rescinded the previous one and the inhabitants were free once again to keep up the tradition.

In 1926, they built the church of Saint Anthony. It was there, that a new priest, by the name of Don Romanus, came to occupy the empty spot left vacant by the death of the previous monsignor.

Don Romanus was in the eighties He had dark complexion, grey hair and brown eyes. He also bore a scar on the forehead. Perhaps, he had an accident in his younger years. The indigenous population held him in high respect and, at times, they liked to refer to him as "the foreigner," he had a high command of the language and his accent was perfect. He could pass as an Italian if nobody mentioned his past. After all, he had all the somatic features of a 'meridionale.' No one knew exactly where he came from, but the local community did not care. It was rumored however that he had a different name before he moved to Alberobello. Whatever it was, they considered him one of them. It is interesting to note that if anyone asked him his origin, he would reply without hesitancy, "I am from heaven." After a while, the villagers abstained from asking him that question.

Don Romanus was a splendid example of charity and compassion and a protagonist of the Gospel of Christ on hearth. He spent his summer vacation in Africa working in camps contaminated with malaria assisting sick people. His parishioners feared for his health because previous priests, who ventured in that area of the world, died of that disease.

At home, he was held in high esteem by the people in jail. He visited them quite often bringing them a word of comfort and faith. He loved to bake cookies and share them among the detainees who devoured them in no time. He bragged being the best baker in town and the bakers laughed at his claim. He also enjoyed playing cards with the prisoners and kept their spirit up by telling them stories full of humor. He would hear their confessions once a week, but it was not uncommon for him to rush at the most odd hours to confess someone on the verge of death. In doing so, he skipped meals and sleep to accommodate their requests. He was also a vehement sustainer of marital sacredness.

In one of the many confessions that he heard during the week, a woman accused her husband of being a fragrant violator of woman's self-assertiveness. The confessor replied, "My dear, marital obligation does not eradicate autonomy. It defines certain rules behind which one cannot and should not go. Being mutually supportive does not suggest that one of the spouses has to watch helplessly or passively to a narcissistic behavior."

"But, Father," she responded. "My husband has one thing in mind and I have to serve him immediately."

"Well, my view on this is very clear. There has to be a mutual commitment to sexual relationship, which I realize, is a biological drive, but cannot be a man's exclusivity even though, nowadays, man are very instinctive. The foundation of a happy marriage is not just one aspect of it, but a reciprocal obligation."

Don Romanus was particularly affectionate with the children and he never wasted an opportunity to shower them with a loving, tender care. He provided food for the needy, bought books for those who could not afford it and even provided lodging for a youngster who ran away from home. He built a small recreational center for them. Among the most revered ones were a basketball court and ping-pong table.

For the older folks, he built a bocce field. The week-end was so busy with activities that it became impellent to schedule the time activities. The prelate also organized bocce tournaments that attracted people from all over the region. No one spoke negatively about Don Romanus. One Sunday, during a soccer game, a melee broke out in the field. He got up from his seat and ran in the center court to sedate the ebullient emotions of some players. In one intervention, he got a black eye from one of the players who,

erroneously, hit him instead of his rival. The players were infuriated by the presence of the priest during the fist fight. They shouted, "For cry sake, do not interfere with our game." The spontaneous outburst of hanger would soon be replaced with an act of contrition. The priest ran after the ball, gave a couple of distorted kicks and the crowd roared with laughter. The referee resumed the game after the players shook hands.

Winter months were the most difficult of the year for the youth. Don Romanus would try to keep them busy with baking, theaters and ping-pong. The parents were so appreciative that in harvest time donated to him all sort of produce that he would store for the cold days.

Girls and boys ready for marriage requested Don Romanus to celebrate the nuptial ceremony. They came even from nearby towns. After the war, Scarman and Barabbus did not return to Rotondi anymore, but they succumbed to menial job opportunities being available in the South. A man, whom they helped to escape from the concentration camp, ran into them casually after the war in their town where he went to investigate some types of olive trees. At first, the two men declined the invitation, but upon a second meditation, decided to follow him in his olives groves in Alberobello. For a few years, they lived on the farm in an old barrack. Later, they bought an old and small apartment, a few blocks away from the cathedral.

One early Sunday morning, Felix made up his mind and took the train for Alberobello. After Mass, people discussed the weekly business and future plans between one expresso coffee and a card game. Gypsies were hanging around the cathedral begging or offering their purported talent in foreseeing the future by reading the palm of peoples' hands. He approached a group of them in front of the church and inquired about his benefactors. An old lady pointed to a nearby street. "I just saw them in that corner a few minutes ago." She finished talking and stretched her hand. Felix dropped some coins and followed the path described. Nobody was there except a woman knitting at the entrance of her house. He made the same inquiry and the lady responded, "I talked to them about fifteen minutes ago. You may be still on time to catch them, there." She stretched her hand and Felix did the same as before. For the next hour, he scouted the whole area, but of his friends he found no trace.

Felix did not wish to return to his hometown empty handed. He lodged the whole week at the hotel.

During the night, he had a rough time sleeping. Out of all the dreams he had, one remained fixed in his mind. When he got up, he spent most of his time developing a plan on a huge white sheet. On it, he drew many small squares and in each one of them he wrote a name. By the time he finished, he felt satisfied of his accomplishment.

The cathedral was at the city center not far from the hotel where he was lodging. One morning, he knocked at the door of the rectory. The secretary, a lady in her late fifties, took her sweet time to arrive, "May I help you?" she asked in a sweet low voice.

"Well, I would like to speak with the priest, if you don't mind it."

"You mean, Don Romanus. Right?"

"I guess," he replied.

"May I ask you the reason for seeking a private meeting with him?"

"To be honest, it is a personal matter."

"I see," she answered. "You mean a confession, right? If it is what you are looking for, I am sorry to disappoint you. He does not hear confessions until six o' clock this evening."

"Not really," tried to explain Felix.

The secretary scrutinized him from the top to the bottom and said, "My dear, Padre is very busy. He has no time for frivolous talks."

In saying that, she was about to close the door. Felix stopped it just on time, "Listen, my case is rather urgent. I need to talk to him."

She moved his hand away and said, "You don't understand, my son. At his age, Padre has curtailed many activities. Years are heavier than stones if you know what I mean."

Felix pulled some money bills from his pocket and put them in her hands, "I am sure that this medicine can alleviate any discomfort coming from his age."

The secretary's face suddenly brightened. She closed right away her hand and said, "Please, come in. Make yourself comfortable on this chair. It is old, but it is a chair. I will make sure that Padre will join us shortly."

Don Romanus was in his eighties. His black hair and brown eyes somewhat blended in with his dark skin. He walked at a slow pace and leaned on a cane. An incident, that occurred many years ago, left him with a knee injury that prevented him to walk straight. Every year, he spent a couple of weeks at the island of Ischia to undergo mud baths that, according to him, made him feel much better. (More will be said of him later.)

Upon entering in the waiting room, Don Romanus greeted the visitor by saying, "Welcome to this modest abode. From the first information I have, it seems that you want to get married."

Felix kissed his hand and replied, "I came here for something..."

The priest invited him to sit down. "Stand up for too long will make you grow taller," he joked.

Felix laughed. He tried to start the conversation, but he was visibly nervous." The priest said, "Take a deep breath. Nobody is rushing you."

Finally, Felix took courage and said, "Yes, Father, you are right. I want to get married." He opened up a large scroll and laid it on the table. "Here, I have outlined date, time and all the arrangements for a splendid religious ceremony."

Don Romanus put on his eye glasses and examined minutely the paper and exclaimed, "This is an impeccable masterpiece of a matrimonial ceremony. I am spellbound. Only a genius can produce such work. I am proud of you,"

"I am elated for your approval," said Felix.

"Not so fast," replied the priest.

Felix face discolored instantly. He became pale and showed symptoms of nervousness. "What's wrong with it?" Felix complained. "Why do you think it is incomplete?"

"There is someone missing in the puzzle, my son," explained Don Romanus.

"The bride, you mean?"

"Exactly! The space for one protagonist is vacant. She should be here with you."

"She lived in Argentina. It takes time to come here."

"Then, I need a proxy from her. I cannot proceed without that document."

Felix became suddenly pensive. He twisted his lips in search of an answer that never surfaced on the screen of his memory. The priest got suspicious and interrupted his thoughts," What kind of wedding are you planning to have anyhow? I start to believe that you have no bride."

Felix took a deep breath as to relieve his tension and said," Father, this is a special wedding. I dreamed of it for a long time." "A dream?" queried the priest. "May I remind you that a marriage is between a man and a woman? Genesis reminds us that God created man and woman. From the New Testament, we learn that Jesus attended with his mother and his disciples a marriage between one man and one woman. Finally, his mother married a man by the name of Joseph." The priest closed his eyes for a short while. He put back his glasses and added, "My son, you don't need to be a theologian to understand the quintessence of the matrimony."

Felix kept on biting his nails. When he noticed that Don Romanus was staring at him, he stopped and muttered, "I still believe that it can be done."

At that point, the clergyman raised slightly the tone of his voice, "My son, what you are asking is absolutely preposterous, inaudible, utterly anomalous. A man does not marry with himself or with another man. Is it clear?"

"No," interrupted him Felix. I did not state that. I said that, considering the circumstances, I still could marry with my spouse."

"Without her physical presence?"

"Why not?"

The priest gave symptoms of losing his proverbial patience. "My dear, the church is a divine institution. You cannot reduce it to a surrealistic vision. A wedding is a triangular celebration between two spouses and God. It is not a dream."

Felix was not willing to give up the notion that he could still carry out his plan. The priest got up ready to leave. Felix held him back,"

Father, you cannot do abandon the boat in the middle of the ocean. You do not know the immense significance that I owe to my plan."

The priest looked at him and shook his head, "You are obtuse of mind." Felix pulled a bunch of dollars from his pocket and put them in his hand. "What is this for?" inquired the prelate.

"The anticipation fee for my wedding..."

The priest returned him the money. Felix pushed his hand back. "The wedding must go on," he stated.

The priest was astonished by such an insubordination and determination. He handed the money to the secretary and said, "Very well. If you wish that the ceremony goes on like any other, I will prepare the announcements and let my secretary make the floral arrangements. Remember that I want to be paid just the same. You will be responsible for all the payments."

Felix shook hands and said, "Agree."

The priest had already arrived at the threshold of his office. He stopped and turned around, "do you know that both of you have to come to confession for the wedding to be valid?"

Felix was taken by surprise, "Don Romanus," he pleaded "Can't you give her a dispensation?"

"Why should I do that for?"

Felix dropped something in the secretary's hand and asked, "Father, maybe, she can go to confession to her parish.

The priest smiled and said, "I accord you that dispensation."

Felix had made a long list of distinguished guests. Among them, there were listed two gypsies, the only ones from their clan. With the aid of a local newspaper, Felix was able to locate his two friends by sending the invitation to the postal office. When Scarman and Barabbus opened up the envelopes, they did not understand those graphic signs. They brought them to the coffee shop to someone to read them. The cards players and the coffee drinkers stopped their activities when they heard the news. They were shocked and offended that those two gypsies had been preferred to them. The two men became speechless. They were stunned and jubilant at the same time. What made things worse was the name. They had no idea who person who had invited them. Without making any comment, they took refuge underneath a oak tree at a short distance from the plaza.

"Boy, this man has showered us with an honor, but he also loaded us with a high responsibility," said Scarman.

"What are you talking about? We go there to eat big, my partner. You sound worried. I do not understand you. It is going to be the greatest day of our life."

"I am not sure if we should attend the wedding in the first place," remarked Scarman.

"Are you thinking about the clothes that we have to wear?"

"I know that you have dirty and shiny suits. By the way, I am not going to ask you to borrow one."

"What's wrong with that? We are partners. Aren't we?"

"Stop being foolish!"

"What's bothering you, man?"

"I tell you. First of all, we don't know who invited us."

"What do you care? We have been invited to eat and drink. We won't have this opportunity for the rest of our life and you are you are creating a lot of problems."

"The second question concerns the gift. Do you have any money?"

Listen to him! If I had money, you would know it." Then, he placed the index finger on his nose and continued, "I have a marvelous idea!"

"Which is?"

"Let's sell the chalice and we will be able to make a monetary gift. How does it sound?"

"Terrible!"

"Why is it?"

"I have a counter proposal. Let us give him the chalice as a gift."

"We can't do that! It costs a lot of money. If we sell it, we can use most of the money for ourselves."

"It won't work. As you know, that chalice possesses a mysterious power."

"If it is so," protested Barabbus, "Why we don't have any of it?"

"If you feel in that way, let's donate it to the church. Whoever the priest is will use it during the ceremony. That will be only a temporary gift. After the ceremony, the priest can give it back to us."

"You have a genial idea, but with one shortcoming. We will look like two peasants if we request the chalice back. The news will spread rapidly in town and they will scorn us. They will consider us as the scum of the society. It is far better if we tell the groom that the chalice is our gift to him, but on three conditions. First, it has to be used for the wedding celebration. Secondly, it must be part of the offertory gift."

"What's that?"

"It means that I will carry it to the altar, while you carry the dish or the chalice with the water. Thirdly, it must remain property of the church. How does it sound?"

Barabbus remained pensive for a while. His mind seemed to be elsewhere. He scratched his head and said, "I don't buy it. That chalice may put us in jail."

What are you talking about?"

"The church has a list of all stolen sacred objects. If they recognize it, we end up behind the bars."

"How in the world are they going to find that out after so many years...?"

"Easy, priests know how to recoup their stolen pieces of art."

Barabbus raised the index finger on his lips and said, "I have a greater idea. If they discover that it belonged to a church in Costantia, we just say that we found it and we are giving it back."

"Marvelous, fantastic, fabulous!" responded his friend. "This is a good reason to get rid of it."

"No! Don't you remember that we swore to use it for that boy's wedding? We kept it all these years and now we are going to give it away like this?"

His friend covered his face and said, "How do we know who is this mysterious groom? What if he is...?

He did not finish the sentence. The two stared at each other. Neither one said a word. They were both stunned.

Monday, was a day off for Don Romanus. Usually, he paid a visit to some of his relatives in the suburb. Scarman and Barabbus decided to consult with him. At the rectory, they knocked at the door and waited for the someone to open. The secretary looked through the curtains of the window and when she saw that they were gypsies, she returned to her cleaning activity. The two men heard a noise, but no one came to the door. After waiting for a while and ringing the bell, repetitiously, at times, they made an exterior tour of the building to ascertain the presence of someone. Disconcerted and disappointed, the two men took their way home.

Down the street, they stumbled in an old, blind man who stretched his hand for money. Scarman said, "Friend, you are not the only one who is begging. We are in the same boat. I am sorry, we cannot help you. They were on the verge of departing when Scarman said to his partner, "Why don't we ask him how to deal with that problem?"

The old man heard him and asked, "What's in your mind?"

The two gypsies got startled. They mumbled something and moved away. The blind man grabbed one of them and said, "Tell me. What's bothering you?"

Scarman and his buddy looked at each other in a mood of astonishment. Barabbus was hesitant to speak. He pulled back his friend and said, "We have nothing to lose. This man really seems to foretell the future.

"Let's find out if he can help us." He turned to the blind man and asked, "If you had to attend a wedding, what gift would you bring?"

"Nothing!" replied the blind man.

The gypsies laughed. "Nobody goes to a wedding without a gift. It is not polite," responded Scarman.

"Since when, both of you have learned to be polite?"

The two friends again looked at each other with surprise. The blind man added, "Let me put it in this way. If I have nothing, how can I bring a gift?" He raise his cane and added, "This is not the point," he added. "What is your question? Hurry because I am a busy man," he reminded them.

"I can see it," responded Barabbus.

Scarman said, "Listen, our friend. We had a dream. We dreamed of being invited to a wedding and we were wondering on the kind of gift it would be proper to bring."

"That depends on financial status. If you can afford thousand dollars, well..."

"I wish I had thousand dollars," replied Scarman.

"We are on the verge of starvation, my friend," added his buddy.

"What should I say," protested the blind man. "I stay sitting on this chair all day waiting for someone to drop a coin in the hat and many days I hear no tinkling."

"If that's the case, I am going to contribute something," replied Barabbus. In saying that, he dropped some change in the man's hat." Bless your heart," replied the blind man upon hearing the noise.

"The truth is," said Scarrman, fragmenting his words from time to time. "We have something very dear to us. It is a chalice. Actually, they are two, but one went back to the owner."

"Where in the world did you get the chalice?" said the blind man in a very altered tone of voice.

"It's, it's..." Scarman could not finish the sentence.

"I see. You stole it in a church long time ago and now you want to create an environment of impunity around you. Your crime is also the result of an inadequate control by the church institution."

The two gypsies looked at each other petrified. Scarman whispered in his friend's ear, "We better get a hack out of here. Where did he learn all of this fancy language? This man can cause a lot of problems us." He was ready to grab the cane from him and him on the head, but his buddy held him back.

The blind man, realizing that he had caused a controversy between the gypsies, said, "The idea of giving a chalice as a gift is a very noble one."

Barabbus stopped him, "Perhaps, you misunderstood. We do not want to give the chalice to the spouses, but to the priest to use it during the celebration. We bring to what they call altar the chalice where they put the wine. We saw it a long time ago. After the ceremony, the chalice would become church property."

"So, you would not bring any gift to the bride and groom?"

"Eh, no!" protested Scarman. "The chalice is priceless."

The blind man waited a while before he responded. "So, what do you say, my friend?" inquired Barabbus.

"Before I respond to your question, I have a question for both of you. Are you Catholics?"

Both men stared at each once again. Barabbus asked, "What do you mean by that?"

"You see? I have a reservation. Neither of you is a practicing Catholic. I am afraid that the priest may reject your participation in the offertory gift on the basis of your religious background."

"This sounds Turkish to me" protested Barabbus.

"Let me put it straight," replied the blind man. "I believe that a non Catholic person is forbidden from holding the chalice with the wine. There are theological implications."

"I don't understand that language. I only know that the chalice is mine," objected Scarman.

"What about me?" responded Barabbus quasi confused.

"Wait a second! It is our wedding gift to the spouses, but it has to go to the church. This is the agreement we stipulated; otherwise, I will sell it" said Barabbus in strong terms.

"I will not allow anyone to send the chalice in the fire, whatever it costs me, even my blood."

The harsh language used by Scarman startled the blind man who right away tried to assuage Scarman's hanger. "I am sure they will honor your agreement."

Barabbus felt tension around him. Instead of abating it, he increased it by imposing his request. "What is going to be my role there? Am I supposed to offer water? What am I going to do with water? If I bring wine, I may be able to drink it."

"Don't listen to him!" Interjected Scarman."

"As I understand," explained the blind man in a mild tone, "You have rudimentary knowledge of your Muslim religion, maybe a null notion of it."

"Hardly any," responded Scarman without hesitation.

"Can you imagine about other religions," replied the blind man.

"I am fully aware of it" responded Barabbus.

Scarman turned to his partner and said, "You are lucky if you can offer the chalice with water. If there were no water to carry, you would be standing next to a politician and you would learn a couple of big words and use them at the first chance among ignorant people. The blind man realized that the two interlocutors were getting involved in an unnecessary argument and cautioned them to cool off their ire "Do you realize that this is a question of faith? It is not discrimination. Talk to the priest to hear his reaction."

"O.K." replied Scarman. I go along with you. If the priest asks us about our religious belief, we just tell him that we are like him."

"You can't lie," rebutted the blind man. "Can both of you tell me where you really stand in terms of faith? You made a vague mention to Muslim before."

Scarman interrupted him, "We can tell him that we are considering ourselves to be on an explorative stage"

"This idea sounds logical. Let's put it in that way," responded Barabbus. "Maybe, the priest will be satisfied."

"The blind man replied, "My friends. As long as you are construing dreams, it is valid. I was talking about real life events. The two gypsies remained in silence for a while. Some people gathered around them. The gypsies gave a pat on the blind man's shoulders and left.

The following day, they were sitting in front of their house busy polishing the chalice. A lady, passing by, stopped him and said, "If you don't want it, I can free you from this unnecessary weight. Metals cause diseases in summertime."

"Lady," replied Barrabbus, with an irritated tone, "I hold it with both hands because here there are many thieves. I do not want anyone to touch it. The woman tried to touch the chalice, but he held her hand back.

"Lady, I repeat. It is not for sale and, if it were, you would not have the money to pay for it."

The woman looked at him with disdain. She realized that she could not pursue her objective and walked away. They had just finished, when a taxi stopped in front of them. The passenger paid and got out. The two gypsies looked at the stranger and asked him if he were looking for someone. The man's eyes were fixed on the chalice. Barabbus pulled it away from his sight by hiding it behind his back. "Why? Do you want to buy it? There is no price for it. So, forget it!"

Suddenly, Felix felt dizzy. His head spanned around until he reclined against the wall. The gypsies asked him if he needed any help. He did not answer. They felt uneasy at the sight of the stranger. Felix had intention of taking time to think, to regain his strength and restart the inquiry. He took a deep breath. The two gypsies were watching and waiting for his next step. Felix started to shiver. Scarman approached him and asked him."What's wrong with you?? Don't you feel good? Do you want a glass of water?"

Felix replied in fragmented sentences, "I was ha...ving drea...ms a...bout thin...gs happen...ed long ti...me a...go."

"Can you spell out your dreams?" inquired his interlocutor.

"I was li...ving a tumul...tu..ous moment of my li..fe."

Scarman pressed him on, "Keep on going. We can wait."

"I ex...changed you for a mo...ment with a couple of men from your eth..nic group who saved my life."

The two men looked at each other with increased interest and were determined to get to the end of the story. Scarman kept on pressing, "Where? When? Talk to us!"

Felix loosened the knot of his tie. The sweat was running down his face. Barabbus offered an old newspaper sheet. Felix declined the invitation and wiped his brows with a handkerchief he pulled from the back pocket of his pants. "As I was saying," he continued, "It happened at Buchenwald in the last weeks of the war."

When the gypsies hear the name of the concentration camp, widened the orbit of their eyes so deep was their interest in the story. Felix said, "Two gypsies, who were guards at the camp, helped me to escape.

I remember very well that one of them held a chalice tightly to his chest and patted it. Clearly, he ascribed a lot of importance to it. I did not have the time to find it out. At one point, he realized the scrutiny that I was giving to it and hid it in a hole in the wall of the barrack. I promised them that, some day, I would invite them to my wedding."

"How come you did not search for them?" asked Barabbus.\

"I remained in Germany for a few years after war. Later, I moved to Brazil, where I got married. My wife's premature death drove me back to my roots."

"How come you did not look for them?" inquired Scarman, more curious than ever to get to the details.

"How could I? I only knew their first names. Still, I don't know if they are alive. Finally, I took somebody's suggestion and I asked for assistance to the post office. They promised me to do their best, but at this point I am not sure if they received my invitation."

Barabbus replied, "I am sure they received it. The post office has professional people working in the office."

"Well, I tried. It would be a day of great joy to meet them again."

"You said that you know their names. Can you tell us who they are? Maybe, we know them," asked Scarman.

"One of them had a scar on his face and was named Scarman. The other name was Barabbus."

Felix notices that streams of tears flowing down their cheeks and felt confused and uneasy. He asked them the reason for weeping. One of them replied, "I am Scarman." "And I am Barabbus," responded the other. In saying that, he raised the chalice and added, "And this is the same chalice you saw then."

Felix tried to reply with a strong defense, "No, it is not true! It is not possible! I don't believe it."

"You better believe it!" responded Scarman.

At that point, it made no more sense to insist because the gypsies reminisced on some events that involved Felix. Blocked by so much evidence, he threw his arms around them and cried, "My friends, my saviors."

The emotion lasted for sometimes. At the end, the two gypsies invited Felix to their poor adobe that they had bought with a pension from Germany. Felix courteously refused. Instead, he took them by the arms and led them to the best restaurant in town.

CHAPTER **XLV**

Faith and Hypocrisy

Felix visited Don Romanus to finalize the wedding arrangements. For the band, the prelate suggested a local one, but Felix kindly declined the offer and told him that he had another plan.

"I am going to hire a friend of mine, Bruno Capisani, a great tenor from La Scala of Milan."

"What are his credentials," asked Don Romanus.

"One who sings at the most famous theater in the world needs credentials?" responded Felix somewhat surprised at the priest's question. "But if you are curious to know something about his past, I will mention solely that during a concert in Moscow, he received ten minutes of standing ovation. If this does not suffice, I will inform you that at The Assumption feast at St.Cecilia in Solvay, New York, he sang the Ave Maria with such a pathos that moved many people to tears. A man asked for special permission to his health institution to be released on that day so he could listen to the tenor." No, no," was quick to respond Don Romanus, "It is your choice. It was mere curiosity on my part. I never heard of him."

"In terms of interpretation, a music director told him that he was second only to Di Stefano."

It was time to wrap up the church decoration, when the priest queried, "Do you have someone in mind who will do the offertory gift?"

Felix responded calmly, "Indeed, I do. I met them in a coffee shop a couple of days ago. It will be a good experience for them. Let's put in this way. They are a bit rustic, illiterate…., but they can walk down the aisle. They may not come to confession…That's what I mean."

Don Romanus remained perplexed. He was quick to explain that it would be appropriate for all the components of the wedding group, including the best man and honor girls, to go to confession."

Felix responded in a low tone, "Father, they are giving a gold chalice as a wedding gift with the precondition that it would be used during the ceremony, that one of them would carry it during the offertory ceremony and that after it would turn it to you as a gift. In other words, it will belong to the church.

"In that case, the confession issue can be waived. Obviously, if an individual is atheist, he would make the whole act void. Similarly, if an individual, being of another religious background, would volunteer to bear the offertory gift would invalidate his involvement." In simple language," added the agent, "You are saying that if someone does not believe in the rite, he should not volunteer."

"Correct!"

"Forgive my theological ignorance," pleaded Felix, 'What about if an individual does it vicariously and upon subsequent reflection, he may come to believe?"

"That's possible," explained Don Romanus. "But, one has to be careful. Let's not confuse faith with apples. You can taste an apple and if you don't like it you throw it in the garbage. Faith needs preparation, reflection and sincerity before we make any commitment. Later, you may increase the fire with action….Remember that you are dealing with God. When the Immensity comes to you in the form of bread and wine, it is a very serious matter."

"I beg your indulgence for the last time, Father, but if these two individuals are engaged in the sole offertory gift?"

"I repeat. It could be regarded appropriate if the person is on his way to conversion. It is simple hypocrisy to be engaged in religious matter when your heart and soul are absent. Why do it in the first place?"

"I only know that they believe that this chalice possesses a mysterious power, a divine power."

"In that case, there is the presupposition that they believe in God."

"Amen!" yelled Felix, "We will come to talk to you about the flowers and carpet arrangements later." He got up and left.

"Don Romanus laughed and accompanied him on his way out.

On Saturday morning, the Cathedral was in ferment. Some women were busy decorating the altar; others were cleaning the pews; another group of men was stretching the red carpet in the central foyer. They created two lines of gardenia flower vases on each flank of the isle. The general manager ordered his assistants to tie bouquets of flowers in every pew. His main objective was to create an atmosphere of order and a flowering harmony. The first rows were reserved according to the social ranks. The offertory gifts rested on a small stand behind the last pew.

In the garage, the chauffeur was shining the car and the sign "Newly Wed." The restaurant was active in preparing the food. The reception invitation was extended to one-thousand guests. The band had already transferred the musical instruments in the corner of the huge hall. The stage was set.

Chapter XLVI

The Lonely Wedding

At two o'clock in the afternoon, the cathedral bells rang with a festive accent and resounded through the neighborhood. The sun illuminated the façade and gave to it a golden appearance. The air was still and the sky was a vault of glass. The trees, alongside the avenue, seemed to be more part of a painting scenery than part of a real life vegetation. For the time being, the weather showed clemency and retired over the mountains. It showed up again the following day in full force.

Guests and friends streamed toward the cathedral on foot and in luxurious cars. They were all dressed up in high attire. As usual, high social ranking women made an abundant display of their gold arrays. The photographers were positioned in the key areas and waited patiently for the arrival of the spouses. Suddenly, a long line of cars appeared on the main avenue. The car decorated with flowers and with a sign stopped in front of the church. The rest of the cars parked in the parking lot.

The conductor of the car stepped out and rushed over the passenger side to open the door.

Felix was dressed in complete white and a blue bow tie. A red rose appeared prominent on the top left side of the jacket. In the little pocket next to it, emerged a flaming red handkerchief. Felix was flanked by two men decently dressed up, but not conspicuously elegant. As they arrived at the main door entrance, the choir began to sing. Tenor Capisani was waiting for the bride to sing the Ave Maria. The priest and his assistants heard the music and walked out of the sacristy. Each took a seat on the altar and waited for the bride. The sight of the groom was greeted by the guests with a long and standing ovation. Felix genuflected before the altar and took seat at his chair. The public was waiting for the bride's arrival, but she did not show up. Disappointed by the delay, some of them got up willing to return home and show up at the reception. It was at that point that Don Romanus stood up and spoke, "Dear guests, the bride is not here, but the show goes on. The reception is expected to take place as usual. The groom will take full responsibility of the events as we agreed." Loud and spicy comments reverberated throughout the vaults. "This is inaudible," commented a lady whose neck was surrounded by a large, gold necklace. "Where is the bride?" asked another lady. "Is this a wedding?" questioned a gentleman sarcastically. The priest approached Felix. His face expressed the disappointment of the crowd. He leaned over him and whispered in his ear, "You wanted it in your way, didn't you? I have never officiated to a wedding without a bride. This is a farce, a comedy." He raised his voice, so that, the crowd which was filling the aisle on the way out, could hear. They all turned around to listen. "The church is a reality, not a dream." The sweat fell down his brow and he wiped it with a cloth that the deacon passed over to him. Felix blubbered something that no one understood. His two best men looked disconcerted. The people from the main isle pressed toward the altar. It appeared that the priest's health was their main concern, but he assured them of his stable conditions.

Felix was kneeling on the pew reserved to him. The priest decided to change his plans and begin the liturgical function, hoping in his heart that the groom was playing a joke on everybody as far as the bride was concerned. Every so often, he launched glanced to the seat reserved to her, but each time it was empty.

He had inverted the ceremony sequence. He planned first to bless the ring, prior to the exchange of vows, followed by the homily and the Eucharistic adoration. In absence of the bride, he started the homely, "My brothers and sisters, we are gathered here to assist at the marriage between Felix and...." He forgot the name and stopped. He looked at Felix, who said, "Esp..." The priest continued, "Esp.." Then he proceeded, "As you can see, we have lost control of space and time. With the creation of Adam and Eve on in the Garden of Eden, those two elements could be conceited only on an abstract level because God had extended to our progenitors the status of eternal being. With sin, appearing on the scene of human history, geographical space, as we know it today, and time, as we intend it, acquired the meaning that we give now.

Both were marked by man's birth and death."

Some people from the crowd began to question whether or not such a language was appropriate for a wedding ceremony. The priest acknowledged the first symptoms of disapproval, but continued anyhow, "My sons, that cycle was completed with the coming of the Messiah. God accomplished his earthly involvement of the human race in space and time.

In the last two thousand years, man has made tremendous progress in technology. He has landed on the moon and has landed a rover on the Red Planet distant millions of light miles from us. Thus, time and space do not portray the same relevance as before. They have been circumscribed. Without a blow, man can reach any area on the globe with a blink of an eye. The computer has allowed us to shorten distance and time by touching a few keys on the keyboard. God has allowed us to partake in the creation process."

This time the annoyance from the public became more evident, but the priest raised his voice and was able to quell down the opposition for the time being. "Now, I come to you, "he said, lowering the tone of his voice. "When a man and a woman get married..." A man from the crowd exclaimed, "Finally, he is coming back to us. Now, he is talking our language."

The priest concluded, "By the physical communion of two human beings, a man and a woman, a new human creature is born. Through the birth, man recreates the creation process of God and space and time recreate themselves. Man alone cannot accomplish this miracle. He needs a woman. A new birth is the quintessence of this union. Many times, we fly too high with our imagination. Like a computer, we cut space and time, with our fantasy, but many times we dwell too long in it. We have to come back to our human reality, to our values of space and time; otherwise, we feel the consequences of such a sudden transition." He paused, pulled up his shirt and checked the wristwatch. Felix looked at his side seat and he only saw empty space. A man rose on his feet and had the audaciousness of addressing the priest in this way, "Father, I believe I have the key that opens the door to this mystery." Don Romanus was never challenged in a nuptial ceremony and was quite surprised to see a man making that assertion. He reflected on it for a moment. The marital rite, actually, had not started yet for the absence of the bride, but odd situations like this one did not bother him. He was old and had acquired much wisdom and patience in his priestly mission. Maybe, to kill time, or perhaps, to grasp the opportunity to teach to such a vast audience, he did not object to get engaged in a theological conversation. "How can you unlock the code that reveals woman's motivation not to accept marriage as in this case?" He asked with a smile.

The intruder responded, "Women don't like to get married because they like to run a six or even ten miles races. Men and women are no longer marathon runners. There is a logical reason why Felix does not have a spouse on his side. In this country, we say 'If I can use my friend's car, why should I buy it? Do you know what I mean?"

"Perfectly!" responded the priest. "First of all, I disagree with you that a marriage life is a marathon. It is true that a marathon is a longer commitment than shorter races, but it is not a lifetime running activity because it finishes after twenty-four miles. Those who take this position do not fully explain a life of union between a man and a woman. Marriage is a whole life commitment where death is the finish line. Only in that context, we can consider it eternal, but only after the extinction of human life. The priest took off the eyeglasses and rubbed his eyes. The expectations of what he was going to say were high. "You see, a long lasting engagement is essential for the harmony of a family. The repercussions of a healthy family are reversible on the social asset as well."

A woman said, "Father, we don't want to be men's slaves anymore. I, for one, have no intention of giving up my freedom." The priest explained, "I hope you are not the same woman who came to confession the other week. In that occasion, I emphasized that renouncing oneself for the benefit of another person, means exactly what it implies, the availability of oneself twenty-four hours a day and submission for the entire life to the spouse. As you can see, it is not a short race."

A young girl protested, "Father, this is pure man egocentricity, man chauvinism."

"No, you misunderstood. The sublimation of one's love for the benefit of another should not be seen as a one way street. There has to be a mutual understanding of each partner giving up his or her rights for the other; otherwise, it will not work. Other than being unjust, it would be deleterious to the person who receives all the time not to recognize his or her reciprocal responsibilities of respect, love and honor."

The same girl replied, "Forgive me, Father, as long as this imaginary bride is not here yet, I take the opportunity to expose my view. We are human and we view the language in a different perspective. Complete submission to the other is not even for contemplation in my future. This means that even too much love can lead to misery."

"Wait a minute!" responded Don Romanus. "It has to be logical."

A young man who had d listened attentively up to that time raised his hand and said,

"I like to taste the apple before I buy."

The priest got a bit annoyed at that, "The problem with young people like you is that parental authority is insipid. It has lost substance. The view that the new generation has toward love is too reductive. Man thinks he is the center of the universe without responsibilities and duties, but only hands out, privileges and conveniences."

Another young man interjected, "Father, as long as this hypothetical marriage is not taking place. I think that it is very innovative of you to transform it into a religion class, but, don't you concur with me that cohabitation is less risky? You can live with a girl for ten years and you quit if you don't get along."

You have an egotistic view of marriage. First, you rob the youth of a young girl and, then, you abandon her. Is this civil and human to you? We are witnessing the mystification of sex. There is too much pre-marital sexual activity going on. Boys and girls look for excitement, for the exploitation of the body. They are not following a civic or religious code. They are being driven by impulse. Everything is a carnival. Look at the girls! They spend much time putting on makeup, for games, dances. They are turning every aspect of life into a spectacle.

The man who sat next to Felix, wishing to marry him, interrupted the conversation and said, "Father, you never answered my question."

Don Romanus replied, "When Adam saw Eve, said, 'This one, at last, is bone of my bones and flesh of my flesh ...that's why a man leaves his father and mother and clings to his wife, and the two of them become one body.' (G., 2:23-24). This is unequivocal and simple language." Then, he concluded, "My dear brothers and sisters, love is the symbol of the cross between a man and a woman. All the rest is demagogy and politics."

The audience understood the metaphor and approved his lecture, but their attention suddenly changed focus. The priest rose on his feet and looked intensely toward the main door. People turned around altogether. Expressions of marvel emerged from their lips and roared throughout the three naves. A woman, in a splendid white veil appeared at the end of the isle and moved slowly toward the altar with a gentle pace.

At a signal of the choir director, tenor Capisani began to sing the Ave Maria and the crowd quieted down its exuberance. Everybody was spellbound by the splendid voice of the singer and by the bride's beauty. Those who were standing in the lateral isles rushed to their seats. Many stepped on each other's feet. The priest too participated in the latest switch of the events. In the process of leaning forward to follow the bride's slow approach, his eyeglasses fell down on the floor. Of course, those nearby made some salacious comments. One lady suggested that he was sleeping, while an old man contradicted her stating that, perhaps, he was absent mind. Felix, in the meantime, was immersed in deep thought and did not realize the turn of the events. One of his best men touched him on the arm. A sacred silence reigned in church. He opened his eyes and saw his bride next to him. The sight of Espera, dressed in a wedding gown next to him, overwhelmed him. Overpowered by emotions, he broke down in tear. His first love had finally come back to stay with him for the rest of their life. His lady smiled, took a small, silk handkerchief and wiped his yes. Felix could not resist the temptation of hugging her and the crowd stood on their feet to give them a tumultuous welcome.

The bride's presence on the altar gave Don Romanus a reason to take a deep breath and begin the ceremony. The lung embracement between the two future spouses continued, oblivious of what was going on around them. The priest coughed once, twice. Both of the two love birds did not catch on and continued in their love effusion of feelings. To normalize the situation, the priest's last resort was to tap on their shoulders and, gently, invite them to prepare for the exchange of wows and rings.

As soon as the bride and the groom, along with the audience, were able to control their emotions, the priest resumed his official role. It was time for the offertory gifts. Scarman picked up the glass containers of water and wine, while Barabbus carried his chalice. Both walked toward the altar, where Don Romanus was waiting for them. The two gypsies looked at each other and began to perspire. Their hands trembled when they handed the sacred objects to the priest. In the act of raising the chalice during the consecration, the priest noticed the letter, 'J.' A moment later, he lifted up the 'new' chalice and noticed the matching letter 'C.' A sudden temblor shook his body. His hands became unsteady and the chalice started to rotate among his fingers until he was unable to hold a firm grip on it and dropped it on the floor. The shaky hands made the wine sprinkle on the altar and his sacred garments. The rest of it spilled out of the chalice at the time of the impact on the marble pavement. Don Romanus was almost petrified. He looked at the other chalice and fumbled something, but nobody understood him. The air was still and the congregation observed a funereal silence. The atmosphere was laden with suspense. The priest made a last effort to stare at the two gypsies, but his knees buckled and took a couple of steps backward. He leaned against the wall and put one hand on his heart. The audience jumped on his feet. Each face spoke the same language of astonishment. Don Romanus' assistants helped him to sit on a chair for a few minutes, but when he tried to get up, he did not have the strength. The deacon, a stout man of around fifty, tried again to sustain him in a standing position, but the old man was wobbling. Scarman and Barabbus did in that moment what nobody expected. They walked toward don Romanus and fell on his feet. "Don Fernando," said Barabbus in a humble tone and with tears streaming on his cheeks. At the sound of his real name, Don Romanus' eye bulbs widened and rotated in a counter clock movement. When they finally slowed down the pace, Barabbus continued, "Forgive us. We have sinned against you and against your church. We are not part of your corral, but even if we were, we would not be worthy of your forgiveness. The chalice that we preserved at all cost and that we brought back to you is a sign of our sincere repentance."

Felix and his wife were speechless and held back their breath waiting for a benign response from Padre, who did not make any immediate pronouncement. He was still deeply and emotionally touched. Espera broke the rules and got up, "Padre," she said in a gentle voice, "My husband and I cannot imagine how much you suffered all these years. The scar of the wound is still open in your heart. I presume that they have shared in your suffering." The two gypsies started to sob. The crowd was following the evolution of the human drama in silence, then, they became vociferous and demanded the gypsies' absolution. Don Romanus, moved to pity, touched their heads and said, "Get up! I am a man like you. If they forgave you, there is no reason why I don't have to." The crowd shouted in jubilation, "Hurrah, don Romanus! Hurrah, our Padre! Hurrah our pastor!" In the middle of the consecration, don Romanus felt an unusual spiritual warmth crossing his entire body. Bands of an intense, luminous light passed through the windows and invaded the interior of the church. A wind lifted him up and kept him suspended from the floor for a couple minutes. The crowd cried out "Miracle! Miracle!" The two gypsies were watching in awe. In their minds, there was no more doubt. They knelt before don Romanus and declared that they had seen the light for the first time in their lives. The priest invited them to a standing position and the two gypsies asked to be baptized. The crowd responded with shouts of joy, "Today, the Holy Spirit has come down to visit us in honor of Felix and Espera."

Considering that the course of the events was taking another unpredictable twist, the priest hurried to close the ceremony with the exchange of rings and wows.

From the audience, a dozen of husky young men picked up Scarman and Barabbus and raised them on their shoulders in triumph.

Chapter XLVII

The Final Truth

The church had been transformed into a market of happiness. It resembled a plaza were everybody talked to each other. Loud voices were a commonplace, but when the priest stretched out his arm, people observed the most rigorous silence. A blind man opened his way in the main isle, which was still crowded, by moving his cane left and right. There were pushes and shoves until they realized that the man was blind and made an effort to create space around him and allow him to pass.

The sight of the blind man was seen fastidious by the two gypsies. Their facial expression turned from joyful to serious. They feared that something ominous would come from him. Scarman whispered to his friend's ear, "It's the blind man!"

"Him again?"

"I wonder who invited him?"

"Stupid, you don't invite blind people. They come and go anywhere. Nobody will chase them out."

"I suspect that he is up to no good."

"Maybe, he knows something that no one wishes to hear," declared Barabbus.

"He may know events that occurred at Buchenwald."

"I don't think so."

"I tell you, I bet he came here to send us in jail."

"What are you talking about, idiot."

"Mark my words. I fear that this is not our best day. We should never have accepted the invitation. You fell in love with the chalice and because of it we will be jailbirds pretty soon."

Barabbus scuffed off his friend's ominous premonitions and said, "If you deeply feel that we are risking our freedom, we better leave and now." He grabbed him by the arm and pulled him away.

"Wait!" said Scarman. "If we run away the crowd will consider it an act of cowardice and, then, we really are in trouble."

The police showed up once again Scarman said, "I warned you before. You did not take my advice. We should have gained the exit before. Now, it is too late."

"Maybe, the priest called them. In that case, he would be a traitor. He would lose credibility in the eyes of the parishioners."

Scarman rebutted, "I believe it has to do with our involvement in the concentration camp."

"We were not at fault! We had to survive." He paused for a few seconds. His face looked gloomy. "We better kiss good-by to freedom."

"Unless they hang us...I don't know which one is worse."

The blind man arrived before the altar and raised his can in the air. A lady turned him around, so he could face the priest, and said, "Padre, You wonder why I am here. I came to reveal the ultimate truth."

"And what is the truth that has yet to be revealed?" queried an incredulous Don Romanus.

Felix, still tied to his wife, asked, "Friend, have you come here to disturb peace and happiness? If it is so, save us from that inconvenience."

"To the contrary, I am determined to confirm both of them."

The police came forward and got close to the two gypsies ready to handcuff them. Felix got over concerned and, turning his attention to the blind man, exclaimed, "As you can understand, you have caused turmoil with your proclaimed revelations. The fact of the matter is that you have made no revelation at all. State what you have in your mind and be done with it."

"Even what you don't like to hear?" responded sarcastically the blind man.

Espera hugged her husband and said, "You did not do anything wrong, didn't you?"

"No, my conscience is clear," answered her Felix.

"It must be a mistake or this man is looking for some popularity."

"Stay calm, my love! Everything will be cleared. I have not done anything illegal.."

"Neither did I," said Espera while she was tightening her grip around her husband's waist.

The blind man swirled the cane in the air as to demand attention and said, "Neither one of you, newlyweds, are aware of it, but the time is ripe to reveal the truth."

"We have been waiting for a long time to hear this truth!" shouted a woman from the background.

The blind man raised the cane again and made some geometrical shapes that nobody was able to decipher. The outsiders, sensing that something extremely important was going on inside, squeezed themselves among the crowd in the interior of the church. The blind man pointed the cane toward the entrance. The expectation reached the apex. As he lowered the cane, an old man with a beard and a hunched back started to walk with unsteady pace. Shortly after, an old woman, a bit obese, followed him, holding, occasionally, on both sides of the pews. They walked up toward the altar and stopped at the first pews where they took deep breaths. The whole congregation observed a rigorous silence and the attention was concentrated solely on them. Don Romanus, himself, was disconcerted by the succession of clamorous events and had to use the remaining energy to face the last revelation.

The blind man, like a magician, raised his magic band and said to the lady, "Talk!"

She stared at Felix, who, in turn, reciprocated with her. An internal, mysterious chemical process developed between them. The audience was tense and the time was pregnant with expectations. In that moment, the lady said, "You are my son!"

Felix, who was holding his wife's arm, turned suddenly pale. Espera held him back. Neither one of them made a move. Espera broke the ice, "We cannot take the blind man's initiative or this woman's words as true. What are the proofs?"

"Very well," answered the blind man in a defying tone. He touched the old man with the cane. The man with the beard made a considerable effort to raise his head and looked intensely at Espera. She returned the same deep look to him. He smiled slightly and said, "I am your biological father."

Espera fainted in her husband's arms. The deacon rushed over with a little flask of vinegar and put it under her nose. After a couple of minutes, she showed symptoms of revival, even though she remained under shock. Soon, the church turned into a pandemonium. It looked more like a market than a religious institution. Don Romanus tried to regain control of the situation and invited the audience to respect the temple of God. He was a scrupulous priest who left nothing unresolved. As soon as the audience noise quelled down, he asked with more determination to the strangers to unequivocally prove their claims. Now, the whole attention reversed back to the blind man who raised the cane once again and pointed it toward the two gypsies. "They are the only witnesses who can ascertain if our two visitors are carriers of fraud or truth." He brought the cane to its initial position and waited for a response.

The air was saturated with suspense. The church went through a process of metamorphosis and assumed the atmosphere of a cemetery where only suppressed prayers rose to heaven. Everybody was waiting for the moment of truth. The two gypsies had no choice. They were the first and last protagonists of a turbulent human story. With an act of courage, Barabbus took the floor and spoke very calmly, "Don Romanus,we are condemned to tell the final truth, a truth that for us may mean a life sentence or hanging."

The priest jumped on his feet with renovated vigor and shouted, "No, you are not being condemned! You are called to assume your responsibility as a son of God! Truth must always prevail at all costs! We need it! We urge it to purge our interior and to promote a sane society. We must raise our hopes for a better future; therefore, everyone of us has to stand up and accept the consequences. The church wants to listen, to understand, to find new ways of forgiveness, but let us not make any mistake. It is here to draw a line between good and evil, to be a guide, a luminary and not to bend to social changes."

"Yeaa!" responded the congregation in unison.

Scarman, looked at the novel spouses and said in a trembling, tenuous voice, "What this old man and woman have just testified is true."

The blind man responded angrily, "We are not interested in your words! We urge you to provide proofs!" In saying that, he banged the cane on the floor three times.

Barabbus replied, "Do you want the proof? We will give them to you." He invited both Felix and his wife to stretch foreword their right arms and keep the fingers open. The audience's expectations reached the bursting level. "Look at the marks between the fingers. We made them," exclaimed the gypsy.

Felix and Espera opened their eyes in disbelief. The crowd pressed closer to them to ascertain for themselves that they had scars. "Now, that you have done that," insisted the blind man, "Tell them when you produced those scars?"

The two gypsies did not respond and the blind man's voice became belligerent, "Was it not when you sequestered them from an orphanage? Confess it or I break your neck!"

Neither of the gypsies responded. The audience took it as an admission of guilt and soon the rumor spread that Felix and Espera were brother and sister. Espera's eyes got blurry. Her husband held her against him fearing that she might fall down. Soon, voices of approval grew louder and louder, "They are brother and sister! They are brother and sister!" The guests cried out.

Eventually, order was restored not without some efforts. Scarman waited for the noise to abate and took the floor, "We did not claim nor we claim that they are siblings." Espera took a deep sigh of relief. Scarman continued, "I repeat. We inflicted the minimum pain in making two small incisions and only as an identification purpose of our booty. They were not born of the same mother. We can assure you on that."

Espera whispered to her husband, "I sensed it all way along."

"I did too," responded her spouse.

Across from them, the old man and woman stood there petrified, dragged in the vortex of family events unaware of how receptive would be their 'resurrected' son and daughter.

Felix and Espera must have interpreted their anxiety and ran over to hug them. "Father, why did you give me up?" asked him Espera.

"I did not have the means of survival. I was young and foolish. I was egocentric. I have no excuse, but only words of repentance," he said.

Felix asked a similar question to his mother. "My son, I would not leave you for the whole gold of the world, but those were other times... I was alone and jobless and your father abandoned me. At least, you had something to eat," she admitted in tears.

In the meantime, the police approached the two gypsies and handcuffed them. The two began to shiver and looked at Felix with an expression of 'good-by.'" Felix felt deeply emotional for them. He would have never imagined a sad epilogue on his marriage day. He wiped the tears from his eyes, motioned the police to hold on and addressed the audience, "Family members, guests and honorable friends! Today is the best day of my life, of our life. As you have come to witness, I have conquered the heart of my love and I have found my biological mother. Even my lovely wife had a splendid surprise. She has reunited with her father. We were all lost, but we are back home. We regained our blood, our roots and our love. Those two handcuffed gypsies saved me and thousands of Jews at Buchenwald. Yes, they stole from an orphanage two babies, my wife and me; they kept us hostage for a while, but they treated us with dignity until they sold us to two families. They held the secret for an entire life and for all of that, they should held accountable and be prosecuted in a court of law. Yes, they caused separations and pains and they stole a gold chalice that don Romanus considered to be his most precious prize. But, they gave it back to him. They have already paid a high price for their crime. We are the only ones who should condemn them, but we have decided to absolve them. We want to give them a glimmer of hope for their future; therefore, we advocate for them immediate freedom and a happy return home. The crowd approved overwhelmingly Felix's brief defense with a standing ovation.

Only don Romanus remained silent and apprehensive on his chair until tension escalated once again. The deacon leaned over him and whispered something in his ear. don Romanus stood up and said in an unsteady voice, "Today is a day of remembrance and joy, not of hatred and retribution. At this moment, the church is telling you that love, warmth and unselfishness will help you to grow into complete human beings." Then, he paused for a moment. When he raised his head, he continued, "Who am I to deny absolution to two repented sinners? There is no better unifying force than love and forgiveness, and this is a day for joy and unity. Forgiving someone is not a heroic act, but a deep and simple act of Christian civility. Forgiveness releases the negative emotions that enslave us; it lowers the stress level and promotes cardiovascular health. But, the most significant, incontrovertible contribution is that of setting us free." He looked at the gypsies and said, "You may go and savor Christian love." He made, then, a gesture to the policemen who loosened the grip around the men's wrists.

The crowd went in delirium. A dozen of husky men grabbed both gypsies and raised them on their shoulders. For about ten minutes, they carried Barabbus and Scarman in triumph. Never before, the two gypsies felt such an intimate link of brotherhood with the local citizens.

The deacon whispered something to don Romanus' ear. The priest covered his head with both hands as an expression of surprise and guilt. He stood up and stretched his right hand foreword, "Silence, everybody!" He shouted. "In all this chaos, I forgot to baptize Scarman and Barabbus. Bring them back here! The two men fell flat on their face at don Romanus' feet and received the sacrament of baptism with Felix and Espera being their 'padrini.'

Outside, the sun was spraying its golden dust all over the town. A carriage, with four white horses, approached the church's main entrance. Felix and Espera, wrapped in their radiant love, took their seat and waived to the crowd. The coachman whipped the animals and the carriage drove the bride and groom to Happiness Boulevard. A cool breeze was impatiently keeping a close watch from the mountain until it decided to descend to the town and bring a long waited relief to the people. A girl looked upward and shook her head in an implicit gesture of incredulity. "What a phenomenal love story!" She said to her boyfriend standing next to her. He leaned over and whispered to her, "These are winds of love. They are carrying on their wings a melodious music for us, too."

The following day, what appeared to be a lonely couple of gypsies walking toward the church, it became an endless line by midday. Never before, the local people witnessed a spontaneous flux of the gypsy community reversing toward the temple of God in an evident gesture of conversion of hearts. So it was written and so it is.